112

RED INK

Also by Greg Dinallo

Final Answers*
Purpose of Evasion
Rockets' Red Glare

*Published by POCKET BOOKS

RED INK

GREG
DINALLO

POCKET BOOKS
New York   London   Toronto   Sydney   Tokyo   Singapore

This book is a work of fiction. Names, characters, places, and incidents are products of the author's imagination or are used fictitiously. Any resemblance to actual events or locales or persons, living or dead, is entirely coincidental.

POCKET BOOKS, a division of Simon & Schuster Inc.
1230 Avenue of the Americas, New York, NY 10020

Dinallo, Gregory S.
    Red ink / Greg Dinallo.
        p.   cm.
    ISBN: 0-671-73313-3 (hardcover)
    I. Title.
    PS3554.I46R3   1994
    813'.54—dc20   93-49358
                                                                          CIP

First Pocket Books hardcover printing July 1994

10 9 8 7 6 5 4 3 2 1

Printed in the U.S.A.

For Josephine and Joseph Carrubba,
who were like second parents to me

ACKNOWLEDGMENTS

For technical information and inspiration, I am especially indebted to Shelley G. Altenstadter, Deputy Director of Financial Crimes Enforcement Network; and also to: Brian M. Bruh, Director of FinCEN, for generously allowing me access to his headquarters and personnel; Timothy J. Kruthaupt, Chief Operations Support Division, for his responsiveness and guidance; and Anna Fotias, Congressional and Public Affairs Officer, who from the start made sure I got to the right people and who kept the information flowing.

I'd also like to thank Beth Knobel of the *Los Angeles Times,* Moscow Bureau; Norman Katkov, friend and fellow wordsmith; and special thanks to my editor at Pocket Books, Doug Grad, for his enthusiasm and support, for making all the incisive comments expected of those paid to wield a critical eye, and for doing so with much appreciated tact, restraint, and good humor.

"Communism is the exploitation of man by man. Capitalism is just the opposite."

—*Joke told by a Moscow cabdriver*

1

I t is winter, and it does not wait.

This thought wasn't penned by a Russian poet, but uttered by Boris Yeltsin's chief economic adviser at a news conference I covered a few months ago. He also said that developing a convertible ruble, curbing inflation, stemming capital flight, and increasing private investment are crucial to stabilizing the Russian economy. Saving the worst for last, he warned that the coming months of subzero weather, when the demand for staples is highest and the supply meager, means things will get much worse before they get better.

I've no idea why the line haunts me now, why it rings with such clarity as I enter a Moscow Community Center and make my way to a drafty meeting room where a handwritten sign proclaims—MOSCOW BEGINNERS.

Conversation stops as I take my seat. Everyone else at the long table turns to look at me, some with compassion, others with despair, all with a trace of apprehension. I study the tired faces one by one: A housewife? A taxi driver? A seamstress? An engineer? A nurse? A factory worker? A university student? I'm forced to guess because they're all strangers—strangers with whom I'm about to share one of the most painful moments of my life.

I'm seized by a compulsion to run, to leave the room and avoid it; but I know from years of denial the pain will be far worse tomorrow if I do.

My turn has come.

I stub out my cigarette, grasp the edge of the table, and stand. "My name is Nikolai K.," I begin. My throat is dry from anxiety, and I pause, wondering if the voice belongs to someone else.

Some of the strangers lean forward expectantly. A husband and wife hold hands across the table for support. A balding man with wintry eyes nods encouragingly.

"My name is Nikolai K.," I resume, making an effort to enunciate each syllable. "My name is Nikolai K., and I am an alcoholic."

Applause breaks out. My personal *perestroika* has begun. This once radical idea of self-rehabilitation has become common since the ban on self-expression was lifted; since the new government identified alcoholism as a severe drag on the economy; and since the State's arcane methods of dealing with it— compulsory hospitalization, sulfazine therapy, and imprisonment— were replaced by clinics like Moscow Beginners.

"Why do you drink, Nikolai?" one of the strangers finally wonders.

"To get drunk," I quip nervously.

Silence. Not a chuckle, not a smile, quite obviously not the first time they've heard it.

"Are you employed?" another asks.

"Sometimes. I mean, I write. Freelance."

"Maybe you're creatively frustrated?"

"No, I don't write fiction. I do investigative work. I have an endless supply of material."

"Investigative work," a woman muses suspiciously.

"For *Pravda*," a young fellow cracks, eliciting a burst of derisive laughter from the group.

"Good riddance," the woman next to him chimes in, pleased that the once powerful propaganda rag of the Communist Party has been shut down.

"I disagree. I'm against censorship of any kind. A free press is the soul of a free society."

"Free to destroy lives? To distort history? To print outright lies?" the man with the wintry eyes challenges, recounting *Pravda*'s once daily diatribe.

2

"Absolutely—as long as opposing views aren't censored and libel laws are enforced. Banning anything other than shouting fire in a crowded theater violates the right of free speech."

"Even banning the Communist Party?"

"Of course."

"Well, I'm still glad the bastards are gone. Is that what you write about, Nikolai? Politics?"

"I write about corruption and—"

"Ah, not politics, *politicians.*"

More laughter.

"—and injustice. I write about *Afghanisti,* about striking coal miners, about *Pamyat.*"

The room falls silent. The strangers know about the shabby treatment of veterans, about the epidemic of lung disease in mining regions, about the ultraright-wing group that preaches anti-Semitism.

"Nikolai K.," a wizened man in a skullcap muses, knowingly. "We have a famous dissident in our midst."

"Please, everyone writes of these things now. I'm afraid dissent has become a very competitive business."

"Maybe he's here to write about *us?*" the suspicious woman suggests.

"Should I?" I ask, pretending I've sparked to the idea. "Have I stumbled upon a cell of subversives? A sinister group out to prevent the State from keeping its citizens in a drunken stupor for seventy-five more years so we won't realize just how rotten life in this country really is?"

Most of them laugh this time and settle back in their chairs, seeming to accept me.

I thank them, take my seat, and light another *Ducat.* The first match fizzles. It always does. The Kremlin has technology to incinerate entire cities but can't make matches that work. The tips have so little sulfur you have to strike several at once to get a light. I'm filling my lungs with smoke and wondering who will be next when an attractive woman with pale skin stands.

"My name is Ludmilla T.," she says shyly, directing the introduction to me. Then brightening, she faces her fellow regulars and announces, "Today is my thirtieth birthday."

"Happy birthday, Ludmilla!" several call out, breaking into a chorus of the song.

"So, Ludmilla," the suspicious woman prompts when the refrain fades, "has this been a good week for you?"

"Well, yes; but I had to skip work today. I didn't want to, but I knew my coworkers would bring vodka to celebrate, and I was afraid I couldn't say no."

"You did the right thing," the woman says.

"No," the wizened man protests. "She has to live in the real world. What's going to happen when she's offered vodka on someone else's birthday?"

"He's right. He is. But I couldn't take the chance," Ludmilla protests timidly. "It's not just getting drunk. It's losing control, and then . . . then other things happen."

"What other things?" the woman prompts knowingly.

Ludmilla lowers her eyes, working up the courage to reply. "I . . . I wake up next to men I don't remember meeting. It's as if I have no self-respect; but I do. I know I do, and . . . and so . . ." She pauses, interrupted by an electronic chirping, and looks about curiously for the source.

There's a vulnerable sensuality about Ludmilla T. Something in her eyes and in her movements that pleads, *Take me. Protect me,* and I'm having visions of her waking up in *my* bed. Five chirp-filled seconds pass before I sense the strangers are all looking at me. Damn. It's my beeper.

I fumble nervously for the switch and turn it off. I'm embarrassed, but bristling with curiosity and the need to get to a telephone. "I'm really sorry. Please, don't be offended, but I have to go. Anybody know if there's a pay phone in the building?"

Several of the strangers shake their heads no sullenly. Others shrug and exchange disapproving glances. I force a smile and hurry from the room. The door slams shut with a loud bang as I run down the corridor, my commitment to sobriety already in question, if not my sanity.

Party *apparatchiks* have had beepers for years, but they're still a mystery to the average citizen and hard to acquire. I got mine from Stockmann's, the renowned Helsinki department store whose mail-order catalogue has everything from American razors to Japanese sports cars. It's required reading for Muscovites in the know; and the Tolstoy Express—as the train that arrives at Leningradsky Station from Helsinki each morning is called—is always met by an anxious crowd.

The revolving door spins me into bone-chilling darkness. The temperature must be close to zero. The weather in Moscow is always at its nastiest in March. I make a beeline for a cinema on Taganskaya where there's a pay phone. I don't have to look at the beeper to know who called me. Vera Fedorenko is the only person who has the number. I thumb two kopeks into the slot and dial Militia Headquarters on Petrovka. The phone rings and rings, four, five, six times.

"Dispatcher seventeen," Vera finally answers over the din of the huge room through which all police communications are routed. The electronics-packed space is dominated by a huge animated map of Moscow on which the location and movements of patrol units are charted.

"It's Nikolai. What's going on?"

"Everything. This is a bad time. I can't talk."

"You beeped me, Vera. You beeped me in the middle of my first meeting."

"Oh. Right. Someone just reported finding a body on the grounds of the Embankment."

"The Embankment? Was it somebody important?"

"I've no idea. Just a minute, I've got another call." She clicks off and puts me on hold.

I listen to the hum of the line, thinking about the Embankment. Vera had no doubt I'd be intrigued. The Embankment is an elite housing complex on the banks of the Moscow River where many members of the government reside. It's also where my parents were living forty-three years ago when I was born.

I enjoyed all the privileges—played on the manicured grounds, swam in the indoor pools, dined in the gourmet food halls, and attended Special School No. 19—until the infamous spring of '68, when Brezhnev sent Soviet tanks rolling into Prague, and my father's conscience overcame his fear of reprisal, causing him to be declared an enemy of the State. An intellectual and professor of political science, he'd rejoiced a decade earlier when Khrushchev initiated the period still fondly referred to as "the Thaw"—the official easing of censorhip, repression, and State terror that allowed Solzhenitsyn's *One Day in the Life of Ivan Denisovich* to be published. *"That* was a spring," he would often say, relishing the memory. A memory that sustained him throughout the years of—

"Sorry, Niko," Vera says, coming back on the line, pulling me out of it.

"What about cause of death? Anything on that?"

"No. That's all I have."

"Great. God help you if it's a derelict who tripped over a curb."

"What am I bid for a member of the government who was murdered by a prostitute working for the CIA?"

"Make sure it's an Israeli prostitute and a high-ranking member of the government. I have to go."

"Wait. Should I come by later?"

"Sure."

"You have coffee?"

"Coffee? The food stores haven't had any for months."

"I do. I'll bring some in case this turns into something, and you're writing all night."

I hang up, wondering how Vera is able to acquire coffee, and hurry to the corner for a taxi. Several years ago, there wasn't a cabdriver in Moscow who wouldn't make a U-turn in a traffic jam for a pack of Marlboros—they still come in handy on occasion and I usually carry a couple of packs with me—but American dollars are the coin of the realm now. Cabdrivers can spot them in the dark at a hundred meters. Passengers without them are often bypassed. Everyone haggles the price. I step off the curb, holding my rubles low to the ground. A few empty taxis roar past before an unmarked gypsy finally stops. "The Embankment," I say, leaning to the window.

"Six hundred," the driver grunts.

"Three."

"Five."

"Outrageous," I protest as I clamber inside.

"I know, but I was just by there. The police have it cordoned off. That's going to cost me time."

Cordoned off? Because of a dead derelict? Not a chance. A smile tugs at the corners of my mouth. I might get my wish. If I do, if someone important was murdered, I've got the jump on a big-ticket story. If not, I won't have to worry about resisting my craving for vodka because I'll be too broke to buy any.

2

The Moscow River twists through the center of the city like a nocturnal reptile, its frozen skin shimmering in the moonlight. Centered between two bridges that link it to the Kremlin, the House on the Embankment has the look of an impenetrable fortress. Tonight, its drab facade is ablaze with light from the flashers of militia vans blocking the approach road.

The taxi deposits me at a wooden barricade where uniformed policemen stand, emitting streams of blue-gray breath that match the color of their trench coats.

"Press," I announce over the crackle of radios.

A sergeant blinds me with his flashlight. A flick of his wrist shifts the beam from my eyes to my chest in search of credentials. "No press card?"

"I'm free-lance."

"Sorry, no unauthorized personnel."

Before I can protest, a brilliant flash cuts silhouettes out of the darkness behind him—a fleeting glimpse of uniformed men gathered around a car. The photographer's strobe flashes again, taunting me.

"Who's in charge here?"

"Senior Investigator Shevchenko."

Shevchenko? I may get my wish. Valery Shevchenko is a

7

senior *homicide* investigator. "Ah, we go way back. Tell him Nikolai Katkov's here, will you?"

Another flash erupts. This time from within the car. The passenger window looks like it's been hit by a rotten tomato. The grisly image sets crimson circles whirling in the darkness.

"Look, if I don't get this story, I'll write that the militia suppressed it. It's your call, Sergeant—" I'm making a show of checking his name tag when headlights sweep the area and a Moskvitch sedan coasts to a stop. The door opens and Valery Shevchenko's narrow face thrusts upward into the cold air.

I once teased him that he shares his surname with a famous poet who advocated Ukrainian independence from Russia, and a high-ranking U.N. diplomat who defected to the United States. He winced, and replied that if not for such misfortune, he'd be *Chief* Investigator Shevchenko by now. My sources tell me it's because he's too good to waste on administrative work and isn't enough of a bastard. I'm counting on the latter.

"What do you want, Katkov?" he growls impatiently.

"A little cooperation would be nice."

"Something tells me you've already had some."

"Come on, Shevchenko. I'm trying to earn a living."

He scowls, then turns to the sergeant who opens the barricade. "Good work. We can't have unaccredited reporters running loose at crime scenes, can we?" Shevchenko starts forward, then pauses. "Certainly not without supervision." He motions me to follow, then charges across the parking area past the massive building where curious faces press against frosty windows. A shaft of light rakes his face, accentuating the lines and deepening the hollows. He looks weary.

The militiamen guarding the car step aside as Shevchenko approaches and leans into the Volga with his flashlight. The beam moves from the open driver's door, to the ignition, where the keys still dangle, then on to the windshield, passenger window, and roof liner that are spattered with blood, bits of tissue, and gray matter. He backs out slowly, pausing to sort through the items in a sack on the passenger seat—Western cigarettes, razor blades, blank audio cassettes among them—then crouches to examine a splotch of blood on the ground below the door, from which a reddish brown smear arcs across the pavement. It leads Shevchenko to the far side of a concrete wall where the beam from his flashlight finds a man's corpse: fully clothed, on its back, head twisted sharply to the right, resting in a glassy pool of crimson ice that encircles it like a halo.

Shevchenko crouches studying the details. The hole in the left cheek is cratered and scorched, indicating a large-caliber pistol fired at close range. The eyes are open and shifted hard right, as if staring in shock at the gaping wound on the side of the skull. The tailored topcoat and sport jacket are thrown open, exposing a freshly laundered white shirt and silk tie.

Shevchenko stands and slowly drifts back toward the car puzzling something out. "The killer is waiting in the darkness—rushes forward—opens the door—and fires," he whispers in bursts, acting out the moves with precise gestures. "Then, instead of fleeing, pulls the body from the car and drags it behind the wall. . . . He lets it trail off. The militiamen nod like a pack of loyal dogs. Shevchenko asks himself, "Why?"

My heart sinks. The obvious answer isn't one rich in political intrigue. "Care to venture a guess?" I ask, pencil poised to jot down: Motive, robbery.

"No. You?"

He knows what I want and is getting some perverse pleasure out of making me sink my own ship. "Well, he probably didn't want to be spotted going through the poor fellow's pockets."

"He?" Shevchenko taunts, surprising me. "Have you detected something that rules out a woman?"

"No. It was just a figure of speech. You have reason to suspect it was?"

He smirks, still toying with me; or so I suspect until he shifts his flashlight to the victim's left wrist. A metallic glint appears. "Sergeant."

The sergeant crouches to the body, pushes up the shirt cuff, and removes a gold wristwatch. He slips it into an evidence envelope and follows it with a wedding band; then he checks the victim's pockets, taking a fold of rubles from one and a leather wallet from another, handing the latter to Shevchenko.

"Well, I guess robbery wasn't 'her' motive," I joke, delighted the intrigue remains.

"Vladimir Vorontsov," Shevchenko says, scanning the victim's driver's license. "Correction. Vladimir Illiych Vorontsov. I wouldn't want to be accused of withholding information from the press." He examines the wallet's contents, pausing curiously at a plastic laminated card that he palms before I can get a look at it. "Who found him?"

The sergeant grins. "A puppy. His owner was walking him after dinner. She lives in the same wing as Vorontsov. Said he's a widower; his daughter and grandchildren moved in with him a few months ago."

Shevchenko nods and walks toward the building at a brisk pace. "Took in his daughter and grandchildren," he muses sarcastically as I follow after him. "Evidently, the new government hasn't solved the housing shortage or divorce rate yet."

"Evidently, you preferred the old system."

He shrugs. "I had a life then."

"A life?"

"Yes, a life. If the KGB was still in business, they'd be handling this and I'd be home with my wife and daughters."

"Care to guess where *I'd* be?"

He chortles, entertaining visions of the gulag, and starts up the steps to the entrance. "You want a story? This rush to democracy is pushing violent crime through the roof. Six hundred thousand more incidents this year than last. Write about that. Just don't forget to mention the Party always claimed it went hand-in-hand with capitalism."

"Come on. It contradicted their propaganda, so they denied it existed."

"No. No, this used to be the safest city in the world, Katkov. Everyone was so terrified of the KGB, they toed the line, and you know it."

"Not everyone."

"True. There'll always be a few—dissidents." He spits it out like an expletive, and puts a shoulder into the massive wooden door.

I haven't been in these buildings in over twenty-five years, but nothing's changed. The creak of hinges, the hiss of steam, the orange glow of chandeliers—I'm overwhelmed with familiar sensations as I follow Shevchenko across the lobby into an elevator. The slow-moving lift deposits us in a third-floor vestibule. He steps to a door and presses the buzzer. A petite woman in her early thirties appears. She seems gentle and refined: salon-styled hair, silk blouse, designer suit, clearly a woman of privilege.

"I'm Senior Investigator Shevchenko," he says, displaying his militia badge and identification. "This is Mr. Katkov. He's a journalist. May we come in?"

"Why, is something wrong?"

"Vladimir Vorontsov is your father?"

She nods, her eyes widening apprehensively.

"I'm afraid it's very bad news."

The color drains from her face as she leads the way to a living room decorated with elegant European furniture, silk draperies, and Persian rugs. It's a grand room. Very grand—my entire apartment could easily fit inside it—and very much like the one where I played as a child. I'm so caught up in the memories that a few moments pass before I reach a sitting area at the far end of the room where Shevchenko is briefing her.

"My God," she wails when he finishes. "Why would anyone do something like that?"

"I'm hoping you can help us find the answer, Mrs.—"

"Churkin. Tanya Churkin," she replies, overcome with grief. "He was late. I knew something was wrong. I just knew it."

Shevchenko nods with understanding and directs her to a chair. "You said he was late?"

She nods sadly.

"On returning from where?"

"His lodge meeting. He gets together with his cronies. They drink. Relive old times. You know."

"And where is this lodge?"

"In Khimki Khovrino near the Sports Palace."

"Quite a long drive," Shevchenko observes. "Did your father have any enemies you know of?"

"No. No, he was a good person."

"No ex-wife, no girlfriends, jilted mistresses, anything like that?"

Her tear-filled eyes flare with indignation. "No. And I don't like what you're insinuating," she snaps, her back straightening in the chair.

"I meant no offense, Mrs. Churkin. Someone shot your father in cold blood. The motive is crucial to tracking down his killer."

"The answer is still no. He was devoted to my mother. She died about a year ago. He still isn't over it. I don't want his good name sullied by you"—she shifts her glare to me—"or anyone else."

"That's not why we're here, Mrs. Churkin, I assure you," Shevchenko replies.

She nods, her lips tightening into a thin line.

"Now, can you think of anyone who might want to hurt him? Anyone he didn't get along with?"

"No. He was well liked by everyone."

"What about his coworkers?" Shevchenko glances at me out of the corner of his eye and produces the laminated card he palmed earlier. "According to this, he was employed at the Interior Ministry."

My brows twitch with intrigue. Mrs. Churkin's fall. She nods sadly.

"In what capacity?"

"As a foreign trade representative. He was usually posted abroad to one of our embassies; but lately, he's been working out of Ministry offices here in Moscow."

"Did he ever take work home from the office?"

"Sometimes. His things are inside." She stands and leads the way to a study that overlooks the river. One wall is covered with floor-to-ceiling bookcases, another with citations and photographs that span a long career in government service: Vorontsov with various heads of state, with generals and dignitaries, with world business leaders, on the fringe of a large group gathered around Brezhnev, with a smaller group that includes Gorbachev and Shevarnadze, with Boris Yeltsin and former U.S. Ambassador Strauss.

Shevchenko crosses to a desk where several neat stacks of papers are aligned. After a perfunctory review, he slips the official-looking documents into a briefcase that he finds next to the desk. "Someone will have to identify the body, Mrs. Churkin. You may do it now, or tomorrow at headquarters. I imagine you'll want to come by to claim his personal effects."

The finely tailored woman hesitates, chilled at the thought. "Yes. Yes, I think tomorrow would be better."

"Should you need to reach me in the meantime . . ." Shevchenko gives her one of his cards with the defunct red star insignia. Then, briefcase in hand, he leads the way from the apartment into the elevator. After the door closes, he pulls a flask from inside his trench coat, thumbs the hinged cap, and takes a long swallow. Vodka may be colorless, odorless, and tasteless, but my senses are undeniably tantalized. Shevchenko notices my hungry stare. "Long night," he says, offering me the flask.

"Thanks, no," I reply, though my throat craves the long, satisfying burn. "But I could use a ride."

"Sorry. I'm returning to headquarters."

"That's what I figured."

He glares at me as the elevator door opens, then charges through it into the lobby. By the time I catch up, he's bounding down the steps outside the building.

"Come on, Shevchenko," I protest as we cross the parking area. "You'll get home to that little family a lot sooner with some help; not to mention the time you'll save answering my questions now."

"Unfortunately, there *are* other reporters in Moscow, Katkov. I'll still have to answer theirs."

"No, you don't."

"You suggesting I deal with you exclusively?"

"I expected a senior investigator with twenty years on the force would demand it."

"Twenty-four years."

"All the more reason. Of course, if what I've heard about your itch to make chief is wrong . . ."

He opens the door, tosses the briefcase inside the Moskvitch, and whirls to face me. "I'm up to my ass. I don't have time to play games. You'll clear every draft with me prior to publication. You'll remove anything I find objectionable, anything I want withheld from the public, anything that might threaten to derail the investigation. Agreed?"

"Agreed."

"You're a terrible liar, Katkov." He slides behind the wheel, slams the door, and jerks his head, indicating I get in.

The House on the Embankment fades in the mist that hangs over the river. There's little traffic at this hour, and about fifteen minutes later we're approaching Militia Headquarters, a crenelated fortress near the Hermitage Gardens. The uniformed sentry at the entrance to No. 38 Petrovka recognizes Shevchenko and raises the gate arm, allowing the sedan to enter without stopping. Six stories of dark brown sandstone tower over a treeless courtyard paved with cobblestones. It's a forbidding presence.

The senior investigator's office is on the fourth floor, deep in a maze of depressing corridors. Gray-green walls, poor lighting, a small, rain-spattered window, and a scarred desk, on which Shevchenko drops Vorontsov's briefcase, do little to change the mood.

"No motive—no suspect," he announces, reciting the axiom glumly, as he begins sorting the documents.

"You've eliminated thieves, mistresses, neighbors, which leaves, what? Professionals. It would be fair to allege it was the *mafiya*. Some kind of a hit. No?"

"No."

"Come on. He was killed with a pistol."

"Would you have preferred a shotgun?"

"A hand ax. I understand it's the most commonly used weapon in homicides."

"Because firearms are illegal and hard to get. There's always an ax handy."

"Unless you're a professional. Then it's—"

The phone rings, interrupting me.

"Shevchenko," he answers wearily. His shoulders sag as he listens. "Yes, I'm still here. . . . I'm sorry, I meant to. I didn't get a chance. . . . Yes, I know it's late. Tell them I'll see them in the morning. . . . Katya, I'm doing my best. It's hard to— Katya? Katya?" He sighs and slowly lowers the phone.

"Old lady's pissed off at you, huh?"

He glares at me. "Stick to business, Katkov."

"Fine. I was about to say, it's rather obvious we're looking at a premeditated murder here."

"I didn't say that and don't write that I did. I said cold-blooded murder. That's all I'm saying."

"Why?"

"Because there are pieces that still don't fit."

"Removing the body from the car . . ."

Shevchenko nods smugly before adding, "And the sack of sundries on the seat."

"What makes that a problem?"

"Time. He leaves the office and goes shopping at one of those trendy emporiums that sell Western goods. The end of the working day. Their busiest time. He'd have to take a number and queue for at least an hour, maybe two. Then time to drive all the way to Khimki Khovrino, time to eat, drink, and be merry, and time to drive home. *All* in time to be killed sometime before eight forty-eight. I'm sure dispatcher"—he pauses and retrieves a report from his desk—"Vera Fedorenko recorded the time of the call accurately."

"I wouldn't know," I say offhandedly, thinking the son-of-a-bitch never misses an opening. "Far as the body being removed from the car is concerned, maybe Vorontsov dragged himself out."

"With half his cranium missing?"

"A reflexive action. Like a chicken without a head. Whatever, I still think somebody shut him up."

"No comment." He tosses a document aside, and begins perusing another. "Not until I know exactly what he was up to at the Interior Ministry."

"Well, since you work for the Interior Ministry, I'm sure you have your ways of finding out."

"And I've no doubt you have yours, Katkov. You'll let me know what you turn up."

"I'll let you know who buys my story. You can read what I turn up."

He bristles, then checks his anger in reaction to something in the documents. "I don't think we're going to need sources to find out what he's involved in."

"You found it?"

"Privatization," he says with the disdain usually reserved for the word *capitalism*. "These reports were prepared by the Committee for State Property."

"The committee *empowered to sell* State property. The committee overrun by corrupt bureaucrats ripping off the industries they've been managing."

"Fucking hypocrites," Shevchenko exclaims, nostrils twitching at the stench of scandal. "They buy businesses with money stolen from the Party and make huge profits reselling them to Western corporations."

"For *dollars*—dollars that never enter the economy, as I understand it."

"It's called capital flight, Katkov. There are dozens of deals here. From high-tech to agriculture, and everything in between."

"So, which one was poor Comrade Vorontsov trying to rip off?"

Shevchenko shrugs and smiles enigmatically. "Maybe all of them. Maybe none."

"None?"

"*None.* I don't get paid to jump to conclusions like you, Katkov. I get paid to assemble and evaluate facts." He kicks back in his chair with a prescient air and ticks the points off on his fingers. "A man of apparent stature and integrity. Rampant political corruption. Documents that cover a broad range of State industries. Agreed?"

"Agreed. Your point?"

"It's possible Vorontsov had the documents because he was reviewing them."

"A watchdog?"

Shevchenko nods. "He's probably as dirty as they come; but it's also possible he died because he was about to blow the whistle on someone."

"But someone blew it on him first."

"Someone with a lot to lose." He looks off for a moment, then grins at a thought. "You know what's *really* intriguing about this?"

"Impress me."

"The motive. I mean, why do Russians kill each other, Katkov? Love, hate, politics—"

"—a bottle of vodka."

"Precisely. That's been about it up until now. Now, we have greed. Money. That's a brand-new one."

3

The Zhdanov-Krasny metro line zigzags beneath the city from the suburbs in the northwest, to the power corridors of central Moscow, and on to the industrial districts in the southeast. Lyublino, a working-class enclave where breathing is more hazardous than smoking, is a long way from the House on the Embankment. Indeed, this drab, polluted area I call home is at the end of the line in more ways than one, which means I can sleep on the train without missing my stop.

But I'm not sleeping tonight.

Despite the hour, my mind is racing to recall all I've learned about the privileged life and violent death of Vladimir Illiych Vorontsov. I can't write fast enough. Item by item I scribble it down in my notebook, along with the endless questions that come to mind:

Was Vorontsov a watchdog, or not? If so, which State assets did he suspect were being illegally sold?

Who were the buyers? The *apparatchiks* who managed those assets? Officials in the Interior Ministry? Foreign consortiums? All of the above? Ministry officials in collusion with outsiders?

Whom did Vorontsov report to? Who were his subordinates? Was he clean or dirty?

It will take weeks, maybe months, to answer them all. The

longer the better, as far as I'm concerned. This is a major scandal. At the least, I'm looking at a lead story and a series of follow-ups.

The train bends through a curve with a chilling screech and rumbles into the station. I slip out the door before it fully opens and charge up the escalator into early morning darkness. The frigid air is thick with noxious fumes billowing from the industrial stacks across the river in Brateyevo. I light a cigarette, thinking there's probably more sulfur in my lungs than on the matches, and head south beneath crackling power lines that stretch to the horizon.

Five years ago, after my last imprisonment for subversive writings, I moved from Perm 35 in the Urals to an apartment in Lyublino to write about the deadly living conditions. To my horror, the air smelled like sulfazine—a vile, fever-producing drug used by prison quacks to cure alcoholism—and I couldn't wait to finish my work and leave; but principle and poverty have conspired to keep me here. The baroque mansion where I live stands in gratifying defiance of the State's monolithic housing units, and the caretaker, whose family owned the house before the State divided it into dozens of cramped apartments, always allows me a few months' grace on the rent.

The harsh industrial odor gives way to the scent of perfume as I enter the vestibule. Vera's delicate fragrance draws me up the twisting staircase, gradually blending with the strong smell of coffee. "Hi," I say brightly, as I come through the door. "Sorry to be so late, but—"

That's strange. The sofa, where I expect to find Vera curled up with a book, is empty. The blanket she keeps tucked around her legs, tossed aside. My dog-eared copy of *I Claudius* is on the end table next to a butt-filled ashtray and a half cup of black coffee.

"Vera? Vera, you here?" I slide back the curtain that separates the sleeping alcove from the main living area. No Vera. The bedding hasn't been disturbed. I've just taken off my parka when I notice the bathroom door is closed. The tub. She probably took a bath and fell asleep. It wouldn't be the first time. I open the door slowly to avoid startling her, but the tub is also empty. Signs of Vera everywhere, but still no Vera.

I call her apartment. No answer. Maybe she had to go back to work. Militia Headquarters has my number. They've called her here before when they were shorthanded. Why didn't she beep me or leave a note? I call the dispatcher's office. But before I can explain, the woman who answers informs me Vera finished her shift and lectures me on the rule against personal calls. I hang up and take stock of the apartment.

Nothing appears to be missing. Even my library of subversive literature, as it was called not long ago, seems untouched. Controversial works smuggled in from the West—Sakharov, Solzhenitsyn, Hemingway, Nabokov, Shakespeare, Orwell, Sartre, Voltaire, Churchill, Locke, Lincoln, and countless others I risked my freedom to acquire, along with binders bursting with articles pirated from wire services—are all as I left them.

Did I take them out of hiding too soon? Did Vera's hunger for knowledge have consequences she never anticipated? A familiar hollowness is growing in my stomach. Perhaps, unlike winter, our newly won freedom is neither inevitable nor lasting.

The pot of coffee on the stove smells earthy and tart. I turn on the burner and pace anxiously as it heats, fighting my craving for alcohol, fighting to keep my imagination from getting the best of me. Vera probably got tired of waiting and went home; she's probably still on the Metro. I haven't had coffee in months, and the first swallow goes down like vodka after a week on the wagon. I'm savoring the second when someone raps on the door.

Vera? Why wouldn't she use her key?

Another salvo of knocks rattles the latch. "Mr. Katkov? Mr. Katkov, it's Mrs. Parfenov," an elderly voice calls out.

I open the door to find the old *babushka* who cares for the building, clutching at her bathrobe in the unheated corridor. "It's three in the morning, Mrs. Parfenov. I know I'm a little behind in my rent, but—"

"They took her away, Nikasha." She has the shaken look of those who have seen the Secret Police come in the night, though these things don't happen anymore.

"Took her away? Who?"

"Men. Who else?"

"Men? What did they look like? In uniforms?"

She shakes her head no, and maneuvers past me into the apartment. Her cloudy eyes dart about, taking stock of the place.

"Did you hear anything?"

"Yes," she says angrily. "They made an awful racket on the stairs. Woke me up."

"I mean, what they said."

"No. I watched from behind the curtains. They put her in a car." She cocks her head curiously and sniffs at the air. "What's that?"

"Coffee."

"Ah," she whines with suspicion. "I thought I recognized it. You have a source?"

"Vera does."

"Maybe that's why they arrested her."

"For buying coffee on the black market?"

"They're cracking down, Nikasha." She punctuates it with a chop of her bony hand, turns toward the door, then pauses and turns back. "There's something else I wanted to talk to you about. . . ." Her face twists with the confusion of age. "Aggghh, it escapes me."

"Something about Vera?"

"No. No, I'm quite sure it wasn't."

"The rent?"

"No. I know you're good for it. Don't worry, it'll come to me." She smiles weakly and shuffles out the door, her breath trailing behind her.

Did Shevchenko say *if* the KGB was still in business?! My gut is a knot of pain now. I lock the door and pull the curtains. I know better, but I place calls to the Militia and the KGB anyway. Anonymous calls. Neither has a record of Vera's arrest. That doesn't mean they don't have her. It's always been difficult to get information on citizens who've been arrested. I know the frustration all too well. I wrestle with it for a while, then do what I always do when I can't do anything else. I roll a sheet of paper into the typewriter and get to work.

V. I. Vorontsov, a longtime servant of the Motherland who spent years in constructive and frank discussions of the prospects for the development of trading and economic exchanges with the Western powers, was shot to death in his car last evening. This heinous act of hooliganism, this cold-blooded murder of a high-ranking Interior Ministry official raises many questions about the Committee for State Property.

Thought to be rife with the most criminal type of corruption, the CSP may be contributing mightily to the rapid flight of capital that is stifling economic growth. Furthermore . . .

As Vera anticipated, the coffee keeps me sharp, and the pages continue to roll out of the typewriter, despite the distraction. I've lived with these fears and uncertainties all my life. If they interfered with writing, I'd have never published a word. I'm leaning back in my chair, searching for an appropriate phrase, when a ray of light that has found its way through the smog announces it's morning.

I try Vera again with the same result. The next call is to a friend at the Interior Ministry. Yuri Ternyak is a respected economist who studied at the Institute of National Economic and Scientific-Technical Progress under a defiant genius named Shatalin who taught free-market theory. His disciples labored in cautious obscurity until the Communists fell and the new government engaged them to draft market-oriented reforms. Schooled in contemporary monetary policies and management techniques, many also find themselves conducting liaison with Western bankers, businessmen, and entrepreneurs doing business in Russia; though Yuri, a shy fellow who prefers academic solitude to corporate wheeling and dealing, has concentrated on formulating policy rather than implementing it. Our friendship began twenty-five years ago at Moscow State University, where he ran an underground literature exchange that has kept my library well stocked. More importantly, he's been a reliable source of information. In the past, we met in parks or on public conveyances to avoid KGB surveillance. Now, we talk more openly—but not today; not after what happened to Vera.

"You know the name Vorontsov?"

"Vaguely. I've heard it mentioned," Yuri replies over the crackling phone line.

"Heard anything lately?"

"Not that I recall."

"Get me what you can on him, and meet me at GUM."

"I can't. My schedule's jammed. I'm crazed."

"Come on, Yuri. It's important."

"I'm sorry, but I'm about to go into a meeting, and then I have to—"

"*Yuri.* Yuri, it's really important. I wouldn't ask otherwise."

He lets out a long breath and sighs. "All right. GUM. About noon?"

I'm not surprised that Yuri is pressed for time; he's been working round the clock as of late. But the fact that the Ministry isn't buzzing with news of the murder piques my curiosity. I ask him to have his secretary transfer my call to Vorontsov's office. The woman who answers says he called in sick. I'm not sure what to make of that. A cover story was standard procedure under the old regime. Either something's wrong, or Shevchenko is keeping the lid screwed on even tighter than he promised.

I jot down a few thoughts, then head for the Metro station. An hour later, I'm fighting my way through the crowds in GUM, the massive department store opposite the Kremlin. Sound bounces off the marble floors and vaulted glass roof like ricocheting billiards. The noise level is almost deafening. Yuri and I have had many meetings here without fear of being overheard. It's almost twelve-thirty by the time he joins me on one of the pedestrian bridges that arch between the shopping arcades.

"Sorry. The phone rang just as I was leaving," he explains; then, puzzled by my clandestine behavior, he lowers his voice and prompts, "So, what's going on?"

"They took Vera from my apartment last night."

Yuri's face pales. There's no need to ask who. His trimmed mustache, sharp cheekbones, and close-set eyes usually give him the look of a mischievous rodent; but he's deadly serious now. He's about to reply when he stiffens with fear at something he sees behind me.

I glance over my shoulder to see a compact man charging in our direction. Trench coat, fedora, face of stone. Hallmarks of the KGB. They are never alone, preferring to hunt in packs of three. I'm looking about frantically for the others. Yuri is poised to run, but they've trapped us on the bridge. I'm beginning to think it's a long way down when the man hurries past us without so much as a glance and brightens at the sight of a woman who runs into his arms, giggling like a schoolgirl.

Yuri sighs, relieved. I could drain a half liter of vodka without coming up for air. We hear of the KGB's demise. Even see signs of it. But decades of intimidation will take decades to forget. We take a moment to settle down, then walk to the opposite end of the bridge in silence.

Finally, Yuri lights a cigarette and briefs me on Vorontsov: sixty years old; born in Zhukovka, an elite suburb of Moscow; studied economics at the Plekhanov Institute, attended MGIMO, the prestigious Institute for International Relations; a member of *nomenklatura,* the privileged Party hierarchy; served in embassies in London, Berlin, Tokyo, and Washington, D.C.; currently in charge of oversight for the Committee for State Property.

"Oversight? I thought the CSP was autonomous?"

"They were—until the corruption got out of hand and the Interior Ministry got into the act."

"Vorontsov's a watchdog?"

Yuri nods again. "One way of putting it."

"Clean or dirty?"

"I've no idea. Why?"

Yuri is clearly shaken when I brief him on the murder. "You realize what you have here?"

I nod solemnly.

"It threatens the development of a free economy. As it is, the G-Seven countries are hedging their bets, and private investment is lagging; but this—this—internal corruption—not a renegade Congress, not betraying Yeltsin or taking over the White House—is what will bring the new government down. Declaring emergency rule and dissolving parliament have bought him time but Yeltsin still has to deliver. If he doesn't, we can kiss it all good-bye, and hard currency along with it. No dollars, no francs, no pounds, no marks, nothing." He pauses, stunned by his own assessment, then his eyes capture mine with concern. "I'd handle this very carefully if I were you."

I nod again, trying not to commit my heart to it. We reach the end of the bridge, and begin walking along the upper shopping level.

"Where are you taking it?" he asks. "The *News?*"

Moscow News was the breakthrough newspaper of Glasnost. The first to exercise freedom of the press, to support political reform, to be published internationally—in England, France, the United States; and in Israel in Russian—but it has since fallen into weak, cautious hands.

"Do you still subscribe?" I challenge, already knowing the answer.

"No. I've switched to *Independent Gazette,*" he replies with a grin, referring to the nonpartisan investigative journal that wants to be *The New York Times,* but comes closer to the *New York Post.*

"Oh, how come?"

"Well, I think the *News* has become staid. It's lost its independence."

"I agree. Why did you suggest it?"

"It just seems more suited to your style."

"Staid?! Not independent?!"

"You know better than that, Nikolai. The *News* has maturity and substance. The *Gazette*—it's trendy and hot. Of course, I'm sure they'd be interested."

"Yes, but everyone takes articles to them. It's a buyer's market."

"Then where? *Commersant? Argumenty i Fakty? Ogonyok?*" he prompts, listing popular liberal journals.

"Pravda."

"Pravda?!" Yuri echoes with a derisive snort. Shoppers in a nearby queue react as we board the down escalator. "I thought *Pravda* was out of business?"

"Temporarily. It's coming back as a political journal. Exposing the scandal would give it legitimacy. That alone would be news."

"The sort of news that'd get the wires to pick up the story," Yuri offers, aware that for years Western wire services have been publishing dissident writers and paying them in hard currency instead of rubles.

"Exactly."

"Even so. *Pravda* is a defunct Communist rag. Their circulation is in the toilet."

"Which makes it a seller's market."

"No. Which is why they pay so little."

"They'll pay plenty for this."

"Come on, no one takes them seriously. You know better than I, the joke has always been that *Pravda* means truth."

"The only way to stop the laughter is by proving it, by finally publishing truth. I'm going to offer them the best chance they'll ever have, and they're going to jump at it."

"If you're right. *If* this alleged corruption can be proven. *If* you are able to—"

"Enough. I have a good feeling about this, Yuri. A very good feeling. It's going to change my life."

"Or end it."

"This is new? We've been dealing with thugs for years. Stalin's thugs, Khrushchev's thugs, Brezhnev's thugs. They're all gone, and we're still here."

"True," he says thoughtfully as the escalator deposits us in a crowd of shoppers scurrying from one queue to the next. "But it's much more difficult to identify them now."

4

S he isn't here," Mrs. Parfenov rasps, her birch-twig broom moving in crisp whisks across the cold pavement.

"Thanks. It's been over twelve hours. I still haven't heard anything."

She nods gravely, working a small mound of litter to one side of the staircase.

"Has anyone else been here?" I prompt casually.

"You mean those men, don't you?"

I nod.

She stops sweeping and grunts no. Then her eyes cloud, and she snaps, "And before you ask, I still can't remember."

"What? What you wanted to tell me?"

She nods, annoyed with herself, and sends me inside with a wave of her broom.

No perfume, no coffee, and no surprises this time. The apartment is dark, cold, and empty. I spend several hours working Yuri's information into the story and fine-tuning clumsy paragraphs. A rush comes over me as I roll the last page from the typewriter. Not because I'm finished. No, this is the beginning, not the end. The sheet of carbon and the copy go into separate trays on my desk; the original, paper-clipped with the other original pages, into a slim, leather briefcase.

My wife gave it to me over twenty years ago when I sold my first story to a French wire service. Faded and scarred, it endured my career far better than our marriage, which ended when my activism endangered her promising medical practice. I snap the tarnished latch and hurry from the apartment, my excitement tempered by Vera's disappearance and Yuri's unnerving observation about thugs.

It's barely midafternoon, but smog and the early dusk of winter have already plunged Lyublino into darkness. Headlights come from behind me, projecting shadows across the gritty facades. My pulse quickens, then settles as the vehicle passes. Not a militia van. Not a KGB troika in a Zhiguli. Just a taxi cruising for fares; but there are no takers among the browsers at the kiosk opposite the Metro station. It's one of the few that actually sells newspapers. Most are mailed because *Soyuz Pechat,* the state supplier, won't pay merchants enough to carry them. But this one gets a fair price from commuters who must leave for work well before their mail is delivered.

I spend the subway ride to *Pravda* checking afternoon editions for stories on Vorontsov's murder. Not a word in any of them. Shevchenko has kept his promise. The escalator at the Belorusskaya Station in north-central Moscow launches its bundled riders into an icy drizzle. It's a short walk to the pedestrian underpass that leads to Leningradsky Prospekt; and about half a mile to Pravda Ulitsa and the journal's gloomily efficient offices at No. 24.

The elevator is in use. I charge up the stairs to the newsroom. Every surface is covered with copy and piles of photographs that threaten to topple. The furniture, lighting, cast-iron radiators, and chatter of manual typewriters are all right out of the fifties. Indeed, everything here is dated. Everything except the faces. Young and diligent, their eager eyes are riveted to the pages in their typewriters.

I snake between the desks to a row of offices at the far end of the newsroom. A chunky middle-aged man with hair that rolls back from his forehead in tight waves sits behind a glass partition labeled EDITOR. Round spectacles bridge his nose giving him the look of a well-fed owl—an "owl" I recognize. This is a stroke of luck beyond anything I could imagine.

Sergei Murashev is a highly respected journalist. Like many Party intellectuals afraid of being shipped off to the gulag, he kept a low profile until the political climate changed, then came out swinging. He was a charter subscriber of Yuri's literature exchange, and we've worked together on and off over the years. At the moment, Sergei is editing copy with a vengeance and doesn't notice me in the doorway.

"What am I bid for a juicy political murder with a terrific scandal and an inside source?"

"Nikolai!" he exclaims as he bolts from his chair and circles the desk to greet me.

"You're the last person I ever expected to find here, Sergei."

"Ah, it's a marriage of convenience. They couldn't find anyone to take the job; and I've grown unashamedly accustomed to food, clothing, and shelter."

My eyes dart to front pages from past editions displayed on the wall behind him. In typical *Pravda* style, each headline is subordinated to the masthead, which depicts Lenin's profile and proclaims:

> Proletarians of the world, Unite!
> Communist Party of the Soviet Union
> PRAVDA
> Established the 5th of May 1912 by V. I. LENIN
> Organ of the Central Committee of the CPSU

"I'm surprised those aren't long gone," I prompt.

"They were. I put them back."

"You did what?"

"I don't ever want to forget; and I want to make damn sure those kids know." He inclines his head to the newsroom, then gets to the matter at hand. "You really have something for me?"

I nod and slip the pages from my briefcase. "Something special."

Sergei's brows arch with anticipation. He settles in the tired cushions of his chair, pushes his glasses onto his forehead, and starts reading. His eyes widen, his jaw tightens, and he begins to fidget. Minutes seem like an eternity.

"Powerful," he finally pronounces. "Powerful, important, and shocking."

"Thank you."

His head cocks challengingly. "You're positive about this conspiracy to rip off State assets?"

"*Shevchenko*'s positive. Really, Sergei, it's no secret the place is overrun with corruption."

"And you're also positive Vorontsov was killed because he was going to blow the whistle?"

"He was head of the IM's oversight committee. Look, he was either onto it or into it. We're talking political scandal no matter how you slice it."

"Good. I'm not interested in doing street crime."

"Nor am I."

"Shevchenko's working with you?"

"*Only* with me, if that's what you mean."

Sergei nods and chortles at something that occurs to him. "I can see it in the *Washington Post* now: FORMER COMMUNIST PARTY NEWSPAPER EXPOSES CAPITALIST PRIVATIZATION SCHEME."

"We should be so lucky. I'm more interested in *Pravda*'s headline."

He hunches down in the chair, rocking back and forth thoughtfully, then eyes twinkling with mischief, Sergei announces, "MURDER FOR PROFIT."

It's a stroke of genius. I laugh out loud with delight. "They've never seen that one in *Pravda*."

He grins with satisfaction, then knocks his glasses down onto his nose and picks up the pages. "Now for the hard part," he says awkwardly. "This is a great story, Nikolai, really; but the writing, it's . . . it's stilted."

"Stilted?"

"Yes, you know, full of *Novoyaz*," he groans, using slang for government-speak. "We don't use phrases like 'longtime servant of the Motherland' or 'heinous act of hooliganism' any longer. We don't *think* the CSP is rife with corruption, Nikolai. We *know* it. Correct?"

I nod, angry with myself.

"Then why not say it outright?"

"Too many years of trying to outsmart *glavit*," I reply, cursing decades spent cloaking the truth in officially acceptable language to slip it past KGB censors. "Old habits die hard."

"Tell me about it. I'm the worst. The syntax has to be more contemporary now. More conversational. More, more . . ."

"Westernized."

He nods emphatically.

I'm crushed and about to argue that it's a rough draft, that I can easily fix it, when it dawns on me Sergei knows this. He also knows it's a hot story. Editors are notorious for finding huge problems with free-lance copy, notorious for their "it's great but needs a lot of work" negotiating technique. It's an old ploy to keep the price down. I casually gather the pages from his desk and open the flap of my briefcase. "Well, Sergei, if you think it's beyond repair . . ."

"Beyond repair?!" He pulls the pages from my hand. "This is a lead story—front page—above the fold."

"A series of follow-ups on Shevchenko go with it," I declare, pressing the advantage. "The investigator tracks down and apprehends suspects, files charges, testifies at trials . . ."

"A case history as seen through the eyes of a cop," Sergei says knowingly.

"An ambitious cop."

Sergei waggles his hand. "I hear he's not enough of a prick to make chief."

"Me too. Still, every exclusive has its price. Speaking of which . . ."

"Hold it right there. I took this job on several conditions. A hefty discretionary fund was one of them. You'll be well paid. I promise you."

"How well?"

He kicks back in his chair, studying the ceiling. "Oh, say . . . a hundred twenty-five thousand rubles."

"That's very poor discretion, Sergei."

"I hasten to remind you it's ten times the average weekly wage."

"Ten? Did I just hear you say ten? Now *that's* a good number. Yes, ten times the *monthly* wage."

"Five hundred thousand rubles?!"

"For the lead, and two follow-ups at two-fifty each."

"No. No, two-fifty for the *lead,* and seventy-five for each follow-up."

"Why don't we make it easy for your bookkeepers and round it off to an even three for the lead, and a hundred per follow-up?" I extend a hand.

A long moment passes before Sergei's meaty fist latches onto mine. "Fair enough. Five hundred thousand."

"That's what I said."

Sergei laughs and tosses his pencil at me. "Now all we have to do is get this 'Westernized' in time for the morning edition."

"I'll do it here. Just give me a desk where I can—"

"Oh, no. No, not necessary. You were up all night working on it, right?"

"Yeah, but—"

"You look it."

"I'm fine. Really."

"Enough. Your face has the pallor of newsprint. A tired writer produces tired copy, my friend. This needs energy and pace."

"Then who? You?"

He smiles enigmatically and takes his time lighting a cigarette. After filling the space above his desk with smoke, he reaches to the intercom box next to his phone and depresses the talk button. "Drevnya? Drevnya, get in here, will you?"

On the other side of the glass partition, a young reporter pushes back from a desk and makes his way through the newsroom. Thatches of brown hair fall over his forehead and collar. In his blue jeans, T-shirt, and vest, the kid looks like he's just come from a rock concert in Sokol'niki Park. Unlike the old-timer at Moscow Beginners, he hasn't the slightest glimmer of recognition when Sergei introduces us. Dissidents have no cachet with this generation.

"Katkov has brought us a story," Sergei explains. "An exclusive one. Something that will get this paper off the mark. But it needs your touch."

The young lion nods smugly and scans the pages with an expression that has "stilted" written all over it. "Looks like an easy fix." He forces a smile and exits, then, as an afterthought, calls back over his shoulder, "Hell of a piece."

"He's good. Very good," Sergei says, sensing my uneasiness. "He can dig out a story, he can verify facts, he can write, and he's not afraid. None of these kids are. They don't give a damn what the Kremlin thinks. Some of the best young journalists I've come across in years."

"You forgot to mention his strong handshake, bristling energy, confident demeanor, and intense eyes. Naturally, I disliked him immediately."

Sergei laughs heartily. "If it makes you feel any better, he punches up my material too. He'll punch me right out the door if I'm not careful. You know why they call political upheavals 'thaws,' don't you?"

"A metaphor for spring; a coming back to life."

"No. It's because getting through them is like walking on thin ice."

"Come on. You've got nothing to worry about, and I'm sure the kid'll do a fine job." I turn to leave, feeling as dated as the furniture.

"Wait!" Sergei beats me to the door and closes it. "Get that shade, will you?"

I'm reaching for the tasseled pull when my eyes dart to the kid in the newsroom. He's at his desk, but he's not typing. He's talking—animatedly—on the phone. I'm wondering what he's up to when I hear the clink of glassware behind me. Sergei is removing a bottle of vodka and two tumblers from a sideboard behind his desk.

"Stolichnaya?" Though vodka is more available in Moscow than meat and fresh vegetables, the government reserves the finest for export only.

"Never drink with *two* other people, Nikasha," he jests, quoting a popular saying as he pours. "You won't know who the informer was."

"Unless one of them brought Stolichnaya."

"Of course. The one with black-market vodka broke the law. He wouldn't be working with the police. So it would have to be the other one."

"Not necessarily . . ." I lower the shade over the glass partition. "There's always a chance the one who broke the law has already been caught."

He smiles thinly and nods in acknowledgment. *"Zadrovnye,"* he says, handing me one of the glasses. He knocks back the vodka, smacks his lips, and looks at me, wondering what I'm waiting for.

So am I. Hell, I've been working my ass off. I have it coming. What *am* I waiting for? Vera's approval? Probably. This Moscow Beginners stuff was her idea. Where the hell is she when I need her?

A couple of hours later, I find out. I'm heading home on the Metro when my beeper goes off. I still don't know exactly where Vera is, but chances are she isn't dead—and isn't in Lubyanka, Lefortovo, or the gulag. I'm halfway up the stairs to

my apartment when the scent hits me. "Vera?!" I call out as I
lunge through the door, which is unlocked.

As I pictured last night, Vera is curled up on the sofa, reading. Her soft platinum hair is swept over one shoulder, the
blanket tucked around her legs, the carbons of my article in
her lap instead of a book.

"What happened? You okay?"

"Bastards!" she exclaims bitterly as she sets the pages aside
and runs into my arms, her flawless White-Russian skin flush-
ing with rage.

"Who are you talking about?"

"Shevchenko. A couple of his goons busted in here and
hauled me away."

"Shevchenko? Why?"

"He didn't like me tipping you off."

"Are you kidding? He was thrilled. We—"

"That's not funny."

"I'm serious. We made a deal. He's giving me an exclusive;
and I'm giving him a promotion, so to speak."

"*Chief* Investigator Shevchenko," Vera intones knowingly.
Then, gesturing to the pages on the sofa, she adds, "If that
doesn't do it, nothing will."

"Rather good, isn't it?"

"Damned good." She lets out a long breath and shrugs, baffled. "I don't get it."

"The only thing that makes sense is Shevchenko wanted to
make sure I know who's calling the shots."

"Well, you always said you were a liability I couldn't afford.
I'm starting to think you're right."

"He fired you?"

"No. Docked me a couple of days' pay, though."

"Gosh, I'm sorry. I didn't know what to do. I called your
apartment, I called the militia, I even called the goddamned
KGB."

"The Security Directorate," she corrects.

"Whatever. They'll always be KGB to me."

"Neither had a record of my arrest, right?"

"Right."

"They stashed me in the drunk tank." That explains it. As
part of the new commitment to increase personal freedom and
change the police state mentality, Moscow's sobering-up sta-

tions are no longer being run by the militia. Of course, they've become the perfect place to confine citizens without any record of their being in custody. "After spending the night watching the scum of the earth barf their brains out, I got a two-hour lecture from Shevchenko about not revealing information to outsiders."

"I'm still glad you did."

Her demeanor softens, and she breaks into a satisfied smile. "This is the one, isn't it, Niko?"

"Uh-huh. I can live off it for a year."

"You already sold it?!"

I nod emphatically. "A series of follow-ups too."

"Come on, come on, who?"

"Pravda."

"Pravda?!"

"Don't laugh. Sergei is there. They're paying five hundred thousand."

"Five hundred?! That's fantastic."

"Enough talk," I say, pointing to a clipping from an old issue of *The New York Times Magazine* that's pinned to the bulletin board above my desk.

"I know, I know," Vera says, beating me to it. " 'Planning to write is not writing. Outlining a book is not writing. Researching is not writing. Talking to people about what you're doing, none of that is writing. Writing is writing.' E. L. Doctorow."

"You have it memorized."

Vera's eyes roll. "A parrot would have little choice around here."

"Can you say, 'Make love to me, Nikolai'?" I ask, pulling her into an embrace.

"Maybe."

"How about, 'Tear off my clothes, Nikolai. Bwaaak! Tear off my clothes, Nikolai. Bwaaaak! Bwaaaak!' Can you say that?"

She emits a lusty giggle and kisses me. All of a sudden she breaks it off and glares at me accusingly.

Damn. The vodka. She's detected the vodka.

"Stolichnaya. How could I say no?"

Her soft eyes narrow and harden like gemstones.

"Sergei wanted to celebrate. I couldn't insult him. I only had one."

"That's one too many."

"Come on, Vera, I'm fine."

"Oh, yeah?" she challenges seductively, grinding her pelvis against mine. "I'll be the judge of that." She buries her hands in my hair, spins me around, and pushes me down on the bed, her mouth devouring mine, her hands tearing at my clothes. Thank God Sergei insisted the kid do the rewrite. Soon, passion soaring, we're naked and tangled in the bedding like writhing snakes. It doesn't get much better than this. No, life has never been so good. Never.

Hours later, I've no idea how many, I awaken to the strong smell of coffee and a rustling sound. My hand searches the bed for Vera to no avail. I push up onto an elbow, squinting at the daylight coming through the curtains. "Vera?"

No reply.

I finally locate her in a chair by the window. She's fully dressed and is frantically turning the pages of a newspaper. "Vera? Vera, what the hell are you doing?"

"It's not here."

"What?"

"*Pravda.* I couldn't wait for the mail. I bought a copy at the newsstand. I can't find it. It's not on the front page, not even below the fold."

"It has to be." I stumble out of bed and tear the paper from her hands—as if looking for it myself, as if willing the article to be there will make it so. But it isn't. Not on the front page, not opposite the editorial page, not anywhere that an important story would be found. Finally, near the bottom of a column of obituaries, I find a small headline: V. I. VORONTSOV KILLED BY THIEF.

"Killed By Thief?!" I exclaim, my voice ringing with disbelief. "By M. I. Drevnya?!"

"Who?"

"The wiseass kid who did the rewrite!" I explode, throwing the newspaper across the room in disgust.

5

Drevnya is at his desk, typing furiously as I charge across the newsroom brandishing the paper. "What the fuck is this?!"

He recoils and swivels in his chair to face me. "Take it easy, Katkov, take it easy, okay?"

"Soon as you explain what happened to my story!"

He retreats, propelling the chair backward with his feet, then stands to confront me. "Look, I can understand why you're pissed off, but—"

"Pissed off?! Pissed off is hardly—"

"Hey, hey?!" Sergei's voice booms. He weaves between the desks and pushes his way through the group that encircles us. "What the hell's going on here?"

"Good question!"

"Ask him," the kid counters, jabbing a finger at my chest. "He's the one who's going bonkers!"

"You little shit!" I lunge for him, but Sergei steps between us and burns me with a look. "Let's do this in my office."

I'm seething, the veins in my neck throbbing like fire hoses. I take a moment to settle, then nod grudgingly and follow after him.

Sergei closes the door and gathers his thoughts. Then like

a teacher forced to reprimand a prize student, he says, "I'm disappointed in you, Nikolai. You're better than this."

"The feeling's mutual. You should have called me."

"I just did."

"Bullshit!"

"I spoke to Vera. You can ask her. It's barely eight-thirty. You expect me to wake you in the middle of the night? 'Hi, Nikolai, I have some bad news.' "

"What news?! Vorontsov was murdered to keep the lid on a privatization scandal. Where'd this nonsense about a robbery come from?!"

"Look, Niko, you're going to have to accept that this story isn't what you thought."

"You didn't answer my question."

"The kid has initiative. Yesterday afternoon, he—"

"That's a polite word for it!"

"Yesterday afternoon," Sergei resumes evenly, "before starting his rewrite, he called Vorontsov's daughter to check some facts, but—"

"He wasn't supposed to check facts! He was going to 'Westernize' my syntax! Remember?!"

"Yes, Nikolai, of course I do," he says, measuring his words as if dealing with a surly toddler. "Now, hear me out, will you?"

I splay my hands and drop into the chair opposite his desk with a sullen nod.

"Thank you. When Drevnya called Mrs. Churkin, she was leaving for Militia Headquarters and couldn't talk. But the kid has some connections there or something so he arranged to meet her. Needless to say, identifying her father's body was upsetting. Drevnya comforted her and, shrewd journalist that he is, just happened to be at her side when she claimed Vorontsov's personal effects and discovered something was missing."

"Come on. I was at the crime scene. Nothing was missing. His billfold, his watch, his—"

"I know—I know," Sergei interrupts.

"Then why does the fucking obit say a thief stole his valuables?!"

He stares at the ceiling for a moment, deciding. "That was a cover."

"A cover?!" I exclaim, jumping to my feet. "A cover for what?"

"For what was actually stolen."

"What is this, some sort of guessing game? Come on, god-dammit, what was stolen?"

"I don't know," he replies, averting his eyes.

"You're insulting my intelligence, Sergei, not to mention your own. If the kid was with her, he knows what was missing."

His head bobs sheepishly, then with a sigh, he concedes, "You're right. Shevchenko asked us to withhold it. You know, to weed out the nuts who always confess to these things."

"You can tell *me,* for Chrissakes."

"Right now, I wouldn't trust you with the time of day. Besides, I told you, I've no interest in street crime. I ran the obit, and I'm done with it. You'll have to talk to Shevchenko."

"Oh, I plan to, but I'm talking to you now. We had an agreement, Sergei. It's my story, and—"

"No. No, Nikolai. We didn't run your story. The kid dug out the facts, it fell apart, and I spiked it."

"You should've consulted me."

"I didn't think you'd want your by-line on an obit."

"Depends on whose it is."

"That a threat?"

"Take it any way you want."

He stares at me, hands on hips, then shakes his head in dismay. "You don't know when someone's trying to do you a favor."

"I know when I'm being screwed."

"I'm sorry you feel that way."

"You should be."

I charge out of the office loaded for bear—a bear named Shev-chenko. Militia Headquarters is less than a mile from here as the crow flies; but the railroad tracks and Ring Road triple the distance. Yesterday's icy drizzle has turned into stinging sleet. There isn't a cab in sight. I hunch down into my parka and head south toward Uspenskiy, a narrow street behind the Hotel Minsk that winds east toward Petrovka.

About a half hour later, I'm at No. 38. I'm not sure whether it's because Shevchenko put my name on the list of approved visitors, or the red-cheeked sentry is anxious to return to his shack, but I'm cleared through the gate without incident. A sergeant at the desk in the lobby explains Shevchenko isn't in yet and directs me to a waiting area.

I shake the sleet from my parka, light a cigarette, and begin pacing. The revolving door spits out a steady stream of shivering employees. I'm grinding my fifth Ducat into the terrazzo when Shevchenko arrives. He spots me out of the corner of his eye and makes a beeline for the corridor that leads to the elevators.

"Investigator Shevchenko?!" I call out, vaulting a low partition to intercept him.

"Katkov, please."

"I thought we had a deal?!" I protest, purposely raising my voice. Everyone within earshot reacts. He stops and looks around uncomfortably. "Well?!" I prompt in a tense whisper.

"*Had* is the operative word," he replies through clenched teeth, directing me into an anteroom off the lobby. "I had something at stake too, remember?"

"Until somebody promised you more!"

"Not true. I'm as pissed off as you are, Katkov. This was the best shot at chief I've ever had." He slaps his briefcase on the table and goes about removing his trench coat.

"Come on. Who got to you?"

"*Nobody.* This reporter from *Pravda* was here when Vorontsov's daughter showed up to ID her father. He—"

"I know. His name's Drevnya. You should have told him to take a hike!"

"And violate his rights?!" Shevchenko exclaims, pretending he's shocked. "Really, you're the last person I'd expect to suggest that. Of course, there was a time I could've locked him up and thrown away the key. But times have changed. Haven't they?"

"I don't think Vera Fedorenko would agree. Do you?!"

"Fedorenko . . . Fedorenko," he repeats, needling me. "Doesn't ring a bell. Was there something else you—"

"*Pravda*'s obit said Vorontsov's valuables were stolen. You and I both know they weren't. Now, I want to know, what *was?*"

His jaw sets and his eyes sharpen with a warning. "Off the record."

An exasperated groan comes from deep inside me. "Off the record."

"His medals. He was killed for his medals."

"His medals?"

"Yes, they're solid gold, highly prestigious, and worth a small fortune on the black market. Somewhere in the neighborhood of thirty million rubles. The killer didn't want to tear them from Vorontsov's jacket and risk damaging them. So he—"

"He?!"

"Or she," he concedes indulgently, "dragged the body behind the wall, where, without risk of being seen, they could be removed with care. That piece fits rather neatly now, wouldn't you say?"

"What about the time discrepancy? That fits rather neatly now, too?"

"Perfectly. Vorontsov didn't spend an hour or two shopping, because he didn't have to take a number and wait in a queue. He bypassed it completely because he was wearing the right medals."

"Come on, that protocol crap went out with the *apparatchiks*. Nobody gives a damn about medals anymore."

"I beg to differ. You're familiar with the names Krichevsky, Komar, and Usov?"

"The poor bastards who were killed in Red Square, protesting the coup. Yes, I am. I was there. Where were you? Cheering on the conspirators?"

"The point is, your buddy Boris-don't-call-me-an-apparat-chik-Yeltsin—free-marketeer and champion of democracy, mind you—awarded the Hero of the Soviet Union to each of them posthumously."

"An acceptable lapse in judgment."

"That was no lapse, Katkov. This society has been medal-crazy since czarist times. Like it or not, the damn things are part of our culture. We award them for everything from having babies, to bravery in combat, to growing cabbage; and we wear them like oil-rich Arabs festooned in gaudy jewelry. You think the new order is going to change that?"

"I'm counting on it."

"Don't be naive. Last week I saw a picture in a Western magazine of Soviet Jews who emigrated to Israel. Dozens of them. All diehard refuseniks who couldn't wait to forsake their country for a miserable patch of desert. Yet every last one was proudly wearing his medals. *Soviet* medals."

"Sounds to me like you have a little problem with Jews, Mr. Investigator."

"Katkov."

"Marx was a Jew. Did you know that?"

"Yes," he hisses impatiently, baring tobacco-stained teeth.

"Not all of us want to live in Israel, believe me. This Jew, for one, is going to stay right here and make your life miserable."

"Don't do this, Katkov. Don't make it personal."

"You're the one who's making it personal. You want me to accept that there's no political angle here just because you say so?"

"No. Because the facts don't support it."

"You're saying they support that some thug just happened to see a guy with a chest covered with satin and brass leave his lodge hall? Followed him? Shot him? And stole his medals?"

"Yes, I am. A tipsy guy, by the way." Shevchenko slips a sheet of paper from his briefcase. "Preliminary toxicology report," he says as if holding the Communist Manifesto. "Vorontsov's blood alcohol level was point one three. He was legally intoxicated."

"So is most of Moscow at that hour."

"It made him an easy target."

"If he was wearing his medals. Just because his daughter said so doesn't mean he was."

"I sure hope you're challenging me to prove it."

"Bet your ass."

Shevchenko smirks, scoops up his things, and blows out of the anteroom. I follow, as he walks briskly to the end of the corridor and down a staircase. The pungent odors of urine and disinfectant intensify with each step. They come from a dank warren of cells and caverns in the basement, where prisoners and evidence are stored.

In the latter section, boxes, envelopes, folders, and large individually tagged items are stuffed onto rows of shelves behind wire-mesh fencing. Shevchenko fills out a requisition form and slips it to a clerk. The dour fellow fetches a large paper sack, which he exchanges for Shevchenko's initials. The investigator drops it on one of the tables and ceremoniously removes Vorontsov's blood-spattered sport coat.

"I thought his daughter claimed his things?"

"She did. That's how we know about the medals. She took one look at this and asked what we'd done with them. I'd no choice but to retain it."

"Because it proves he was wearing them."

Shevchenko nods slyly and pushes the coat toward me. "See for yourself."

The fabric is a heavily textured wool. I give the area next to the lapels a careful once-over. There are no impressions, no fading, no pinholes, tears, or marks, nothing to indicate there was ever one medal affixed to it, let alone a chestful. "Sorry. I don't get it."

Shevchenko opens a drawer where examining tools are stored and removes a magnifying glass. "Try the lining."

I turn the jacket inside out and slowly move the lens over the imitation silk, zeroing in on the area behind the breast pocket. And there, puckering the fibers in neat rows, are dozens of pinholes.

"See them?" Shevchenko prompts.

I look up and nod glumly.

"According to his daughter, he was the proud holder of three Heroes of the Soviet Union, two Orders of the Red Banner, the Order of Lenin, and enough secondary military and civilian decorations to adorn half the members of Parliament."

I'm beginning to get a hollow feeling when something dawns on me. "Hold it. That still doesn't prove Vorontsov was wearing the medals when he was killed. They could've been removed ages ago."

"Good, Katkov. Very good. That was *my* question. And Mrs. Churkin had the answer. It's a new coat. As a matter of fact, she helped her father transfer the medals from another a few days before."

The hollowness returns with devastating impact. Homicide not withstanding, a billion-dollar government scandal has turned into a two-bit robbery. The lead story, the series of follow-ups, the wire service sales, the five-hundred-thousand-ruble fee, the professional satisfaction—all blown away. But as the senior investigator would say, there's still one piece that doesn't fit. "What about those documents?

"Vorontsov's?"

"Uh-huh. The Committee for State Property. Something's going on."

Shevchenko begins folding the coat. "Undoubtedly. But you're making this into something it isn't."

"What about your theory that he was hit because he was going to blow the whistle on someone?"

"I was wrong."

"You were right, dammit. You said you thought he was a watchdog, and he was."

"True," he says, preening. "But it's not relevant to my case. The fact remains that Vorontsov was wearing his medals when he left the house and wasn't when he was found. My report will state: Crime, homicide. Weapon, nine-millimeter Stechkina. Motive, robbery. Have I made myself clear?"

"What's clear is those documents should be turned over to the guys who handle this kind of stuff."

He burns me with a look and shoves the folded sport coat into the evidence bag.

"Come on, I know there's a department here that—"

"Look, Katkov," he interrupts, ignoring the suggestion, "despite my fondness for the old guard, I'm not going to bring charges against the new one, especially against the ministry that employs me, or against the CSP's privatization program, which, I'm man enough to admit"—he pauses, barely able to say it—"might, *might,* be the key to pulling our economic chestnuts out of the fire. Are you?"

"Yes, if it's infested with corruption."

"And you have evidence of that?"

"No, but I know what might," I reply pointedly. "And I'd be more than happy to run with it, if they happened to fall into my hands."

Shevchenko's eyes flare. He knows what I want. "I can't do that."

"Sure you can. We go up to your office. You accidentally leave the documents on your desk and head for the john while I get acquainted with the nearest copying machine."

"Not a chance." He sweeps the bag off the table, pushes it through the window to the clerk, and charges out of the evidence room.

"Okay, back to square one. If not you, who?"

"Pardon me?" he challenges, stepping up his pace.

"Come on. Which section handles white-collar scams?"

"Economic Crimes."

"Thank you. Why not give the documents to them?"

"Because the *Interior Ministry* is investigating irregularities at the CSP. If Vorontsov's superiors determine his suspicions are valid, they'll take whatever steps are necessary to—"

"You don't really believe that."

"Sure I do. Maybe they already have." He starts up the staircase, lighting a cigarette.

I'm right on his heels, thinking he knows better, knows that whatever Vorontsov uncovered probably goes from the top down, knows the bureaucrats can't be trusted to investigate themselves. Furthermore, his evasiveness suggests he has an ulterior motive. And I know what it is. "Who's in charge of Economic Crimes, anyway?" I prompt offhandedly.

He reaches a landing and starts up the next flight. "Fellow named Gudonov."

"Doesn't ring a bell."

"He transferred from Central about six months ago."

"Would that be *Investigator* Gudonov?"

Shevchenko nods. "Around here, he's become known as Incinerator Gudonov."

"Incinerator?"

"Uh-huh. Black-market money transactions fall in his area. He hauls whatever he confiscates down to Sanitation and burns it. Claims it's a deterrent. Fucking grandstanding, if you ask me."

We climb a few more steps. "So, is that Senior Incinerator? Or Chief Incinerator?"

"Senior," Shevchenko replies apprehensively, sensing where I'm headed.

"And how long has Senior Investigator Gudonov been on the militia?"

"We were in the same class at the IMPC."

"Where?"

"Interior Ministry Police College."

"An old rivalry then."

His shoulders go up.

"Would you say he's an ambitious fellow?"

"A snake."

"Professionally frustrated?"

"Extremely."

"How many openings for chief are there?"

"Not enough."

"And if you gave Gudonov these documents, you'd be handing him the promotion while you'd be stuck solving a two-bit homicide."

"I don't have to put up with this. Get it into your head: The documents came from the Interior Ministry, and I'm returning them. Now, if you'll excuse me, I'm late for a seminar."

"A seminar? Keeping up with the latest in thumbscrews and eavesdropping devices, are we?"

"No such luck," he replies with a disgusted scowl. "Try sitting through a lecture on how law enforcement agencies can better share information, sometime." He forces a smile and walks purposefully toward a set of double doors at the end of the corridor.

"That's exactly what I'm talking about," I exclaim, right on his heels as he pushes through the doors. "Sharing information. Those documents are—"

"That makes two of us—" a voice interrupts sharply. It's a woman's voice, angry and amplified, speaking Russian with what sounds like a heavy American accent.

I freeze, realizing I've followed Shevchenko into a lecture hall filled with law enforcement personnel, who turn and stare at us.

"—And unless I'm mistaken," the woman goes on, glowering at me from behind the lectern, "I'm the expert in this area."

"Just what I need," I say, as we move down the aisle toward her. "Maybe you can convince this thickhead to cooperate."

"Oh, no. No, that's your job. That's what this seminar's about," she replies, coming out from behind the lectern with her microphone. She's tall, larger than life, with large Mediterranean features; large jumble of coarse black hair; large gestures; indeed, everything about her that counts is large. "And I've several workshops planned where you'll be putting these data-sharing techniques into practice. But for now, I'd appreciate it if you'd both take your—"

"There won't be anything to share if we wait," I interrupt. "He took the documents from someone's apartment, and—"

"They're evidence," Shevchenko protests, turning to the stage. "Look, this man isn't even a—"

"Evidence?!" I explode, cutting him off in the nick of time. "You're the one who said they weren't. They're the victim's property!"

"I don't think he's up to claiming them. Do you?!"

"His daughter is! And I'd be more than happy to—"

"Gentlemen?! Gentlemen, please," the woman pleads, maintaining a professional demeanor. "Maybe a practical lesson would be valuable at this time. If your colleagues agree, perhaps we can—"

"Colleagues?!" Shevchenko roars as an affirmative murmur rises from the audience. "This clown isn't a police officer. He's . . . he's a journalist!"

"A journalist?" the speaker sneers, realizing she's been snookered. Her coal black eyes lock onto mine like angry lasers. "What's with you media people, anyway? Is it an international conspiracy, or do you all share a genetic defect?"

"Actually, it's an eating disorder. We have this obsessive hunger for truth."

"Yes, and a nasty habit of publishing it without any regard for the consequences." She shifts her gaze to the audience and resumes, "Speaking of the media—with all the crime and narcotics coming out of Eastern Europe, effective media relations and control are all the more vital. I'll be dealing with it in tomorrow's session. I call it: Debunking the Power of the Press and Other Myths. But it'd be a shame to pass up an opportunity for a hands-on demonstration now." She looks off to one side of the stage and nods.

Two uniformed militia officers, each about the size of my refrigerator, stand and lumber up the aisle toward me, to applause.

6

No way, Niko. Not a chance," Vera replies when I bring up the subject of Vorontsov's documents.

We're in McDonald's on Pushkin Square, having lunch with Yuri. It's an extremely large space with vast expanses of glass and brightly colored plastic, a short walk from Militia Headquarters and the Interior Ministry. The concept of queuing at a window to place your order is perfectly suited to Muscovites, who are accustomed to waiting in line for everything. But after a lifetime of eating boiled potatoes and beef, the richness of french fries and cheeseburgers takes some getting used to, especially, I imagine, for residents of the apartment building directly above. Despite the culture gap, a hoard of middle-class locals are gorging themselves on fast food—inexpensive fast food—that most of them can't afford. For the three of us, the noise level is more than worth the price of admission.

"Come on, Vera," I protest. "You're in thirty-eight Petrovka every day. I've got to get my hands on those documents. You could at least try."

Her lips tighten into a defiant line.

"*Vera.*"

"I get caught this time, it'll cost me more than a couple of days' pay and a night in the drunk tank."

"Something I don't understand. . . ." Yuri says. He pauses, savoring a spoonful of chocolate ice cream as he puzzles it out. Along with sharing my passion for political reform, he's as addicted to ice cream as I am to vodka; and his search for the perfect flavor and texture has taken him to every *kafé morozhenoye* in Moscow. "If Vorontsov was killed to cover up a scandal, why take his medals?"

"For openers, to make it look like a robbery so the militia will bark up all the wrong trees. Which is exactly what I think Shevchenko's doing."

"Possible. And?"

"Their value. How much do you think a professional would get to take Vorontsov out?"

"I don't know," Yuri muses, contemplating the dollop on his spoon. "Five hundred, maybe a thousand rubles."

"If he's lucky. But in this case the shooter gets even luckier. He whacks Vorontsov, then spots the medals. Suddenly, he's looking at two, maybe three hundred thousand. Not a bad bonus."

"Not a bad theory, either," Vera concedes. "Anything else?"

"No, just that and the documents," I reply, with a forlorn expression to make her feel guilty.

"Don't do that to me, Nikolai. I'm warning you, it's not going to work."

"I'm crushed." I clutch my chest as if shot in the heart, then shift targets. "What about you, Yuri?"

"Me?"

"Yes. Shevchenko's returning the documents to the IM. You should be able to get your hands on them."

"Impossible."

"You never had trouble before."

"That's because I could always bribe someone with a copy of *Playboy* or *Dr. Zhivago*. But now, now you can buy them on the Arbat." Yuri's brows arch in amazement that such things are for sale minutes from the Kremlin on a thoroughfare that has been closed and turned into a pedestrian mall. Lined with shops and cafés, where artists, musicians, hustlers, and restless teenagers hang out, it extends more than a mile from Arbat Square to the Foreign Ministry. "It's out of the question."

"Maybe I'm missing something here, but when you were an outcast, you could; now that you're an insider, you can't?"

"Nikolai," he groans, implying I should know better. "Despite all the restructuring, the IM is still highly compartmentalized; access to documents is as restricted as ever. Besides, I don't have to tell you, I'm a theoretician, not a salesman. Privatization deals aren't my area."

"Nothing like having friends come to your rescue."

Yuri methodically scoops the last bit of ice cream from his cup, then seems to have a change of heart. "All right. I'll look into it, but don't hold your breath. Frankly, the way hard-liners are hanging on, I'd forget the whole thing if I were you."

"No," Vera pipes up. "No, I think he should forget the documents—and focus on the medals."

"The medals? Why?"

"Well, if you can find them, there's a good chance you'll eventually find the killer. And he's going to turn out to be either a thief or a hired assassin."

"That would settle it one way or the other."

"And if he is a hired gun, once he's cornered, maybe he can be convinced to identify who paid him."

"Maybe. But I'm a writer, Vera, not a militia interrogator. Remember?"

"If I wanted to be sleeping with a cop," she says, smiling at a thought, "I'd have little trouble finding one."

"Nobody's stopping you."

Vera stiffens, stung by the remark. "That was uncalled for," she protests with an angry flip of her hair. "I was just kidding."

I reach across the table for her hand, but she pulls it away. "I'm sorry. I'm not feeling very good about myself lately."

She sighs and raises a brow at Yuri, who nods knowingly. "Do we have to listen to this?"

"Come on, remember how I used to say a dissident is a citizen who has the guts to say what everyone else is thinking. And you used to say—"

"Who has the *stupidity*," Yuri interrupts, beating me to it. "Yeah, I remember. It was a joke."

"I know, but sometimes I think you were right."

"You're infuriating, you know?" Vera challenges. "The Communists are out, democracy is in, you finally have a free society, and you're still not satisfied."

"It's not how I thought it would be."

"Give the country a chance, Nikolai. These things take time."

"No, I meant for me. It's different."

"In what way?" Yuri prods gently.

"Every way."

"*Every* way?"

"Writing. Okay? My style is stilted. I have to fight for every angle, every sale. I mean, making the *apparatchiks* squirm used to be fun, but it's become a chore. I never used to think about making money, and I always seemed to have enough. Now, it's all I think about, and I'm always broke."

"Well, speaking of a job," Vera intones a little too self-righteously, "maybe you should stop feeling sorry for yourself and get one."

"You mean on a newspaper?"

"Don't look so insulted. It's a perfectly respectable way to earn a living. I bet Sergei would hire you in a minute."

"I'm not so sure about that. I'd have to revamp my syntax and get a face-lift first. Besides, after being on my own all these years, the mere thought of writing on assignment . . ." I splay my hands and let it tail off to emphasize my distaste for the idea. "Of course, I could do a free-lance piece on the black market in medals. It'd—"

"Why didn't I think of that?" Vera interrupts facetiously.

"Where would you take it?" Yuri prompts.

"*Independent Gazette.* They'd buy it in a minute."

"So would the wire services," Vera encourages. "They love all that Moscow subculture stuff."

"And I suppose you just happen to know where the black-market medal dealers hang out?"

"No. Why would I?"

"Well, since you've been so adept at keeping me in coffee, I thought maybe on one of your excursions into the Moscow netherworld you came across . . ."

"No such luck."

"What about that athlete?" Yuri prompts.

"What athlete?"

"That one you wrote about. Arkady—Arkady something, wasn't it?"

"Arkady Barkhin?"

"Yes, yes, that's it. Barkhin. He might have a line on it."

"He might, but I haven't seen him in years. Besides, he's probably dead."

It wouldn't be from old age if he were. Arkady Barkhin was a promising decathlete before a knee injury ended his career. He'd be in his mid-thirties now. I met him years ago while writing an article that exposed the government's practice of discarding athletes who are injured or past their prime. The famous ones find jobs as trainers and coaches, but the rest—selected in childhood by Goskomsport to stock local, national, and Olympic teams—are unskilled, uneducated, and unemployable.

Women marry, gain weight, and have children. Men peddle their brawn and physical skills to the *mafiya,* working as enforcers and loan collectors in the rackets that have spread like the plague to every Russian city and suburb. Their days are spent in gyms coaxing atrophying muscles to life, nights hanging out in restaurants and cafés from which protection money is extorted. These aren't proud old-timers, but a thirty-something group of embittered jocks who earn a living as crooks and killers.

When I last saw him, Arkady Barkhin was well on his way to becoming one of them.

Medals. A black market in medals. I've no doubt it exists—there'd be a black market for toenail clippings if there were a demand for them—but I haven't the slightest idea where to find it. Of course, the denizens of Moscow's underworld are no different than others. They live in shadows, prey in darkness, and keep on the move to stay one step ahead of the militia—which sort of narrows it a little. It's hostile territory, regardless. Yuri was right. If anyone can give me an entrée and safe passage, it's Arkady Barkhin. All I have to do is find him.

I can't imagine it will be this easy, but I dig his number out of my files and call him. The woman who answers says she's had the number for years and has never heard of Arkady Barkhin. To make matters worse, despite a widely publicized contract with a Western supplier, Moscow still doesn't have a comprehensive telephone directory. Furthermore, before giving out a number, the 09 information service requires the caller know the citizen's full name and address—which leaves me with my story notes. Hastily written years ago, they contain the names of restaurants and cafés where I'd met with Barkhin and other athletes who'd been junked by the government.

I take the Metro back to the city and spend several evenings making the rounds of *mafiya*-infested night spots. The resident thugs are easily identified by their Levi's, leather jackets, and Adidas running shoes. They dismiss my inquiries about Arkady Barkhin with shrugs, glazed eyes, and in some cases, what seem to be convenient memory lapses. My next stop is in the Arbat District.

What functions as a shopping mall by day turns into a freak show after dark. Despite the sub-freezing temperature, the pimps, prostitutes, and supporting cast of con artists are out in full force, feverishly hawking their wares to score as many johns and take as many suckers as possible before the police shut them down. Even locals can lose their way in this labyrinth of twisting streets and alleys, and it takes me a while to get oriented. I'm being hustled by a rock groupie with purple hair selling back-issues of *Rolling Stone* when I turn a corner and spot a weathered sign that whispers KAFÉ SKAZKA.

It's a grim cavern of cracked plaster that reeks of tobacco and stale beer. At this hour, the customers are few and silent, the pain of empty lives temporarily deadened. Loners hunch over a slab of stained marble that serves as a bar. The more gregarious commiserate at rickety tables on twisted wire chairs. In a corner far from the window, a group of athlete-enforcers stare blankly into their vodkas in search of past glories.

I'm dying for a drink, but continue to resist the urge and order what must be the evening's tenth glass of mineral water.

The bartender, a rotund fellow with a face veined like a road map, fills a mug with Borzhomi and slides it in my direction. "Get you anything else?"

I slip a pack of Marlboros from my pocket and place it on the bar. "Some information."

His eyes dart longingly to the cigarettes, then harden with suspicion. "See that?" He points to the disclaimer that warns smoking can be hazardous to your health. "It goes double for guys like you."

"I'm not looking for trouble. Just a friend."

"There are a lot of cafés in Moscow, pal."

"Yeah, well, I'm hitting all his old haunts."

The bartender shrugs and wipes up a spill with a damp cloth, imparting a momentary luster to the marble.

"The last time we were in here," I resume, as he works his way down the bar, "my friend sold the owner on the benefits of paying for protection."

That gets his attention. Ditto for the desultory characters in the far corner. The sound of eyeballs clicking and necks snapping is followed by the rumble of chair legs and squeak of athletic shoes.

I'm not surprised. Neither is the bartender. He hurries off to clear a distant table as the pitted mirror behind him darkens with swaggering men.

A wall of leather closes around me. A gloved hand beats mine to the Marlboros. I turn on the barstool and find myself staring at the words ELECTRO SHOCK THERAPY. The name of the popular heavy metal band is printed on a skin-tight T-shirt that clings to the thug's chest. Neo-Nazi stubble covers his head. Sunglasses bridge a broken nose. Hooked and scarred rather than flattened, it's clearly from battles fought on ice, not canvas.

"You're looking for a friend in the protection racket?" the thug demands, pushing his face to mine. The sunglasses are so close I can see the designer logo on the lens reads *Ray-Ban*.

"Uh-huh. Haven't seen him in years."

"You know who he worked for?"

"Nobody. He was putting together his own operation. His name's Barkhin. Arkady Barkhin."

"Never heard of him," he says impassively, though his eyes could be wide with recognition behind those Ray-Bans. "Any of you?"

As I expected, the knuckle-draggers flanking him grunt *"Nyet,"* in unison.

"Well, thanks anyway. No harm in asking." I force a smile, chalk up the Marlboros to the cost of doing business, and turn back toward the bar.

"Don't count on it," Ray-Ban threatens, spinning me around to face him.

My gut flutters and begins to tighten. "Pardon me? Have I missed something here?"

"Yeah, asshole, like the whole point."

"Which is?"

"Friends always know where to find you. Enemies have to ask."

"Look, Barkhin and I lost touch."

"Bullshit." He removes the cellophane wrapper from the cigarettes with an angry flick of his wrist. "You owe him money or something. Right?"

I'm getting the feeling he knows more about Arkady Barkhin than he's telling and am tempted to explain, but think better of it. If owing Barkhin money is what's on this thug's mind, I might as well go with it. "Yeah, matter of fact I do. I'm looking for him so I can settle my account."

"Shame." He pushes a Marlboro into the corner of his mouth and lights it. "I earn a living off people who welsh on debts."

"Nothing personal. I take mine seriously."

"Good. So do we. Come on, let's have it," he demands, motioning with his hand.

"Have what?"

"The cash. I'll make sure your friend gets it."

Damn. I should've seen that coming. There's no getting away with a white lie in this game. "But you said you didn't know him."

"I don't," he cackles, drawing raucous laughter from his colleagues. "But my time's worth a lot more than a fucking pack of Marlboros." He pockets the cigarettes and signals the others with a nod. Hands grip my arms like vises and pin me to the bar. Ray-Ban goes through my pockets and takes my wallet. He eyes the few rubles with disdain. "What the fuck you think you're paying back with this?"

I doubt he'd be pleased to hear that I went along with the idea to manipulate him, or, assuming he can read, that I once wrote a story in support of washed-up athletes like him. No, I'm writing another story now and have no choice but to play it out. "I don't have the money on me. I wasn't sure I'd find him. I didn't want to chance carrying it."

He snorts derisively. "Get him out of here." He throws the rubles on the floor and stalks off with my wallet in the direction of the phone.

The thugs jerk me from the stool then, all in one motion, hustle me to the door, and gleefully shove me into the street.

My arms break the fall, but the ice-cold cobblestones are ungiving. I lie there for a moment reevaluating my position on discarded athletes, then head for the Metro station on Kropotkinskaya. It's the Kirov-Frunze line. Not the Zhdanov-Krasny. Not mine. But I've had all the electroshock therapy I can stand for one night and want out of the Arbat as fast as possible. I take the train north to Lubyanka Square station, until recently Dzerzhinsky Square, site of KGB Headquarters. Several Metro lines interconnect here. The arched colonnades, ornate chandeliers, and prerevolutionary murals go by in a blur as I dash between trains, then settle down for the long haul to Lyublino.

The evening was a total loss. Worse than total. I have less now than when I started: no Marlboros, no wallet, no ID, no money, and no information on black-market medal dealers.

The train lurches. The lights dim briefly. I stiffen, eyeing my fellow passengers with suspicion. A leather jacket on one. Running shoes on another. Sunglasses on a third. Ordinary citizens? Low-level gangsters? Weary workers? I hate to admit it, but Shevchenko was right. Moscow has traded one set of tyrants for another. We used to live in fear of being victimized by the police, now we fear being victimized by criminals. Victimized by ourselves.

8

It's almost midnight when the train pulls into Lyublino Station. Nearly an hour and a half after I kissed the pavement outside Kafé Skazka. Vera's shift ends soon. I'm counting on her to tend to my bruised ego, aching muscles, and zero bank balance, not necessarily in that order.

Gusts of Arctic wind disperse the smog in wispy layers as I walk to my apartment. The streets are empty except for a few scavenging cats and a tradesman's van, its dim headlights glowing like balls of yellow cotton. I'm at the corner when I notice a sedan emerging from a darkened side street.

Reflections of refinery lights in the waxed finish catch my eye. Reflections? Moving across sleek forest green lacquer? In Lyublino? Not a chance. Sooty, dull, unpolished wrecks are the rule here; and most residents can't afford one, not even a broken-down *razvalina,* let alone a spanking new *konfekta* like a Volvo.

I quicken my pace, crossing to the other side of the street, when it dawns on me. A Volvo?! Volvos are favored by Moscow's midlevel gangsters. I break into a run. The sedan accelerates and cuts me off. For an instant, I'm eyeball to eyeball with the driver. It's him! Ray-Ban. Still wearing his designer shades.

"Katkov?!" he calls out as the car dives to a rubber-burning stop. "Katkov, wait!"

Why? To get my ass kicked?! I sprint toward the intersection. The two thugs from Kafé Skazka pile out of the car and pursue. I turn into a street lined with boarded-up houses and shuttered storefronts. An alley flashes past. I reverse direction and duck into it before the thugs turn the corner. Barely a meter separates the soaring brick. The alley is so narrow and dark I almost missed it. Maybe they will.

I had no intention of threatening them, but I've obviously hit a nerve. Why the sudden paranoia? Do they know Barkhin? Is this a rival mob? Did they get into a turf war with Barkhin's people and muscle them out? Maybe he *is* dead. My adrenaline surges, forcing painful memories to surface, memories of being hunted. The pit bulls worked for the KGB, not the *mafiya,* and the threat was a stint in the gulag, not eternity in a shallow grave; but this is no time to quibble over details. The feelings of terror are the same.

Ray-Ban's thugs dash past the alley. An instant later, one returns, squinting into the darkness. My heart sinks. I freeze against the gritty bricks, holding my breath. "Katkov?" he calls out. "Katkov, we want to talk."

About what? Carrying me out of here feet first? No thanks.

He takes a few uncertain steps, leaning left and right to get an angle on the shadows; then, to my relief, he backs out of the alley and hurries off.

I've just begun searching for a way out when I hear the thump of air-cushioned running shoes and whisk of denim behind me. He's back. With his colleague. Two lumbering silhouettes are pushing long shadows in my direction now! I run deeper into the alley. It zigzags wildly, but never branches, never intersects with the streets. Several buildings have steel service doors. I put a shoulder into one, but it won't budge, nor will the next or the next. I scan the darkness frantically. A pale red glow spills across the pavement just beyond the last building. All of a sudden it changes to green. A neon sign? A traffic light? I take the turn on the run, and there, at the far end of the alley, is what looks like an intersection.

A car flashes past.

It is an intersection! If I can make it into the streets, I've got a chance of losing them. But then what? They'll be all over my apartment. Ray-Ban is probably heading there right now. Vera's place! Her roommates will be pissed off, but I could stay there for a while. I'm sprinting down the narrow chasm when I sense something in the darkness. A pattern. Vertical lines. Black against blackness. There and gone. And there again. I put on the brakes an instant before running into a wrought-iron fence. Topped with spikes and barbed wire, it keeps me from the street not ten meters beyond.

The thugs keep coming. Walking rapidly now, not running, they advance confidently, without any sense of urgency as they close in.

There's no way I'm going down without a fight. I whirl and lunge between them, throwing a punch at the one nearest me. He blocks it, grasps my wrist, and snaps my arm up behind my back. The other puts a pistol to my head.

"Easy, Katkov. Take it easy," he advises. "Didn't you hear what we said? We want to talk."

The glint of the muzzle flickers in the corner of my eye. I'm terrified. Exhausted. I can barely catch my breath, barely get a word out. I nod eagerly. "Sure. Whatever you say."

Instead of blowing my brains out or beating me senseless, the thug lowers the pistol, and they march me from the alley in silence. Headlights bend around the opposite corner as we reach the street. The Volvo dives to a stop next to us. The thugs push me into the seat and clamber in on either side. The doors are still open when Ray-Ban floors the accelerator. The Volvo heads west on the Outer Ring, cutting across the outskirts of the city.

The silence continues.

They said they wanted to talk, but they're not talking. I haven't the slightest idea what's going on or where we're headed, but it isn't long before my imagination cooks up a few scenarios: They lied, so I wouldn't struggle, wouldn't scream, so they wouldn't have to kill me in the alley and carry my body out to dispose of it. Shrewd bastards. Sporting of me to save them the inconvenience, to sign up for a trip from which I'll never return.

The Volvo turns off into the Frunze District, where the Moskva loops back on itself, encircling Luzhniki Stadium. Ray-Ban maneuvers through desolate streets awash with litter and stops in front of an abandoned building. Heavy bronze doors, deep-set windows, and a peristyle of bloated columns that support a peaked roof suggest the graffiti-scrawled edifice was once a bank. The greenish stain of metal letters that were once affixed to the granite confirm it.

Ray-Ban and his thugs escort me to the entrance. He presses a buzzer. A security slot opens, revealing wary eyes. Then with a portentous shudder the huge door swings back into a brilliantly illuminated vestibule. It takes me a few moments to become accustomed to the light. Instead of the rat-infested hovel I expected, the well-dressed guard clears us into a tastefully decorated anteroom where my head fills with the smell of alcohol and perfume. Or is it formaldehyde and funeral wreaths? The thugs remain behind as Ray-Ban leads the way through several more doors where the rhythmic thump of music rises.

The last opens into a private club. They've been sprouting all over the city lately to service the new class of free-market entrepreneurs and their guests: clubs with names like Olimp, Atlant, Warrior, and Chernobyl offer everything from gourmet food and wine to erotic revues, rock music, and what are billed as "sensual massages."

But few Muscovites have ever imagined, let alone visited, one like Paradise: Towering palms and lush floral arrangements are set against murals reminiscent of Gauguin's Tahitian landscapes. Wispy clouds seem to drift lazily across a vaulted ceiling. Colorful parrots stock a circular aviary. Indeed, it's a tropical paradise. The last time I encountered anything like this was twenty years ago in Havana on my honeymoon. Nothing in terminally gray Moscow can compare with the club's sunny opulence or sultry floor show.

The dancers, all exotic Latin women, are writhing suggestively to an infectious merengue beat, leaving no doubt their skimpy halters and hip-hugging sarongs are destined for removal. Seated on semicircular tiers are Moscow's well-heeled elite, members of government, diplomats, entrepreneurs, owners of local cooperatives, and an assortment of foreign business types. All are valiantly trying to guide food and beverages to their mouths without taking their eyes off the stage—all except those in the adjacent casino, who are captivated by the whizz of roulette wheels and clatter of chips.

The Paradise Club is right out of Las Vegas. Not that I've been there. My knowledge comes from a friend—a former member of a SALT inspection team stationed in Nevada—who smuggled a risqué travel brochure past Customs inspectors.

Ray-Ban leads the way to a corner booth where an elegantly dressed man with a phone pressed to his ear presides over the action. A magnum of champagne, a crystal flute, a bowl of caviar, and my wallet are arranged on the table in front of him. Young women with the stunning looks of fashion models are perched on either side. Rich, powerful, venerated, it's immediately obvious he's a crime boss, but it takes a moment for me to realize that the handsome, deeply tanned fellow, the *vor v zakone* of the local mob, is Arkady Barkhin.

He finishes the call and glances up. "Nikolai Katkov," he says thoughtfully.

"Arkady." It catches in the back of my throat and is barely audible.

"I hear you've been looking for me."

I nod apprehensively, my eyes darting about the dazzling interior. "In all the wrong places."

"Everyone finds their way here, eventually."

"Some more easily than others, I imagine."

He smiles indulgently. "I also hear we have some unfinished business."

"No. No, that was his idea," I hear myself saying, indifferent to Ray-Ban's reaction. I'm concerned about Barkhin now, concerned he'll be offended by my raising something as trivial as black-market medal dealers; but this is no time to choke. "Actually, Arkady, I was hoping you could—"

"Don't try to back out of it," he interrupts, glaring at me. "I hate unpaid debts. They fester. They get in the way of business. They destroy friendships. It's time, Katkov. Time to settle up." He leans back, taking his measure of me, then his eyes soften with amusement. "But as I remember it, I don't hold the marker. You do."

My heart flutters with relief, then accelerates in disbelief. "Me?" I finally squeak.

"Yes, I'm the one in debt here," Barkhin replies, embellishing the moment as he gestures to the club. "See this? I worked hard for it. Busted my ass, believe me. Had some luck too. But you don't get to the top without owing somebody something. In my case, none of it would've happened without you, Katkov." He lets it hang there mysteriously and reaches inside his jacket for his wallet. His manicured nails pluck something from one of the sleeves. It's a yellowed newspaper clipping, which he unfolds carefully, making certain the fragile creases don't tear, and places it on the table in front of me. "Remember this?"

It's been almost ten years, and it takes a moment to recognize my own article. I can't imagine how an exposé on the treatment of over-the-hill athletes could have anything to do with Barkhin's success.

"I don't mean the part about being junked by the State," he explains, sensing he's puzzled me. "Oh, we were really getting screwed. It had to be said; and it took guts to say it, a lot of guts, but—"

"*Stupidity,* according to some."

"No. No, it helped. Things got a little better. But what you said about athletes and free enterprise . . . If it wasn't for that, I'd still be working out of the Skazka."

I light a cigarette, trying to recall what I said. The match fizzles. I'm about to strike another when Barkhin produces a butane lighter with an air of self-importance, just in case I don't know they're a status symbol. PARADISE CLUB is printed on the barrel. A stylized parrot serves as the *P.*

"The part I'm talking about is right here." He stabs a forefinger at a short paragraph bracketed in faded red marker. "I mean, when I read that retired athletes in the West were making it big in business, that their itch to compete, their work ethic, their let-the-best-man-win mentality were the keys to their success, a light went on. It dawned on me that, unlike the average Russian who was taught to shun individual achievement, athletes have what it takes to make it in a free market. It changed my life."

"I couldn't be more pleased," I reply, amazed how a few sentences in a twenty-five-hundred-word article—sentences I can barely recall writing—can stick in a person's mind and have such impact. I do vaguely recall they were an afterthought. Something I threw in there to needle the *apparatchiks* at Goskomsport. And ten years ago, neither I, nor Barkhin, nor the brainwashed bureaucrats had any reason to believe they would ever be anything more.

"No kidding," he goes on enthusiastically. "It really kicked me in the ass. Made me stop whining. Made me realize I didn't need pity or a bigger pension. Made me believe in myself. And,

as they say—" He pauses dramatically, playing to his fawning
models. "The rest is history."

History indeed.

His gratitude is such that after returning my wallet and apolo-
gizing for his thugs' behavior, he dismisses the ladies and insists I join him. I spend the evening fending off glasses of
champagne as he chronicles his rise from a one-man protection
racket to an entrepreneur operating a string of what he refers
to as "service companies." It's almost four in the morning by
the time he runs out of gas and his thoughts turn to other
matters. "I always end the evening with a nice piece of fruit,"
he confides enigmatically.

"Fruit?"

"Tropical fruit." He inclines his head toward the stage and
grins lasciviously. "Smooth brown skin, flesh filled with juices
and ready to explode. Which one made your mouth water,
Nikolai?"

"Which *one?*"

He chortles and cups his hands out in front of his chest.
"You recall the spinner with the coconuts?"

"Oh, I recall lots of coconuts, Arkady."

"The turned-up ones." His forefingers point skyward. "The
hot little Chiquita who was on the left?"

"Ah, yes."

"Absolutely insatiable. She's yours."

"Thanks," I reply, momentarily tempted by the fantasy. "But
I have a lovely bunch of my own. And they're more than I
can handle."

"Then what? How can I thank you? Money? A job? Name it."

"A source."

"A source?" he echoes with an incredulous cackle. "Who
else but a journalist would trade the best fuck in Moscow for
information?"

"A *dissident* journalist."

He cackles again; but when I reveal my intention to write a
story about black-market medal dealers, the levity ceases, and
his eyes narrow with concern. "Still taking risks, aren't you?"

I nod.

"You'll need an inside source."

"Preferably."

"Done," he says smartly, scooping up the phone. "It's not one of my operations, but I know someone who can take you in."

After the night I've had, I'm delighted just to be alive, let alone a step closer to finding out whether Vorontsov's death was the result of scandal or theft. It's a short-lived high, tempered by the fact that, either way, the person who took those medals is a cold-blooded killer.

9

Moscow always looks like a ghost town in the early morning hours—eerie, silent, unpopulated—as if hit by one of those structure-friendly bombs Kremlin saber-rattlers used to justify decades of massive defense expenditures and painful food shortages.

It looks even gloomier through the tinted windows of Barkhin's Mercedes as we race west on Komsomolsky Prospekt. A Lada sedan stocked with his fruit tarts and the Volvo of leather-jacketed thugs follow. The fast-moving caravan recalls the days when traffic would be held so the Premier and his entourage of Zils could traverse the entire city without stopping.

But we're not going to Red Square.

No. After making the arrangements, Barkhin insisted on dropping me off, and we're on our way to the Lenin Hills and a meeting with his contact in the black market. He pops open an attaché and removes a computerized list of companies. "Look," he says proudly. "My own little mutual fund. You know, you should write another story—'Ten Years Later.' I mean, you were right on target."

I force a smile, loath to publicize my role in birthing a predator, no matter how innocently. I'm not solely responsible. I may have awakened Barkhin's ambition, but Communism created his attitude, and democracy the opportunity to unleash them; and unleash them he did—upon his fellow citizens, which is the part that bothers me.

"Blow your own horn a little, Katkov," he urges, sensing my ambivalence. "You can do one on Arturo too." He gestures to his chauffeur, an athletic-looking Cuban who doubles as a bodyguard. "He came here ten years ago to coach baseball and stayed."

"It sure as hell wasn't for the climate."

"Try the economy."

"The what?"

"The economy. It's booming compared to Cuba's."

"If you prefer hunger to starvation."

"His government offered him a bicycle to go back. I offered him a job. You blame him?"

"They tried to bribe him with a bike?"

"Uh-huh. Cars are useless there. The country is literally out of gas."

"So the elite pedal, and the peasants walk."

He nods glumly. "Thanks to Castro. They could all be driving one of these, if he wasn't such a thickhead. See, we don't have a quick fix, but they do. Always have. It's a long shot, but last year when I was there, I made some contacts who think he's seriously considering taking the plunge."

"Into what?"

"Tourism."

The caravan is on Vorob'yovskoye Shosse now, climbing into the heavily wooded terrain that surrounds Moscow State University. The area has a breathtaking view of the city as well as the distinction of being selected by black-market medal dealers as the site of this week's get-together. According to Barkhin, they set up shop at dawn just prior to the militia shift-change, when the officers are tired and anxious to get home. The Mercedes turns into a narrow service road and stops opposite a forest of evergreens.

Barkhin lowers the window and winces at the blast of frigid air that rushes into the car.

A moment later, a short man in a pin-striped coat and tweed cap cocked forward on his head, giving him the look of a Bolshevik elf, emerges from the trees.

"That's him. His name's Rafik. Good luck."

"Thanks, Arkady. Thanks a lot."

"Thank you, Nikasha." He holds my eyes with his, then squeezes my hand to communicate his sincerity. I slide out of the Mercedes and close the door. "Katkov?" Barkhin leans to the window and tosses me a butane lighter. "Keep in touch."

The caravan glides off into the dense mist that drifts between the hills. When I turn around, Rafik is gone. I hurry toward the evergreens. Halfway there, the silence is broken by an unnerving chirping sound. It's my beeper. Vera must be wondering if I'm dead or alive. I can't say I blame her. I've spent half the night doing the same.

I'm nearing the evergreens when Rafik reappears amid the craggy trunks. There's something mysterious and instantly appealing about him—a serene confidence that gains my trust. The scent of damp pine needles fills my head, as he leads the way to a clearing where dozens of vehicles are parked. Bikes, motorcycles, cars, vans, pickup trucks.

The dealers are surprisingly young, most in their late teens and twenties. Their merchandise sparkles in the early light, displayed on blankets that are spread across tailgates and hoods, on rectangular panels that stack neatly in attaché cases, and on the linings of coats that they open as if revealing their manhood. It's like a gypsy bazaar: facile minds, quick hands, wary eyes, the exclamations of shock and disbelief when a price is quoted; then rapid-fire bargaining, the rustle of currency, and jingle of metal as deals are struck and money and medals change hands. Buyers waste no time in leaving once the transaction is completed. Dealers waste none shifting their attention to the next customer. Rafik leads the way to a small group gathered at the tailgate of a truck and introduces me.

"You want to write about us?" a young dealer with shoulder-length hair asks warily. "Why?"

"To earn a living."

"Fair enough. What's in it for us?"

"Police harassment!" someone shouts. "Yeah, they'll be all over us!" another exclaims, causing several to back away.

"Hold it! Hold it," I object as Rafik corrals them. "You mean the militia doesn't know about your operation?"

"You kidding?" Long-hair snorts. "We make sure we keep one step ahead of them."

"A little *vzyatka* goes a long way," a compact fellow says smugly, using slang for graft.

"Then my story will have customers, not cops, beating a path to your door."

"He's right," someone mutters grudgingly. "Yeah, yeah, he is," another enthuses. An impromptu conclave, with much whispering and sagacious nodding of heads, follows. "Okay," the long-haired spokesman announces when they adjourn. "But no names. Agreed?"

"Agreed. Where do you get your merchandise?"

"From people who need cash."

"Give me an example?"

"Sure," one of the teenagers with an Iron Maiden T-shirt and squeaky voice pipes up. "My uncle had all kinds of medals from the war. When he died, my family sold them, took the cash, and went on a shopping spree. We got a new car, a TV, VCR. My sister got braces, and I got these." He gestures proudly to his high-topped basketball shoes with built-in air pumps. "I also got into the business."

"But that can't be your only source of supply?"

"What do you mean by that?" Long-hair asks, his eyes narrowing with suspicion.

"Well, from what I hear, some medals are worth a lot of money. They could be stolen like jewelry, couldn't they?"

"Stolen?!" he snaps, offended. The dealers move forward threateningly. "Are you accusing us of fencing stolen goods?"

"No. No, of course not. It was a poor choice of words," I explain, my mind racing for a way to defuse the situation. "For the sake of argument, why don't we say medals that were— lost—then found by an enterprising individual—and sold to you?"

Uncertain looks dart between them. Several nod grudgingly. "It's possible," Long-hair concedes.

"Would there be a way to identify them?"

"You mean to determine if a medal or group of medals are the same ones that were lost?"

"Uh-huh."

"It depends." He turns to one of the displays, selects several medals, and explains, "You can see right here: Some are numbered, some have initials on the back, some even have names, others are blank. Why do you want to know?"

"Just curious," I reply matter-of-factly. Their reaction to my comment about stolen medals makes talk of murder and government scandal unwise. "Who are your buyers, by the way?" I ask, purposely changing the subject.

"All kinds of people. Collectors, metal brokers, pensioners."

"A lot of them are into *blat,*" another pipes up. "You know, special privileges, beating the long lines at markets, getting into shops closed to the average citizen."

"They come in handy on a crowded train or bus too," a third chimes in. "Not to mention scoring tickets to rock concerts and soccer finals."

"Sounds good. I wish I could afford some."

The group breaks into easy laughter. The tension evaporates. As a joke, the squeaky-voiced one gives me a *znachki,* the cheap commemorative lapel pins sold to tourists at kiosks. Some have a picture of St. George slaying the Dragon. Others, the image of the Kremlin. This one has a small photo centered in a five-pointed red star—a photo of Lenin as an infant which evokes more laughter. The mood gradually turns businesslike as several of the dealers notice customers hovering about. It's a perfect time to disengage.

Rafik and I are moving off when he cups a hand over his mouth as if revealing a State secret and whispers, "Nationalism."

"What about it?"

"It's on the rise. What do you think this madness for medals is all about? When things get bad, people get nostalgic. They want to relive past victories: Bolshevism, World War Two, Stalin, Sputnik. The Communists will make a comeback. Mark my words."

"You left out the gulag."

"With good reason."

"Perm thirty-five," I announce, sensing where he's headed.

"Chistopol," he fires back. "Three years for—"

"—crimes against the State," we say in unison, breaking into laughter at the absurdity of the catch-all charge; but our levity is short-lived. Rafik's eyes glaze. So do mine, as visions of the gulag come back with chilling clarity: the rough concrete cells—two steps wide, three steps long—less than twenty square meters for two men; a dim light bulb, an open toilet, wooden planks for beds. No windows. Not even bars. Just a solid iron door. I can still hear its chilling clang—and still shudder at the screech of the *kormushka,* the slot through which coarse black bread, boiled potatoes, cabbage, or a thin gruel masquerading as kasha were thrown as if to animals. The monotonous, mindless work. Sweltering heat. Bitter cold. Disease. No contact with the outside world. No visitors. No daylight. No mail.

"Never again," Rafik says, pulling me out of it.

I smile wanly. "While we're on the subject . . ."

"The gulag?"

"No. Crimes against the State. If some medals *were* stolen, what are the chances of establishing a chain of custody?"

"You mean, find the dealer who bought them and work back to the thief?"

"Uh-huh."

Rafik's head cocks suspiciously. "There's more on your agenda than food and rent, isn't there, Katkov?"

I nod.

"Good luck."

"Look, I'm not out to make trouble. Frankly, this story began with a . . . a certain incident, and I'm trying to sort out the motive."

"Incident?" he flares. "I'm not into riddles. Speak plainly or forget it."

"Murder. Plain enough?"

"Someone lost more than their medals."

"Yes. I want to find out if it really was a robbery, or a shrewd way to cover another reason for killing him."

"You have the poor bastard's name?"

"Vorontsov. Vladimir Illiych."

Rafik's brows rise and fall. He's mulling it over when the darkness is split by the sweeping headlights and acid blue flashers of police vans. This sets off a frantic buttoning of coats, packing of cases, and rolling of blankets and sends dealers and buyers scattering to their vehicles. Amid roaring engines and screeching tires, those of us on foot literally head for the hills and cover of dense foliage.

"You have a car?" I call out on the run. There's no reply. I glance over my shoulder. Rafik's gone. Vanished as mysteriously as he'd appeared.

I'm dashing toward the evergreens when several of the scattering dealers up ahead suddenly reverse direction. A phalanx of uniformed officers with revolvers and riot guns comes out of nowhere and fires a volley of warning shots. We freeze in our tracks, hands over our heads, as the officers advance in an ever-tightening circle. They frisk us and confiscate our IDs as several large vans with barred windows roll into the clearing.

A sergeant begins calling out names, checking them off on his clipboard as each prisoner is handcuffed and put in the van. He goes through about ten before getting to mine.

"Katkov?"

"Here," I reply, disgusted, as I cross toward him. "Look, I'm a journalist. I'm not involved in anything illegal. I'm covering a story."

"Get in." He shoves me toward the door.

"You're making a big mistake. Senior Investigator Shevchenko's a friend of mine."

The sergeant cocks his head skeptically.

"He is. I'm telling you. Get him on the radio. Give him my name."

That does the trick. The sergeant takes my arm and leads me through the trees. The sun is creeping over the horizon as we emerge. It sends long shadows across the hills, and silhouettes a tall figure in a trench coat who's overseeing the operation. Son of a bitch. It's the senior investigator himself. This is his show. As we're crossing toward him, two officers, who have the long-haired dealer in custody, beat us to Shevchenko.

"I'm sure we can work something out here," the dealer says cockily. He pulls a wad of U.S. dollars from his raincoat, removes the rubber band, and starts counting off hundreds. He stops at ten.

Shevchenko turns away and lights a cigarette.

The dealer adds ten more.

Shevchenko exhales impassively. After five more hundreds join the stack, he reconsiders, nods thoughtfully, and pockets it.

The dealer smiles and starts to turn away.

Shevchenko signals the officers. "Take him. Add attempting to bribe a militia officer to the charges and bag this as evidence."

"You bastard!" the dealer cries out, resisting the attempt to cuff him. "You fucking bastard!"

"Add the use of disrespectful language as well."

The officers smirk and ratchet the cuffs tight against the dealer's wrists. The sergeant prods me forward as they lead him away. "This one claims he knows you, sir."

"Up early today, Mr. Investigator?" I tease.

Shevchenko looks at me blankly for a long moment. "What's his name?" he asks, deadpan.

My eyes roll. "Come on, Shevchenko."

"Katkov, Nikolai," the sergeant growls.

Shevchenko's brow furrows. "Doesn't ring a bell." He whispers something to the sergeant, smiles thinly, and walks away.

The sergeant hustles me to a prisoner van, shoves me inside, and slams the door. Angry medal dealers crowd two long benches that face one another. There must be at least a dozen of them. Their eyes burn with hatred, leaving no doubt who they think is to blame for what happened. Fortunately, their hands, like mine, are cuffed behind their backs.

The van shudders to life and chugs off. It's gone a short distance when one of the dealers spits at me. Then another. And another. Finally, the long-haired one rears back and kicks me in the ribs, inciting the others, who leap from the benches. I bull my way into a corner of the van, kicking wildly to keep them at bay. My heel catches one in the chest, driving him back into the others, but there are too many of them. A boot slams into my groin. A knee connects with my forehead. I howl, racked with pain, and crumple to the floor. They're out of control now, shouting, stomping, spitting, calling me names.

I'm convinced I'm going to die when suddenly the van dives to a stop, sending the dealers tumbling forward in a tangled heap. The door opens, revealing the muzzles of two riot guns.

"Okay! That's enough! Settle down" the sergeant shouts. He scans the group for a moment. "You," he says, pointing his weapon at me.

"Me?" I ask weakly, wiping the blood that seeps from the corner of my mouth.

"Out. Move it."

I extricate myself and crawl eagerly to the door. The cops help me to the ground and slam it shut. Then they hustle me around to the cab, shove me inside between them, and drive off.

"You okay?" the sergeant asks gruffly.

"Great. They damn near killed me."

"There wasn't any chance of that happening."

"Could've fooled me. Thanks anyway."

"Don't thank us. It was Investigator Shevchenko's idea. He figured they'd take it out on you. He said to let it go on just long enough to teach you a lesson."

"Well, I'm a very fast learner."

"Good," the sergeant says with a malevolent sneer. "Your education's just begun."

10

'm making notes, but I'm in a cell in the bowels of 38 Petrovka, not a classroom. I've got plenty of material for a piece on the black market in medals. The crackdown will make it all the more interesting, assuming I get out of here to write it. Fortunately, Shevchenko decided not to put me in with the dealers, and I've got a cell all to myself. I've been cooling my heels in this dank, wretched-smelling pigpen for over four hours when the jailer delivers a cell mate.

Bald, bearded, and rotund, the poor fellow looks like a refugee from a monastery. He throws his coat on the wooden bench in disgust, looks the place over, and scowls at me. "So, what are you in for?"

"I got caught in a sweep of medal dealers."

"Ah, a black marketeer."

"No, I'm a free-lance journalist. I happened to be in the wrong place at the wrong time. You?"

"Exploitation of meat."

"*Spekulatsiya?*"

"*Da, spekulatsiya.* I bought beef in Smolensk at a very low price, and sold it in Moscow for a big markup."

"And they arrested you? Sounds like you're a smart butcher to me."

"Tell them that."

"I will."

"Actually I'm an engineer."

"An engineer? You sure don't look like one," I say in English, falling back into an old habit acquired during my years in the gulag. It was automatic with a new cell mate, a subtle way to expose informers, since most political prisoners spoke some English while most KGB plants were illiterate dullards who didn't. We nailed several that way, until the warden caught on and imported English speakers to spy on us. We also spoke it so the guards wouldn't understand. Sometimes we'd talk about the weather just to piss them off. "Where'd you get your degree?"

"Degrees," the meat peddler replies in English, his voice ringing with defiance and pride. "Both from Moscow Polytechnic Institute."

"A fine school."

"Finest school," he corrects, continuing in English. "Then the whole hell broke loose. One minute I am having career, and the next, nothing."

"Defense cutbacks?"

"Yes, yes, cutbacks. The obsession with having democracy. It makes everything ruined."

"That's a matter of opinion."

"You are in favor?"

"All my life."

"So was I. So was family. Until they learned what will be the cost. Until wife won't be having the dress. Until son won't be having the cassette player." He pauses and smiles in a way that indicates he's about to make a clever point. "Until they see Viktor hawking the meat to make the ends meet." His smile broadens. "Pun intended."

"Very good, Viktor."

He preens. "Now, they long for Communists."

His English isn't as good as mine, but it's more than adequate. I'm not surprised. Most university graduates in our age group speak it. Those who were fortunate enough to be raised by educated parents and sent to elite schools, as I was, do so quite well. I've resumed my note-making when a familiar voice calls out, "Katkov?"

It's Shevchenko. He stands outside the cell with a smug grin, enjoying the sight of me behind bars.

"You just here to gloat, or what?"

"No. Someone vouched for you. I can't imagine why." He nods to a guard, who unlocks the cell and leads me out.

"What about him?" I ask, gesturing to Viktor.

"Not a chance," Shevchenko replies sharply, as the cell door clangs shut behind me and we start down the corridor. "He doesn't have a knack for merely being underfoot like you. He's a grifter and has to be taught a lesson."

"You're very big on lessons these days, aren't you, Mr. Investigator?"

We pause at a security door. His eyes sweep over my bruised face and disheveled clothes. A smile tugs at the corner of his mouth. "You've got a lot to learn."

"Makes two of us," I retort sharply.

The door rumbles open, and he leads the way past a massive outprocessing area. A mesh fence contains the surly mob of prisoners, lawyers, friends, and relatives who are lined up at three windows where clerks work with listless detachment. It's like shopping in a department store: one line to place your order, one to pay, and one to pick up the goods.

I recognize several medal dealers in the crowd. Unfortunately the long-haired one recognizes me and lunges at the fence like a wild man, his fingers clawing at the mesh, hair snapping around his face. "Informer! Fucking informer!" he shouts, making the obvious assumption when he sees me with Shevchenko. "We're not finished with you yet, Katkov!"

I ignore him, hurrying after Shevchenko, who's at the elevator, impatiently thumbing the call button. "How come that nutcase is getting out, and Viktor isn't?"

"Because Viktor-the-grifter exploits food."

"Come on, he's not a grifter, he's a speculator. Guys like him are what make free-market economies work."

"I don't think I'm up to this, Katkov."

"You'd better be. You're going to have to live with it for the rest of your life. The bottom line is—and by the way that's a term you should become familiar with—instead of prosecuting Viktor, you should set up five more speculators in the meat business."

"That's ridiculous. Why?"

"Because more meat will be available, and competition will drive the price down. You know a lot about laws. This one is called supply and demand."

Try as he might, Shevchenko can't stop his brows from arching. "Very clever. But it has nothing to do with Vorontsov's murder. That's what's keeping me here till midnight and getting me out of bed at five in the morning to bust medal dealers."

"Your old lady still getting pissed off?"

"None of your business."

"Business. Very good. Your free-market vocabulary is expanding."

"The bottom line is," he says pointedly, "this may not be a scandal, but it's still a homicide. And I've got to solve it."

"By locking up medal dealers? The poor bastards are only trying to earn a living."

"So am I. It sends a signal. They know they'll be harassed until someone comes up with information on Vorontsov's killer."

"You're assuming they have it."

"No. I'm assuming that squeezed hard enough they'll make it their business to get it."

The elevator deposits us on the fourth floor. We navigate the labryinth of depressing corridors to Shevchenko's office.

"In case you're wondering, I'm sparing you the humiliation of being processed like a common criminal." He falls into his chair like a rag doll and pushes my paperwork across the desk. "Sign these." There are at least a half-dozen forms. Vera is listed as the person who vouched for me. I begin scrawling my signature beneath hers. Shevchenko leans back, staring at the ceiling, deep in thought. "She's moving out," he says softly.

"Pardon me?"

"My wife. She's leaving me. She and the children."

I'm caught completely off guard, taken by his surprising vulnerability and willingness to share it. An awkward moment passes before I regain my composure. "I'm sorry."

Shevchenko shrugs forlornly, then, shutting me out, swivels around and stares at a photograph of his family atop a file cabinet behind him. "You'll find Miss Fedorenko downstairs."

I whisper, "Thanks," and hurry from the office. While searching the maze of corridors for the elevator, I turn a corner and catch sight of a familiar face through the window of a confer-

ence room. It's Drevnya, the kid from *Pravda*. He's writing furiously on his notepad while an obese man in a rumpled suit
circles the table, slashing the air with emphatic gestures as he
talks. His back is to me at first; then, reversing direction, he
reveals himself to be a repulsive fellow with thick lips, scarred
complexion, and small eyes that briefly catch mine. I've no idea
who he is, but Sergei said the kid has connections here. I guess
he does.

Vera is waiting in the lobby, reading another book from my
library when I join her. She looks up and frowns with concern.
"You look awful."

"Long night."

"You should've called."

"I know. I'm sorry. I didn't mean to worry you."

"I mean when I beeped you."

"Oh," I exclaim, recalling it vaguely. After all that's happened, it seems like a week ago. "Too much going on. I
couldn't. Why?"

"I was on duty when the Lenin Hills operation got the
green light."

"Why'd you wait so long?"

"Well, it didn't seem important at first. Then when you
didn't show up at the apartment, I thought maybe you'd gotten
a line on the dealers. Obviously, by then it was too late."

"The story of my life."

"You're your own worst enemy, Nikolai."

"What does that mean?"

"Nothing."

"*Vera.*"

"This isn't the time or the place."

"Come on," I say, directing her aside. "You know how I hate
it when you play these games."

"Okay. If you really want to know, why can't you take a job
like a normal person?"

"You're really hung up on that, aren't you?"

"Most people are."

"That's not the answer, and you know it. Besides, I'm not a
normal person."

"Thanks for sharing that with me."

"What you see is what you get, Vera. I can't be someone else.
I thought you respected me for it."

"I did. I mean, I do. I—"

"I don't need this."

"Neither do I, Niko. I can't keep bailing you out of trouble. I can't keep funding your crusades. I—"

"You wouldn't have to if you'd get me copies of those documents like I asked."

Her eyes flare as if something just dawned on her. "God. That's all you care about, isn't it? That's all I am to you. An inside source. A spy. Well, I'm sick and tired of it. Tired of taking chances. Tired of"—she pauses, face reddening with anger, eyes welling with emotion—"tired of being used."

"Vera, I . . ."

She turns and starts walking away.

"Vera? Vera, listen to me, dammit." I catch up and take her arm.

She jerks it loose, throws her head back defiantly, and strides across the terrazzo to the revolving door that spins her into an icy haze.

I'm torn between going after her and going back to Shevchenko's office and suggesting we commiserate over the contents of his hip flask. Instead, I take a few moments to convince myself Vera will get over it—she always does—light a cigarette with a cocky flick of my new butane lighter, and head for my apartment. I've got a story to write.

11

It's past noon when I get to Lyublino. I walk down Kurskaya
from the Metro, looking over my shoulder. It's an old habit,
acquired twenty-five years ago—June 16, 1968 to be precise—
the day the KGB arrested my father. A Saturday. The Jewish
Sabbath. It was no accident. His outspokenness on the Prague
issue is what landed him in the gulag, but his cultural heritage
is what kept him there. Though the recent dismantling of the
Secret Police has taken the edge off my paranoia, that rabid
medal dealer quickly sharpened it.

My apartment is like a meat locker, the radiator silent and
cold like Mrs. Parfenov's aging brain, which can't remember to
turn on the heat. I bang on the pipes with a wrench I keep
handy, put up a pot of coffee, and roll a couple of sheets of
paper into the typewriter with a worn carbon.

Rafik's point about the rise of nationalism is a perfect angle
for the story: Despite the change from enslaved to free society,
life for the average citizen has taken a turn for the worse. No
wonder the nostalgia for the past. No wonder the demand for
medals is such that thieves kill for them, dealers assault those
who endanger their operation, and the police are faced with a
rise in violent crime.

I write it, rewrite it, and polish it, fighting my inclination to

sugarcoat bitter pills with government-speak. Countless cigarettes and cups of black coffee later, it's finished. Six double-
spaced pages. Fifteen hundred words that bristle with energy—
that are my best shot at getting a line on Vorontsov's killer.

I've been beaten, arrested, jailed, and dumped by Vera, and
I'm still no closer than when I started. I've been hoping she'd
stop by on the way to work, but no such luck. I slip the pages
into my briefcase and head for *Pravda*. Sergei is in a meeting
when I arrive. I'm talking shop with another free-lancer when
he emerges from a conference room.

"Sergei?" I call out, hurrying after him as he recognizes my
voice and quickens his pace. "Sergei? Sergei, wait. You were
right."

That stops him. He turns to face me, jut-jawed, head cocked
challengingly.

"Look, I'm really sorry about what happened. I acted like
a jerk."

"That's one word for it. Anything else?"

"Yes. I need a favor."

He groans.

I slip the pages from my briefcase.

Sergei snatches them, pushes up his glasses, and scowls.
"The black market in medals? I thought I made it clear I'm not
interested in street crime."

"I'm not asking you to buy it, Sergei. I'm asking you to read
it. I need a critique."

His face softens like a parent with a prodigal child. "No
more *Novoyaz?*"

"You tell me."

He lumbers into his office, plucks a pencil from a mug as he
rounds the desk, and goes to work. His expression seems to
soften in tribute. "Better, much better," he finally mutters, pencil darting across the pages. He's nearing the end when he recoils and looks up. "Shevchenko had you arrested?"

"Uh-huh. Claimed he was making a point."

"What point? Why would he . . ." Sergei pauses as the pieces
fall into place. "You're not letting go of this Vorontsov thing,
are you?"

I shake my head no and smile.

"Dumb. But I'd be disappointed if you had," he says enigmatically. "Why is it any skin off Shevchenko's ass?"

"It complicates his life. He's overworked, he's got trouble at home, he—"

"Who doesn't?" Sergei cracks, his pencil resuming its journey. "Where you going to submit this?"

"I was thinking about *Independent Gazette.*"

"Good. You know Lydia?"

"Lydia?"

"Lydia Brelova," he says, scooping up the phone and dialing as he talks. "Best Metro editor in the city. Young, smart— Lydia?" he says effusively when she answers. "Sergei Murashev here. Crazed. What else? Listen, I've just come across a piece that's more your thing than mine." After briefing her, he hangs up, explains I've got a shot at tomorrow's edition, and offers me a typewriter to do the rewrite.

I'm about to get into it when something dawns on me. "By the way, Sergei, the other piece?"

"Other piece?" he echoes, a little evasively.

"Yes, the one on Vorontsov. I'd like it back, if it's handy?"

"Oh? Oh, yes, of course." I'm probably reading into it, but he seems to be going through the motions as he shuffles a stack of files on his desk. He comes up empty and shrugs. "Funny. I could swear it was here."

"You think maybe the kid has it?"

"Drevnya? It's possible. He's covering a story. I'll check when he gets back." Sergei chuckles to himself, savoring a thought. "He's a pip. Always out there, digging. Relentless."

"Try ruthless."

"That too. They all are. You remember when we had that kind of drive?"

"What do you mean, 'we'?"

Sergei laughs and points me to the newsroom. "Better get started; you'll miss the deadline."

I settle at a desk and make the changes. About an hour later, I'm leaving the building when a taxi pulls to the curb and Drevnya jumps out, nose buried in the pages of his notebook. He's preoccupied, bristling with journalistic zeal. Like he's onto a story and can't wait to get to his typewriter.

What story? I wonder. Where's he been? What's he up to? Why do I feel threatened, dammit? He heads for the door, pretending he hasn't seen me. After our last encounter, who'd blame him? "Hey? Hey, Drevnya? Got a minute?"

The kid pauses and eyes me apprehensively. "No. I'm on deadline," he replies, keeping his distance.

"Me too," I fire back, which seems to disarm him. I make a brief apology and ask about my Vorontsov article.

"Sergei has it," Drevnya replies, clearly puzzled.

"You're sure?"

"Uh-huh. He asked me for it."

I was right. Sergei is up to something. But I don't have time to go back upstairs and get into it now. "Ask him to call me if it turns up, okay?"

It's a short Metro ride to *Independent Gazette,* the gutsy, Western-style journal that took over where *Moscow News* left off. Hidden in a courtyard near Lubyanka Square, where the Russian tricolor flies in place of the statue of secret police founder Felix Dzerzhinsky, the *Gazette*'s efficient offices are alive with youthful energy and the hum of word processors.

Sergei was right. Lydia Brelova is immediately taken by the article. She's a decisive woman who knows what she wants and drives a hard bargain to get it. I'm in no position to argue. Besides, after paying my rent—Moscow Telephone takes forever to track delinquents, so the phone bill can wait—I'll still have enough left to bury the hatchet with Vera over dinner, if she doesn't bury one in me first. Then I remember she's working tonight, so I head over to Yuri's, instead.

His tiny one-room flat on Begovaya is located in a run-down area of the city—but it's still in the city. Moscow has always had a critical housing shortage and those who don't want to share living space with relatives or, as is often the case, total strangers, have two choices: live in a polluted suburb like I do, or in a "closet" like Yuri—though I expect his new status at the Interior Ministry will soon result in an upgrade. The floor-to-ceiling bookshelves are stuffed with economic treatises, among them works by Adam Smith, Robert Solow, Milton Friedman, the three Johns—Kenneth Galbraith, Maynard Keynes, Stuart Mill—and a treasured, *samizdat* copy of Samuelson's *Economics* that I recall Yuri acquired in the days when studying Western economic theory required courage and guile.

He's on the phone with his mother when I arrive. She lives alone on a farm in Sudilova, several hours north of the city by car. For as long as I've known him, every Saturday morning without fail, Yuri drives out to see her; and several times each week, she calls to remind him to come. After hanging up, he mentions he's had no luck with Vorontsov's documents, but promises to keep trying. I've been so caught up in the medals, I'd almost forgotten about them. Besides, once this story hits the streets, I may not need them.

We celebrate with a few beers.

I've been up over thirty-six hours and on the wagon considerably longer. The alcohol hits me like a sledgehammer. I spend the night on his sofa and pick up a copy of *Independent Gazette* in the morning on the way home. I've stopped counting how many times I've seen my by-line in print, but I still get a little rush. This one is cut short by a man in a trench coat, leaning against a Zhiguli across the street from my apartment.

Tall, slim, his angular face masked by sunglasses, he flicks a cigarette to the ground and steps on it as I approach, then follows me with his eyes—or so it seems. It's not the medal dealer who threatened to get me, but that doesn't mean this guy isn't one of them. I'm climbing the steps of the old mansion, telling myself it's another flash of paranoia, when a shadow ripples across Mrs. Parfenov's curtain. Is she keeping an eye out for him or me?

"Nikasha," she says effusively, emerging from her apartment as I enter the foyer.

I know what she wants. "The rent," I announce, producing a wad of rubles before she can ask.

She stuffs them in the pocket of her apron without so much as a glance, then turns to the door behind her. "Come in for a minute, Nikasha. Come in. I want to show you something."

"This isn't a good time, Mrs. Parfenov."

"She's not up there," the old *babushka* says, sensing I'm anxious to find out if Vera's here. "Take a minute. Please, it's important."

Important? Maybe she's finally recalled whatever it is she hasn't been able to remember. I follow her into a musty room filled with baronial furniture that dwarfs her. On the tired cushion of an armchair, I notice a copy of *Independent Gazette* open to my story.

Mrs. Parfenov shuffles to a closet and fetches something wrapped in a moth-eaten Army blanket. She cradles it like a swaddled infant and places it on the table in front of me. Then carefully folding back the coarse wool, she reveals a lacquered hardwood box. Her bluish fingers undo the latch and open it like a book. Both halves are lined with black velvet. One contains a rust-stained pistol. The other, dozens of gleaming medals with brightly colored ribbons. They're arranged around a small, enameled frame that holds a photograph of a handsome young man replete with mustache, mutton-chops, and military uniform sporting officer's epaulets.

Mrs. Parfenov's eyes come alive with distant memories and search mine for a reaction.

"Your husband?"

"Sasha," she says, nodding with pride, her fingers skimming reverently over the medals. "He fought in the revolution; and in the civil war too; then he fought the Nazis. My Sasha . . ." Her eyes glisten and her voice cracks with emotion. "My Sasha fought for Russia. The real Russia. A place where people would help one another. Where everyone would be equal. Where no one would go hungry or be without clothing or shelter. He fought for a dream."

For a socialist fairy tale, is what comes to mind, though I'm so taken by her lucidity I don't dare say it. It's as if reading my story sent an electric shock through her brain, revitalizing long dormant neurons.

Her cool hand takes hold of mine. "You see, Nikasha, we loved our country, not our government."

"I remember my father saying that at his trial."

"Yes, there were some dark days; but you *shestidesyatniks* are all alike," she says, referring to the generation that saw hope in the last political thaw. "You think we wanted purges? You think we wanted to live with fear and ugliness? We're no different than you. All we wanted was a better life. Was that so terrible?"

"No, Mrs. Parfenov, it wasn't."

She nods, vindicated. "That's why my generation still believes in Communism. The new order is for the young: those with no stake in the past and the strength to face painful change." She pauses and shakes her head in dismay. "My life has gotten more difficult lately. Much more."

"So has mine. But I believe that it will get much better in time."

"Time," she echoes with a sarcastic croak. "Time is a luxury the elderly can't afford. We sacrificed to give life to the *Rodina.* Now she is sacrificing us." She sighs resignedly. "But that's how it is with one's children, isn't it?"

"I wouldn't know."

She stares blankly, signaling her inertia has returned. The silence is broken by a truck that lumbers to a stop outside, making the casements shudder. She goes to the window and pulls back the curtain. A moving van is backing into a space in front of the building.

I'm more interested in the Zhiguli across the street. It's still there, but the man in the trench coat isn't. "Someone moving in?" I ask, relieved.

"Out," she replies impassively. Then her posture straightens, and she looks up at me. "Ah, yes, I know what I've wanted to tell you, Nikasha," she announces, pleased at having finally remembered. "At the end of this month—" A distant phone rings, interrupting her. She squints in search of the thought, then loses it and glances to the ceiling. The muffled ring is coming from directly above us, from my apartment.

I excuse myself, dash up the stairs, fumbling for the key, then swiftly unlock the door, and dive across the desk for the phone. "Vera?!"

"No—Lydia," comes the reply, accompanied by an amused giggle.

"Oh? Oh, hi," I say, glad the "city's best metro editor" can't see my sheepish expression.

"There's a Mrs. Churkin here looking for you. She wants to talk about your story."

"Churkin? Mrs. *Tanya* Churkin?"

"That's right. I told her you were free-lance and suggested she write a letter to the editor, but she insists she has to talk to you. I said I couldn't give out your number without permission."

"She's there now?"

"Uh-huh. Won't take no for an answer. I'll put her on, if you like."

"No, I want to do this in person. I'll be there in about an hour. Don't let her leave."

I've no doubt this is the break I've been looking for; no doubt that after reading my story Vorontsov's daughter recalled something disturbing, something she doesn't want to take to the mi-litia, who were too quick to decide he was killed for his medals, whom she doesn't trust. Why else would she come to me?

I hurry from the apartment, stopping briefly at the Zhiguli. A half-dozen cigarette butts are crushed into the macadam. All Marlboros. All half-smoked. I work my *Ducats* right down to the filter. The fellow in the trench coat is either a foreigner or a Russian who's beating the system—like the medal dealers.

The escalator deposits me on the crowded Metro platform where a man leans against a column reading a newspaper. A man in a trench coat! *The* man in the trench coat! Is he out to get me? If he is, why is he stalking me? Why hasn't he made his move? If wants me to squirm for a while, if that's how he gets his kicks, he's sure as hell succeeding.

I drift toward the opposite end of the platform. He watches me over the top of his newspaper, then drifts in the same direc-tion. I quicken my pace, weaving between the other passengers. As soon as I've put some distance between us, I step back into one of the arched seating alcoves, and slip out of my parka. Then I turn it inside out, put it back on, put up the hood, and remove my glasses.

The station is a blur without them, but what looks like a woman with a rambunctious toddler hanging from one fist and shopping bags from the other comes toward me and takes a seat.

I settle on the bench next to them and wave at the child. He screeches playfully in reply. My gut tightens as the soft-edged silhouette of a trench coat moves into view on the platform. The child screeches again and lunges at me, almost toppling off the bench. He's still screeching as I catch him by the seat of the pants and swing him into my lap.

The man in the trench coat reacts to the sound and glances over his shoulder at us. He's looking for unkempt hair, wire-frame glasses, and a beige parka; but I'm wearing a dark blue one with a hood now, and have just acquired a lovely family. He anxiously sweeps his eyes over the other passengers in the area as the whoosh of air rises and the train pulls into the station. The woman takes the squirming child from me and smiles in appreciation.

"Why don't I help you with those," I suggest, hefting her

shopping bags without waiting for a reply. I casually escort my "wife and son" onto the train. The man in the trench coat moves off down the platform in search of me. There's no sign of him during the ride to Moscow or walk to *Independent Gazette,* though I've no doubt he's as adept at concealment as he is at intimidation.

12

etro editor Lydia Brelova, a gaunt, frizzy-haired woman with smiling eyes, shows me to a small conference room where Vorontsov's daughter is waiting. Refined, composed, and well-dressed, in contrast to *Independent Gazette*'s frantic T-shirt-and-jeans staff, she sits primly on the edge of one of the folding chairs that ring the table.

"So what do you have for me, Mrs. Churkin?" I ask, anxious to get down to business.

"Have for you?" she wonders.

"Uh-huh."

"Nothing. Why?"

"I'm sorry. I'm a little confused. As I understand it, you insisted on seeing me."

"Yes, about my father's medals. I want you to help me find them."

"That's very disappointing."

"What do you mean?"

"Well, for one thing, I'm not sure that's why he was killed. It might've been related to his work."

She recoils slightly. "His work?"

"He was investigating the CSP. Surely you've heard of the corruption. The speculation is he either was about to expose, or was involved in, a privatization scandal."

"Speculation?!" she snaps, stiffening with anger as she stands and advances toward me. "I warned you about destroying his name!"

"Only he could do that. I was hoping you had some information that might settle it one way or the other."

"There's nothing to be settled as far as I'm concerned. I'm interested in recovering his medals, nothing more."

"That's the militia's problem."

"They're corrupt and inept. They won't find his killer, let alone his medals."

"I agree. Though in all fairness, Investigator Shevchenko turned down a bribe right in front of me. I think he's trustworthy."

"Maybe. But you wrote the story. You're the one with the connections."

"Yes, and making them damn near got me killed. If there's one thing I learned, it's that tracking down stolen medals is next to impossible."

"I don't see why. My father's name was on them."

"You're sure of that?"

"Positive."

"Then forget it. I asked about them. No one had them. You're wasting my time."

"You talked to every medal dealer in Moscow?"

"Of course not."

"Well, one of them must have them."

"Maybe. Then again, maybe they've already been sold to a private buyer."

"Fine. I'll buy them back from whoever has them. They're very important to me."

"So is my life. You really think I'm going to put it on the line again? Just so you don't have to queue at the local market?"

"That was uncalled for! I could buy any medals on the black market if that were the case. They're, they're—" She stops, overcome with emotion, and crosses to the window. The afternoon light warms her complexion and paints the courtyard below with long shadows. She settles down and turns to face me. Her eyes capture mine with undeniable sincerity. "My father's medals are his legacy, Mr. Katkov. They represent something, something unique—a special time—a world we'll probably never see again."

"Let's hope not."

She groans, disgusted. "Their value is sentimental. Can't you understand that?"

I nod contritely, reflecting on Mrs. Parfenov. "Yes, as a matter of fact I think I can. I'm sorry, Mrs. Churkin. I was out of line."

"Does that mean you'll find them for me?"

"I wouldn't stand a chance," I reply, though I'm suddenly aware it might give me another shot at finding out if Vorontsov's killer was a thief or assassin. "But I know someone who might. *Might.* And if he does, it will be expensive."

"I have money."

"Hard currency?"

She nods. "My father traveled extensively and lived abroad for many, many years."

"I understand. There's a chance the dealers will take it and run."

"It's a chance I'll have to take," she says, her moist eyes hardening with resolve.

I cross to the phone, slip the butane lighter from my pocket—the number of the Paradise Club is printed on the barrel—and call Arkady Barkhin in search of Rafik. Barkhin hasn't seen him since that morning in the Lenin Hills, but suggests I try Kafé Graneetsa, a bar in Serebryanyy-Bor. The desolate island is situated at the end of a canal that connects the Moscow River with the Volga. Its resident dockhands and rivermen work the ferries and cargo vessels that sail northern lakes and the pleasure ships that take Western tourists on cruises to St. Petersburg.

Tanya Churkin offers to give me a lift. Her zeal and brand-new Lada make quick work of the journey, and we're soon crossing the Khoroshevsky Bridge onto the island. The bullrushes and milkweed that grow in the shallows are locked in ice.

Dusk has fallen by the time we arrive at the Graneetsa. It's a typical waterfront dive of rough-hewn wood, coiled hawsers, and portholes that serve as windows. The air has the stinging bite of deep winter, as I leave Mrs. Churkin in the car and cross to the entrance. The interior is alive with the clank of mugs and dull thunk of darts. I stand just inside the door, scanning the crowd for Rafik. He's nowhere in sight. The aroma of perfumed prostitutes working the rivermen thickens as I make my way to the other end of the bar. Still no sign of him. I'm about to give up when I spot a familiar cap bobbing in the midst of a raucous group of dart throwers.

"Katkov!" the diminutive fellow exclaims when he sees me. "I read your article. Nice job."

"Thanks."

"I never thought of myself as 'the mysterious fellow in the evergreens,' but I'm glad you kept my name out of it."

"That was the deal."

He nods, studying me with suspicion. "You didn't come all the way out here to get patted on the back."

"I hope not."

Rafik's expression brightens. A flick of his wrist sends his last dart at the board; then he directs me to a table away from the action, where I brief him. *"Vayluta,"* he replies, using slang for hard currency. *"Vayluta* is the key."

"Don't be so sure. Those dealers were pretty pissed off. Damned near killed me. They might not be interested in doing business."

"They'll be killing each other to take your money, believe me."

"Shevchenko seemed to think the medals are worth somewhere in the neighborhood of thirty million rubles."

"At the current rate, that's damn near thirty thousand dollars. You're sure your client can come up with that much?"

"Yes. More, if need be."

"Lots more, if we don't play this right."

"You mean the instant whoever has them knows we want *those* medals and only those medals, he'll know he has no competition, and the price will . . ." I pause, catching sight of a man who slips in a side door. It's the guy in the trench coat. He walks toward us calmly, pulls a handgun from a shoulder holster, and starts firing.

I dive beneath the table, turning it on its side like a shield. Rafik pulls a small revolver from a pocket and scurries to the end of the bar, returning the fire. Rivermen and prostitutes are screaming and running for cover as more blinding flashes erupt. Six, seven, eight sharp cracks in rapid succession. The bullets splinter wood and ricochet off concrete. I'm curled up, flinching in terror at every pop and ping. Then silence, smoke, the smell of cordite, and the sounds of furniture being moved and people getting to their feet. I crawl out from behind the table slowly.

Several rivermen are crouching over the gunman's body, which is sprawled on the floor. Blood bubbles from a hole in the center of his chest, pooling in the folds of his trench coat. He's clearly dead, and those around him waste no time helping themselves to his valuables.

I push past them and find Rafik slumped against the bar, clutching his abdomen. His shirt is drenched with blood that runs between his fingers.

"Call an ambulance!" I shout at the crowd.

"No," Rafik growls through clenched teeth. "No hospital. They report gunshot wounds. They—"

"Call, dammit, call!"

"Don't," Rafik pleads again, grimacing in pain. "The militia. They'll—"

"You want to die?!"

He nods emphatically, struggling to get up. "Better than prison."

"You're not going to jail, and you're not going to die either." I help him to his feet and start toward the door.

Tanya Churkin must be serious about recovering those medals because, despite the commotion, she's still waiting when I emerge from the bar with Rafik. Her jaw drops as we stumble toward the car. She isn't thrilled at the idea of getting blood all over the upholstery of her new Lada, but she helps me settle Rafik in the backseat anyway.

"You know the Yushkov House?" I ask, referring to a famous building in Old Moscow.

"Of course," she snaps haughtily, wheeling the car around.

"Good. We're going right across the street. Sixty-three Myasnitskaya."

"Why?" Rafik rasps apprehensively, his ruddy face turning pale as the car accelerates. "What's there?"

"A doctor."

"Better be one we can bribe," he jokes weakly.

"One we can trust."

"You're sure?"

"No. But I was married to her once."

13

Tanya Churkin's Lada races along the Garden Ring, the tree-lined boulevard that circumscribes the spider-web of streets spun from the city's hub. She turns off at Kirova and weaves through the darkened neighborhoods of Old Moscow. The chromatic facades are faded now, pale pastel hues overpowered by the Lada's headlights.

"It's the last one on the right," I say as she angles into Myasnitskaya. "Turn into the alley."

Like many buildings in this historic area that are being restored, No. 63 is sheathed in scaffolding, and the adjacent alley is littered with construction debris. Mrs. Churkin maneuvers next to a staircase that leads to the service entrance. She sets the handbreak and hurries up the steps ahead of me to open the door.

"Time to plug that leak," I say to Rafik, moving him into a sitting position. A weak smile creases the corners of his mouth. He's ashen and barely conscious. I'm getting an arm under him when Mrs. Churkin returns on the run. "The door's locked."

"Damn. Stay with him." I dash up the stairs and try it to no avail. Light spills across the scaffolding from nearby windows. I climb onto the rickety structure and peer into a doctor's waiting room. Every chair is occupied. Several patients queue at a desk where a harried nurse prioritizes files. My ex-wife was right. Getting rid of me and my political baggage paid off.

The shade on the next window is fully drawn, but a gap at the side affords a view of the examining room. Alexandra Sereva, the woman who promised to love, honor, and cherish me until death, sits at a desk jotting in a file. She's between patients. Alone. Something's finally gone right.

I'm about to knock on the window when she stands and crosses toward the door, lab smock billowing stiffly behind her. I rap sharply on the window. She pauses and looks about as if unable to place the sound. I knock again, louder, insistently. She zeroes in on the window and advances with caution.

Her shadow falls across the shade.

"Alexandra?!"

It suddenly goes up.

We're face-to-face for the first time in years. She's startled, her wide-set eyes blinking in disbelief at the sight of a man on the scaffold—at the sight of *me*. The frosty pane that separates us frames her classic face like a painting. She's still attractive as ever, still radiant with Hippocratic goodness.

I'm drained, fixated on the life slipping away in the Lada. I'm not sure what I feel. "The service door's locked," I shout, gesturing toward it frantically. "The door, Alexa. Open the door."

"Come round front," she orders loudly, unable to imagine why I'm slinking about alleys and peeping in windows.

"I can't. It's an emergency, dammit. Come on, Alexa. Open the fucking door!"

She's momentarily taken aback, then nods and moves off, glancing back at me with uncertainty.

I jump to the ground and hurry to the Lada. Mrs. Churkin helps me remove Rafik; then, without a word, she drives off, sending bits of litter swirling in the darkness. I'm carrying Rafik up the stairs when the deadbolt retracts and the door opens.

"My God," Alexa exclaims at the bloody sight cradled in my arms.

"Someone shot him. I didn't think it'd be a good idea to drag him through the waiting room."

"You should've taken him to a hospital."

"I can't."

Her brows go up.

"You don't want to know."

"In that case, I can't help him."

"Come on, he's going to die, for Chrissakes!" I push past her and hurry down the corridor.

"Nikolai?!" she says sharply, right on my heels. "Nikolai. The law requires I report gunshot wounds."

"If you happen to think of it."

"That's not funny. I won't do anything illegal."

"I'm not asking you to. Paperwork falls through cracks, files get lost, assistants forget to fill out reports." I turn into the examining room and lay Rafik on the table beneath the fluorescents. His face is the color of week-old snow.

"I won't," Alexa insists, taking his pulse instinctively. "I mean it."

"Fine. We'll wait here until he dies, and then you can report whatever you want."

"You're right," she concedes with that sexy pout I still find alluring. "He's barely alive." She takes the phone and stabs a finger at the intercom. "Nina? I think I'm coming down with something. . . . Uh-huh. A nasty headache. . . . Yes, they'll have to be rescheduled. . . . No, you can leave when you're finished." She hangs up and glances to me. "Lock the door."

I know what's coming. I've seen her in action countless times. Swift, precise, decisive, she could handle this in her sleep. I throw the latch and step aside as she fetches an emergency kit from a cabinet, sets it on a cart, removes an IV unit, tears off the sterilized wrapper, and plugs it into a bag of saline that she hangs on a mobile stand.

Rafik is silent and motionless now, his eyes half-lidded and unfocused as Alexa buzzes around him. She cuts one of his sleeves to the shoulder, searching anxiously for a vein. Nothing. "Lost a lot of blood."

"Can you replace it?"

"If I had some. If I knew his type. If I—"

"What about that stuff you used to—"

"—had any plasmanate," she continues without missing a beat. "Hard to find these days. The saline'll replete his intravascular volume, but it's no substitute for the red stuff."

She lets Rafik's arm hang from the table, then ties a length of rubber around the biceps. A faint, bluish ripple rises just above his wrist. Alexa inserts the stylet, feeds the intracath up

the vein, and cranks the valve wide open. She whirls to a cabinet. Surgical gloves snap and squeak as she pulls them on, then
douses Rafik's bloody shirt with disinfectant.

"I don't know, Niko," she scolds, as she begins cutting away
the loosened fabric. "I haven't heard from you in years, and
when I finally do, you're up to your ass in trouble."

"Déjà vu, I know."

She pauses, allowing her expression to soften. For an instant
her eyes have the adoring affection they had when we first met,
when she admired my outspokenness and shared my belief in
a free society. "I should've let you die," she says mischievously, before her eyes narrow in concentration and she peels
away the last of the fabric, revealing the wound.

I'm staring at a nasty puncture in Rafik's gut, but it's mine
that I see. It's been over twenty years, and the once-jagged scar
is smooth and shiny now, but Alexa's remark makes the memory of that cool, autumn morning painfully fresh.

I'd just graduated from Moscow State University when Egypt
and Syria invaded Israel on the eve of Yom Kippur. The Kremlin sent massive arms shipments to the Arabs and I wrote an
editorial for an underground paper urging dissidents to march
on Red Square in protest. The KGB showed up in force and
came at us with billy clubs. The blow that struck my scalp hurt
like hell, but did little damage. I was getting to my feet when
an angry voice shouted, "Jew bastard!" Then a searing pain
erupted in my side, and I realized I'd been stabbed.

Before the pit bulls could finish me off, friends intervened
and rushed me to a hospital. Despite the trauma, I was quite
taken by the young woman who was waiting for me in surgery,
taken by the compassionate eyes that peered over the top of
her mask and the reassuring voice that came from beneath it.

"You're going to be fine, Nikolai," she said, holding my hand
as the anesthetic took me under. I thought about her constantly
during my recovery and pursued her upon my release. Alexa
spent ten years blaming my writing and political activism for
ruining her medical practice. And I spent the next ten blaming
her ambition and willingness to put up with tyranny for our
divorce; but, in all fairness, my alcoholism had as much to do
with it, if not more. I've never admitted that to her. I've never
had the—

The harsh chatter of adhesive tape pulls me out of it. "Cut this, will you? Nikolai? Nikolai?!"

I take the scissors and snip the tape that she uses to secure a bandage beneath Rafik's rib cage. "He going to be okay?"

"If he gets to a hospital."

"Come on, Alexa."

"He's severely exsanguinated. Probably still bleeding internally. There's no exit wound, which means the bullet's still in there. And I've no way to remove it or assess the damage."

"There's no more you can do?!"

"He needs blood, Nikolai. He needs surgery. A hospital is his only chance."

"What's the point of saving his life if he's going to spend it in prison?"

"This is no time for riddles. He's got a couple of hours, maybe less. Don't waste them."

"I promised he wouldn't die and wouldn't go to jail. I might as well make good on one of 'em. Get your car. I'll meet you in the alley."

"I don't have a car. Not one that runs anyway."

"You have a waiting room full of patients and you can't afford to get your car fixed?!"

"Like everyone else in this damned city, Niko, most of my patients are out of work. And when they're broke, I'm broke!" She turns on a heel, crosses to her desk, and calls for an ambulance. Then she fetches a blanket and covers Rafik. "He an old friend?"

"No. Why?"

"Well, you seem so worried about him. I—"

"I worry about everyone who spent time in the gulag," I interrupt, a little too pointedly. "I'm sorry, Alexa. It's been a long night. Poor bastard was helping me with a story."

She nods knowingly. "It could've been you, couldn't it?"

"Should've been."

"You're going to run out of lives one of these days, Nikolai."

"I already did . . ." I say, pausing before delivering the punch line. "I died the day you left me."

"A guilt trip. I should've known. You haven't changed a bit, have you?"

"Sure I have."

"For example?"

"I don't drink anymore."

That gets her attention. Her eyes latch onto mine, prying the truth out of me the way they used to.

"Well, not much anyway."

"Alcoholics either drink or they don't," she says sharply. "There's no in-between."

"I'm trying."

She groans, exasperated. "Talk about déjà vu."

"It's different. Really. You ever hear of Moscow Beginners?"

Her eyes widen with surprise. "You've been going?"

"Uh-huh. A friend told me about it. She kept bugging me to look into it."

"It's nice to have someone who—"

"Where the hell's that damned ambulance?!" I interrupt, preferring not to get into it with her.

"Take it easy. It's only been a few minutes."

"See. Another change. I'm much more impatient, not to mention incompetent—according to the 'teenagers' who staff *Pravda* these days."

"Well, you sure haven't lost your knack for writing things that piss people off."

"That wasn't it. I was doing a story on black-market medals. The militia put the squeeze on them. They blamed it on me."

A horn sounds in the alley.

I hurry down the corridor and open the door. Two emergency technicians are coming up the steps with a gurney. By the time Alexa finishes filling out the transmittal form, Rafik—oxygen mask over his nose and mouth, IV bag swinging from a hook on the gurney—is on his way down the corridor to the ambulance.

"Take care of yourself, Nikolai," Alexa says as the ETs shove the gurney inside.

I force a smile and climb in after it.

"I mean it, Niko," she says poignantly. "I do."

One of the ETs slams the door. The ambulance bounces down the alley, turns into the street, and accelerates toward the Ring Road, emergency flashers strobing in the darkness. A short time later, as the ambulance snakes through traffic, Rafik's chest suddenly arches against the restraints. Then he expels a massive amount of blood into the oxygen mask and goes limp. His head lolls to one side and stays there, blank eyes staring up at me. Through me.

The ET puts a finger to Rafik's neck, then shines a light in his eyes and closes them. "Save it," he calls out to the driver, who backs off the gas and flashers in response. The ambulance slows and changes direction, heading toward downtown. A short time later, it clears the main gate at Militia Headquarters and circles around to the morgue. Attendants remove Rafik's body while an arrogant clerk in a militia uniform deals with the ETs, who turn over the paperwork and leave.

"He was shot?" the clerk asks me, after reviewing Alexa's transmittal.

"If that's what it says."

"You don't know the circumstances?"

"No," I reply, wanting no part of a homicide.

"You his next of kin?"

"Good Samaritan."

"Put that down and explain it," he says, pushing a form across the desk. "You can't leave until I run it past the duty officer."

"I told you I wasn't a witness."

"That's for him to decide."

I cook up an innocuous story and scribble it on the report. He methodically separates the copies, putting several into cylindrical carriers that vanish with a whoosh into a network of pneumatic tubes. Ten minutes later, I'm lighting my third *Ducat* when Shevchenko comes through the double doors. "Katkov," he calls out. "Saw your name. Thought I'd say hello."

"It's been that kind of night."

He produces a copy of my report. "It says here you found an injured stranger in the street?"

"That's correct."

"And since you just happened to be in the vicinity of your wife's office, you took him there."

"Uh-huh. She did what she could for him. We were on the way to the hospital when—"

"So it says," he interrupts, casually adding, "I didn't know her office was in Serebryanyy-Bor?"

"Serebryanyy-Bor? It's not. It's in—" I bite it off, realizing he set me up.

"My people covered a shooting there today. In a bar. *Mafiya* style. The way they do it in America. One dead. One wounded.

The latter, according to witnesses, was a short fellow named Rafik. He was with a third man, unidentified; described as"—he pauses, making a show of checking his notes—"lean, dark blue parka, unruly hair, wire-rim glasses."

"So? We all have a double out there somewhere."

"And *we* have a body, a pistol, and experts who I'm betting will find your friend's prints all over it, not to mention ballistic markings that prove it was the murder weapon."

"Get to the point, will you?"

"You're an accomplice to murder, Katkov."

"What?! I was the fucking target, for Chrissakes!"

"You?"

"Uh-huh. The guy followed me around all day. Rafik saved my ass. No thanks to you."

"What the hell does that mean?"

"The medal dealers. You heard that guy threaten me. They thought I set them up."

"That's what happens when you stir up trouble for a living. You're an action junkie, Katkov. You crave it. All you media people do. You get high on it, and then you crash." He pauses and looks to his clipboard. "What's this Rafik got to do with it?"

"He was my connection." It dawns on me the shooter wasn't following me to make me squirm, but because the medal dealers wanted to take out both of us. "Rafik was there that morning. They must've blamed him too."

Shevchenko nods thoughtfully, then studies me.

I've a feeling he's knows more than he's telling and is deciding what to do about it. "Come on, don't hold out on me. We still have a deal, if this is what I think it is."

"It probably isn't," he says unconvincingly. "Regardless, we're still working on it." His eyes dart to his watch. "Sorry. I'm in the middle of something." He signs off on the report, and leaves with a spring in his step, setting the double doors swinging on their hinges.

I wait while the clerk completes his work, then hurry outside, anxious to get the smell of formaldehyde out of my nostrils. The temperature has dropped below zero and the sky is gray with the promise of snow. I walk past the line of cars parked along the wall and out the gate, deciding to treat myself to a cab.

Ten minutes later, I'm still waiting for one when headlights illuminate the courtyard, and a car emerges. Shevchenko's car. It comes in my direction on the other side of Petrovka and stops at the employees' entrance. A woman steps from the shadows in the recessed doorway. Her walk is familiar. Unfortunately, so is her face. Too preoccupied to notice me in the darkness, Vera crosses to the car and gets in next to Shevchenko.

I feel as if I've been punched in the gut. He said he was in the middle of something! This sure as hell explains it, along with Vera's endless supply of coffee. I'm seized by an impulse to get roaring drunk and confront them. But it's a short Metro ride to the community center, and if there was ever a time for a session at Moscow Beginners, it's now.

"Nikolai K.!" the heavyset fellow with the wintry eyes enthuses, clapping me on the back as I enter the meeting room. "How've you been doing?"

"Lousy. I'm in a rotten mood. Frankly, I'd rather be getting drunk."

"So would I," Ludmilla T. says with mischievous eyes that make brief contact with mine.

"So would we all," the old fellow in the skullcap chimes in. "Want to talk about it, Nikolai?"

"Nothing to talk about. Even if there was, ten years of talk wouldn't change a thing."

"How do you know?"

"Yes, why not give it a try?"

"You don't have to be afraid with us."

"I'm not afraid."

"Of course you are," the old fellow says gently. "The way to overcome fear is to meet it head-on."

"Maybe he's not ready," Ludmilla says vulnerably.

"Are *you*?" one of the younger men challenges.

"No," she whispers. "I may never be."

"I can relate to that," an older woman says. "I hate confrontations. Especially with myself."

"It's like picking at a wound," another observes. "It never heals."

I couldn't agree more. It was a mistake to come here tonight. I've too many wounds, too much pain. I'm drifting off, trying to tune them out, when an uneasy feeling comes over me, a feeling I'm being watched. I look up to find stern, hypnotic eyes staring at me from a poster. Beneath the life-size image of an ascetic-looking man, identified as "The Founder," is flame-scorched typography that proclaims:

DIANETICS
CHURCH OF SCIENTOLOGY
MOSCOW STATE UNIVERSITY WINTER SESSION
REGISTER FOR CLASSES NOW

It's a depressing sight. No sooner do we topple the statues of Lenin, then we rush to replace them. Rafik was right. Little has changed. We're still eager to be wooed by charismatic men who claim they have all the answers. Oh, we applaud democracy, but it's religion—an infallible hierarchy to tell us what to do— that we crave. I've no doubt this guy, Hubbard, and others like him, will have a field day with the current craze for self-improvement.

"You'll have to excuse me," I say, having decided that maybe Alexa and Vera can't accept me warts-and-all, but I can. I know who I am, I know it's futile to fight my nature, to be someone I'm not.

"No pain, no gain, Nikolai," the old man warns.

"As my ex-wife would say, 'That's why God made anesthesia.'" I head for the door, turning a deaf ear to the group's exhortations to remain.

Heavy snow is falling as I leave the community center. I've gone about a block when I hear the crunch of footsteps behind me. A figure bundled in greatcoat, fur hat, and boots moves into view as I turn the corner. The snow obscures my view, but it looks like a woman, a tired woman, paying me no mind. Is her blank gaze the result of an exhausting day's work? Or of professional schooling intended to conceal she's tailing me? I'm tempted to duck into an alley until she passes, but I'm sick and tired of jumping at every shadow and sound. It's a few blocks to State Liquor Store No. 12. If she's there when I come out—if she *is* surveilling me—I just might confront one of my fears and offer to share my bottle of painkiller with her.

14

I'm running down a long, narrow alley. It's dark and still except for the glint of steel and threatening movements of the person stalking me. I keep running, deeper and deeper into pitch blackness. The towering walls suddenly converge. There's no way out. I'm trapped, backed into a corner. The assailant charges, shoves a pistol against my chest, and pulls the trigger with a vengeful sneer. A deafening explosion! Blinding blue-orange flashes! Glimpses of a face! A peaked cap set at a jaunty angle.

"Bastard!" Rafik shouts. "Fucking bastard! You promised you wouldn't let me die!"

Searing pain tears through my body. I stumble in the darkness. A door! There's a door! My fists pound on it frantically. No one responds. I'm on the verge of passing out. My arms drop from exhaustion but the pounding continues.

Another gunshot!

The pounding intensifies!

I scream and sit bolt upright, drenched in sweat. My tongue feels like it's made of wool. My head like it's being crushed in a slowly tightening vise. My eyes, wide with terror, are staring at the door to my apartment. Someone's knocking on it. I crawl out of bed, stubbing my toe on an empty vodka bottle that goes spinning across the floor. I'm halfway there when I hear a key in the lock.

It's Vera. She recoils at the sight of me. Then her eyes react to something and flare with anger. "Who the hell is that?!" she demands, slamming the door closed after her.

"Who's who?" I wonder meekly, head throbbing.

"That!" She stabs a finger at the sleeping alcove.

I squint at the bed, trying to resolve the blurred image. Christ! There's a woman tangled in the sheets! A naked woman! Legs drunkenly askew, a breast exposed, one arm hanging over the side of the bed, the other bent at an angle over her face.

"I don't know," I rasp, shuddering at the sight of hastily removed clothing and yet another empty bottle as it starts coming back. "Last night . . . yes, yes, there was this woman . . . she, she was following me. I thought she was, anyway. But she wasn't. She—"

"You picked up a woman on the street?!"

"Yes. Wait. No. I'm not sure," I stammer, leaning into the alcove for a closer look. There's something familiar about her. As a matter of fact she looks a hell of a lot like what's-her-name. God, it is what's-her-name.

Ludmilla T. stirs, pushes up onto an elbow in a lemon-vodka haze, then collapses with a groan.

"No, she's not from the street, Vera," I say, foolishly expecting to mollify her. "She's from Moscow Beginners. Yes, that's where she's from."

"You go there to get rid of a vice, Nikolai!" Vera screeches, yanking the curtain to close off the alcove. "Not to pick one up!"

"Hey, people who live in glass *dachas* . . ."

"What the hell does that mean?"

"Come on, Vera. I saw you! He finally make chief? That it?"

"Chief? You can't mean Shevchenko?!" Vera's about to launch a fusillade of indignant denials when someone knocks on the door. Several sharp, authoritative raps.

Vera opens it brusquely, revealing a tall, good-looking woman in a down-filled overcoat, standing in the corridor. Vera's eyes narrow and burn with anger—*"Another* woman?!" written all over them. "It's over, Nikolai! I mean over!" She takes a folded newspaper from under her arm and throws it at me. It whizzes past my head and hits the wall above the dresser. Vera turns on a heel and blows out of the apartment. "Take a number, honey," she says to the woman standing in the doorway.

"Vera?! Vera, wait!" I'm stumbling down the corridor after her when it suddenly strikes me that I'm stark naked. I put on the brakes and slink back to my apartment, palms cupped over my shortcomings.

The woman greets me with an amused smile. She is tall and zaftig, as my father used to say, with large features that seem familiar. "Nikolai?" she echoes with uncertainty, flinching as the door in the foyer slams, rattling the glass. "Nikolai Katkov?"

I nod numbly, trying to place her, and slip into the apartment in search of my pants.

She gives me a moment to find them, then follows. "Gabriella Scotto, Special Agent, United States Treasury Department," she announces in heavily accented Russian, displaying her identification.

"We got rid of the KGB. Now we have Americans with badges knocking on our doors."

"I don't believe *they* knocked."

"They didn't ask permission to come in, either."

"Could we talk for a few minutes?"

"If you insist," I reply in English. "But I'd rather we massacre your language than mine."

"Fair enough," she replies, sounding a lot like a tourist I met from a place called Queens. "My agency is interested in a story you wrote. They think it might tie in with something they're working on."

"Really?" I wonder, unable to imagine what the U.S. Treasury and black-market medals dealers could possibly have in common. "You came all the way from Washington to talk to me?"

"Of course not. Please don't feel flattered. I happened to be here giving a seminar, and my people asked me to—"

"Militia Headquarters," I interrupt, finally placing her. "The data-sharing expert."

"That's me."

"I knew you looked familiar. You're wasting your time, by the way. The only thing a Russian cop values more than his gun in his fiefdom. Sharing just isn't part of his vocabulary."

"Thanks for the warning," she says, breaking into a confused smile. "I'm sorry, have we met before?"

"Collided."

Her brow furrows as she tries to remember.

"Debunking the Power of the Press . . . ?"

"And Other Myths," she adds with a scowl. "The journalist with the eating disorder."

"Hunger for truth."

"Sorry. Didn't recognize you without your bib."

"You're welcome to borrow it."

"Oh?"

"I have a feeling you're about to eat your words."

"Look, Mr. Katkov, I dragged my butt all the way out here, and—"

"I've seen better, Agent Scotto. Believe me."

"Okay. Okay," she says, exasperated. "We can spend the next hour insulting each other, or we can spend it doing business. What do you say?"

A loud moan comes from the sleeping alcove before I can reply.

Agent Scotto's eyes widen with concern and sweep to the curtain. "Who's that?"

I shrug sheepishly. "I'm afraid we just met."

"I think I'm starting to understand. That was your girl-friend before?"

"Was," I reply glumly.

"I've been there," she confides with a hint of empathy. "Played both parts. More than once."

I'm thinking Special Agent Scotto has a healthy lustiness that makes it easy for me to believe her when Ludmilla T. moans again.

"We better insult each other someplace else," Scotto suggests. "Trouble is, where? This berg makes my old neighborhood look like a country estate."

"Where did you grow up? In Queens?"

"Bensonhurst. That's in Brooklyn. You sound like you grew up in London."

"Well, frankly I've never been out of Russia. Not every Englishman who lives here is a spy, you know. My parents hired a tutor when I was a child. He was from Dover, as I recall. You like country estates?"

"Not particularly."

"You'll fancy this one. Give me a few minutes."

I slip behind the curtain. Ludmilla hasn't moved. I pull the covers over her, then quickly freshen up and dress. I'm sitting on the edge of the bed pulling on my boots when she stirs.

"Hi," she whispers, sleepy-eyed.

"Hi. You okay?"

She smiles weakly and nods.

"I'll be out for a while. Place is yours. There's some coffee in the cupboard."

"Coffee?" she mouths, brightening.

"Make enough for two." I blow her a kiss and return to the parlor in search of my parka. Agent Scotto locates it on the floor behind an armchair and tosses it to me. "You don't work on a word processor?" she wonders as we leave the apartment.

"I wish. Every time I save enough money, I run out of coffee and cigarettes."

"Among other things," Scotto sneers, noticing the vodka bottles on the way out.

The air is unusually clear, thanks to a wind shift that took the smog south along with the snow. It left a crystalline patina in its wake, giving Lyublino an uncharacteristic sparkle.

"So, Agent Scotto," I begin as we walk north on Kurskaya. "What does Moscow's black market in medals have to do with your Treasury Department?"

"Medals?" she wonders with a puzzled frown. "What're you talking about?"

"My article. *Independent Gazette* published a story I wrote on black-market medal dealers."

"Never seen it. The one they faxed me from D.C. is about a guy named Vorontsov. He was murdered to stop him from blowing the whistle on a privatization scandal."

My jaw drops. That's the last thing I expected. "How'd your people acquire it?"

"Picked it off your wire service."

"ITAR?"

"We call it RITA."

Either way, it's an acronym for the Russian Information Telegraph Agency, formerly TASS. "That's rather puzzling. The story never ran. It was spiked. . . ." The pieces suddenly fall into place. "Sergei."

"Who's he?"

"The editor who spiked it. I wanted the story back. He claimed he'd misplaced it. I had a feeling he was up to something. Now I know what."

"He sent it to the wire service? Why? Why wouldn't he run the story himself?"

"Because the militia blew it out of the water."

"And he never told you he sent it to RITA?"

"Not surprising. He's a rather cautious, secretive fellow. Out of necessity, mind you. We all were. I guess, like most of us, Sergei still hasn't completely shaken the old ways of doing business. He's also a friend. Maybe he didn't want to get my hopes up in case it didn't fly."

"It just might. We knew it'd been spiked, but we weren't sure why. So we weren't sure who to trust. That's why we came to you first."

"Quite smart."

"I get paid to be smart. Those documents you mentioned in the story, you still have access to them?"

"No, but not for lack of trying."

"Well maybe I can—"

"You had your chance. You blew it."

"Pardon me?"

"You recall that day at Militia Headquarters?"

"Oh, no," she groans, as it dawns on her.

"Oh, yes. They were the bone of contention."

"Guess I owe you one. This Investigator . . ."

"Shevchenko."

"He still has them?"

"I doubt it. He said he was returning them to the Interior Ministry."

"Shit." Her brow knits with confusion. "I thought he worked for the Interior Ministry."

"He does, but he's at thirty-eight Petrovka, not Ministry Headquarters on Markskaya. That's where the Oversight Committee's located. The documents belong to them, and I imagine that's where Shevchenko sent them. Keep in mind, the Interior Ministry's a massive bureaucracy. It's got more subdirectorates, departments, and administrative sectors than you can count. The joke used to be that half of Moscow has to work at the IM to keep an eye on the other half."

A knowing smile cracks Agent Scotto's face as we turn the corner and come upon the Durasov Estate. Built on a wooded lakefront by a family of aristocrats, the eighteenth-century mansion now houses the Oceanographic Institute. Its spired, snow-dusted dome caps two intersecting wings that form a Greek cross, giving it churchlike scale and presence. "Wow," Scotto exclaims as we walk down the drive lined with towering poplars. "Now, that's what I call a weekend retreat."

"That's precisely what it was a couple of hundred years ago."

She stops walking and catches my eye. "You'd have to launder a hell of a lot of money to build it today."

I nod thoughtfully, reading between the lines. "That's what this is about, isn't it? Money laundering."

"Interdicting it. That's FinCEN's specialty."

"Who?"

"FinCEN—Financial Crimes Enforcement Network—it's a federal task force that gathers financial intelligence. We have personnel from Customs, IRS, Secret Service, Postal Inspection, FBI, BATF—"

"I'm afraid you left out KGB," I say, facetiously.

"We're working on it. Right now we can access American commercial, financial, and law enforcement data banks; but we're going global."

"Information-sharing expertise."

"And analysis. I'm Deputy Director."

"A bureaucrat. Russians abhor bureaucrats."

"So do I. I'm a cop by trade, Katkov, an eighteen-eleven—licensed to carry a weapon."

"Rhymes with double-o-seven."

"We had it first," she says with a sassy smile. "Twenty years in the field. Border patrol. Undercover drug enforcement. I was running a network of informants when they put this operation together and bumped me upstairs."

"Sounds like you rather miss getting your hands dirty."

"Any agent pushing a desk who says otherwise is full of it." She stops walking and sits on a bench overlooking the frozen lake, then emits a reflective sigh. "Trouble is it gets on more than your hands. Anyway, the case I was telling you about: Some funds FinCEN's been tracking surfaced in a deal to build a pipeline from Siberia to Western Europe. The broker on the Russian side was a V. I. Vorontsov."

"That makes sense. He was an accomplished trade representative. This country is drowning in red ink. I venture to say hard dollars for oil is one of the keys to recovery."

"Yeah, but the pipeline deal's being put together with dirty money. If Vorontsov was responsible for oversight and brokering it at the same time, we have a classic case of the fox in the hen house."

"Maybe. Then again, perhaps he was working both sides of the street."

"You mean undercover?"

"Precisely. Can you think of a better way of conducting oversight than being at the table when the deal is going down?"

"Several. You have any proof he was murdered to stop him from blowing the whistle?"

"No. But I'm pretty damn sure he was."

"Why, because it'll sell more newspapers?"

"No, dammit. Because somebody tried to kill me yesterday."

That stops Scotto cold. She's all ears now.

"I thought I knew why, but my story running on RITA changes things. If you lifted it off the wire, maybe other people did too?"

"People threatened by it?"

I nod.

"Okay. Then why did Vorontsov's obituary say it was robbery?"

"The medals. Some are quite valuable. To make a long story short, he was wearing them the night he was murdered. The police figured someone killed him for them, but now I'd wager that's not the case."

"Well, then maybe I should touch base with Shevchenko. See if he learned anything about sharing information."

"I wouldn't count on it if I were you. He said these matters are usually handled by Economic Crimes, anyway. Mentioned an investigator named Gudonov."

"Thanks but no thanks."

"You know him?"

"Not really. We had a run-in at the seminar. He's an arrogant jerk."

"So is every other cop I've ever met—"

She glares at me.

"—in Moscow."

She smiles. "Anything else you can think of?"

"Not really, no."

"Well, we're dealing at the highest levels of international finance here. Not the sort of stuff you pick up in the street. But you can reach me at the embassy if anything surfaces." She stands, takes a deep breath of cold air, and walks to the edge of the lake.

"For what it's worth, Scotto, your people ever come across the name Barkhin? Arkady Barkhin?"

"Barkhin? No, I don't think so. Who is he?"

"The local mob boss. Moscow's very own *vor v zakone*. He operates a private club, among other things. All the high-level deal makers who come to town fancy it."

"You mean businessmen, bankers, government types?" she prompts, in her rapid-fire cadence.

"Yes. It's called the Paradise."

"Sounds very mystical." She breaks into a little smile at something that occurs to her. "That's mystical as in religious experience, not mythical as in—"

"The Power of the Press and Other Myths," I interject.

"Very good."

"Tough language."

"We're a tough bunch. What's the story on the Paradise?"

"Palm trees and parrots, gambling, floor show, best cuisine in town."

"No kidding?"

"Uh-huh."

"Sounds like my kind of place."

15

ix! The hard way!" The stickman calls out in English as
the dice come to rest. Like most of the staff at the Paradise,
he's a young Cuban.

"Yeah!" Agent Scotto exclaims in a husky growl. She jerks
her fist backward in a victory gesture that one of the caged
parrots seconds with a piercing squawk.

It's midafternoon, though it could be two in the morning in
the windowless club that's buzzing with activity. Scotto is having a ball. I'm strung tighter than a balalaika. We've been here
an hour, and still no sign of Barkhin or his athlete-turned-
enforcer types. Not that I'm sorry. The thug who tried to kill
me was probably a discarded jock. If the medal dealers didn't
hire him, who did? Barkhin put me onto Rafik; Barkhin sent
me to Kafé Graneetsa; Barkhin, and only Barkhin, knew both
Rafik and I would be there—but there's nothing that links him
to Vorontsov or a privatization scandal. Furthermore, I know
why the medal dealers were pissed off; but Barkhin's motive,
if he has one, escapes me. And why take out both of us? Why—

"What do you think, Katkov?" Scotto asks, pulling me out of
it as the stickman rakes the dice toward her. "Let it ride?"

"Let it ride?" I echo forlornly, eyeing the stacks of chips that
can be bought only with hard currencies, preferably dollars.

Indeed, they're critical to our economy, and, along with other schemes to acquire them, the government declared gambling for rubles illegal, punishable by imprisonment and/or a stiff fine. "Well, I guess you could. Then again, you could give it to me and make believe you lost it."

Scotto laughs, then scoops up the dice and begins shaking them to the beat of congas that comes from the dining room where the floor show is starting.

"The player's point is six," the stickman shouts as gamblers lean to the table, covering the felt with chips. "Six is the point. No more bets."

"Come on six," Scotto urges, blowing on her fist before tossing the dice.

"Six!" the stickman exclaims after several rolls. "Six! Pay the shooter! Pay the line!"

"Katkov? Hey, Katkov?!" Arkady Barkhin's voice rises over the din as the stickman pushes stack after stack of chips toward Scotto. The crowd parts. Ray-Ban is on point. Arturo the driver brings up the rear. Barkhin shoulders his way toward me, greeting several regulars en route. "Katkov, what the hell are you doing here?" His enthusiasm seems genuine, as if he's not at all surprised that I'm alive.

"Touring Moscow's hot spots with a friend," I reply, making the introductions.

"Gabriella Scotto," Barkhin repeats musically as he sweeps his eyes over her. "Italiano?"

"Italian*a*," she corrects, emphasizing the *a*. Then in her New York-accented Russian she explains, "On my father's side. My mother's family came from Kiev."

Barkhin's brows go up. "Really? So did mine," he offers in a puzzled tone. "No offense, but your accent, it doesn't sound like . . ."

"Hey, if you grew up in Brooklyn, you'd talk Russian like this too."

"So," Barkhin says with a laugh, "how do you two know each other?"

"Gabriella's a tourist. She—"

"I work for Nikolai's cousin," Scotto interrupts as if she's been saying it all her life. "He insisted I look him up when I got here."

"Why don't I have cousins like that? What kind of work?"

"He has a restaurant in Brooklyn. Brighton Beach."

"Little Odessa."

"Uh-huh. I manage the place for him."

"She's in the restaurant business, her mother's family's from Kiev, we're practically related," Barkhin gushes, taken by her— *really* taken, since I don't have any relatives in America, let alone a cousin who's a restaurateur. "I'll bet you could teach my staff a thing or two. If you feel like picking up some pocket money while you're here, I'd be—"

"Thanks, I already have," Scotto counters. "Cash me out will you, Nikolai? I've got to make a pit stop." She tips the stickman, scoops the rest of the chips into my cupped palms, and hurries off.

"Be careful, Katkov," Barkhin warns after she's gone. Is he that sharp? Did he nail her as a cop that fast? I'm thinking he wasn't taken by her at all when he grins lasciviously and explains, "She could fuck a man to death." He winks and leads the way between the gaming tables toward the cashier's cage, where a Latina in a sexy costume smiles from behind thick glass. To my surprise, Barkhin continues past it and starts down a marble staircase. "Unfortunate about Rafik, wasn't it?" he says offhandedly.

Is he sincere? Is this a shrewd cover? Is he thinking, "The shooter was supposed to get you too"? Is that what's going to happen now?! "Sorry, Arkady. I really screwed up. The guy followed me. I thought I'd lost him, but—"

"No, I shouldn't have sent you to the Graneetsa in the first place. The medals aren't out there."

"They aren't?" I'm not all that surprised, but he's caught me off guard. "That's very interesting. How do you know?"

"I offered to buy them. The dealers would've turned in their mothers for what I put on the table." The staircase takes us to a corridor, sheathed in marble and lined with heavy wooden doors.

"What about the shooter? Anything on him?"

Barkhin shakes his head no. "I came up empty."

"Then he probably wasn't a local." The numerous Marlboros crushed into the pavement come to mind. "You think he might be a foreigner?"

"Yes, from Minsk, Sverdlovsk, or Tbilisi," Barkhin replies facetiously, rattling off capitals of former Soviet states. "Who knows? Every little town has a gang that's trying to muscle into the big time now." He stops at one of the doors and unlocks it with a key.

We enter an elegant office that contrasts with the tropical decor of the club. Thick Persian rugs. Floor-to-ceiling hardwood paneling. A huge, carved desk piled with papers. A computer terminal. A vase of fresh flowers. And—with the touch of a button that sends a section of wall panels sliding aside—a gleaming, case-hardened-stainless door to a bank vault.

Barkhin stands there, admiring it like a new car. "Is this the perfect place to open a casino, or what?" Then, as if conducting a symphony, he sets the tumblers, spins the wheel that retracts the dead bolts, and throws the opening lever. Two and a half meters across, a meter deep, its weight measured in tons, the door pivots aside smoothly on two immense hinges. We step through the circular opening into an enormous space. Deep bays of shelving units line the walls. Each hard currency nation has it's own labeled section. The United States—stocked with dollars of every denomination—is by far the largest. Counting machines are aligned on a table in the center.

Barkhin switches one on. "Five hundred sixty dollars," he announces seconds after I deposit the chips in the hopper; then he crosses to the appropriate bay, counts off a neat stack of bills, and slaps it into my palm with a grin. "Don't bring her back."

"Why not? You might get even?"

He laughs, then closes up shop and escorts me back to the dining room, excusing himself to greet some new arrivals. Scotto is already seated in a booth near the stage, watching the show. I slide in next to her and drop the money into her outstretched palm.

"Thanks. Not a bad haul, huh?"

"More than a year's wages for the average Russian. Where'd you learn to gamble?"

"Brooklyn. Where else? My uncle Angelo taught me. My mother wasn't thrilled, but—"

"Did you say her brother's name is Angelo?"

Scotto nods matter-of-factly. "He was a bit of a hood but a great guy."

"I thought you said your mother was Russian?"

"I also said I work for your cousin in Brooklyn," Scotto replies with a grin. "She's Sicilian. My relatives come from Palermo."

I lean back, studying her as it dawns on me. "You're really quite good, aren't you?"

"Uh-huh," she says matter-of-factly. "I'm a professional. I'm trained to think on my feet. To take control. To speak Russian. To—"

"To lie like the devil himself, and—"

"*Her*self."

"—and make it seem like the truth."

"Yeah, if the situation calls for it."

"I imagine it becomes difficult to know which is which after a while."

"Enough. You're starting to sound like my husband."

"Your husband?"

"Yeah. I'm married. God, you'd think I said I have AIDS or something."

"Sorry, Scotto. I'm afraid you don't quite come off as the domestic type."

"I'm not. He is. We've been separated for a while. I don't know where it's going." She pauses, then with a knowing smile asks, "So, what'd your buddy Barkhin have to report?"

"Report?"

"Come on, I gave him the chance, and you and I both know he took it."

My respect for her acuity goes up another notch. She went to the ladies room because she knew Barkhin wouldn't talk in front of her. "He said Vorontsov's medals aren't for sale on the black market."

"Then you're probably right about robbery not being the motive. What else?"

"Whoever tried to kill me wasn't a local."

She's nodding thoughtfully when champagne and caviar arrive. "Winner buys," she says, peeling off bills. The waiter explains it's complimentary, fills our glasses, and pockets the twenty Scotto slips him. "By the way," she says offhandedly when he's gone, "you ever come across the name Rubino? Michael Rubino?"

"No. Can't say that I have. Sounds like someone from your old neighborhood."

She smiles and shakes her head no. "It's R-u-b-i-n-e-a-u," she explains, spelling it out. "Used to be Rubinowitz. That was a lot of years ago. He was working for Meyer Lansky at the time."

"Lansky? The one who ran the rackets in Cuba?"

"The one and only. Rubinowitz was being groomed to take over the operation, but Castro beat him to it, so to speak. He hung in there until Lansky retired, then changed it to Rubineau and went on his own. Done very well; runs a chain of hotels now: Vegas, Atlantic City, Tahoe, Reno . . ."

"Something tells me *he* could teach Barkhin's people a thing or two."

"Something tells me he already has."

"Why do you say that?"

She smiles and takes a long swallow of champagne, then tilts her glass in the direction of a large table. "Because he's sitting right over there."

I casually shift my position to see a group of Western businessmen, easily identified by their heavily starched shirts and tailored suits. They're buzzing about a trim, aquiline man in his early sixties who listens more than he speaks, responding with a decisive nod or shake of his head. Rimless glasses combine with graying, neatly parted hair and a deep tan to give him the look of a natty investment banker. "The fellow sporting your complexion and my nose?"

"Uh-huh."

"I have a feeling I've seen him here before." Then gesturing to the Caribbean decor, I joke, "I guess he's into reliving old times."

"Or recreating them," she says suspiciously.

"You're watching him too?"

"Oh, yeah." Agent Scotto locks her twinkling eyes onto mine and breaks into that amused smile. "FinCEN's watching lots of people."

16

Darkness has fallen, and it's well below zero when Scotto and I leave the Paradise. On a night like this, it'd be worth being fucked to death just to have her sensuous body smothering mine with its warmth, but she doesn't offer, and I don't ask. Instead, she wishes me luck and, with a sarcastic cackle, says to look her up if I live long enough to visit my cousin in Brighton Beach; then she hails a taxi and takes her winnings and biting sense of humor back to the U.S. Embassy.

I'm walking to the Metro, wondering if FinCEN's watching *me,* when I start having second thoughts about returning to my apartment. Last night I was angry, depressed, and drunk, not to mention with a woman. What's more, the hitman was dead, and I vaguely recall thinking it'd be a while before the medal dealers found out he'd blown the assignment. But now I'm pretty damned sure they didn't hire him, and I'm concerned whoever did might find someone else to finish the job. No. No, my apartment is off-limits. It isn't safe, and—Ludmilla! Damn, I forgot all about her.

I find a public phone and dial my number. There's no answer. She probably got tired of drinking coffee alone and went home. I sure as hell hope so. I've no idea where she lives, which is unfortunate, because neither does whoever's trying to kill me. It'd be a perfect place to stay for a while. Any place is better than mine. Even Vera's. I know I'm asking for trouble, but I call her at work anyway.

"Hi. It's me."

"I'm busy, Niko," she says curtly.

"I'm in trouble. I need a place to stay."

"Hey, I did my bit. I didn't even get a thanks. Ask one of your other girlfriends to help you."

"They're not my girlfriends. Come on, give me a chance to explain. I—"

"I told you, Niko. It's finished." The line clicks and goes dead.

"Vera? Vera, you there?" I slump against the wall of the booth, feeling sorry for myself, then drop the receiver on the hook, jam my fists into the pockets of my parka, and head off into the darkness.

I wander about the city, cold, tired, and hungry, wishing I could afford a hotel room. About a half hour later, I find myself in front of Yuri's apartment. His window is dark. He's not back from work yet. I climb the three flights, nauseated by the smell of boiled cabbage that fills the stairwell, and camp out on the landing. Several hours pass before I hear the trudge of footsteps.

"Why don't you get it over with and move into your office?" I tease as his head rises into view.

"Believe me, I've thought about it." He holds up a mesh sack stuffed with canned goods. "I snuck out early tonight. My mother always gives me a list of things to bring on Saturday."

"How's she doing?"

He waggles a hand. "She's old. She's lived a long life." He shrugs philosophically and leads the way inside. "By the way, I'm sorry, but there's no way I can get them," he says, referring to Vorontsov's documents.

"It's okay. Really. I—"

"I tried everything, believe me," he rushes on, removing his coat and gloves. "I wouldn't be surprised if they've been destroyed."

"Figures. Thanks for trying." I settle in a chair next to a radiator that could heat the Kremlin. The whole apartment is barely larger than my sleeping alcove but on days like this, I'd trade in a minute. "Actually, I dropped by because I need a place to stay."

"Oh? Why, what's going on?"

"Well for openers, I fell off the wagon and into bed with another woman."

Yuri winces, sending the ends of his mustache to the corners of his eyes.

"Naturally, Vera caught me."

"Naturally."

"To make matters worse, she was smack in the middle of a tantrum when another woman shows up. Tall, vivacious, *bronskis* out to here."

"Naturally," he cackles, starting to loosen up.

"Vera takes one look at her, throws her newspaper at me, and takes off. So, there I am, nasty hangover, one woman in bed, one at the door, and one on the run. I'm not sure what to do. So, I go after Vera. I'm more than halfway down the hall before it dawns on me I'm stark naked . . ."

Yuri's laughing so hard he can hardly speak. "I'm sorry," he finally says. "How'd you get hooked up with . . ." He lets it trail off, suggesting I supply her name.

"Ludmilla. Moscow Beginners. I couldn't handle it. Neither could she. We ran into each other at Liquor Store Twelve over on Vekova; ended up at my place drunk as skunks."

"And the rest is history," he concludes, still laughing.

I nod sheepishly and laugh along with him.

"Now," Yuri says, suddenly more serious, "I know why you can't stay at Vera's place. You want to tell me why you can't stay at yours?"

"Someone's trying to kill me."

"Naturally," Yuri says with a solemn nod. He has the patient look of someone who's spent his life raising a child who can't seem to stay out of trouble.

"I've no idea who."

Yuri nods again, then fetches a carton of vanilla ice cream and two bowls. He plops a large scoop in the center of each and drowns them in peach brandy. "Might as well fill your veins with alcohol and save the embalmers the trouble." We spend the rest of the evening doing just that and discussing my encounter with Agent Scotto.

The next morning it's so cold, frost covers the windshield of Yuri's Lada. But by some miracle the engine starts, and he drops me on the Kremlin side of the Krymsky Bridge on his way to work.

My fear of assassins gives way to nostalgia at the sight of an old building on the far bank. Dingy and gray, hidden by the massive bridge abutments, the four-story edifice—current home of MGIMO, the prestigious Institute for International Relations—once housed Tsarevich Nikolay Lycée, a school founded in 1868 by my great-grandfather M. N. Katkov. I recall my parents being proud that he taught democratic principles and once traveled to America; and as a child I spent hours watching the river ferries and wondering if any of them went there. They're not going anywhere today. The frozen Moskva has them locked in its wintry grasp, a thick, monolithic sheet of ice that will hold them captive until spring.

A bone-chilling wind snaps me out of it as I come off the swaying span. It's a short walk to the House on the Embankment. I hurry through the lobby with the familiar sounds and smells and take the elevator to Tanya Churkin's apartment.

A girl of about seven, clutching a Barbie doll, opens the door and leads the way inside to Vorontsov's study. Mrs. Churkin is on a ladder, handing things down to a pale-faced boy who stands amid piles of books, papers, photographs, and numerous boxes. He's a few years older than his sister and eyes me with appropriate suspicion.

"I'm sorry. I hope this isn't a bad time," I say as Mrs. Churkin climbs down to greet me. "I didn't know you were moving."

"We're not," she explains in a tone that suggests she wouldn't mind it. "I can't come in here without getting upset. And the children—they're in one small room. Now they can each have their own. My husband, I mean ex-husband, was supposed to do this. But . . ." she scowls and lets it trail off.

"I understand."

"You have some news for me?"

I nod solemnly. "He died. I should've taken him to a hospital."

"Please," she protests. "I've enough misery. I'm interested in my father's medals. Nothing else."

"They're not for sale."

She pauses, her arms filled with books, and looks at me with a mixture of hope and uncertainty. "Does that mean you found them?"

"No. It means I was right all along. They're not on the black market. Never were. Never will be."

"Why not? Why steal them otherwise?"

"To make your father's murder look like robbery."

"More speculation?" she flares, throwing the books to the floor. "Or have you proof he was involved in this . . . this scandal you mentioned?!"

"No, but I'm betting he was. Of course, which side of the street he was working is another matter."

"What are you suggesting, Mr. Katkov?"

"That your father was either ripping off the government, or about to blow the whistle on someone who was."

"I assure you it was the latter."

"That's for the militia to determine."

"Then we have nothing more to talk about," she says, turning her attention to the packing.

"I guess not," I reply, winking at the children, who aren't sure what to make of all this and keep their distance. I'm about to leave when I notice a briefcase on the floor next to the desk. It looks like the one Shevchenko used to take Vorontsov's documents back to his office. My pulse quickens at what it might contain. "The police returned your father's briefcase?"

"Yes, when I picked up his things."

"Have you been through it?"

She shakes her head no.

"Mind if I have a look?"

She studies me, deciding, then shrugs in a suit-yourself gesture.

I put it on the desk and discover a bulging manila envelope inside, the kind the police use to store evidence. It contains: a watch, wallet, ring, currency, loose change, checkbook, keys, pens, pencils, a pack of cigarettes, a paperback novel, and some business correspondence—everything but the elusive documents.

I turn my attention to the briefcase. The file dividers and pockets are all empty, as are the four penholders. However, one of them feels rigid, as if a pen had been inserted upside down in the leather sleeve, then removed, leaving the cap behind. I press my thumb against the bottom to force it out. The object won't budge at first; then all of a sudden it breaks free, shoots through the air like a tiny missile, and goes rolling across the polished floor.

The children giggle and scurry after it. The boy elbows his sister aside and retrieves it for me.

My eyes widen with intrigue. What I thought was a pen cap turns out to be a cigarette lighter—a butane cigarette lighter from the Paradise Club.

17

Shevchenko sits behind his desk staring at the lighter, his hands wrapped around a mug of tea. Steam wafts from a kettle gurgling on a hotplate beneath the window. It's so cold, the drops of moisture that roll down the glass freeze well before reaching the sill. "Really, in his briefcase?" he says, expelling a thoughtful breath. "I had one of my men examine it."

"Don't be too hard on him. It was easy to miss."

"He doesn't get paid to miss," Shevchenko snaps. "What do you think it means?"

"That Vorontsov wasn't anywhere near his lodge hall the night he was killed. He was—"

"He wasn't," Shevchenko interrupts smugly. "As a matter of fact, several of his cronies told us he hadn't been there in months."

"No kidding? I can't imagine why, but all of a sudden I have a funny feeling he'd been going to the Paradise Club instead."

Shevchenko scowls and picks up the lighter. "So? It's a known hangout for free-market fanatics. All the *apparatchiks* go there to make deals and be wined and dined by Western businessmen."

"It's run by the *mafiya*."

"So is every other club in Moscow. I don't see that this changes anything."

"Vorontsov lied to his daughter about where he was going. Why?"

"Because he didn't want her to know he liked to drink expensive champagne and watch naked women dance. He might've been fucking one of them for all we know."

"I don't think he'd want her to know he was brokering a pipeline deal that was being put together with laundered money, either."

Shevchenko leans back and studies me out of the corner of his eye. "A little tidbit from one of your infamous sources, no doubt."

"A huge tidbit, and you know it," I reply, sensing what's coming next.

"Yes, Agent Scotto is a very impressive woman," he says with a little smirk. "She dropped by yesterday afternoon. She told me about the pipeline scam. She also mentioned her people picked your article off the wire service."

"And what did you tell her?"

He thumbs the cap from his flask and slowly pours some vodka into his tea. "Why do you think I had anything to tell her?"

"You said you were working on something, remember?"

"I also said it was probably nothing."

"Come on, she wouldn't have come to see you if it weren't for me."

"True," he muses, grudgingly. "It's still probably nothing; but one of the medal dealers we busted put us onto a shoe factory in Zuzino, a very productive one that's being privatized." He pauses, then sarcastically adds, "As a free-market advocate, I'm sure you know how these deals work."

"Of course, and I'll be happy to explain it to you," I retort, matching his tone. "The employees have first crack at buying the business. If they vote no, the government can sell it to outsiders. Got it? Good. Where does the medal dealer fit in?"

"His sister was the factory's bookkeeper. She was sleeping with the manager; that is, until she found out he was married and was screwing her so she'd doctor the books for him, and he could screw the workers."

"The factory would look like a loser; the workers would vote no; and the outsiders who paid off the manager would buy it."

"Precisely."

"But Vorontsov got wind of it, threatened to blow the whistle, and the manager killed him."

"No," he says, with a pregnant pause. "No, your friend Rafik did that."

My jaw slackens. "Run that past me again, will you? Rafik killed Vorontsov?"

Shevchenko nods matter-of-factly.

"How do you figure that?"

"I'll show you." He takes a swallow of spiked tea, then steps to a file cabinet and spins the combination lock on one of the drawers.

My mind is racing, trying to sort the pieces: The manager hired Rafik? The outsiders hired him? Whoever—they had a prominent government official killed so they could buy a shoe factory? The more I think about it, the less sense it makes. It's not worth the risk. Not big enough. I hunch down in my parka, taking a moment to regroup. Footsteps echo in the corridor. A vaguely familiar voice joins them. My eyes drift to the open door, catching a glimpse of two men who walk by at a brisk pace, engrossed in conversation. It's Drevnya, the brat from *Pravda*, and his militia connection.

I'm about to ask Shevchenko who the repulsive-looking fellow is when he slams the file drawer closed with a loud bang. "We searched Rafik's room. We didn't find anything to indicate who he was working for, but we did come across these." He slides the contents of an evidence envelope onto the blotter in front of me. There, glittering beneath the desk light in all their splendor, are Vladimir Illiych Vorontsov's medals.

I'm overwhelmed, my curiosity about Drevnya's connection obliterated. I stare at them stupefied, still unable to accept Shevchenko's conclusion. "You sure they're Vorontsov's?"

Shevchenko nods, turns one over, and pushes it toward me. "Got his name on them."

"Look, Rafik knew I wanted them, and he knew the market, right? Maybe he managed to acquire them and was playing a game to jack up the price. He was obviously a grifter. And he—"

"A grifter?" Shevchenko interrupts with a derisive cackle. He removes a computer printout from the file folder and drops it in front of me. Neat paragraphs of data fill the space between Rafik's picture and fingerprints. "According to our records,

Rafik Obolenskiy—one of several aliases, by the way—was a trained assassin; did KGB wet work for years. Became a free-lance contractor when the agency was dismantled."

I'm stunned, barely able to speak. "But . . . but he said he was in the gulag. He . . . he . . ."

"He was. It's on there somewhere. I believe he worked as an informer for a while." He pauses, then unable to pass up the opportunity to needle me, adds, "I'm sure you'll agree he was an expert at gaining confidences."

"Must've written the book on it."

"Well, it's hard to accept being so taken in, but facts are facts. We had his pistol from the bar. Nine-millimeter Stechkina, by the way. That and the medals prompted us to fire some test rounds and compare them with the slug that killed Vorontsov." He slips a photograph from a file on his desk and hands it to me. The two greatly enlarged slugs are side by side. One is slightly deformed. Arrows and handwritten notations point out the key areas. "As you can see, the markings are identical."

I shake my head, feeling totally duped.

"They were keeping you close, Katkov. You had this thing for the medals. Rafik was the perfect baby-sitter."

"They? Who are they?"

"I've no idea. They probably figured killing a journalist who was crying scandal could backfire, give credence to the allegations. When you wouldn't let go, they realized they had no choice."

"Okay, but why kill both of us? Why not have Rafik just get rid of me?"

"Because he was the link to whoever hired him. They decided to sever it. It's an occupational hazard in his business. Who knows? Maybe they were pissed off he took the medals. Maybe they were afraid he was going to sell them to Mrs. Churkin. Maybe they didn't count on the hitman being killed. I have a feeling he was supposed to come up with the medals, not us."

"I can't believe it," I mutter as it dawns on me. "Arkady Barkhin. I played right into his hands."

"Perhaps, but I doubt this is all his doing." Shevchenko's tone suggests he knows more. He takes a cigarette and methodically taps it on the desk, packing the tobacco.

"Why? Come on, dammit. Stop toying with me."

"Well, why does your story threaten him?" he asks rhetori-

cally. "I mean, what's Barkhin's tie to it? Some meetings Vorontsov had at his club? Not enough. Besides, Barkhin has an army
of thugs at his disposal"—he pauses and lights the cigarette
with Vorontsov's butane, letting smoke stream from his nostrils,
then he grins smugly and resumes—"and therefore no need to
import a hitman from Israel."

"The guy in the trench coat was an Israeli?"

Shevchenko nods emphatically. "He was staying at the National under the name Goldman, but we know he used a phony
passport to check in because Passport Control has nothing
under that name or number."

"Then chances are the passport he used to enter the country
was phony too, which means he could be from anywhere."

"A reasonable conclusion. I entertained it myself until the
coroner issued her report. As always, Olga's incisive eyes went
right to the critical detail and detected that the corpse was
circumcised—*recently*. My sources in the Jewish community
tell me the ritual was dropped here ages ago, but it's—"

"Indeed. The day your heroes in the Kremlin outlawed
religion."

"—but it's become somewhat mandatory for men who've emigrated to Israel. Sort of a barbaric, middle-age rite of passage,
if you will." His face twists with imagined pain. "No wonder
you've chosen to remain here, rather than join them."

"Come on, you'd be lost without me."

Shevchenko smiles, savoring the thought.

"Let's get back to the shooter. It's possible he used to work
for Barkhin and was brought back in to wipe the slate clean.
No?"

"Anything's possible. As soon as we get an ID on him, we'll
know if he was one of those discarded athletes you're so
fond of."

"Regardless, the same people who hired Rafik must've hired
him too."

Shevchenko exhales with a sarcastic snort. "Brilliant. We've
just narrowed the suspects to everyone who saw your story on
the wire."

"That's right," I say, getting a little annoyed. "Which elimi-
nates everyone involved in the shoe factory deal. Nothing about
that in my story, or in Vorontsov's documents, as I recall."

"See, I told you it was nothing." He forces a smile, then

shudders at the cold and crosses to the thermostat. He turns it all the way down, then all the way back up, as if trying to trick it into sending up more heat. The valve on the radiator emits a weary hiss and sputters mockingly. "Where were we?"

"Narrowing suspects. Did Agent Scotto mention the name Rubineau?"

"As a matter of fact, she did. I'd never heard of him. She had nothing to connect him to Vorontsov. I mean other than that he hangs out at the Paradise when he's in Moscow. Have you?"

"No. You're the investigator. Anything in those documents on him?"

He shakes his head no. "I went through them several times. I don't recall seeing the name Rubineau, or Rubinowitz, for that matter."

"You told that to Scotto?"

"Uh-huh. She wanted to see them anyway."

"That makes two of us."

"As I told her, they've been returned to the Interior Ministry."

"Really? When was that?"

"A few days ago."

"As of last night, they still hadn't shown up."

"I have the transmittal right here." He rifles the file and removes a green form with numerous checked boxes and initials. "Once again, you've been talking to the wrong people. Another infamous source?"

"A highly reliable one. He's betting they've been destroyed. So am I."

"What if they were?"

"What if they were?" I echo incredulously. "You sound like you could care less."

"It's out of my hands."

"Come on, there's a lot more going on here than a robbery, and you know it. I came this close to having the bullet holes to prove it, and you don't care?!"

"Sorry, Katkov. This isn't a crime prevention unit. It's Homicide. You have to be dead before I get involved." He grins and snickers at his own joke. "Besides, once the story runs, there'd be little point in killing you to shut you up, would there?"

"Let's not forget you have a little stake in this story too."

His eyes glaze.

"Am I missing something here? What about your career? What happened to making . . ." I pause as the reason for his indifference dawns on me. "The promotion went to Gudonov, didn't it?"

Shevchenko nods resignedly.

"Sorry," I mutter, my compassion tempered by the memory of seeing him with Vera.

"Don't worry, I'll stand by our agreement," he says, mistaking the reason for my attitude. "Now, if you'll excuse me . . ." He lets it tail off and begins scooping the medals back into the envelope. "I have an appointment."

"You had one the last time I was here. You two must've really hit it off."

He pauses and looks up, clutching a fistful of medals. "What do you mean by that?"

"Nothing," I reply, wishing I hadn't said it.

"I don't know what your problem is, Katkov. If you've got something to say to me, say it."

"Vera Fedorenko."

He looks at me blankly. "What about her?"

"The night I brought Rafik to the morgue? You both left in your car. Ring a bell?"

His face tightens in disdain. "It was a purely professional matter."

"Sure it was."

"You disappoint me, Katkov. Sophomoric jealousy isn't becoming in a man of your stature. You may recall I'd taken some disciplinary action against her, and—"

"Unwarranted action. Unnecessarily harsh action."

"That's what Miss Fedorenko thought too. She was in my office appealing it when you dropped by with Rafik's corpse."

"And . . . then what? You decided to take her out to make up for it?"

"No. To keep us from getting frostbite. We were both cold and decided to continue elsewhere. I'm always looking for an excuse to get out of this meat locker. And as you know, I've been dining alone these days, so . . ." He lets it tail off and shrugs matter of factly.

I challenge him with a stare.

"Believe what you like, Katkov," he says, putting the last of the medals in the envelope. He glances to his watch and frowns, then shoves a clipboard at me. "Sign right there."

"Why? What for?"

"These." He hands me the envelope. "Rafik's dead. We can't prosecute his corpse. They're useless as evidence now. I was planning to return them to Mrs. Churkin before picking up my daughters. Thanks to you, there isn't enough time. It's the least you can do."

I'm caught completely off guard, and it takes a moment for his real motive to dawn on me. "It's true. You *aren't* enough of a bastard."

"Pardon me?"

"Some people said that's why you wouldn't make chief. They were right."

"Perhaps, but I don't see the connection."

"Well, you could always return the medals tomorrow yourself, couldn't you?"

"Uh-huh. Guess I could."

"So?"

"You're going to make me say it, aren't you, Katkov?"

I nod, suppressing a grin.

"Okay," he grumbles, turning away from me to fetch his hat and coat. "I thought maybe you'd like to be the one to do it."

I search the pockets of my parka and find the lapel pin the medal dealer gave me. "Shevchenko?" I wait until he turns and toss it to him. "Thanks."

He snatches the *znachki* in midair and opens his palm. His eyes widen at the image of the infant Lenin centered in the red star—the curly blond locks and cherubic face bearing no resemblance to the fierce-eyed orator. Then he smiles at a thought and says, "The way things are going for your buddy Boris, this one may soon be more valuable than those."

18

A high-ranking government official—dead.

A former KGB assassin—dead.

A hitman brought in from Israel—dead.

A Russian journalist—almost dead.

A Moscow *mafiya* chieftain.

A powerful unknown collaborator.

A U.S. Treasury agent.

A set of documents that vanished.

A ritzy gambling club.

A privatization scandal.

A pipeline being built with laundered money—all pieces to the same puzzle; the kind that front-page stories are made of; the kind that will give Sergei a chance to use his witty MURDER FOR PROFIT headline along with an arresting photograph of the medals. Mrs. Churkin will have to wait. Instead of returning them as planned, I return to Yuri's and begin writing. I've no fear of being scooped. Shevchenko isn't talking. Excellence, not speed, is my only criteria, and I spend the next two days writing.

Though he couldn't acquire the documents, Yuri does get something important from the Interior Ministry for me—a brand-new package of carbon paper. Saturday morning, he's up at the crack of dawn to drive out to his mother's farm. I've worked most of the night and have reached the point of diminishing returns.

"Mind if I tag along? Maybe the fresh air'll clear my head. Besides, I haven't seen your mother in ages."

"I know. She always asks about you," Yuri replies as I fetch my parka and turn toward the door. "By the way, chances are pretty good I'll be out there the whole weekend."

That stops me. My eyes cloud with guilt and drift back to the typewriter. "The whole weekend?"

"Uh-huh. I promised her I'd clean out the barn. Don't say I didn't warn you."

"Thanks. On second thought, I'd better not."

"Figured you'd say that." Yuri fetches some items he bought for his mother and heads for the door.

He's halfway through it when I make an impulsive decision. "Yuri? Yuri, hang on." I slide the rough pages and writing materials into my briefcase, tuck Yuri's typewriter under an arm, and hurry after him. "Do me good to get out of the city for a few days."

We head north on the Yaroslavl Highway in Yuri's aging Lada. It's a two-hour-plus drive, and I spend the better part of it looking over my shoulder. He's intent on his driving, but eventually notices.

"What's wrong?"

"Nothing. Old habits die hard when people are trying to kill you."

"I'd almost forgotten."

"I'd be a fool to think that *they* have."

We maneuver through Sudilova's knotted streets and swing west into the Ustye Valley. We've gone about ten kilometers when Yuri turns in to a dirt road guarded by a wind-lashed tree. There's no name on the mailbox. Yuri's mother has lived here all her eighty-six years, and the postman needs no reminder. The road forks at a stand of frost-dusted pines. One leg meanders down a gentle slope to the barn and outbuildings, the other to the weathered farmhouse made of stone and split logs.

"Nikasha!" Mrs. Ternyak exclaims, embracing me as if I were her own. Stocky, with a deeply lined face, cracked hands, and cataracts that give her a perpetual squint, she's Mother Russia incarnated. She spends the weekend at a cast-iron stove, filling the house with incredible aromas. Yuri spends it cleaning out the barn as promised. A curious task, since the fields haven't been plowed in decades, and there's little reason to think this spring will be any different. I spend it watching snowflakes fall past the windows and filling blank pages with almost as many words. I'm making some minor revisions when Yuri returns from an excursion to the local collective where groceries, clothing, and hardware are sold.

"It's done!" I exclaim, as I rip through the last sentences. I strike the period key with a triumphant flourish, then crank the pages from the typewriter, and whirl to face him. "Want to read it?"

"I already have," Yuri replies enigmatically. He looks shaken.

"What do you mean?"

He tosses me a newspaper. It's yesterday's *Pravda*. I stare at the headline in disbelief. Set above the masthead, three all-too-familiar words proclaim MURDER FOR PROFIT.

I feel as if I've been disemboweled. The hollowness quickly turns to anger when I see the by-line reads M. I. Drevnya. It's all here—the information I gave to Shevchenko, the information he gave to me, and more: comments from anonymous sources impugning Vorontsov's integrity; charges that *apparatchiks* in the Interior Ministry—who joined the Party out of ambition, not patriotism, and easily switched ideologies—have been embezzling Party funds to buy profitable businesses; and allegations that Vorontsov was killed because he found out about it and was blackmailing them. But it's Gudonov of State Crimes—hailed as the militia's canny new chief investigator—who's credited with breaking the case, not Shevchenko; and a leaked internal memorandum that's cited as the source.

"I'm really sorry," Yuri says, his voice breaking. "It's beyond comprehension."

I shrug, too stunned to reply. Shevchenko may have upheld our deal, but Sergei sure as hell didn't. How could he do this? How could he let this fucking kid steal my story?! How could he give him that headline?! Sure, Sergei said he was relentless, ruthless. But I never dreamed . . .

A surge of adrenaline fuels my outrage. I toss the paper aside, grab the phone, and dial *Pravda*. "Sergei Murashev," I bark when the switchboard operator answers. "When do you expect him? . . . He was what? . . . You're kidding. . . . Yeah, you can give him a message for me. Tell him Nikolai Katkov said he's an unethical son of a bitch!" I slam down the phone, fuming, unable to comprehend it all.

Yuri flinches and questions me with a look.

"Sergei was fired."

Yuri's mustache bristles as if electrified.

"Guess who got the job?"

"The kid."

I nod solemnly.

"What are you going to do?"

I'm devastated. My shoulders sag in reply. Except for the first time I was shipped off to the gulag, I've never fallen this far this fast. "Kill him with my bare hands."

"Well"—Yuri says, pausing until he's certain he has my attention—"maybe whoever's been trying· to kill you will save you the trouble."

He's right. The kid's name is on the story, not mine. Even if they wanted revenge, I wouldn't be the target. I almost smile. "Yeah, maybe they will."

Sunday afternoon, we drive back to Yuri's apartment in gloomy silence. He settles in front of the television with his trademark bowl of ice cream. I've lost my appetite; the mere sight of it makes me queasy. *Novosti,* Moscow's evening news program, is in progress. Boris Yeltsin's image fills a screen behind the anchorman, who reports:

"Emerging from yet another rowdy session of Parliament, a beleaguered President Yeltsin refused to comment on rumors that G-Seven governments are about to renege on a billion-dollar aid package. He also claimed he hadn't seen a story in *Pravda* alleging a scandal at the Committee for State Property, but emphasized that capital flight must be stopped and private investment substantially increased for the economy to stabilize and grow."

The word *SCANDAL* in bright red letters slashes across the screen as the image of Yeltsin fades.

"However, Chief Investigator Yevgeny Gudonov held a news conference today to confirm that the CSP is under investigation. He also used the opportunity to voice his displeasure with the media."

My eyes bug at the image on the screen. The man holding

court with reporters is the rumpled, repulsive-looking fellow I'd seen at Militia Headquarters with Drevnya. It's not beyond comprehension now. Sergei was right. The kid was connected—connected to Gudonov! Incinerator Gudonov. I'd like to incinerate him!

"This is a serious, sensitive matter; not a media feeding frenzy," Gudonov lectures in a gruff voice. The image zooms in to a close-up, revealing a gold cap flashing amid his widely spaced teeth. "And it will be handled with the care and discretion it deserves."

"Militia shorthand for cover-up," Yuri chirps.

"Furthermore," Gudonov goes on, clearly enjoying his moment in the spotlight, "the person responsible for leaking a confidential militia memorandum will be identified and dealt with harshly."

"Sure he will," Yuri mutters. Gudonov's smugness leaves little doubt as to the identity of the culprit.

"Conniving bastard," I hiss bitterly, as the pieces fall into place. "Shevchenko filed the memo. Gudonov got his copy, revised it to suit his purposes, and used the kid to put out the story." I stare at the screen numbly. The images blur. The words disconnect. I'm seized by a compulsion to wash my hands of the whole damn thing. Returning the medals to Mrs. Churkin would be a good start. I call her several times, but there's no answer. She must be away. At her country *dacha*, no doubt. I haven't been back to mine in almost a week. It's cold, depressing, and out of the way, but all of a sudden I miss it. I'm like a wounded animal. I want the comfort of my own cave to lick my wounds and heal. Yuri offers to drive me, but we discover the street has been plowed, and the Lada is buried in snow up to its door handles. We spend a half hour digging it out, only to discover it won't start. In a cruel joke, winter always saves the worst for last when Muscovites have had their fill of snow and subzero cold.

I wait until morning and treat myself to a taxi again. Its windows are gray and gritty like the sky, like the passing streets, like all of Moscow at this time of year, like my mood. Lyublino does little to brighten it.

A moving van is parked in front of my building when I arrive. Two men are coming down the steps, carrying a rolled-up rug on their shoulders. I have the cabdriver circle the block in case whoever's been trying to kill me hasn't seen Drevnya's by-line in *Pravda* yet. No Israelis in trench coats. No discarded athletes in leather jackets. No Volvos with thugs in Ray-Bans. The building isn't being watched.

This time, when the taxi turns the corner, the men are struggling to carry a chest of drawers down the steps. The cabdriver stops in the middle of the street next to the van. I stuff a wad of rubles into his fist and get out, hurrying past the movers. Wait a minute. That dresser. There's something familiar about that dresser. "Hey? Hey, what're you doing with that?"

"Carrying it to the van," the gaunt one replies with a facetious snarl. "Why?"

"Because it's mine. I didn't make any arrangements to move. There must be some mistake."

"No mistake, comrade," the mover growls. "I have a work order to clean this place out and put everything in storage."

"You sure you have the right address?"

He lets go of his end of the dresser to show his exasperation. It lands with a dull thump and settles into the snow as he trudges to the front of the truck and yanks open the door. "Number eleven Kurskaya, second floor rear, Katkov?" he asks, brandishing a clipboard.

"That's me." I'm totally baffled. For the first time in years, I'm caught up in my rent. So I know I'm not being evicted. "I don't care what that says. Put that dresser back where it belongs. Put it all back," I demand, noticing they've already loaded most of my other furniture.

"Sure, soon as you pay the charges."

"Charges? Look, just get it through your head, I'm not paying for anything. Put it back or I'm calling the police."

"Be my guest. You have ninety days. After that, the stuff can be sold to cover the charges. If it doesn't, and you can't come up with the balance, *we* call the cops. That's the law."

"Look, I don't know what's going on here, but—"

"Nikasha? Nikasha?" Mrs. Parfenov calls out. The old *babushka* is standing in the vestibule, waving a folded newspaper at me.

"Just a minute, Mrs. Parfenov," I shout, loath to abandon my belongings.

"Nikasha? Nikasha, it's important."

"Don't leave until I come back," I warn the movers as I hurry off across the icy pavement.

"Someone was looking for you," Mrs. Parfenov hisses when I join her.

"You know who?"

"It was a few days ago. I don't remember," she croaks, then admonishing me adds, "I haven't seen you for almost a week."

"I'm sorry, I . . . I was away. What did they look like? Did they have a fancy car? Leather jackets? Running shoes?"

She shrugs, her eyes darting about warily. "I think there were two of them. Maybe three."

"You think? Were they tall, short, fat, skinny?" The movers charge past us into the building for more booty. "Any chance it was the militia?"

Mrs. Parfenov shrugs. "Sunglasses. Sunglasses and a shaved head." She shuffles into her apartment. Sunglasses? Shaved head? I hurry after her, wondering what Ray-Ban was up to. The place is empty except for a chair with a broken leg and some packing crates.

"What the hell's going on around here?"

She tucks the newspaper under her arm and sits on one of the crates. "I told you. Sunglasses and a shaved head."

"No, I mean with the movers." My frustration soars at the sight of my desk being carried through the vestibule. "They're taking all my things!"

"Oh, that," she says as if I'd mentioned the weather. "We all have to be out by today. The new owner must've hired them to—"

"New owner?" I interrupt, flabbergasted.

"The building's been sold. You know."

"No. No, I don't know."

"Of course you do. You're the one who told me, it's legal to own property now." She shakes her head disapprovingly.

"Yes. Yes, I know that, but—"

"One of those groups you're always talking about. What do you call them? Free . . . free something?"

"Free enterprise?"

"Yes, *maklers*," she hisses with disdain, using the German word for broker that has become part of our language. "Young smart alecks. They were here once. They said they bought the building from the State."

"From the State?"

She nods matter-of-factly.

"But your family owned the building before the Communists confiscated it, didn't they?"

She emits a wistful sigh. "My grandfather built it."

"Then you have first claim. They can't do that."

She sighs resignedly. "They can do anything they want, Nikasha. It's too late now. They've already bribed someone to transfer the ownership documents. You know those bastards at ZHEK," she says, cursing the clerks at the Housing Administration. "Why didn't you say something before?"

"Because this is the first I'm hearing about it," I reply, on the verge of losing my patience.

"Oh, I know I mentioned it."

"No. No, Mrs. Parfenov. Not to me. I think I'd remember being told I was being put out on the street. I have a feeling you may have been on the verge several times, but—"

"You're always so preoccupied, Nikasha. You probably forgot. Don't feel badly. Some of my friends can't seem to remember anything either. It happens when you get older. I'm sure my time will come. Anyway . . ." She pauses, trying to recall what she was going to say. "Oh, yes, yes, the building. I was telling you about the building. I think they're going to knock it down and put up a café to sell cheese-and-tomato pies to the refinery workers." She hands me a mailer that proudly proclaims this will be the site of Moscow's newest Pizza Hut.

I gather what's left of my wits, then climb the stairs to my apartment. It's empty, eerie, as if I've never lived here. If I didn't know better, I'd swear the KGB has just done one of their notorious *obysks*. Like most encounters with the Secret Police, these began with a knock on the door in the middle of the night. Sometimes it was just ripped from its hinges. Then, pushing aside the terrified occupants, a horde of agents entered the apartment, searching it top to bottom before carting off everything in sight. Items identified as evidence of criminal behavior—items like forbidden books—were meticulously catalogued. I take a few moments to regain my composure, then charge downstairs. Mrs. Parfenov shuffles after me, wrapping herself in a shawl.

The movers have finished and are swinging the van's big door closed. I convince them to wait until I retrieve my typewriter and a suitcase, which I quickly fill with clothing from the dresser.

Mrs. Parfenov and I watch as the van rumbles off, cutting tracks deep into the fresh snow. She tightens her shawl and studies me with knowing eyes. "You know, Nikasha," she finally says, with an amused smile, "when I was a little girl and couldn't get my way, my mother had a saying—a perfectly wonderful saying. Of course, I didn't think it was so wonderful then. You know what it was?"

"No, no, I've no idea."

Her eyes crinkle as if she's forgotten it; then she wags a finger at me and rasps, " 'Be careful what you wish for, you just might get it.' "

I nod forlornly, wishing I had her mother's sagacity. "So, you have a place to stay?"

"I have a sister in Leningrad," she replies in a tone that leaves no doubt she can't bring herself to call it St. Petersburg.

"Well," I say after an awkward silence, "thanks for everything, Mrs. Parfenov. Take care of yourself." She smiles, wraps her bony arms around my torso, and hugs me with surprising strength. I tuck the typewriter under one arm, grab the suitcase, and trudge off toward the Metro, my briefcase swinging from the other.

The wind turns the snow into a swirling haze. A perfect metaphor for my increasingly surreal existence. Homeless. A busted career. Down to my last ruble. I'll probably end up like those lost souls who stand on street corners hawking their belongings to buy groceries. I feel terribly alone, rudderless, as if I'm starting life all over. I'd call Vera, but she'd probably hang up on me again. Moscow Beginners. Yeah, maybe Ludmilla will be there. If that doesn't work, I could always spend another night or two at Yuri's. I've taken about a half-dozen steps when Mrs. Parfenov's voice cuts through the silence.

"Nikasha? Nikasha? I almost forgot," she says, slipping the folded newspaper from within her shawl as I reverse direction. "I found this behind the dresser when they moved it."

"Behind the dresser?"

She nods.

"It's a week-old newspaper, Mrs. Parfenov," I say, recalling Vera's rage when she threw it at me. "What am I going to do with it?"

"Well, I thought maybe you'd put it there for safekeeping or something."

"For safekeeping?"

"Those men who were looking for you? You know, I thought maybe you were afraid they'd search your apartment."

"Did they?"

"No, but if they had, they might've found this." She removes a rubberband from around the newspaper and unfolds it, revealing an envelope inside.

I set the typewriter atop the suitcase, then open the envelope and remove the contents. My eyes widen in total shock.

"Is it something important?"

I nod emphatically, the words catching in my throat. "I got my wish, Mrs. Parfenov," I finally reply, unable to believe I'm actually holding Vorontsov's documents. "I just got my wish."

19

M rs. Parfenov?" Yuri exclaims in disbelief as I slip the documents from my briefcase onto his desk. The Interior Ministry is a turn-of-the-century edifice of epic proportions, and Yuri's office is considerably larger than his apartment. Reams of printouts covered with mathematical computations and economic forecasts—produced by an antiquated computer and daisy-wheel printer that chatters like a machine gun—are piled on every surface and tacked up on walls, encircling the room like miles of bunting. "How the hell did that old *babushka* get her hands on them?"

"Vera," I reply glumly, going on to explain about the newspaper.

Yuri tilts backs in his chair and studies me curiously. "What's wrong? You should be thrilled."

"I am."

"You have a funny way of showing it."

"Half of me is; the other half feels like shit. I mean, Vera took a big chance for me—Shevchenko'd lock her up and throw away the key if he knew—then she finds me in the sack with Ludmilla, for Chrissakes."

"Naturally," Yuri says, still unable to contain his laughter at the thought.

"Come on, Yuri, think of how she must've felt. Besides, I really miss her."

"Well, call her and tell her that."

"I tried. She hung up on me."

"I'm sorry," he says solemnly, realizing it won't be easily smoothed over. "I miss her too."

Melancholia turns to anticipation as we spread the documents on a small conference table and begin reviewing them. They're all unsigned drafts with blank spaces where names and signatures will be inserted. They confirm Vorontsov was overseeing deals with companies wishing to invest in various Russian businesses and industries. The investors run the gamut from small businesses to multinational giants: IBM, ITT, ATT, ITZ, TWA, Amex, Exxon, Levi Strauss, Caterpillar, Agritech, GM, GE, CNN, Royal Dutch Shell, Pizza Hut—but that's it. There's nothing in the documents that indicates illegitimate money sources are involved; nothing that smells of capital flight; that connects the deals to Seabeco, Galaktik, Istok, or any of the other companies with foreign charters founded by former Party officials to move money out of Russia; or that even hints at corruption, let alone implicates Barkhin or anyone else. It's a waste of time. A crushing disappointment. Shevchenko was right.

We're staring at them in gloomy silence when Yuri's phone rings. "Ternyak," he answers, in a voice laden with uncharacteristic authority—but the phone continues ringing. He groans, slams it down, and scoops up another. But the ringing continues. The victim of ancient technology that dooms those important enough to have multiple lines to working at desks covered with phones, Yuri unearths another, and yet another from beneath the papers and printouts in a frantic hit-and-miss routine bordering on slapstick. "Ternyak—Ternyak—Ternyak— Ah," he replies, brightening when finally greeted by a voice instead of a dial tone. Then, seeming a little self-conscious, he lowers his voice and says, "Uh-huh . . . uh-huh . . . of course. I have someone in my office. I might be a little late." He hangs up and pushes the phone aside. "It's a conspiracy. I mean, I don't know how they do it, but somehow it's always the last one I pick up."

I smile at the irony and begin gathering the documents. "So, who is she?"

Yuri looks puzzled.

"The phone call. Sort of sounded like a date."

"I wish," Yuri replies with a wistful sigh. "It was just someone confirming a meeting."

"Sure it was. Come on, stop being so evasive. What's her name?"

"Igor," he replies with a chuckle. "My policy team is meeting tonight to get ready for a meeting tomorrow; after which, we'll have a meeting to review the meeting, and schedule more meetings." His eyes roll in dismay. "If talk could drive this economy, we'd make Japan look like Honduras. Sorry, where were we?"

"Throwing in the towel." I'm about to put the documents back in my briefcase when something dawns on me: We identified all the companies except one—ITZ. Neither of us have any idea what it stands for. The documents, dealing with privatizing State distribution systems—trucking, shipping, rail freight, air cargo, and warehousing—are filled with phrases like: ITZ will do . . . ITZ will receive . . . ITZ will guarantee . . . ITZ will have access to . . . But unlike other companies that are first identified by their full name—International Business Machines ("IBM") will provide—with initials being used alone for the sake of brevity thereafter, ITZ is never fully identified.

"*I* probably stands for International," Yuri suggests, printing the three letters on a pad.

"Probably. Then again, it could be Institute, Independent, Inter, Intra, Intelstat, Interstellar—"

"Okay, okay," Yuri interrupts like an impatient parrot. "Let's stick with International for now. What about *T*? Transport, Telephone, Telecom, Telesis, Technics, Thermodynamics . . ."

"Thermonuclear, Telegraph, Television, Trans, Tri, Trade, Transfer, Transworld, Technology, Techtonics, Tactics, Textile . . ."

"Enough," Yuri says, quickly jotting them down. "What about *Z*?"

"Zoo, Zipper, Zone . . ."

"Zephyr, Zinc . . ."

"Zilch."

Yuri nods. "Tough one."

I fetch an English dictionary from the bookcase behind his desk, and turn to the *Z*s. "Zenith, Zircon, Zither, Zurich . . ."

"International Telecommunications Zurich," Yuri suggests, taking a stab at a combination.

"Institute of Trade Zagreb."

"International Textile and Zipper."

"International Technology and . . . and . . . and what? Zinc? Zirconium?"

"Zoology."

"Zucchini."

"Independent Transport . . . something or other," Yuri suggests halfheartedly; then his eyes brighten with a thought. "Maybe it's a law firm? The Ministry's overrun with attorneys lately."

"Not surprising. An active legal system is as crucial to making democracy work as a free press."

He throws up his hands in protest. "Please, these lawyers are driving us crazy. From what I've seen, ITZ probably stands for Inept, Tedious, and Zany."

"Well, as long as we're indulging in lawyer-bashing— Ignominious, Tautology, and"—I scan the dictionary for an appropriate pejorative that starts with Z—"and Zoanthropy."

"Zoanthropy?"

"A form of mental disorder in which the patient imagines himself to be a beast."

"How about, Illusive, Temperamental, and Zaftig?" Yuri fires back.

"Attorneys?"

"No. My ex-wife." More laughter before Yuri sags in capitulation. "Forget it, Nikolai. This is ridiculous. We're wasting our time."

I'm prone to agree. But his joke has brought Agent Scotto to mind, which reminds me of something she said, which, if I'm not mistaken, solves the puzzle.

Yuri notices the smile spreading across my face. "What? Come on, I know you have it."

I shake my head no, savoring the irony. "It doesn't stand for anything, Yuri."

"It doesn't?"

"That's why it's not identified like the others. I take the pad and pencil from him, and in front of the letters *ITZ* I write the letters *R-U-B-I-N-O-W*—so it now reads *RUBINOWITZ*."

"Rubinowitz?" Yuri wonders, clearly baffled. "I don't get it. Who's he?"

"Michael Rubinowitz. That was thirty years ago. Now known as Michael Rubineau. Hangs out at the Paradise. Runs a chain of hotels in America—"

"I still don't get it."

"—connected to the Jewish mafia."

Yuri's brows arch with intrigue. "I get it now. You think he had Vorontsov killed?"

"I don't know. Shevchenko said he didn't think Barkhin was behind it."

"You realize how big this is, if you're right?"

"Well," I say, glowing with satisfaction, "it's a lot bigger than a shoe factory in Zuzino."

"What're you going to do? Go to the cops?"

I shrug; then my mind starts racing, and I hear myself say, "Yeah—an American cop."

"That woman?"

"That illusive, temperamental, zaftig woman," I reply with a grin, crossing to the phone. "You have the number for the U.S. Embassy handy?"

Yuri fetches his little black book—leatherbound, chock-full of alphabetized phone numbers and addresses, and stuffed with odd slips of paper on which others are scribbled, awaiting entry. It's among his most valued possessions. Westerners say the same of their Rolodexes and Filofaxes, but it's not the same. They haven't lived in closed societies, in cities without telephone directories. Their black books haven't been their only link to family, friends, and business associates through decades of secrecy and oppression. Yuri dials the number on one of the phones and hands it to me.

"Yes, I'm trying to reach Special Agent Scotto. Gabriella Scotto ... That's right, with your Treasury Department. A group called FinCEN. ... Oh ... Yes, please. ... Uh-huh ... uh-huh. ... Thank you."

Yuri questions me with a look. "She's gone?"

I nod glumly. "Back to Washington. They gave me a number for her."

"Good. Call. Be my guest. On second thought, better wait till you get back to my apartment. It could take hours to get an overseas line."

"I know."

"What does that mean?" Yuri challenges, picking up on my lack of enthusiasm. "You're giving up?"

"No. No, just thinking. I'm out of work. I've got no place to live. People have been trying to kill me. Might be a good idea if I got away for a while."

Yuri recoils slightly and makes a face. "You mean to America?"

"Why not? My great-grandfather went over a hundred years ago. I've never been out of Russia. Maybe it's time."

"How? Airfare alone is more than a million rubles. And in case you've forgotten, along with being homeless and unemployed, you're also broke."

"I don't need to be reminded, believe me; but you're forgetting about these." I remove Vorontsov's medals from my briefcase. "They might be my ticket out of here."

"You're going to sell them?"

"The thought's crossed my mind."

"How much are they worth?"

"Thirty thousand."

"Dollars?"

I nod.

"You could do a lot of traveling on that," Yuri muses, running his fingertips over his mustache. "And you wouldn't have any trouble selling them?"

"On the black market? They'd be gone like that."

"Yes, Nikolai, I'm quite sure they would," he says disapprovingly.

"What's that mean?"

"Nothing."

"Come on, Yuri. I know that tone. You're accusing me of something unethical."

"Yes. Frankly, the thought of selling them makes me uncomfortable. It's not like you. The medals belong to Mrs. Churkin. I thought you were—"

"Of course they do."

"Well, then you should return them."

"I am," I say with a little smile. "I don't recall saying, I wasn't. I said they might be my ticket out of here."

There is a newspaper on the mat in front of the door to Mrs. Churkin's apartment when I arrive. She doesn't respond to the buzzer, and I return to the lobby and settle in one of the big leather chairs. They feel smaller than they did thirty years ago, but they smell the same. The musty odor conjures up distant memories, unpleasant ones of my father being led away, of my mother crying, of being forced to move in with relatives, of the disgrace. I'm lost in my thoughts when the huge door creaks open and the children burst through it, pulling me out of the reverie. Mrs. Churkin is right behind them, carrying a chic, pastel blue shopping bag that proclaims ESTÉE LAUDER. Her eyes flare at the sight of me, leaving no doubt she's seen the story in *Pravda.*

"I have some good news, Mrs. Churkin," I say, hoping to defuse her anger before it erupts.

"Blackmail?! My father was a blackmailer!" she exclaims as she blows past me, shooing the children toward the elevator. "That's good news?!"

"I didn't write that story." She stops dead in her tracks and turns to face me. "Any of it."

"You started it," she counters, thumbing the elevator button angrily. "You were supposed to get his medals for me. You—"

"I did," I fire back.

She tilts her head and stares at me skeptically.

"I have them right here," I explain, holding up my briefcase.

Her eyes flicker with hope that turns slowly to delight. "Oh. Oh, that's wonderful."

The moment is broken by the rumble of the elevator door rolling open. The four of us pile in. As soon as we enter the apartment she sends the children off to their rooms, then takes the envelope from me, crosses to the dining room table, and sits down. Her hands quickly undo the clasp and open the flap. She pauses momentarily, then gently slides the medals onto the white lace. A colorful pile of satin and gold shimmers in the soft light. She picks up one of the medals, straightens the ribbon, and sets it down, reverently. She does the same with another and then another.

"Did your father ever mention the name Rubineau?"

She shakes her head no, her attention riveted to the medals that she's arranging in neat rows as if pinning them on a jacket.

"What about Rubinowitz?"

"No, not that I recall," she replies, looking up at me, her eyes glistening with emotion. "Why?"

"Well, I'm betting that's who your father was involved with—blackmailer, coconspirator, whistle blower, I've no idea."

"I don't recall seeing either of those names in the story."

"They weren't."

She sighs with impatience. "What do you want, Mr. Katkov, money?"

"No, Mrs. Churkin. I want the truth."

"So do I. I've little hope of ever finding it."

"Depends on where you look."

"You know where?" she asks, picking up on the inference as I intended.

"USA."

"America?" she wonders, a little awestruck.

I nod.

"Well, we're all free to travel now. Why don't you go there and find it?"

"I plan to, but there are a few things I have to work out. First, this is ugly business and could get uglier. It's important you understand that instead of clearing your father's name, I may end up proving he was every bit the corrupt *apparatchik* they claim he is."

She nods smartly. "I don't care. I have to know. What else?"

"I don't have a ruble to my name."

Her eyes narrow, then shift from mine to the medals and back, softening with understanding and admiration. "I didn't know there were any honest men left in Moscow, Mr. Katkov."

"Thank you. Nikolai. Please."

"Nikolai," she repeats with a friendly smile. "Let me know how much you'll need."

20

First thing in the morning I head over to the U.S. Embassy, a rococo, mustard-colored building on Tchaikovsky Boulevard, to get a visa. It's not as easy as I thought, and I return to Yuri's apartment without it. As he predicted, it takes almost the entire afternoon to get a call through to Agent Scotto in Washington, D.C.

"Run that by me again," her dusky New York accent crackles over the line. "You need a special letter from me to come here?"

"Your embassy does. Someone in the United States has to vouch for me. No letter, no visa, I'm afraid."

"What about your cousin in Brooklyn?" she jokes.

"Even if I had one, Scotto, I'm coming to see you."

"Hey, with what's going on in my life these days, Katkov, flattery'll get you everywhere. Mind telling me why?"

"I have some information."

"No kidding? What kind of information?"

"The kind you've been looking for."

"Don't play games with me, dammit. Come on, what do you have?"

"Vladimir Illiych Vorontsov's documents."

"Geezus. What's in 'em? What do they say? Stuff about that pipeline deal?"

151

"Not so fast. If I tell you now, there's no reason for me to come, is there?"

"What is this? Some ploy to get FinCEN to pay for your trip?"

"No, that's all taken care of. It's a ploy to earn a living. I give you the documents when I arrive, and you give me first crack at whomever and whatever they give you. Deal?"

"I don't make deals, Katkov. Especially with journalists. They all seem to have a problem when it comes to taking sides."

"You know, you'd make a rather good Communist, Scotto. They think the media exists to pump out propaganda for the State."

"Where do I sign up?"

"I'm afraid they've been outlawed, but you're in luck. We've been puppets for so long, there's not a journalist in Moscow who *isn't* taking sides now. I'm offering to take yours."

"Big of you."

"I'm quite certain you'll be more than delighted when you see the documents. Are you going to send me the letter or not?"

She emits an exasperated groan. "I'll pouch it to our embassy. You have the name of the immigration officer you saw?"

"Of course, his card's right here." I give Scotto the name, then turn my attention to getting a passport—a passport for foreign travel.

For the last sixty years, all Soviet citizens were required to carry an *internal* passport containing two crucial items: the residency stamp on page fourteen was used to restrict where we could live; and the infamous Item Five, which listed ethnic background, was used to discriminate against non-Slavs and Jews when they sought employment and access to government services. As part of the commitment to individual liberties, the internal passport has been declared unconstitutional and replaced with a plastic-encased identity card that contains neither item—though there are those who view the magnetic data stripe on the back with suspicion.

Of course, the internal passport had nothing to do with travel abroad. An exit visa—routinely denied to most citizens, especially Jews who were dubbed *refuseniks*—was required to leave the country. These have also been outlawed by the reformists, and only the standard traveler's passport is required now.

Unfortunately, the Foreign Ministry is swamped with applications, and the issuing process can take up to a month, sometimes longer. I spend countless days standing in lines, filling out forms, and dealing with a succession of envious, mean-spirited passport officers. They have nothing but disdain for those able to travel—and the power to delay or deny one's application.

My evenings are spent in Yuri's apartment, helping him catalogue books in his library, and thinking about Vera. I'm tempted to call her back but, despite knowing that I was in trouble, despite knowing I needed a place to stay, she's neither beeped me nor even contacted Yuri. He gently suggests that, since she's shown little interest in my whereabouts or well-being, and since, with any luck, I'll soon be leaving Moscow, a lengthy cooling off period might be in order.

After more than three weeks of tedium at the Foreign Ministry I finally make it to the window where passports are issued. Looking at the bright side, instead of being in winter's grasp when I arrive, Washington—unlike Moscow, where harsh weather lasts well into April—will now be basking in spring. A gray-faced bureaucrat rolls a blank into her typewriter and asks for my identity card. She stares at it for a long moment, then looks up. "This is your current address?"

Is it a routine question? Or does her unnerving tone mean she already knows the answer? If she does, if it's a setup and I'm caught giving false information, new government or no, it might forever disqualify me. If she doesn't, I'd be a fool to admit I'm between apartments and don't have an address. Along with my ethnic background, it's the sort of technicality the KGB would've used in the past to turn my life into a nightmare; and I've no doubt it's the sort of thing this brain-dead *apparatchik* would use now to turn me down. I steel myself, and, as offhandedly as possible, reply, "Of course it's current."

She thinks it over for a moment, making me squirm, then nods matter-of-factly and begins typing. After filling in the blanks, she affixes my photograph, and embosses it with the government seal. Each step is done with painstaking deliberation intended to make the process take as long as possible. Finally, she folds the booklet in half and hands it to me with an insipid smirk.

I can't believe my eyes. Instead of the Russian tricolor, the ruby-red cover is imprinted in gold with the Hammer and

Sickle. The letters *CCCP* parade above it, and *Union of Soviet Socialist Republics* below. "Hey, haven't you people heard? We're neither Soviet nor socialist anymore."

"That's nothing to be proud of," the passport officer snaps, making me glad I lied. "We're issuing these until the new government decides on a new coat of arms. If they wait much longer, they might not have to change it." She snorts at her own joke and holds out a hand. "I'd be happy to take it back."

I force a smile and resist the temptation to say "Eat your heart out, *comrade,*" then head for the United States Embassy. It's only a few stops on the Metro. To my relief, the immigration officer has the letter Scotto sent him and agrees to expedite my visa. I pick it up at the end of the day along with my passport and a copy of the letter. The next evening Yuri drives me, my briefcase, typewriter, and several pieces of luggage to Sheremetyevo Airport twenty-five miles northwest of downtown Moscow. I suspect his generosity has much to do with finally getting me out of that tiny apartment as saying bon voyage.

Just after midnight, Aeroflot SU-317 takes off in a raging snowstorm and soars high above the clouds, taking my spirits with it. I've left the thugs in trench coats and Ray-Bans behind. I'm no longer lonely, homeless, and unemployed. I'm unleashed, unencumbered. For the first time in my life, I feel free.

The jetliner heads due west, crossing the Baltics, the southern tip of Sweden, and the North Sea to Great Britain and a brief stopover in Shannon, Ireland; then it continues on over the stormy North Atlantic to the United States. Eighty-four-hundred miles and fifteen hours after takeoff, the wide-bodied IL-62 descends over the Virginia countryside, where the graceful sweep of plowed roads slices through fresh snow.

Snow? I press my face to the window in disbelief. Yes. Snow, as far as I can see. Not only doesn't winter wait, but regardless of the season it seems to follow wherever I go. So much for the cherry blossoms I've heard so much about. A short time later, the intercom crackles and the pilot explains that a freak cold front pushed down from Canada over the weekend, turning April showers into wet snow.

Cool morning light streams into the cabin as the plane banks, and the intersecting runways of Dulles International appear off the left wing. My guidebook says it was named for John Foster Dulles, Secretary of State during the 1950s. It fails to note that his policies fueled the Cold War and led to America's disastrous involvement in Vietnam. I recall how his Soviet counterpart, equally responsible for instigating those decades of tension and distrust, and our disastrous involvement in Afghanistan, was held in similar esteem.

Snowflakes stick to the windows as the Ilyushin touches down and taxis to the terminal. I'm coming off the boarding ramp, numbed by the long flight, when the public address system comes to life. "Will arriving passenger Nikolai Katkov please proceed to inspection station number six?" a soothing female voice requests in Russian. "Arriving passenger Katkov to station six, please?"

I enter the brightly illuminated terminal, where a sign proclaims UNITED STATES DEPARTMENT OF IMMIGRATION AND NATURALIZATION. Another prohibits smoking. Long lines of weary passengers snake from stations one through five; but not from six. No, six is roped off and unused. A uniformed officer stands behind the counter. Is he waiting for me? Is it possible I'm getting VIP treatment? I can't believe it, but it sure looks like Scotto has pulled out all the stops.

"Mr. Katkov?" the stocky fellow prompts with a friendly smile. "Welcome to the Untied States."

"Thank you. It's my first visit."

"Yes, we know. We just have a few questions." He examines my passport and visa, then raises his eyes. "You're a freelance journalist?"

"Yes," I reply jauntily, getting my second wind. "I'm working on a story."

"I see; but you don't have a job, per se?"

Something in his tone makes me uneasy. "I don't work for one newspaper, if that's what you mean."

"What about your address in Moscow? Can you tell me about that?"

My gut tightens. I've good reason to be uneasy now. "Precisely what do you want to know?"

"Our embassy did a routine check. It seems the address in your passport isn't current. As a matter of fact, they were informed the building was recently vacated and is being demolished. Is that accurate?"

"Yes, well, you see, that address was copied from my identity card. I can't get a new one until I have a new address; but I won't have a new address until I return to Moscow and find a new apartment. I believe it's what you Americans call a catch-something-or-other."

"Twenty-two," he says, unmoved. He lifts the phone and dials an extension. "Mac? Cosgrove here. . . . On this Katkov thing? You were right. We're going to need a secondary . . . no, actually he sounds a little like an Englishman. . . . Uh-huh. On our way."

Cosgrove directs me down a corridor and into an office where a stern-looking fellow in trifocals sits behind a desk. A name-plate identifies him as W. T. MACALISTER. A gold badge is pinned to his white military-style shirt. Impressive insignia perch on the epaulets. He takes my passport and visa from his colleague, who leaves the office with the ticket stubs for my bags.

"So," MacAlister says. "You're a journalist?"

"Yes. The immigration officer at your embassy said there shouldn't be any problem as long as I had this." I slip Agent Scotto's letter from my briefcase.

"Treasury Department." His lips purse thoughtfully as he reads. "You realize this letter isn't on official stationary, Mr. Katkov?"

"Of course, it's a copy. Your embassy retained the original. Agent Scotto's meeting me here. She'll authenticate it for you."

He nods, then lifts the phone, and asks that Scotto be paged. "You see, Mr. Katkov," he says in a patronizing tone, "the average person thinks a visa gives them permission to enter the country. It doesn't. It merely entitles them to *request* it on arrival."

"Is there some reason why it shouldn't be granted in my case?"

"Possibly." He folds the letter and returns it. "Your profile suggests you might be here to find work—illegal work—and it's my job to make that determination."

"Illegal work? I don't understand. I told you I'm already working on a story."

The phone rings. "MacAlister." He listens, grunts, hangs up, and, as if rendering a guilty verdict, announces, "Agent Scotto didn't respond to the page."

"Well, you saw her letter, you—"

"*A copy of her letter,*" he corrects sharply. "Put yourself in our shoes. You're single; you have no family in Moscow; no residence—in other words, little incentive to return. How do we know that you—"

"I have a round-trip ticket!" I interrupt, losing my patience.

"You'll be using it sooner than you think, with that attitude. How do we know that you won't work for American publications?"

"You have my word."

"Mr. Katkov, if I had a dollar for every person who swore they weren't going to work illegally and did, I'd be in Florida working on my short game."

"Your what?"

"Golf. Nicklaus? Trevino? Forget it. The point is, before we can allow you to enter the United States, we need assurances you won't become a burden to the American taxpayer."

"I've never been a burden to anyone, and I don't intend to start now."

"Good, I'll keep that in mind. By the way, I meant to compliment you on your English. Unfortunately, it's another thing that's working against you."

"Against me?"

"Exactly. You'd have no trouble making contacts; no fear of being suspected of doing business illegally. I venture to say the *Post* would welcome you with open arms, regardless."

I'm about to lose my temper when Cosgrove returns and takes his boss aside. After several tight-lipped nods, MacAlister says, "Good news, Mr. Katkov, your luggage is clean. Now, would you empty your briefcase, please?"

I stare at him sullenly, then decide the better of challenging him and do as he asks.

MacAlister sorts through the items methodically, pausing at Vorontsov's documents. His brows rise with suspicion. "What are these, Mr. Katkov?"

"Material for my story. Why?"

"Well, they look like originals to me. Stamped 'received'—by your Interior Ministry, I believe."

"That's correct."

"Care to tell us how you happened to get your hands on them?"

"I have sources like any journalist."

"Sources?" he echoes suspiciously. His eyes shift to Cosgrove's. "You thinking what I'm thinking?"

"Time to get the FBI into this."

MacAlister nods ominously.

The FBI? The fucking FBI?! The nightmare is happening, but the monsters aren't mean-spirited clerks at the Foreign Ministry, or KGB interrogators. No, they're from the U.S. Department of Immigration and Naturalization. "You're making this into something it's not," I protest vehemently. "Call Agent Scotto's office. I'm sure they'll be able to—"

The phone rings. MacAlister is scooping it up when someone knocks on the door. "Thanks for the warning. She's already here."

Girdled in a leather sash and gun belt, from which a sidearm hangs, festooned with decorations, hair tucked up into an officer's cap, a zaftig woman in a navy blue uniform that's frighteningly akin to KGB issue blows into the office.

"Scotto, Treasury," she says, showing her official ID to the two officers. "Sorry I'm late, Katkov. We got a break in a case. I've been going round the clock the last couple of days." She shifts her look back to the officers. "I'm real tired and way behind schedule. Can we get this cleared up?"

"Well, that depends on—"

"Good. I knew you guys'd understand."

Minutes later Scotto and I are marching across an airport parking lot with a baggage handler who's pushing a cart loaded with my things.

"Well, you really got off on the right foot, didn't you, Katkov?"

"I'm afraid they're the ones out of step."

"Sure. This sort of thing'd never happen back in the good ol' USSR."

"There's no such place."

"Come on Katkov, don't be naive. You know what they say about roses and leopards."

"You don't really believe that?"

She grins, leads the way to a salt-spattered sedan with two antennas, and opens the trunk. It's loaded with cardboard boxes. One contains food: cookies, popcorn, potato chips, canned goods, a bottle of vodka, cartons of cigarettes. Another overflows with clothes: jeans, sweat shirts, socks, running shoes, a dark blue windbreaker with TREASURY AGENT printed across the back, and what look like wigs. A third holds equipment: a flashlight, binoculars, tools, softball and glove, Frisbee, a small TV set. Stuffed between the boxes are a sleeping bag, pillow, blankets, an umbrella, a shovel, a bag of rock salt, and skid chains. Scotto shoves the boxes around to make room, then gives up and slams the trunk closed. We load my things into the backseat and drive off, wipers chattering across the icy windshield.

"You do a lot of camping?"

"Camping? I'm from Brooklyn. I hate camping."

"Then what? Your husband threw you out when you separated?"

"No. As a matter of fact he generously offered to bunk with a buddy for a while."

"Ah, you're one of those eccentrics who live out of their cars."

"Sometimes," she replies enigmatically. "We go way back. Eighty-one Buick Skylark. The good old days when cars had trunks. You bring the documents?"

"Was Stalin a butcher?" I indicate my briefcase.

"Good. I want to go through them as soon as we get back to my office, but I've got some business to take care of first. You'll have to tag along."

"That's why I'm here. What kind of business? You wouldn't be making—what do you call them—a bust, would you?"

"A bust?" she repeats derisively. "What the hell would make you think that?"

"Well, you said you had a break in a case; and that's not exactly a cocktail dress you're wearing."

She groans. "First, we call them takedowns, not busts. Second, FinCEN doesn't make them per se. We support other law enforcement agencies with data and analysis. Third, I haven't worn this zoot suit in years, and I hope I never wear it again. Fourth, it's the last thing I'd ever wear to a takedown."

"You have special combat gear for that?"

"You could say that."

"Well, if you don't wear that zoot suit to busts, what do you wear it for?"

"Funerals," she replies glumly. "The break in that case had a high price tag."

21

Special Agent Scotto drives like a Moscow cab driver. Despite snow and rush-hour traffic, she speeds, tailgates, and cuts off other vehicles with abandon.

"Hey, hey, easy does it," I finally protest, losing my bravado to one near-miss too many. "They'll be burying us too."

"Not a chance," she says, turning off the highway into a tree-lined approach road. "You have to serve in the military to be buried at Arlington."

"Arlington—your President Kennedy is there, isn't he?"

She nods solemnly. "One of your heroes, huh?"

"Well, not quite in the same league as Lincoln or Peter the Great, but his speeches were rather inspiring."

"Yeah, to every woman he met. Ask not what your president can do for you, ask what you can do for your president."

I can't help but laugh. "Those are some of my favorite lines—I mean as originally written."

"Mine too, actually. My family hated his guts—the Hoffa thing, I guess—but you're right, he had something special. I'm sorry to say he's about to be joined by Agent Edwin Woodruff—lovely wife, three great kids, one of the most decent people and dedicated cops I've ever known." She smiles, reflecting, then adds, "Played a hell of a second base too."

Iron gates hung from massive stone pillars flank the entrance to the cemetery. A marine sentry in dress blues glances at Scotto's ID and waves us on. The road winds through groves of bare trees that reach skyward in prayer. Beneath them, thousands of headstones march with military precision over white-blanketed hillsides.

Scotto parks behind a line of cars. She gets out without a word and walks swiftly to a hearse, joining a group of uniformed pallbearers. On a signal from the minister, they remove the coffin and carry it at a solemn pace toward the gravesite where mourners wait.

Agent Woodruff's family emerges from a limousine and follows. They're African-American. The possibility never occurred to me. There are few blacks in Russia. Mostly students and diplomats. Certainly none on Moscow's militia. They stand with heads bowed as the honor guard sets the coffin on a platform adjacent to the grave.

I remain in the car. Snow soon covers the windshield. I can't write about what I can't see, can't hear, can't feel. There's a hallowed silence here, and the click of the door latch carries like a gunshot. I make my way past a TV reporter whispering grimly into his microphone, until I'm close enough to see the widow's saddened eyes and hear the minister's words.

I've been in America for barely an hour, and I'm attending a funeral. It's strangely disorienting. Indeed, my body is here, but my mind still isn't. It's drifting to the past, to another wintry day, to another cemetery and a weathered tombstone that proclaims KATKOV. The wail of a bugle pulls me out of my reverie.

Woodruff's widow is holding her head high with defiance and pride now. When the service ends, she and Scotto hug like grieving sisters. Their pain seems nearly equal in intensity. The mourners quickly take their leave, sent to their cars by the numbing cold. Scotto drives in silence, eyes welling with tears that I can't ignore.

"Are you all right?"

"No. It's not fair."

I let it go for a moment and light a cigarette. "Would you like to talk about it?"

She shakes her head no.

"Sometimes it helps."

"It won't bring him back." She takes a hand from the wheel and pulls it across her eyes. "I still can't believe it. Two tours in Vietnam, he gets blown away by a fourteen-year-old in a junkyard in St. Louis."

"A fourteen-year-old," I echo incredulously.

"With an assault rifle. They're putting metal detectors in grade schools, for God's sake. Witnesses said Woody had his gun drawn, but held his fire, just for an instant, just long enough ... damn ..."

"Rather hard to kill a child."

"It's rather hard to kill anybody, Katkov," Scotto snaps, braking hard for a traffic light. The car skids slightly. She bounces a fist off the steering wheel, then sighs remorsefully. "I'm sorry. You're right; and I probably would've done the same thing."

"Not you, Scotto. You're tough as nails, aren't you? You would've blown that child right out of his running shoes."

She smiles. "Maybe, maybe not. The agent backing up Woody had no choice."

"I imagine you two were quite close?"

She bites a lip and nods. "Woody was my partner before I took this job. It's like being married. You squabble, share things, support each other. I asked for him when I got into this case. If I hadn't, maybe ... maybe he'd ..." She groans and lets it trail off.

"Really. You can't blame yourself."

"Yes, I can. I sent him down there."

"To be killed?" I prompt facetiously.

"Of course not. As we say in this business, he was following the money. Trying to anyway."

"Whose money?"

"Drug cartel. We're talking big, real big, you wouldn't believe it if I told you."

"If? I'm afraid we'd better settle this right now, Scotto. No ifs. We're joined at the hip, as they say. You show me yours. I show you mine. Deal?"

"Two conditions," she fires back. "Like the INS guys said, you publish nothing here; and whatever you do publish waits until the operation's over."

"Fair enough. Now, as you were saying ..."

The light changes. She nods and tromps on the accelerator. "Montreal to Miami, New York to St. Louis, we figure the cartel's raking in somewhere in the neighborhood of a hundred K a minute—that's six million an hour, a hundred fifty million a day, fifty billion a year—that's *billion*."

"You're right. I don't believe it."

"But before they can spend it or invest it, they have to launder it; and before they can do that, they have to collect it, count it, package it, and store it until they can move it. The fifty-billion dollar question is 'Where?' We keep looking for it. They keep moving it. We call it Operation Shell Game."

"How does this teenage gunman fit into that?"

"Indirectly. Woody and his partner were checking out a warehouse. The kid was riding shotgun for a drug deal going down in the junkyard across the alley. They just happened on it." She shakes her head in dismay. "We lost him over a couple of crummy vials of crack."

"And the warehouse?"

"Empty, unfortunately. We'd been informed it was being used by a certain corporation—one of several we've linked to the cartel."

"The 'cartel.' Another one of those nameless, faceless words like 'organized crime.' The company wouldn't be called ITZ, would it?"

"No. Why?"

"It has a rather nasty habit of turning up in Vorontsov's documents."

"Really? Never heard of it."

"I'm afraid you have. As a matter of fact, you're the one who put me onto it."

"Me? I think I'd remember."

"Rubineau . . . Rubinowitz . . . ITZ. Follow?"

She whistles, clearly impressed, and makes short work of what's left of the drive to her office.

FinCEN is headquartered in Arlington, a few miles from the cemetery on Fairfax Drive. U.S. and Treasury Department flags hang stiffly from a pole on the corner. The nondescript concrete box would fit right in with the drab housing blocks on Moscow's Kalinin Prospekt. Its four-story precast facade dwarfs a lone tree and a brick building across the street that has a stovepipe chimney from which gray smoke curls.

"Burn, baby, burn," Scotto mutters, turning into the parking lot behind FinCEN. "That damned barbecue's going all day."

"Barbecue?"

"It's a funeral home. They do cremations. Sorry, it's my way of dealing with—" She bites it off when a media horde surrounds the car, pushing TV and still cameras against the windows as Scotto pulls into a parking spot. She can barely get her door open. "Back off, guys. Come on, back off." She slips out and charges across the pavement.

The media pursues, shoving cameras, tape recorders, and microphones into her face. "Can you tell us who you're investigating?"

"Not without tipping them off."

"What was Agent Woodruff doing in that junkyard?"

"Giving his life for his country."

Scotto darts down a colonnade toward the entrance, the reporters at her heels, the questions coming rapid-fire: "Several witnesses claim the kid was trying to surrender when he was shot? Is it true he had no criminal record? What about his family's claim he was unarmed? As Woodruff's former partner, can you tell us how you're feeling right now?"

Scotto stonewalls it until we reach the entrance, where uniformed guards restrain the reporters from following us inside. "That's your competition, Katkov," she growls, glaring at them through the glass door. "I'll make any deal you like, but if you're counting on me to keep those animals from beating you to the punch, you're nuts."

"Mind telling me what you have against journalists?"

"I did, once. Obviously you didn't want to hear it. You all think as long as you tell the truth, you're not responsible for the consequences."

"Sounds like someone burned you rather badly."

"I've lost count. Frankly, I don't know a single person who's talked to a reporter and wasn't either misquoted or quoted out of context."

The lobby is a cramped space with few chairs and a gray steel reception desk that looks like it was lifted from someone's office. A black felt board with letters pressed into grooves serves as a directory. Sections of ceiling tile have been removed, and workmen on ladders are pulling thick cables through a utility chase. The guard has me sign the register, then clips a plastic visitor's badge to my parka.

"That was easy," I remark, following Scotto to the elevator. "No lie detector test, no background check, no strip search?"

"And no smoking," she says smartly, stabbing a finger at a forbidding sign. "As far as security goes, we already pulled your skivvies—twice. Once when I looked you up in Moscow, and again after you called. I think the director has a soft spot for people who did time in the gulag, especially for subversive writings. You'd be cooling your heels in the lobby if he didn't like what he read."

"He actually read my articles?"

"Some of them. He thought the one on athletes was particularly on target. We discard them here too—usually right after college."

The elevator deposits us on the fourth floor in an institutional gray corridor lined with file cabinets. More open ceilings. More workmen on ladders pulling cables. More NO SMOKING signs. Scotto parks me outside her office for a few moments and changes into street clothes, then leads the way to the director's office and introduces me to her boss.

Joseph Banzer is a heavyset fellow with thinning hair, wearing a medium brown suit that blends with the wood paneling behind him. He seems to possess a certain absentminded cunning and comes off more like a distracted law professor than relentless investigator.

"This is very interesting, Mr. Katkov," he says softly as he peruses Vorontsov's documents. "We're familiar with the holding company for Rubineau's hotel operations, but—"

"Travis Enterprises," Scotto interrupts. "It's an acronym: Tahoe, Reno, Atlantic City, Vegas, Isabelle, and Sarah."

"Isabelle and Sarah?"

"His granddaughters," she replies.

"Whatever happened to widows and orphans?"

"*But,*" Banzer repeats commandingly, putting an end to the levity, "we haven't come across ITZ Corporation yet, have we, Agent Scotto?"

"No, it never turned up in our data, let alone linked to Rubineau."

"I'm afraid you won't find a link in those either," I confess a little apprehensively. "It was pure deduction on my part."

"Best kind," Banzer says smartly. He glances at me with a

puzzled look, then shifts it to Scotto. "Where'd you say he was from?"

"Moscow."

He drops a perplexed brow and nods. "That's what I thought you said. Anyway, it'll take some time to run these deals and determine whether or not they're legitimate; but ITZ is either Rubineau's company or it isn't—we can run that one right now." He slips the documents into a folder and heads for the door. "You see, Mr. Katkov," he explains as he lumbers down a corridor, "Systems Integration is the key to FinCEN's operation. That means we have immediate access to multiple data bases, including records of federal law enforcement and regulatory agencies like DEA, BATF, FRB, OCC, OTS, RTC, SEC, not to mention commercial repositories like Dun and Bradstreet, TRW . . ."

Scotto's rolling her eyes. "I covered some of this ground, Chief."

"Oh," Banzer says, a little disappointed at having the air let out of his balloon. "Well, to make a long story short, in partnership with other enforcement agencies, FinCEN detects and supports investigations and prosecutions of financial crimes. Our primary mission is to identify national and international money-laundering schemes, mainly those involving the proceeds of narcotics trafficking. . . ."

Scotto leans to me and whispers, "Right out of his congressional budget proposal."

"Don't remind me," Banzer warns, overhearing. "This damned deficit crunch has cut us to the bone. We're already outgunned and outfinanced. Out-of-business is next, if we're not careful. Budget meeting at two, Scotto. I want you there."

"Been burning a hole in my calendar for a week."

Banzer cuts a corner, pushes through a set of doors into the Operations Center, and wraps up his orientation lecture with "State-of-the-art computer technology's the key to our effectiveness. This place is up and running damn near twenty-four hours a day."

The room is alive with the steady hum of central processors, the zip-zip-zip of printer heads, and the probing questions of analysts who shoulder phones, freeing their hands to dance over keyboards. Rows of work stations—each with computer terminal and communications console—run down the center of the cramped space. Study carrels line the perimeter. There's just enough room between them to roll back a chair. One wall is covered with clocks set to various time zones, another with official-looking insignia, each about the size of a dinner plate. Scotto explains they represent the enforcement agencies that have signed information-sharing agreements with FinCEN.

Banzer turns Vorontsov's documents over to Ops Center Section Chief Tom Krauss, a tall, clean-cut fellow with sharply chiseled features and precise diction. He spends a few minutes at his keyboard accessing a data base before the printer next to his console comes to life. We're all hovering over it like expectant parents. I'm so preoccupied, I unthinkingly pop a cigarette into my mouth. Scotto's look is all the reminder I need. This is going to be torture, pure torture.

Banzer tears off the printout. "ITZ Corporation . . ." he announces with a dramatic pause, "President and CEO, one Michael A. Rubineau . . ."

"Way to go, Katkov," Scotto enthuses.

"Born Grodno, USSR, nineteen thirty-one; came to the USA with his parents at the outbreak of World War Two—"

"He's a Russian," I blurt, energized by the revelation. "A Russian Jew."

Banzer nods and continues. "Magna cum laude, Harvard Law, 'fifty-five; disbarred in 'fifty-eight for consorting with known gamblers."

"Lansky."

"Then," Scotto chirps. "Your friend Barkhin, now. Old habits die hard."

"ITZ," Banzer concludes, "was recently spun off from a subsidiary of Travis Enterprises—a suspiciously complex network of companies, I might add, with offices in New York, Miami, Los Angeles, and Tel Aviv."

"Did you say Tel Aviv?"

"Uh-huh," Banzer replies. "He lives there part of the year, according to his tax returns."

"Well, we know where he's going if things get too hot for him at home," Krauss observes.

"You remember Shevchenko?" I ask, directing the question to Scotto. "According to him, the fellow who was hired to kill me was an Israeli. A Jew who recently emigrated from Russia."

"That doesn't mean Rubineau was behind it," she counters. "Doesn't even implicate him. It's circumstantial at best."

"Unless I'm mistaken, I recall your saying our friend Rubineau was connected to the Jewish mafia?"

"Yeah, thirty years ago. It doesn't mean a thing now. We need hard evidence, something specific even to question him."

"Real hard," Krauss chirps, his eyes taut with frustration. "Just to access information, let alone act on it, we're up against all kinds of civil liberties laws, the due process clause, reams of tight regulatory and statutory guidelines: the Privacy Act, Freedom of Information Act, Bank Secrecy Act."

"We can't just walk in and rip things apart like they do in your country," Scotto adds sharply.

"That's changing, and you know it," I protest a little too defensively.

"What I think they're trying to say, Mr. Katkov," Banzer says in a conciliatory tone, "is that legal restraints come with the territory, and we make every effort to stay within them. Why? Because: a) Individual rights are what this country is all about. b) We might destroy someone's reputation or livelihood if we mistakenly accuse them of wrongdoing. c) We might lose an otherwise solid prosecution on a legal technicality."

"D) Not necessarily in that order," Krauss quips, eliciting laughter from the others. "See, it's not only cops and robbers. It's cops and lawyers. Our position is: If there isn't a law that says we *can't* do it, we *can*. Their position is: If there isn't a law that says we *can* do it, we *can't*."

That stops me for a moment. It gets to the core of democratic rule. There aren't any positions in a dictatorship, only subservience. "Who usually wins?"

"They do," Banzer replies without rancor. "Our successes are in spite of legal restraints, not because of them. Makes it all the sweeter when we win one."

"Well, you folks may need hard evidence to question Rubineau, but I certainly don't."

Looks dart between the three of them before Scotto challenges, "Run that by us again, will you, Katkov?"

"I'm a journalist writing a story on private investment in Russia, correct?"

"If you say so."

"I'll interview him."

"Interview him?" Scotto echoes. She tears off a page from the printout and hands it to me. It lists over a dozen corporate and residential addresses. "That mean you know where to find him?"

"No, but I'd wager one of your computers does."

"Maybe," she muses with a look to Krauss, who nods and takes the printout across the room to one of the intelligence analysts, a perky young woman with short-cropped hair, who goes to work on her computer terminal.

"You said Rubineau tried to kill you," Scotto goes on. "Why would he give you the time of day?"

"Because I'm a Russian, because I'm Jewish, because he missed."

"You sure it was him?"

"No. I don't have any proof but—"

"If he agrees to see you," Banzer interrupts in a prescient tone, "I'd say chances are pretty good it was him. If he won't, I'd say it was someone else."

"Well, one thing you can be sure of," Scotto says with a dramatic pause. "If it was Rubineau, he won't miss twice."

22

catnapped on the plane, and it's barely noon; but jet lag, the eight-hour time difference, and nicotine deprivation have taken their toll. I'm ready to fall facedown on the nearest horizontal surface. I'd settle for the sofa in Scotto's office, but it's going to take some time to track down Rubineau. She suggests the Ramada Inn a couple of blocks away on Stafford. I jump at the chance to get out of the building.

I'm lighting a cigarette with one hand and holding the lobby door open for Scotto with the other when some media stragglers appear and unleash another barrage of questions. She responds with a terse "No comment," and makes a beeline for the parking lot.

"Come on, Scotto, give us something," one whines.

"Yeah, we're on deadline," another shouts.

Scotto stops and whirls to face them. "Okay, here's the lead: Gay KGB spy in Oval Office."

A cacophony of protests rises.

"No kidding. That visit to Russia in the sixties? Clinton had a homosexual affair and defected."

"Come on, Scotto, stop jerking our chain."

Scotto grins wickedly at a thought and gestures to me. "And this is his Russian boyfriend."

Their eyes brighten.

She whirls and leaves me surrounded by hungry reporters, pencils poised, cassette recorders thrust forward. For the briefest of instants I can see the looks darting between them, see the wheels turning, see the questions in their eyes. Is it? Could it? Possibly be? True? Then they emit a collective groan and drop off, as I hurry to catch up with Scotto.

"Don't ever do that again."

"Why not? Can't you take a joke?"

"Not me. Them. They wanted to believe you."

"That's ridiculous."

"You've a lot to learn about journalists."

"I know enough not to make public statements that might come back to haunt me in a criminal proceeding." A trace of that wicked grin breaks across her face. "I might have to revise my seminar. I mean, you guys are even easier to manipulate than I thought." She opens the Buick's door, then pauses and removes a sheet of yellow paper from beneath the wiper. It looks like an advertising flyer. She's about to discard it when her eyes widen. "The hotel's on hold, Katkov," she announces suddenly.

"On hold? Why?"

"Get in and button it, or you're walking." She slides behind the wheel and tosses the sheet of paper into my lap. Printed neatly are the letters J-P-S-E.

I'm closing the door when she starts the engine, backs out of her parking spot, and rockets into the street. She makes a left into Fairfax and runs the light at the next corner, spraying several pedestrians with slush. A series of lefts and rights follow. After we've gone about a mile or so, Scotto slows at the intersection of Jackson and Pershing and pulls to the curb on the southeast corner.

The car has barely come to a stop when a fragile-looking man bundled in overcoat, scarf, and gloves exits a coffee shop, carrying an attaché case. He approaches swiftly, sees me in the front seat, and stops walking, looking around nervously; then he opens the rear door and gets in next to my luggage. "Who's he?" the man asks warily as Scotto pulls away.

"It's okay. He's a friend."

"This isn't a social call."

"Then let's do business. What do you have for me?"

"Nothing. I haven't been paid."

"We're working on it. You heard about Woody?"

"That's not my problem."

"Hey, show a little compassion, for Chrissakes."

"Try telling that to the sharks sometime."

Scotto pulls to the curb, takes her wallet from her purse, removes a number of bills—I glimpse the numeral fifty—and hands them over the seat. "Here. This'll help hold 'em off."

"Thanks, Gabby," he says, genuinely appreciative. "Thanks a lot."

"Get something for me, okay?"

"For *you*," he replies pointedly, glaring at me. "Nobody else. No friends. Know what I mean?" He gets out and slams the door before Scotto can reply.

"As the man said, 'Who's he?' "

"Woody's informant," Scotto replies as she drives off. "Used to be mine. I guess we're back in business."

"He doesn't seem the type, does he?"

"There is no type. He's a traffic manager for a freight company. Coastline Commercial Carriers. Care to guess who owns 'em?"

"That corporation you linked to the drug cartel."

She nods emphatically.

"Why would he do business with you?"

"To keep the loan sharks from breaking his legs. He's a horseplayer with a knack for picking losers, but his information's prime. We figure the cartel's using the freight company to transport the money. He's helping us figure out where."

"Evidently they're operating right under your noses, aren't they?"

"Money laundering's an international business. You think of a better town to make connections? We're betting the cartel made a few in the diplomatic corps."

"Like Vorontsov?"

"Maybe. The pipeline deal is a good example."

"Your snitch put you onto that?"

"No. Operations traced some suspicious wire transfers. We prefer 'informant,' by the way."

"Whatever. Stalin called them Heroes of the Soviet Union. The people they sent to the gulag had other names for them."

"I'll bet."

"Stalin's favorite was Pavel Morozov. A teenager who set the example that nothing came before the State."

"Wait. Don't tell me. He turned himself in for having a subversive thought."

"He turned his father in—for hoarding grain. The man was executed."

Scotto gasps. "Now he's a snitch."

"Thank you. That's what I like about English. It's so precise. You can always find exactly the right word to describe someone."

"Anyone particular come to mind?" Scotto wonders with a grin as the Ramada Inn comes into view.

"Well, now that you mention it, what did your 'informant' call you before? Crabby, wasn't it? It's quite perfect."

"It was *Gabby*. For Gabriella."

"Ah, Gabby—it means someone who talks too much, doesn't it? That suits you too."

"Thanks a lot," she growls, pulling up to the hotel's entrance. "I think this is your stop."

I laugh, then open the door and start to get out.

"Hold it, Katkov," she says sharply.

I sigh with exhaustion and turn back toward her. "Now what?"

Scotto is squinting curiously at the rearview mirror; then she suddenly twists around and retrieves a white envelope that's been placed on the backseat next to my luggage. It contains a sheet of lined paper filled with neat printing. She reads it, then, voice crackling with energy, asks, "You in, or out?"

Instead of getting out, I close the door quickly, whacking my knee on the cellular phone bracket. "Of what?"

She drives off without replying, races two blocks down Fairfax, and swerves into the FinCEN parking lot. In an eyeblink, she's out of the car and running toward the entrance. I'm right on her heels, trying to imagine what earthshaking information the note contains. We enter the lobby. She charges right past the guard. I get stopped. He checks my visitor's tag and insists I sign in again. By the time I catch up, Scotto's already in the elevator, door closing. I scoot past it. "Come on, come on, dammit," she urges impatiently as it rattles, creaks, and stops at every floor.

"He's been looking for you," Banzer's secretary warns as we dash down the corridor toward his office.

"Shit. The budget meeting." Scotto knocks on the door and blows through it, startling Banzer, Krauss, and several staff members. The conference table is littered with computer print-outs and data. One wall is lined with charts that are titled: Cost Effectiveness. Polar Cap V Support. OCDETF Support. An easel holds a card that lists various programs: Support for Local Agencies. Systems Integration. Criminal Referral Data Base. Massively Parallel Processing. Banzer glances to his watch incriminatingly.

"Sorry, boss," Scotto says, a little out of breath. "Got a break on Shell Game."

"Can it wait till we wrap this up?" Banzer pleads. "We need your input here."

"No, we've got less than an hour to move."

"Geezus. Give me the *TV Guide* version."

"Informant reveals cartel-connected trucking company made hundreds of deliveries to East Baltimore factory last year."

"That's it?"

"The factory went belly-up three years ago."

That gets Banzer's attention. "Give us a few minutes, will you?" he says, dismissing the others. "No kidding, three years ago?"

Scotto nods. "It's gotta be a stash house. Last delivery was in November."

"November?" Banzer echoes, reconsidering. "That's months ago. The cash has probably already been moved."

"There's no record of any outgoing shipments."

"So? Maybe the freight company didn't log it. Maybe the creeps used another shipper." Banzer's voice rises in half octaves. "I mean, they buy and sell companies faster than we can . . ." He splays his hands. "Where in East Baltimore? We have a name? An address?"

"That's what we're buying," Scotto replies with a glance to her watch. "I've got forty-eight minutes."

"You? Since when are you working the streets?"

"Since we lost Woody. It's my old informant. I'm it now, and you know it."

"Okay, but you're not rotating back out. Don't even think about it. How much?"

"Twenty-five."

Banzer winces. He kicks back in his chair and steeples his fingers thoughtfully.

"Twenty-five what?" I whisper to Scotto.

"Thousand bucks."

I stifle a gasp. "For a piece of information?"

She nods, disgusted.

"You realize that's ten times the average Russian's annual income."

"Tell me about it." She glances off to Banzer. "Clock's ticking, Joe."

"Okay, but only if it pays off."

"Not gonna work," Scotto protests. "He's checking out a phone booth on the corner of Wilson and Veitch at two-thirty. If the money's taped beneath the coin shelf, he calls me with the info. If not . . ."

Banzer thinks it over, then nods grudgingly.

Scotto takes a thick report from her shoulder bag. It's titled "FinCEN Budget Proposal." "I made some notes." She drops the report on the table and heads for her office. It's not as impersonal as the rest of the place, though a computer terminal holds center stage amid the Toulouse-Lautrec posters, Victorian sofa, and brass coatrack covered with hats. In minutes, she's into a three-way conference call, and has several other lines on hold—a capability that Yuri, and everyone else in Russia with more than one phone line, would give their firstborn to acquire. I use the time to jot down some notes. It's almost two-twenty when a field agent calls from the phone booth to report the money is in place.

Banzer joins us at two-twenty-five. Two-thirty comes and goes. Two thirty-five, thirty-six, -seven, -eight, -nine. Scotto's pacing. Banzer's staring at his watch. I'm dying for a cigarette. We all jump when the phone finally rings. Scotto answers it, gives us a thumbs-up, and jots down the address; then presents it to Banzer. "Your move, Joe."

He stares at it for a long moment. "Hate to mobilize a task force and come up empty again," he says indecisively, pausing to force air between his teeth. "Do we know who owns the building?"

Scotto groans with frustration. "No, we don't; but we know who owns the freight company."

"Yeah, but regardless of who owns them, they have thousands of perfectly legitimate accounts. How do we know a perfectly legitimate company isn't using this building for perfectly legitimate storage?"

That knocks the wind out of her. "You're right, Joe. I'll find out who owns it."

I follow Scotto to Operations. An intelligence analyst accesses a data base in the Baltimore City Clerk's Office and runs the address. "For openers," he says, scanning data on his monitor, "the building is currently leased by Coppelia Paper Products Limited."

Scotto's brows go up. "Limited? They Canadian?"

"Uh-huh. The checks for city services are drawn on a Montreal bank."

Scotto looks off thoughtfully, then shakes her head with disappointment. "I don't recall ever coming across them."

"I have," I interject, suddenly the center of attention. "*Coppelia* is a rather famous ballet, as I recall."

Scotto rolls her eyes, but the analyst nods. "Saw it at the Kennedy Center a couple of years ago," he reflects. "Sort of a romantic comedy. This fickle dude . . . falls in love with a wax doll. . . ."

"Yes, named Coppelia," I chime in. "Of course, she's not terribly satisfying."

"Turns into a puddle in the heat of passion," he quips. "In the end the fickle fool goes back to his main squeeze, and they live happily ever after."

Scotto's looking at us like we're freaks in a sideshow. Guys didn't stand around talking about ballet in her neighborhood. "Great. Joe's right. They're probably storing tutus in there." She grins at the analyst and adds, "I heard they've really caught on at the Bureau lately."

The analyst rolls his eyes.

"Tutus?" I wonder. "Am I missing something here?"

"He's on loan from the FBI," Scotto explains. "Who owns this building?"

"Never heard of them either," the analyst replies. "Somebody called ITZ Corporation."

I can almost hear Scotto's eyeballs click as they dart to mine. A little smile is already tugging at the corners of my mouth. "That's two for you, Katkov," she exclaims, heading for Banzer's office. The look on his face when she tells him is all the approval she needs. She dashes back to her office and goes to work.

I'm ready to drop. I help myself to a cup of Ops Center coffee and drift over to the perky analyst who's tracking down Rubineau. "How's it going?"

"Nothing yet," she replies with an exasperated sigh. "Called a number of places and just straight out asked for him. They all said he's not in."

"I'd say it sounds as if they've been instructed his whereabouts are nobody's business."

She hands me a computer printout. "I also ran an SEC on him."

"A who?"

"SEC. Securities and Exchange Commission. It's a federal agency. Companies that sell stock to the public have to register and keep certain information on file. That's a schedule of Rubineau's board meetings. It lists cities and dates; but there aren't any for at least a couple of months."

"Months?"

She nods resignedly.

"So that's it?"

"No, I still have a few ideas. Hang in there."

I leave wondering what I'd do if she finds him. Call and ask for an interview? The chances of even getting through to him are slim to none. Show up on his doorstep? He could be anywhere, New York, Los Angeles, even Tel Aviv, for that matter. I'm stumped, and too tired for strategic thought. Scotto's on the phone when I enter her office. I flop on the sofa, intending to make a few more notes. The fabric has an intriguing pattern that seems to vibrate with hypnotic resonance. The last thing I remember is thinking I should get a refill on the coffee.

"Katkov? Katkov, you coming?" Scotto calls out, shaking me awake. "Come on, we're taking that factory down."

I push up onto an elbow and squint at the window. It's dark out, not as dark as the inner workings of my brain at the moment, but dark. I grab my parka and stumble after Scotto, gulping what's left of my coffee. I don't know how long I napped, but in that time she obtained a search warrant, completely outlined the operation, and assembled a task force to carry it out; and now, like she said, that factory's going down.

23

According to Scotto, Baltimore is about an hour's drive from Arlington. She makes it in just over forty minutes, taking Route 95 into the heart of downtown. En route, she explains that the task force includes: the Baltimore Police Department, because it's in their jurisdiction; DEA, because the money comes from illegal drug sales; and Customs, because the probability it would be smuggled out of the country is high.

"What? No FBI?" After my run-in with Naturalization and Immigration I can't resist provoking her.

"Not if I can help it," Scotto replies sardonically.

"Really? Care to be more specific?"

"Nothing I can put my finger on. Somehow, they always manage to find a way to ruin my day."

Baltimore looks like a snow-dusted frenzy of brick and aluminum siding jammed onto narrow streets that radiate from a series of inland bays. The Holabird Avenue off-ramp deposits us in the city's depressed eastern district. Littered with decaying garbage, abandoned vehicles, and the cruel irony of street people huddled in the doorways of boarded-up houses, it reminds me of the area around Leningradsky Station that has become a haven for Moscow's rapidly growing homeless population.

Colgate Street, where the factory is located, has already been cordoned off and secured by members of the Baltimore Police Department. We park next to a boarded-up storefront that will serve as a command post. It's papered with faded movie posters and campaign flyers.

Scotto reaches into the backseat and scoops up her shoulder bag. It's an impressive-looking tour de force of black leather with myriad compartments, pockets, snaps, and zippers that serves as purse and executive briefcase. She removes an automatic pistol, extracts the clip, examines it briefly, then slaps it back into the handgrip and jacks a round into the chamber. Her eyes are dispassionate; her hands nimble and steady. A cool professional conducting a precombat check on her equipment— the equipment that keeps her alive. She digs a shoulder holster out of the trunk and slips the pistol into it, then grabs the black windbreaker with TREASURY AGENT printed across the back and heads inside.

Clusters of uniformed and plainclothes officers in tense conversation are sprinkled throughout the space. Each has a radio. The electronic din is occasionally broken by short bursts of dispatch data. Banzer and ranking officers from the other agencies involved are gathered around a long table, reviewing the floor plan of the factory. A wiry black fellow with a mustache, who seems to be in charge, introduces himself to Scotto as Captain Trask of the Baltimore PD, then glances at me curiously. "He one of yours?" he asks in a thin voice that suits him.

"Our guest," Scotto replies without batting an eye. An investigator from Moscow. He participated in one of my seminars. He's doing field follow-up."

Banzer looks away and suppresses a smile.

Captain Trask nods warily, sweeping his eyes over me as he moves off. Moscow? A Russian?

I lean to Scotto and prompt, "An investigator?"

"Isn't that what journalists do?" she replies in a taut whisper. "Investigate?"

"True."

"Didn't you 'participate' in my seminar?"

"All too briefly."

"And aren't you doing field follow-up?"

"I knew there was a name for it."

"I rest my case."

GREG DINALLO

Trask takes charge of a makeshift communications console—another long table covered with portable radios—to check the position and readiness of field units. Each agency has its own frequency; and the sleek, high-tech instruments are crudely identified by pieces of tape on which Customs, DEA, BPD, and FinCEN have been scribbled in black marker. Trask thumbs the transmit button on the one labeled CUSTOMS, but a DEA officer responds. The DEA radio raises the BPD. The mix-up turns the simple procedure into a comedy skit that rivals the Moscow phone system with its separate phone for each line. "Okay, let's do it," Trask finally calls out, laughing good-naturedly. "Let's do it before I become the first black man in history to turn red."

A group of us move back outside to a vantage point from where we can see the factory. The single-story brick building has a vaulted roof and barred windows through which neither light nor movement of occupants are visible. There's no sign; nothing that identifies it as the home of Coppelia Paper Products Ltd.

Members of various law enforcement groups move in and surround it. Some carry sidearms, others riot guns; all wear black windbreakers identifying the respective agency. Each entrance is hit by brilliant spotlights that turn night into day.

"This is the police," Trask announces through a bullhorn that emboldens his squeaky voice. "You're surrounded. Come out in single file, hands on top of your heads."

The windows remain dark. The doors closed. The interior free of movement. No one responds. The announcement is repeated several times before members of a SWAT team, cloaked in black jump suits and body armor, advance on the main entrance. They're carrying what looks like the cannon that inspired Tchaikovsky's 1812 Overture. It's a battering ram. The four officers grasp handles on each side and swing it back and forth, building up momentum. The tremendous impact smashes the door to bits.

The SWAT team moves swiftly into the building. Tension turns to anticipation as they secure it. Scotto is the first one through the door when we get word the factory is unoccupied. Blue fluorescents are flickering to life as Banzer and other agents follow. We're soon stopped in our tracks by a devastating sight. The huge space is empty. Not a stick of furniture, not a box, packing crate, or piece of money-handling equipment is to be found within the painted brick walls, let alone huge amounts of illicit cash waiting to be counted, packaged, and shipped.

Scotto's shoulders sag. She lets out a long breath and swings an apprehensive look to Banzer, who shrugs resignedly.

A routine search of offices and storage spaces gets underway. Scotto opens a door. A staircase leads down into the basement. She finds a light switch and throws it. Nothing happens. We begin our descent. The beam from her flashlight cuts through musty darkness. It reveals nothing but blank walls and a corridor lined with storage rooms. The first few we examine turn out to be empty. We've just entered another when what sounds like the creak of a hinge comes from the corridor behind us.

Scotto freezes and crosses back toward the door. "Scotto, Treasury," she announces. "Who's that?"

There's no reply.

She shuts off the flashlight, slips the pistol from its holster, and signals me to stay put, then eases back into the darkened corridor. Despite the tightening in my gut, I disobey orders and advance to the doorway. My eyes find her faint outline pressed against the opposite wall. Tense, vigilant, she's inching down the corridor toward a door that appears to be slightly ajar. A rustling sound comes from behind her. I flinch. Scotto whirls and turns on the flashlight, aiming the beam and her pistol at the sound. A rat the size of a small dog darts from behind a door. It scurries across the floor right in front of her into a storage room on the other side of the corridor. Scotto shudders, then holsters the pistol, relieved.

We take a moment to let our heart rates return to normal, then resume checking out the storage rooms. The circle of light from Scotto's flashlight moves across something in the distance that glimmers. She stops walking and shifts the beam back and forth over it several times, then advances.

"What's that?" I ask.

She uses the flashlight to reveal the word JANITOR stenciled across a door.

"Oh, I thought you'd found something."

"I did."

"A janitor's closet?"

"No, that." She shifts the beam to an impressive dead bolt

and lock assembly. "Must be some pretty high-priced mops in there, huh?"

Scotto radios for assistance. She's barely clicked off when agents come clambering down the stairs with several banks of work lights. Banzer, Trask, and other command personnel follow, along with the battering ram crew, which makes quick work of the door.

A moldy stench rushes from the space. Hurried scraping noises and what sounds like the intermittent bloops of dripping water follow. We move through the door onto an underground loading dock. There below, in the glare of the work lights—stacked on pallets, on tables, on the floor, stacked almost to the ceiling beneath rusted century-old pipes from which water drips—are bundles of cash, bags of cash, boxes of cash, crates of cash, an unimaginable amount of wet, blackened, crumbling, rotting cash standing in two feet of water with rats crawling all over it. They freeze momentarily in the sudden blast of light, then scurry off with their booty.

We stand in stunned silence, delighted, relieved, and chilled by the squealing, panicking mass of pinkish gray rodents.

"God, how much you think is there?" I finally ask.

Banzer takes a moment to calculate. "Off the top of my head, I'd say we're looking at hundreds of millions."

Scotto grins broadly and nods. "This has gotta be four, maybe five times the size of that hundred we bagged in Detroit last year."

"Five hundred million?" I hear myself blurt in total disbelief. "That's half a billion dollars. They just abandoned it?"

"Sure as hell looks that way," Trask squeaks.

"Probably decided it was too much trouble to mess with it," Scotto deduces. "What does that tell you?"

"It's pocket change."

She and Banzer exchange looks and nod.

"Is this what you needed to nail Rubineau?"

"Nail him?" Banzer challenges. "For what? Leasing his property to people of questionable character? He's not responsible for what they store here." Banzer pauses, savoring a thought, then looks over at Scotto and smiles. "Not yet, anyway."

24

It's after nine by the time I check into the Ramada Inn, a soaring knife-edged tower in Arlington's business corridor. "Smoking or nonsmoking floor?" the clerk asks, leaving little doubt he disapproves of my choice. My color-coordinated room is lavish by Russian standards, with sitting area, writing desk, and a bathroom Muscovites can only dream of.

Shevchenko was right, I do live for that adrenaline rush. Tired as I am, I'm banging away on my typewriter. It takes about an hour to rough out a few page of notes and down a pot of room-service coffee. Vodka would've been a better choice. Between the caffeine and change in time zones, my brain refuses to shut down. I briefly consider ordering a Stoli sedative, but grab my travel guide instead and take the elevator to the Metro station beneath the hotel.

Twenty minutes later, I'm at the Foggy Bottom /GWU Station in downtown Washington. A brisk wind stings my face as I walk south past stolid government buildings toward what my guidebook calls the Mall. Beyond an expanse of snow-dusted lawn, a broad marble staircase rises to a terrace where a Greek temple bathes in the warm glow of halogens. I enter between towering columns and proceed to the base of an imposing statue.

Captured within the cold granite is the soul of a man who freed slaves, presided over a civil war, and saved a nation. Shoulders stooped, head bent slightly forward, face deeply lined, eyes distant and burdened with the weight of monumental responsibility, he seems utterly tired and alone; as if while passing by on this frigid night, he saw an empty chair and sat for a moment to catch his breath.

I'm lost in my thoughts when footsteps break the silence and a long shadow comes from behind me.

"Hey, buddy, you okay?" a husky voice asks.

I turn to find myself face-to-face with a police officer, his concerned eyes aglow against jet black skin. "I'm fine, thanks. How about you?"

"Freezin' my butt off. Couldn't imagine anybody in their right mind be out here tonight."

"Nor could I."

He laughs good-naturedly. "Yeah, but I ain't got a choice. Gonna finish this shift and get me home."

"You live in Washington?"

"Used to. Kind of miss it, but we had to get the kids out of the city. Went into hock to buy us a little place out in Suitland."

"Good for you. 'Property is the fruit of labor. . . . That some should be rich, shows that others may become rich, and hence is just encouragement to industry and enterprise.' You know who said that?"

He frowns as if I'm speaking Russian.

"Him," I say, pointing to the statue of Lincoln.

"Yeah? Never heard that one." He gestures to a tablet where the Gettysburg Address has been engraved. "I kind of like the one about all men being created equal, myself."

"I rather like that one too. Though the idea is just starting to catch on where I come from."

"Where's that, South Africa?"

"Russia."

"No kidding? Thought I picked up a little accent there, but that wasn't it. Well," he says philosophically as he starts to move off, breath trailing behind him, "don't count on it happening overnight."

I linger for a few moments, shaken by his incisive wisdom, then return to the hotel. A red light on the phone is blinking when I enter the room. The message is from the perky computer-tech at FinCEN's Ops Center.

"Got a fix on Rubineau for you, Mr. Katkov," she reports when I return the call. "Picked him up in an FAA data base. Turns out he's got a corporate jet. A Gulfstream. Last flight plan listed LaGuardia as its destination, which means the bird's still cooling its jets in New York."

"Do we know for certain he was on the flight?"

"Uh-huh. First name on the manifest. He has an apartment in the city. The address is . . ." She pauses. I can hear the click of her keyboard. "Four thirty-five Sutton Place South. Odds are that's where he's bunking, but I wasn't able to verify."

"Perfectly fine odds, if you ask me. Thanks."

After a few hours of fitful sleep, a steaming shower, and change of clothes, I take the Metro to National Airport—one stop south of the Pentagon, according to my guide—and board the morning's first shuttle to LaGuardia. Like Immigration, like FinCEN, like the hotel, like the terminal and boarding lounge—the 737's cabin is plastered with NO SMOKING signs. America is well on its way to becoming a nation of disgustingly healthy neurotics.

In less than an hour, the famous skyline appears off the right side of the aircraft. The dense mass of stone, steel, and glass is a stunning sight in the early morning darkness, as is the illuminated antenna that soars from its midst.

"That's the Empire State Building, isn't it?!" I exclaim to the man seated next to me.

He shifts his eyes from his newspaper and nods indifferently as the plane banks and makes a big looping turn north of Manhattan, coming in over an expanse of water to a smooth landing.

A dispatcher greets me as I exit the terminal and ushers me into the backseat of a taxi. There's no need for Marlboros here, no need to negotiate the price; though, as we get into traffic, the driver proves he could go fender-to-fender with Moscow's best. We're soon crossing a spired bridge strung with necklaces of light. The stately span takes us into New York's dark, empty streets, where steam, rising from manhole covers, drifts in an eerie haze. I'm still working on my nicotine fix, lighting one cigarette from another, when the taxi passes a sign that reads

SUTTON PLACE and turns into the gated grounds of a residential highrise.

A uniformed doorman escorts me into the lobby and deposits me at the security desk, where a guard sits staring at a
bank of television monitors. I give him my name and tell him
I want to see Rubineau. He studies the pages of a register,
then slowly shakes his head no. "Sorry, pal. Mr. Rubineau
always notifies us when he's expecting someone. There's no
Kirov, here."

"It's *Kat-kov*. He isn't expecting me, but I—"

"Forget it. He ain't gonna see you."

"I was about to say he might, if he knew I was here. Tell
him it's Nikolai *Katkov,* from Moscow."

"Moscow?" he echoes, warily. "Don't sound to me like you're
from Moscow, buddy."

"Oh? Have you ever been there?"

"Look, I don't care if you're from Santa's workshop, okay?
He ain't gonna see you."

"Well, maybe he 'ain't.' But knowing Mr. Rubineau, I'd let
him make the decision, if I were you."

He mulls it over, then calls Rubineau's apartment and relays
the information. From his tone, it's obvious he's talking to one
of Rubineau's flunkies, who puts him on hold. He bristles impatiently awaiting the reply, then emits a cynical grunt. "Okay,
Kirov. You're on." He shows me to an elevator and waits until
it arrives.

The door opens, revealing a broad-shouldered young man in
a business suit. I stand aside to let him out, but he gestures I
enter instead. As the elevator starts to rise, he turns me to the
wall and frisks me without a word. My pulse quickens. Grave
warnings begin ringing in my ears: "If he agrees to see you—it
was him. If it *was* him—he won't miss twice."

The elevator leaves us in the foyer of a penthouse apartment.
A huge welded-bronze sculpture resembling a menorah covers
the entry wall. Floor-to-ceiling windows frame a panorama of
twinkling lights that extends to the horizon. A glass-enclosed
staircase sweeps to upper levels. Pristine white walls display
priceless art. I'm gawking at a violent explosion of paint, signed
de Kooning, when a commanding voice calls out, "Mr. Katkov,
welcome to New York!"

Tanned, sartorially splendid in a finely cut dark blue suit, striped shirt, and boldly patterned tie, Michael Rubineau seems taller than when I first saw him at the Paradise Club; he bounds down the steps with the vitality and bearing of a man half his age.

"Nice of you to drop by," he exclaims with disarming sincerity as we shake hands. There's a combative sparkle in his eyes and traces of a streetwise cunning beneath the polished veneer. He dismisses my elevator escort with a nod, then leads the way to an intimate dining room. The table is set with elegant silver, china, and glassware for two, not to mention crystal ashtrays. "Why don't we have some breakfast and get to know each other?"

"Sure," I reply warily, as we take our seats. "It's only fair to warn you that people know I'm here. Federal law enforcement people."

"Good. I was counting on it."

"You were?" I say, somewhat astonished. Other than Yuri, only Shevchenko knows about FinCEN. Have I been wrong about him? Is the senior investigator corrupt? Are he and Rubineau somehow connected?

"Really, Mr. Katkov," Rubineau replies, somewhat condescendingly. "I don't have to tell you about the power of the press." He places a copy of *The New York Times* on the table next to me. At the bottom of the front page—beneath a caption that reads: Agent's Death Related to Money-Laundering Investigation—is a picture of Scotto in the FinCEN parking lot. She and the puzzled-looking man next to her are surrounded by reporters. The man has been circled in yellow marker. The man is me. "Have some orange juice," Rubineau urges with a wiley smile. "It's freshly squeezed."

A uniformed maid fills our goblets, then serves blintzes, smoked salmon, and coffee from a cart.

"I'm rather confused, Mr. Rubineau," I say when she's finished. "I'm not identified; we've never met; how did you know that was me?"

"I make a habit of getting to know everyone who can hurt me or help me," he explains, stirring his coffee thoughtfully. "You straddle the line, Katkov. I'm still making up my mind about you."

"An assassin in Moscow gave me the impression you already had."

"Assassin?" he echoes, offended, his eyes narrowing to angry slits. "Where the hell did you get that idea? Mental firepower is my weapon of choice. I select my targets carefully, and I rarely miss."

"I meant no offense, but the fellow in the elevator wasn't frisking me for my IQ."

Rubineau stabs a finger at the newspaper. "Kids with assault rifles. *Kids.* The world is full of violence; the more you achieve, the more exposed to it you become. Athletes, movie stars, entrepreneurs—we're all in the same boat. Unfortunately, guns and bodyguards have become as essential to the conduct of business as women and computers."

I'm thinking it'd be a perfect epitaph when he pushes back in his chair thoughtfully, then crosses to a fireplace. A collection of family snapshots is arranged on the mantel: adoring wife, comely daughter—as infant, college graduate, and bride— giggling grandchildren, proud parents, and the usual assortment of relatives. He selects one and hands it to me. "You know who that is?"

A man in his late sixties holding a shaggy dog in his arms stares at me from within the sleek silver frame. His close-set eyes, long nose, and wide smile give him the bemused expression of a camel.

"Your father?"

Rubineau shakes his head no and smiles. "My rabbi. Eighty years ago when he came to this country his name was Mei'er Suchowljansky."

"Oh," I exclaim, as it dawns on me. "Meyer Lansky, isn't it?"

Rubineau brightens. "He was a great man, an honest man in a dishonest business, and a genius with numbers. Our families came from the same town in Russia."

"Grodno, near the Polish border."

Rubineau's eyes flicker and burn with curiosity.

"I'm a journalist, Mr. Rubineau—an investigative journalist."

"We'll come back to that," he growls impatiently, returning Lansky's picture to its place of honor. "I was about to say Meyer knew all there was to know about business, and he taught it to me. Even the FBI said he could've run General Motors."

"From what I hear, he probably should have."

"He *would* have, had he chosen a different path. . . ." He

takes his seat and, expression darkening, adds, "And been born a gentile."

"Is that why he changed his name?"

"That's two insults, Katkov. Meyer was proud of being a Jew—and so am I. He broke up Nazi meetings in New York during the thirties, and after the war, when Israel was fighting for its existence, he stopped shipments of guns to the Arabs. It killed him when the Israelis denied him residency."

"I imagine they aren't interested in people who don't play by the rules."

"Play by the rules?!" he explodes indignantly. "You know where Israel would be today if they played by the rules? Look, the point is, he advised me not to make the same mistake; and I didn't. I've played by 'em from day one."

"Was that before or after you were disbarred?"

His eyes flare with anger. "That was a travesty. Meyer had a falling-out with some business partners. Italians. They fed me to the sharks to get at him." His eyes drift to the snapshots on the mantel. "For the sake of my family, I *modified* my name; but I was playing by the rules then. And I still am."

His anguish seems to be genuine, but recent events demand it be challenged. "Very well. Then what's half a billion dollars in drug money doing in the basement of one of your buildings?"

"One of my buildings?"

"Precisely. A factory in East Baltimore."

"An up-and-coming town. Prime area for urban renewal. I've acquired a lot of real estate there. I can't rattle off every piece I own."

"I'd wager Mr. Lansky could."

"That's strike three, Katkov. You know baseball?"

"I assume you *can* rattle off the names of your companies. The building in question is owned by ITZ Corporation. Ring a bell?"

"You're a cocky little fuck, aren't you?"

"A necessary evil in my line of work. Is ITZ your company or not?"

"Of course it is. I put it together to do business in Russia. Believe what you like, but my parents were persecuted in Russia just like Meyer's, and yours, I imagine. They left so their children could have a better life. Now that I have it, I'm still interested in making money, but I'm more interested in *how*. In other words, I'm going to do everything in my power to see the country of my birth succeed as a democracy."

"That makes two of us, Mr. Rubinowitz."

He leans back in his chair and smiles wistfully. "There's one difference, Katkov—your people stuck it out. You've got good genes. You've got guts."

"I also had no choice. Now, you didn't agree to see me to massage my ego. What are you after?"

"An even shake. For me and for your country." He pauses briefly, reconsidering. "Make that *our* country. You realize the enormity of what's going on there? It took Margaret Thatcher twelve years to privatize fifteen percent of the British economy. Yeltsin's trying to do it all overnight. He doesn't stand a chance without private investment; but it's hard for investors to think long-term with all this corruption going on. It hasn't scared off Mike Rubinowitz, because it's personal with me, emotional, but it's already scaring the shit out of other guys. Banks that did business with the Soviet Union for years are backing away from Russia now. A lot of them won't even touch loans for grain purchases anymore."

"Yes, unfortunately, but what does that have to do with me?"

"With your line of work. I said we'd get back to it. You've written some interesting things lately."

"Nothing that was published here, or in English, as far as I know."

"You know *The New Yorker?*" He sees my reaction and quickly adds, "No, no, not in there. Great magazine, though, especially if you've got nothing to do, and all week to do it. Anyway, they had a cartoon once of an author cornered by some people at a party. The caption was: 'Loved your book. Heard all about it.' " Rubineau laughs to himself, savoring the irony.

"So, someone happened to mention my stories?"

"It was a little more calculated than that. The point is you can do a lot of damage by making a big deal out of this so-called scandal."

"Me? I'm quite flattered, Mr. Rubineau. But what about the thousands of other newspapers and magazines?"

"You're on the inside, Katkov. You're going to be first. Your story's going to set the tone, and they're going to follow. The

Russian economy—what there is of it—is like a house of cards. One push, one little bit of negative publicity, could bring it down; and that would have a devastating impact on what I'm trying to do."

"Frequenting casinos run by mobsters might have the same effect."

"You mean Barkhin?"

"Precisely."

"You're right. When it comes to hiring hit men, I'd be pointing a finger at him if I were you."

"The thought's crossed my mind. But you still haven't answered my question."

"Moscow's movers and shakers think his club is hot, which makes it a good place to make connections. Just because I do business with him doesn't mean I like him. He's smart and selfish, building his own little empire. Believe me, Arkady Barkhin doesn't give a fuck for Russia."

"That's not surprising. Russia didn't give a fuck for him, either. Nor for a lot of people. It's every man for himself now, you know that. Communism fell and the *apparatchiks* became capitalists overnight. Instead of managing State industries for the Party, they're selling them off as if they were their own." I pause, unable to suppress a grin before adding, "Take our distribution system, for example . . ."

"Hey, I could've 'taken' it; but I decided to pay a fair price instead. Keep your fingers crossed the deal works out, because what's there now is a joke. I mean, what's the point of selling industries to private investors who can run them more efficiently, if they can't get raw materials to their factories? If they can't get their products to market? I'm going to make sure they can. The bottom line is, an integrated distribution system is critical to economic growth. An efficient one can accelerate it; one that isn't can bring it to a screeching halt."

"Yes, as I recall, your Teamsters Union figured that out a long time ago."

"You can question their tactics, but not their performance. You realize, only twenty-five percent of your crops get to market? The rest is either stolen, damaged in transit, or rotting in storage. Profits vanish, prices skyrocket, inflation goes through the roof—twenty-five hundred percent last year—and the public gets screwed. Your shelves aren't empty because you don't produce, but because you don't distribute."

"And because any hustler can get much more selling his product outside the country than in."

"Look, there's nothing wrong with, say, buying oil for a buck a barrel in Odessa and selling it in London for twenty, Katkov. That's what free enterprise is all about. You people better learn it, and learn it fast. That's what brings in capital; and God knows, Russia needs all the hard currency it can get."

"Quite true, but we're *not* getting it. The hustlers are taking more out than they're bringing in."

"Not this hustler. I'm putting in plenty. I'm an ally, not an enemy, and you can tell your friends at FinCEN that all my deals are bona fide."

"They'll find out on their own, believe me."

"Wasting their time. You and I care about our country. These law enforcement types—Russians, Americans—they get their kicks breaking people, regardless of who it hurts." He angrily shoves back his chair and stands. "They're cracking down too hard. Killing entrepreneurial spirit. You have to be a gambler, a con man, a genius, and lucky as hell to get a business off the ground. Believe me, Katkov, it takes steel balls the size of cantaloupes to make something from nothing. . . ." He pauses, his silver mane glowing in the spotlights as he locks his eyes onto mine and adds, "And that's what all those hustlers you're out to destroy are trying to do."

"I'm not out to destroy anyone. Crime and corruption are running rampant in Russia. We—"

"So?!" he interrupts heatedly. "You think it was any different here a hundred years ago?! This country was a hotbed of greed, bribery, and political corruption that makes you guys look like fund-raisers for the B'nai B'rith. It was run by ruthless men with vision and chutzpah who bent the rules and took it to the cleaners: Vanderbilt, Carnegie, Rockefeller, Morgan. Sure, they were robber barons. Did they have a positive impact? Did they build a democratic nation with a powerful free-market economy? Bet your ass they did; and they're still at it. Look at Milken, for God's sake." Rubineau gestures angrily and groans in disgust. "The guy creates a new industry; a financial market that didn't exist until he singlehandedly cooked up the idea of junk bonds; a market that's still making billions for people, *billions*. And what's he get? Some ex-Playboy bunny—who I'm loathed to admit went to Harvard—puts on a black robe and locks him up. If these people don't back off, they're going to snuff out any chance Russia has to develop a free-market economy. Remember, you heard it here first."

Rubineau made the speech, but I'm the one who's winded. I'm far more moved by his passion than his argument, though I can't deny there's a certain twisted logic to it.

He crosses to the window and looks out across the city. "Come here, Katkov," he orders in Russian, waving me over. His tone is softer, familiar, as if he's going to confide something in me. I'm caught off guard by the sudden shift in languages. I'd no idea he spoke Russian, and it takes me a moment to react. "See that?" he prompts, still speaking Russian. He gestures to the shimmering ribbon of liquid copper that splits the landscape. "The East River. That's what most people see, anyway. Not me. I see the Volga. Interesting thing about this planet. The water's all connected. Know what I mean?"

"Yes, yes, I think I do," I reply in Russian, impressed with his accent and fluency.

"Good. I'm glad we understand each other." He breaks into a satisfied smile, taking his measure of me, then shifts back to English. "Now, you didn't come here to listen to me pontificate. What are you after?"

"The truth."

"It's often a matter of opinion. The truth about what?"

"The name Vorontsov ring a bell?"

"It might."

"Really, Mr. Rubineau. You were doing business with him. You know what happened. ITZ documents were found in his briefcase. They put you square in the middle of the very scandal you're asking me to ignore."

"I don't like what you're implying."

"Prove me wrong."

"In my experience, Vorontsov was a fine man and dedicated public servant. I enjoyed doing business with him."

"Legitimate business?"

"That's right. Why? What's it to you?"

"Nothing. It's of no concern to me. To his daughter. She thinks his reputation's been smeared rather unjustly."

"No thanks to guys like you."

"I assume you're referring to journalists. I'm afraid we don't make up news, we report it."

"We? Look, Katkov, I'm not interested in we. I'm interested in you." He smiles thinly, glances again to the family snapshots, then locks his eyes onto mine and, in a threatening whisper, warns, "I'd sure hate for my daughter to find herself in the same boat as Vorontsov's."

25

My return flight to Washington arrives well past noon. I loosen up Mrs. Churkin's purse strings and take a cab back to FinCEN. The driver makes a right into Pollard and drops me off in the parking lot. I'm crossing to the main entrance, savoring a cigarette, when I notice a yellow sheet of paper fluttering against the windshield of Scotto's car. Printed in the same neat hand is another four-letter code for where her informant will meet her.

The security guard in the lobby recognizes me, but has his orders: All visitors must sign in and out, wear badges, and be accompanied by a staff member inside the building. He's about to call Scotto when Tom Krauss returns from lunch and escorts me.

I can see Scotto through the doorway as I approach her office. She's on the phone, pacing back and forth in front of the windows as she talks. I lean against the doorjamb, rather taken by her animated gestures and eye-catching dress. The blue-purple wool sets off her complexion and hugs her generous figure alluringly. It's a marked change from her usual jacket, slacks, and blouse. Furthermore, there's a cheerful, almost bubbly air about her; and though the bureaucratic nitty-gritty of getting search warrants seems to be the topic of conversation, she's twisting a curl of hair around her finger like a schoolgirl. A few seconds go by before she senses my presence and waves me in. Her demeanor is immediately more businesslike and self-conscious.

I stand inside the doorway, staring at her until I have her attention, then hold up her informant's message.

Scotto's eyes widen in reaction. She reaches across the desk and snatches it from my hand. "Hey, listen, something's come up. I gotta drop off." She finishes the call, then changes focus and fetches her coat. "It was on my car?"

"The windshield. Like the last one."

"Thanks." She stabs an arm into a sleeve. "I thought you'd be in here first thing. I tried the hotel a couple of times. Where you been?"

"Sight-seeing," I reply with a little smile.

"Sight-seeing . . ." she echoes flatly.

"Yes, I started at the Lincoln Memorial and worked my way to the Empire State Building."

"Hell of a walk in this weather." She scoops up her shoulder bag and heads for the door.

"I caught an early shuttle out of National."

Scotto stops in her tracks, sensing it wasn't a joke, and questions me with a look.

"You know the little computer-tech in Ops who was tracking down Rubineau?"

"Jennifer."

"Jennifer. She found him in New York. He and I had a rather lovely breakfast."

"You're putting me on."

I shake my head no and grin smugly.

"Geezus." She takes a step in one direction, then the other, torn between Rubineau and her informant. "What'd he have to say?"

"Quite a lot, actually. For openers, you'd be interested to know he thinks cops are basically ruthless."

She makes a face, pretending she's crushed. "Well, I'm sure you put up a spirited defense." The phone twitters. "Damn. This always happens when I'm trying to get out of here." She spins back to her desk and answers it. "Scotto. . . . Yeah, shoot. . . . Uh-huh. . . . uh-huh. . . . You're sure?" She groans, clearly unhappy at the reply. "Okay, thanks." She hangs up slowly, and frowns. "That was Ops. They finished running those ITZ deals. They're legit. All of 'em."

"That's what Rubineau told me. He said you were wasting your time."

"Guess so." She leads the way from the office and hurries down the corridor toward the elevator. "What else he have to say?"

"Well, after a lecture on the sorry state of the Russian economy, he requested I refrain from doing anything that might hurt our country."

"*Our* country?"

"Yeah, Russia. It seems Mr. Rubineau's developed a late-in-life passion for the land of his birth."

"What a pile of crap."

"No, really. He has a rather compelling sincerity. I found him quite credible."

"Well," she sighs, nervously pressing the elevator button, "where the hell do we go from here?"

I sweep my eyes over her and smile. "Someplace quite special, I imagine."

"Katkov," she coos, coming closer to blushing than I ever thought possible. "How nice of you to notice. Nothing like scoring a basement full of cash to warm an agent's heart. I felt so good when I got home last night, I called my husband. To make a long story short, he's got a meeting tomorrow somewhere near Hilton Head. That's a resort in South Carolina. Right on the coast. You'd love it. Anyway, he said he was thinking of taking a couple of days off . . . one thing led to another . . . and I'm flying down with him tonight."

"A couple of days? I just got here."

"I know. I thought about that. But if Marty's thinking we can put our lives back together, I have to give it a try. Besides, think of how much more sightseeing you can get in." The elevator door opens. The tip of her forefinger stabs me square in the chest and keeps me from following. "Far as you go," she says, hurrying off to meet with her informant.

"No friends," I call out as the door rolls closed. "I remember." I stand there for a long moment, thinking about Vera and wondering if there's any chance to put *our* lives back together. It's been a little more than a month since we broke up, but it seems like years. I start drifting back toward Scotto's office, feeling a little empty, then detour to Ops to get a cup of coffee. Jennifer, my favorite computer-tech, is putting in time at a copying machine.

"I want to thank you for tracking down Rubineau for me."

"My pleasure, Mr. Katkov. Put me onto something I wouldn't've found otherwise." She hands me one of the copies she's made. It's the flight plan that Rubineau's crew filed with the FAA. "The D-sched covers everyone who's working on Shell Game."

"The D-what?"

"Distribution schedule, sorry. We sort of have our own language around here."

"Oh. How come? I mean the D-sched."

Jennifer smiles, then takes another copy of the flight plan, fetches a yellow Hi-Liter and draws it across: José Martí International, Havana. "That flight to New York had a Cuban launch pad. You got lucky. Wouldn't even be in our data base if it wasn't an I-F." She reddens slightly and adds, "Sorry, that means international flight."

"Well, everyone gets lucky once in a while. Even me. What's so special about Cuba?"

"It's off-limits to Americans. No diplomatic ties. No travel. No trade."

"Ah, yes, that's right," I exclaim, reflecting on the Paradise Club and Arkady Barkhin's comment about making contacts in Cuba. "So what do you think Rubineau was doing down there?"

"Good question. I was about to ask you. The flight had FAA clearance. That's the—"

"Federal Aviation Administration," I say, beating her to it. "Am I right?"

"Right. It's pretty unusual to get it. Maybe we can find out why Rubineau did." She returns to her work station, brings up a master list of data bases on her computer, and selects STATE DEPT. A column of subheadings appears. She picks the one she wants and initiates a search.

A half hour later, she's still at it when I spot Scotto coming through the door. "Glad you're back. We may have something important here."

"That makes two of us," Scotto says, preoccupied. She tears

a page from a small notepad and hands it to Jennifer. "Run that for me, will you? ASAP. I want to know who owns it."

Jennifer goes to work on her keyboard and soon announces, "Mid-Atlantic Trucking Depot—purchased two months ago by—ITZ Corporation."

Scotto smiles to herself, then swings a look in my direction. "Rubineau didn't happen to mention anything about buying a trucking depot, did he?" she wonders, her voice dripping with sarcasm.

"Quite a few, as a matter of fact—not to mention several airlines and a railroad or two—in Russia, of course."

"This one's in Maryland. Hagerstown."

"Well, as long as we're on Rubineau . . ." I flick the copy of the flight plan onto the desk. "What would you say if I told you he made a trip to Havana recently."

"Havana?" she repeats, somewhat astonished. "How the hell'd he manage that?"

"Good question. I doubt he was on holiday. Jennifer's working on it."

"No, Jennifer just struck out," Jennifer says in her perky way. She points to her monitor, where the phrase ACCESS DENIED pulses tauntingly. "I tried State first, then Commerce. Every time I cross-reference Cuba with Rubineau or his companies, that's what happens. It's really weird."

"Sounds like somebody's got something to hide. Good work. Keep trying." Scotto heads for the door.

I hurry down the corridor after her. "What's all this about a trucking depot?"

"According to my informant, one of their shipping containers, number 95824 to be precise, might be of interest to us."

"I imagine they run hundreds of them in and out of a place like that every day. Why that one?"

"My guy says it's filled with cash—all hundreds."

"He knows that for a fact?"

"Hey, that basement in East Baltimore gives him a lot of credibility. We're talking in the neighborhood of a couple of billion dollars."

"A couple of billion?" I exclaim, flabbergasted.

"Yeah, it rolls at midnight."

"Tonight?"

"Uh-huh."

"Your 'guy' isn't much for lead time, is he?"

"Tell me about it." She darts around a corner, almost colliding with another employee, and makes a beeline for the director's office.

"Way to go, Scotto," Banzer enthuses after she's briefed him. "I've got just one question."

"ITZ Corporation," Scotto cracks, beating him to it. "I already checked."

"You withheld that on purpose, didn't you?"

"Well, I knew you'd ask, Joe," she replies mischievously.

"Okay, smartass. It may come as news to you, but Hagerstown just happens to be one of the hubs of this country's trucking industry. That container could be going just about anywhere."

"Try Atlanta," Scotto replies.

Banzer's expression softens.

"It's consigned to a recycling plant west of downtown, near Fulton County Airport.

"Who's the shipper?"

"Coppelia Paper Products."

Banzer's brows go up. "I'll bet."

"According to the bill of lading"—Scotto pauses and cackles insidiously at what she's about to say—"the cargo is seven tons of scrap paper."

"Makes sense. Covers the cargo and weight. It wouldn't wash if they were into down-filled comforters, would it? Whatever, we're going to recycle it for 'em," Banzer says with a wiley smile; then his eyes narrow. "I want both ends of this, Gabby. That means we set up surveillance at the trucking depot and the recycling plant, and tail the rig with the container between 'em."

"You going to ramrod the Atlanta end?"

"Not if our budget's ever going to get approved. Krauss can fly ahead and handle it out of the local SAC office down there."

"SAC?"

"Special Agent in Charge," Scotto replies. She crosses to a wall-sized road map of the United States. "Looks like I-81 is the main drag south out of Hagerstown: six, maybe seven hundred miles; four states—Maryland, Virginia, Tennessee, Georgia; and umpteen intersecting highways and legal jurisdictions before we get to Atlanta."

"Who do you want to use?" Banzer prompts.

"It's an interstate tail—so no locals, right?"

"Right. Last thing we need is a parade of cruisers at every county line. And no choppers. The driver'd have to be brain-dead not to spot a bird sitting on his shoulder for seven hundred miles."

"Limited range anyway. I figure four units with a mix of Customs and DEA oughta do it. That way we can take turns—"

"*They,* Gabby," Banzer interrupts. "Not we. They. The only thing you're licensed to drive is a desk."

"I'm the agent-in-charge, Joe."

"You're the Deputy Director of FinCEN, dammit."

"Not if you stop me from doing this. Come on. You can get by without me for a couple of days. Make believe I'm off pontificating at some seminar. It's my informant, Joe. That makes me the AIC."

"It's *Woody's* informant; besides, I thought you were taking a couple of days off to go away with Marty."

"Indeed," I reply unthinkingly. "As did I."

Scotto burns me with a look that condemns my disloyalty; then she shifts her lasers back to Banzer. "You ever lose a partner, Joe?"

"Yeah. He keeled over in the middle of a poker game. Massive heart attack. Nothing I could do about it. Neither can you."

"I can do this, Joe."

"Gabby, you're going to lose your husband next. Go away with Marty. Have a good time; put your life back together."

"Joe, I've had a pain in my gut ever since you called me in here and told me about Woody."

"You think I haven't?"

"Don't keep me from this, Joe. Please."

Banzer sighs and glances to me. "You know what's going on here, Katkov? She thinks the more she calls me Joe, the harder it is for me to say no." He pauses and sighs defeatedly. "She's right. Okay, Gabby," he says, his tone sharpening. "But DEA and Customs are on point; you lay back and coordinate. Agreed?"

"Yeah, I guess that'd work."

"Agreed?"

"Agreed."

"And get someone to ride shotgun with you."

"Done."

"Who? What? What do you mean done?"

"Don't ask."

Banzer's eyes widen with understanding and dart to mine. "No."

"I made a deal, Joe."

"No."

"It's a perfect cover. A couple of Russian tourists getting their first taste of—"

"You're coordinating; you don't need a cover."

"Joe."

"No. He's not a professional."

"I take exception to that," I protest. "I venture to say you'd have no knowledge of ITZ whatsoever if it weren't for me."

"I think he's got you, Joe."

"Yes, I'm quite certain I do. By the *karotki volaskiis,* as we say in Russia. If ITZ is tied in to this, I'm tied in to it too."

Banzer's posture slackens in capitulation. "Answer one question for me, Gabby, okay?"

Scotto suppresses a smile and nods.

"I'm the boss. Why do I always lose these things?"

"Because you're more than just a boss, Joe. You're a very smart boss who always makes the right decision."

"Geezus Christ," Banzer says incredulously as Scotto drags me out the door toward her office. "Geezus H. Christ!"

She wastes no time heating up the phone lines. Field strategy, operational briefings, interagency teamwork—it's obviously the stuff that makes Scotto tick, that gets her out of bed in the morning; she's damned good at it. "Right," she says, wrapping up a conference call with DEA and Customs colleagues. "Four unmarked units counting mine. We'll rendezvous outside the depot at twenty-two hundred. That'll give us plenty of time. Oh, and let's see if we can't get everyone on the same radio frequency for a change, okay?" She hangs up, grabs her gear, and charges for the door. "Come on, Katkov. Move it. We've got to stop at my husband's office on the way. This isn't something I can do over the phone."

"Hard to check out of a hotel over it too."

She sighs and hurries to the elevator. We blow through the lobby and dash across the parking lot. The Buick waits patiently in the darkness. We open the doors and jump inside.

"Aw, shit!" Scotto wails, freezing in horror at what the dome light reveals.

I gasp at the repulsive sight of a man's body sprawled across the hood. His anguished face presses grotesquely against the windshield. His eyes are open, blank, and bugged. His teeth are bared in a twisted smile by a cut that goes from the corner of his mouth to his ear. There's a bullet hole in his forehead, and a frozen splatter of blood on the glass that runs along the wiper. It's Scotto's informant.

26

S cotto is shaken but defiantly resolute, and she handles the aftermath with cool efficiency. I check out of the hotel in the meantime, and we're soon heading west toward Hagerstown on the parkway that parallels the Potomac. We're driving in stolid silence when the Buick's headlights sweep across a sign that reads CAPITOL BELTWAY 495 DULLES AIRPORT.

"Oh, shit," Scotto groans, jolted by a thought. "Marty." She scoops up the cellular phone and autodials her husband's office. "Hi, it's Gabby. Is he there? . . . Damn. I was afraid of that . . . no, no, thanks." She hangs up and stomps on the gas. "Damn."

"What's wrong?"

"He already left for the airport. I'm supposed to meet him at the check-in desk."

"Perhaps you might have him paged?"

She considers it for a moment, then sighs, overwhelmed. "I can't. This trip was my thing. I can't just say 'Sorry' and leave him standing there." She shifts lanes abruptly, darts into the interchange, and heads south to Dulles International.

The approach road is clogged with traffic. There isn't enough time to park in one of the lots, hike to the terminal, find her husband, and still make it to Hagerstown on schedule. Scotto drives up the congested departure ramp instead. Harried police officers in reflective vests are trying to undo the gridlock. We finally make it to the United Airlines entrance, where she triple-parks. "My husband's a tall, lanky guy with a mustache and a southern drawl. Sort of talks like this," she says imitating it, before sending me to fetch him.

The check-in area is jammed with travelers. A man who fits the description is standing off to one side anxiously watching the entrance.

"Excuse me. Are you Mr. Scotto?"

"Uh-huh. Well, actually, that's my wife's name," he replies in the drawl Scotto mimicked so perfectly. "I mean her last name's Scotto. Mine's Jennings. Is something wrong?"

"Oh, no. No, she just needs to talk with you."

Marty's eyes roll knowingly. He grabs his carryon and follows me outside, where frustrated drivers are leaning on their horns. One of the police officers reacts and comes in our direction. I get in next to Scotto. Marty circles around to the driver's window.

"Hi," Scotto sighs, drawing it out into several syllables. "Sorry about this. We got a last-minute break in a case."

"Don't do this, Gabby," Marty pleads, almost drowned out by the racket.

"I don't have any choice, honey. I can't go."

"You can't block this lane, either, lady," the police officer cracks. He holds up traffic in the adjacent lane and waves Scotto forward. "Let's go, move it! Move it! Let's get this opened up!"

Marty scowls in disbelief and gets into the backseat. "I thought you didn't have cases any more."

"It's Woody's last case. I'm taking it over," Scotto explains as she pulls away. "Look, I'm not going to lie to you, Marty, even though I'm good at it. I asked for the case. I threatened to resign over it."

"Admirable; but nothing's going to bring him back."

"Hey, I'm tired of hearing that, okay? I have to do it for him, for his family."

"He was your partner, not your husband," Marty reasons in his even-tempered way. "I thought you took this job so we'd have more control over our lives?"

"I did."

"Yeah, I guess so," he concedes, sensing the futility. "You can't be somebody you're not, can you, Gabby?"

"I'm trying. What do you want me to say?"

"Nothing. Drop me off at the terminal, please."

"The terminal?" Scotto echoes in a tone that leaves no doubt it'd be inconvenient. "It'll take a half hour, maybe more in this mess. We have to—"

"Pull over, dammit," Marty snaps, finally running out of patience. Then he shifts his look to me and challenges, "What's *your* wife doing this weekend?"

"I'm . . . I'm afraid I'm divorced," I reply with a shrug, caught off guard. "She—"

"Figures," he cracks sarcastically, assuming I'm in law enforcement, an inspector from Scotland Yard, no doubt. "You think maybe she'd like to go to Hilton Head?" He gets out without waiting for a reply, drags his suitcase after him, and slams the door.

Scotto takes a moment to collect herself before pulling into the stream of traffic exiting the airport. We're soon heading north on the Leesburg Pike, gas pedal to the floor. Fists locked on the steering wheel, eyes riveted to the sweep of headlights up ahead, Scotto drives in tight-lipped silence, leaving little doubt she'd prefer I not break it. About forty-five minutes later, we're moving at high speed on a winding mountain road when she finally says, "He's right. I can't be something I'm not."

"No one can, Scotto. It cost me a marriage ten years ago, not to mention someone else I care about."

"The woman at your apartment that morning?"

I nod glumly. "Vera. I can't blame her. She's caring, supportive. Wants to be put first once in a while. I try, but I get caught up in a story and—"

"It takes hold of you, and all of a sudden you can't see anything else, right?"

"Precisely. I'm starting to believe that people can't change their nature. It makes me quite pessimistic about the future."

"Just be your pushy, pain-in-the-ass self, Katkov. You'll do fine."

"Thanks, but I was thinking of Russia. I'm afraid we may never escape our past. We've let czars and dictators bully us

for so long, we may no longer be capable of governing ourselves, let alone competing in a free-market economy."

"Don't write your countrymen off that easily."

"You don't know them. We have an old saying: 'The tallest
blade of grass is the first to be cut by the scythe.' Russians
aren't risk takers. They're far more interested in guarantees than
opportunities. Listen, I didn't mean to change the subject. I'm
terribly sorry about your husband."

She shrugs matter-of-factly. "I can't be what I'm not. He can't
accept who I am. Neither of us is tuned in to what the other
wants out of life." She drifts off for a moment, then sighs. "I
don't know why I'm telling you all this. It's not your problem."

"Sometimes it's a bit easier with a stranger. You *sure* your
mother wasn't Russian?"

"Positive," she replies, managing a smile. "Why?"

"You know Chekhov?"

"We've lost touch over the years, but I recall his plays are
about relationships, if that's what you mean."

"About people who care deeply for each other, but are unhappy because they can't quite grasp what the other wants out
of life."

"Yeah, well, you don't have to be Russian, do you?"

A sign that reads HAGERSTOWN 35 flashes past. Half an
hour later we're crossing the city line. Banzer was right. If this
isn't the center of the American trucking industry, I can't imagine what is. Panel trucks, step vans, tankers and tractor-trailer
rigs cruise the streets, line the curbs and fill the massive parking lots that flank the highway.

Scotto takes the first turnoff and pulls into a service station.
Spotless and brilliantly illuminated, it's one of four at this intersection. I'm amazed. There are barely a half dozen in Moscow, all located beyond the Outer Ring, where long lines,
outdated pumps, and outrageous prices greet the customer.

While an attendant fills the tank, Scotto rummages in the
trunk, then hurries off to the rest room. A few minutes later,
she emerges in jeans, running shoes, and leather jacket over a
faded sweat shirt that proclaims FORDHAM. After depositing
her weekend outfit in the trunk, she shifts one of the boxes of
snacks into the backseat, slips behind the wheel, and drops a
pair of binoculars and her notepad in my lap. Then she takes

the pistol from her shoulder bag and slips it into the holster she's wearing beneath her jacket.

We're more than an hour behind schedule when we approach the trucking depot. It's located on a wide, litter-strewn street that runs parallel to the highway. Beyond the high fence, trucks of every size, description, and affiliation are neatly aligned on acres of macadam. Countless tractor-trailers with containers in their flatbeds are backed up to a block-long warehouse. Scotto parks near the corner of a darkened cross street from where we can observe the depot's entrance, then uses her radio to contact the other agents and confirm they're all in position.

"Affirmative," one replies. "We've been waiting for you to check in, Scotto. Where you been?"

"Yeah," another chimes in, "we thought maybe you ran off with Dr. Zhivago."

"Eat your hearts out," Scotto taunts, reddening slightly. Then she slouches in her seat to keep a low profile and gestures I do the same.

About an hour later, I'm cold, hungry, bored, and halfway through a fresh pack of cigarettes. "You know, Scotto, I'm really starting to understand why you were so eager to get back into the field."

"Very funny." She pulls a cellophane bag from the box on the backseat and tosses it at me. "Have some popcorn and shut up."

"I'd much prefer a vodka."

"What? And go running down the highway naked?"

"A tactical diversion."

"Oh, yeah, these long-haul rednecks'd really get off on that." She laughs, then glances to her watch. "Trunk's open. Help yourself. Better make it fast." I'm reaching for the door handle when she suddenly has a change of heart. "No. No, on second thought, we're looking at a twelve-hour haul. I don't want you nodding off on me. Forget it."

The hiss of air brakes puts an end to any thought of appealing the verdict. A massive tractor-trailer thunders past the dispatcher's shack into the street. The cab's tinted windows obscure the driver and anyone who might be riding shotgun. According to Scotto, its extended configuration means there's a sleeping area behind the seats. Most important, the trailing flatbed carries a container with large numerals, identifying it as 95824.

"That's the one," Scotto exclaims, starting the engine. As she slips the Buick into Drive and starts creeping toward the intersection, three identical rigs roll from the depot one after the other. Each carries a container on its flatbed. Each container has the number 95824 stenciled on it.

"Son of a bitch," Scotto groans, hitting the brakes as the convoy comes down the street toward the intersection where we're parked.

"How could they know?"

She shrugs, disgusted. "How'd my informant end up kissing the windshield? Besides, that's a lot of cash. Maybe they're being smart, making sure it doesn't get hijacked or anything. Either way, I screwed up. I should've foreseen it. This is what happens when you don't have enough lead time." She's bouncing a fist off the steering wheel in frustration when her radio comes alive with a cacophony of puzzled voices:

"What the fuck?!"

"Am I seeing quadruple here or what?"

"Whoever said 'Assumption is the mother of all fuckups' must've gone to Fordham."

Scotto steels herself, then thinks for a moment and hits the radio transmit button. "Hang in there, guys. This isn't over yet." There's no bravado in her voice, but her tone leaves no doubt that she has an idea. She clicks off and squints into the darkness as the first rig thunders through the intersection in front of us. "Georgia," she says in a tense whisper, leaning forward expectantly as the next approaches. "Virginia. Yeah. Way to go . . ." Then the next. "Arkansas. Okay. Come on, come on. One more." The last rig rumbles past. "Georgia. Shit."

"The license plates."

"Yeah. Check the notes. The one we want's in there somewhere. Come on. Find it. Fast. I hope to hell it isn't Georgia."

I'm flipping through the pages frantically as the convoy of eighteen-wheelers rolls past a sign that proclaims I-81 MARTINSBURG, WINCHESTER, and heads toward an on-ramp at the far end of the street.

"Katkov?" Scotto growls impatiently, through clenched teeth.

"Here. Here it is. Virginia."

"Yeah!" Scotto exclaims.

"Four-three-nine-L-H-T-six-six . . . five? Three? It's scribbled. I can't quite make it out."

"Doesn't matter. That's it. Virginia. That's the rig with the cash." Scotto starts after the convoy, and thumbs the transmit button on her radio. "This is Shell Game Leader to all units. The Virginia rig is mine," she announces. "Each of you take one of the others. Where it goes, you go. Good luck."

Engines roaring, exhaust stacks belching diesel smoke into the darkness, the four eighteen-wheelers accelerate onto the highway and fan out across the lanes. The traffic is fast-moving and surprisingly heavy, considering the hour.

"I'm rather puzzled, Scotto. Why didn't you tell them you know which one has the money?"

"Do I?" she challenges, slipping into the lane behind the truck. "You're positive my guy wasn't wrong? I mean, the poor bastard didn't know zip about four containers with the same number, did he?"

"No, I'm afraid not," I reply with a little smirk. "And since those other agents are on point and you're laying back coordinating, I imagine its only fair to assign the decoys to them."

"You're too smart for your own good, Katkov."

"Thank you. While I'm at it, have you considered the possibility the money might not be in any of them?"

"Uh-huh. But my gut tells me it is. Sometimes, you have to go with it, you know?"

"I knew there was a reason I came to America."

The Virginia rig accelerates as the driver works his way up through the gears and merges into the galaxy of taillights streaking the darkness. Unfortunately, most belong to trucks, making it all the more difficult to follow. We've gone a couple of miles when a delivery van, turn signal flashing, slips in front of the Buick, blocking our view of the rig. The van soon moves over another lane, revealing a stakebed truck piled high with tree cuttings in front of us. The Virginia rig is nowhere to be seen.

"Where'd he go, dammit?"

"I don't know. He was right there a moment ago."

"The binoculars," Scotto orders, warming to the chase. She moves over a lane to give us an angle. "Come on, find him. Virginia plates. White field, black letters."

I scan the traffic up ahead, moving from one plate to the next. Some are poorly illuminated, others not at all. "Maryland,

Washington, that one's rather obscure—ah, here we are—Virginia. Yes, yes, it's Virginia. "Four-three-nine-L-H-T-six-six-five . . ."

"Good. Stay on him."

"Easier said than done. He keeps changing lanes. It's damn near impossible."

"Yeah, we're going to have to do something about that, aren't we?"

"Do something about it?"

"Tricks of the trade, Katkov."

"It must be quite a trick at seventy miles an hour."

"You'd be amazed at what I've done at seventy miles an hour." She glances at me out of the corner of her eye and lets a smile spread across her face. "But this might have to wait."

"What might have to wait?"

"Open the glove box."

I thumb the button. The door flops down and whacks my knee. Half the contents follow: maps, Tampax, a tube of lipstick, ball-point pens.

"Sorry, I've been meaning to get that fixed. There's an ice pick in there somewhere."

"What are you going to do with an ice pick?"

"You're worse than a precocious two-year-old."

I rummage through the glove box. My fingers soon come upon the cold aluminum handle tucked between the scraps of paper and folded maps. Scotto glances over, nods mysteriously, and keeps driving. I stare at the ice pick, trying to imagine what it could possibly have to do with tailing a speeding eighteen-wheeler in the middle of the night.

27

Two hundred miles south of Hagerstown, the concrete inter-state zigzags through rugged terrain that Scotto explains is the heart of the Shenandoah Valley—Blue Ridge Mountains to the east, Appalachian Range to the west. I'm smiling in amazement. Not at the breathtaking vistas she describes, which are obscured by darkness, but at an intriguing thought that occurs to me. "You know, we've been on the road over three hours and not a single checkpoint."

"What're you talking about?"

"The KGB. When they were in business, highways didn't connect cities and towns; they connected secret police check-points. You couldn't drive twenty kilometers without having to stop."

"That's about, what? Fifteen miles?" she says, as a sign flashes past proclaiming: CHARLOTTESVILLE, RICHMOND, NEWPORT NEWS —I-64—NEXT EXIT. "No wonder the place went in the toilet. I mean, what's the point?"

"Intimidation. Iron-fist control of every last citizen. They checked papers at every stop; and if you exceeded the bounds of your residency stamp, you'd be sent back, sometimes imprisoned."

"But not anymore."

"Well, there are still some restrictions, but on the whole, it's improving."

"See, Russia *is* escaping its past. Between that and McDonald's, who knows what they'll cook up next?"

"Pizza."

"A major commitment to the twentieth century."

"A rather costly one. I've been evicted from my apartment."

"I'm not sure I follow that."

"They're tearing it down to build the world's largest Pizza Hut."

She breaks up laughing. "I'm sorry, Katkov. I don't mean to laugh at your expense. It's just that—"

The radio crackles, interrupting her. "Unit three to leader. Unit three to leader. My guy's peeling off," an agent in one of the other pursuit units reports. "Heading east on Sixty-four."

"Copy that. Stay with him," Scotto replies. "Shell Game Leader to units two and four. Leader to two and four. What's your status?"

"Unchanged," agents from both units respond, confirming their targets are still proceeding south.

Scotto signs off and slips the radio into its hanger. "Talk to me, Katkov. Where's our boy?"

"Still in the fast lane," I reply, steadying the binoculars. "I'd say about five hundred meters ahead and pulling away."

Scotto glances to the speedometer that's pushing eighty. "Tell me about it. He's really hauling ass."

"He's what?"

"Hauling ass—moving fast—speeding." She darts into the adjacent lane, expertly weaves between several vehicles, and accelerates into the blind spot a distance behind the trailer. "Now, don't lose him, she orders, activating the windshield washers lest I have an excuse. Jets in the Buick's cowling begin blasting the road grime with sudsy water, then the wipers start sweeping across the windshield. The one in front of Scotto streaks a chilling blood red swath across the glass. She gasps, horrified, and frantically thumbs the washer button until the gory smear is gone.

The eighteen-wheeler is maintaining its high rate of speed, and the Buick is having no trouble holding its own, when several short bursts from a siren alert us to the police cruiser bearing down on us.

Scotto groans, backing off the gas as an explosion of rainbow-colored light fills the air.

"I'm afraid I spoke too soon."

"Yeah, you jinxed us."

"Any chance you can reach them on the radio?"

"I wish. No way we're on the same frequency."

"But the truck . . ." I protest as she begins working her way across the lanes toward the shoulder. "We're going to lose contact with the truck if we stop!"

"We'll lose the whole ballgame if we don't. Every 'smokey' in the area'll be on our ass. Best we can do is get this over with fast and play catch-up." She chirps to a stop, takes her official identification from her purse, and starts to get out of the car.

"Remain in the vehicle!" an amplified voice commands. "Return to the vehicle, now!"

Scotto freezes, drops back into the seat, and slams the door, infuriated.

"Roll down the window. Put your hands on the steering wheel or dash. Keep them there until instructed to do otherwise."

I glance to the side-view mirror. Two police officers in blue-gray uniforms are strutting toward us, jackets girdled in black leather, jodhpurs tucked neatly into jackboots, black wide-brimmed hats tilted forward jauntily. One takes up a position behind me. The beam from his flashlight streams through the windows, sweeping slowly across the Buick's interior. The other officer, a crisp, imposing, square-jawed young woman, leans to Scotto's window. Sergeant's stripes slash across her sleeve. "Evenin', ma'am," she drawls. " 'Fraid y'all can't do that sort of thing in this state. May I see your license and—"

"See this," Scotto interrupts, sticking her ID and badge in the sergeant's face. "Special Agent Scotto, U.S. Treasury. We're in pursuit, we've gotta move, and we've gotta move *now.*"

The sergeant's expression runs the gamut from panic to chagrin and back. "Oh?! Sure, sure. Y'all give me the vehicle's license and description, I'll get it on the air and set up an intercept."

"No! No intercept," Scotto exclaims, panicked by the thought. "Put mine on the air, and instruct your people *not* to intercept me. Say it's official USG business. I don't want to spook this guy, Sergeant. I want him to get where he's going. Understand?"

Scotto doesn't wait for an answer. She slams the pedal to the floor and leaves the officers standing in a cloud of grit from the shoulder. The Buick fishtails back onto the highway, streaking the concrete with rubber; then, in response to Scotto's expert handling, it settles down and accelerates in neck-snapping lurches with each gear change. The speedometer is soon pushing ninety.

I spend the next several hours squinting through the binoculars, darting from one license plate to the next; but Virginia 439LHT665 isn't one of them. It isn't long before my eyes are burning and my stomach is growling. So is Scotto's. We make short work of a bag of chocolate chip cookies—a new experience that may just rival my addiction to cigarettes and vodka. The road signs that flash past read: LYNCHBURG, ROANOKE, PULASKI. The rig's driver could've taken any of these turnoffs, but Scotto is betting on Atlanta.

We're approaching the Virginia-Tennessee border when a garish sight appears in the distance. The tangle of pink, yellow, and lime green neon flashes BRISTOL TRUCK STOP. More eye-catching signs shout: CAFETERIA, LAUNDRY, SHOWER FACILITIES. Others advertise: DRIVE-THROUGH WASH, COMPLETE SERVICE CENTER, 30 REFUELING BAYS. The sprawling main building is surrounded by a broad expanse of macadam where more than a hundred tractor-trailers are neatly aligned.

"He's in there," Scotto says confidently, wheeling onto the grounds.

"What makes you so sure?"

"My fuel gauge and my bladder. Truck or no truck, the guy who built this place figured it's about as far south as you can go without filling one and emptying the other."

Whoever he was, he was right. Scotto isn't the only one in need of relief, and the fuel warning light leaves no doubt the Buick is running on fumes. After dealing with the necessities, we drive to one side of the grounds and begin cruising back and forth between the rows of eighteen-wheelers in search of our target. We soon spot a rig with container 95824 in its flatbed, but the Arkansas plate identifies it as one of the two remaining decoys. Scotto raises the other agents on the radio.

Both pursuit units and both decoys are here; to our delight, so is our target.

"There it is," she blurts when we finally locate it. She parks a distance away in a darkened area between the rig and the main building. "Ice pick," she commands like a surgeon.

I slap it into her palm. "What do you want me to do?"

"Nothing. On second thought, get us some coffee. Lots of it. Black."

"You're sure you're going to be okay?"

"Piece of cake. Anybody hassles you, just play dumb and make believe you don't understand English. That should be easy for you." She winks, then gets out of the car and walks swiftly toward the truck.

I watch until she disappears behind the trailer, then zip my parka and head for the cafeteria. Laughter and loud voices erupt as several drivers come through the door and lumber across the tarmac, expelling puffs of breath into the cool air. The bearded one in the quilted vest and cowboy boots splits off and comes in my direction. I wait until he passes, then glance over my shoulder. It looks like he's headed toward our rig. Each step he takes tightens the knot that's forming in my gut. Damn. He *is* headed for it, right for it. He pauses at the cab, rubs a smudge off a chrome fuel cap with the cuff of his jacket, then begins checking the rig's tires and undercarriage prior to hitting the road. There's no way I can warn Scotto without making him suspicious; but maybe I can distract him, ask for directions or something? I hurry after him, but Scotto emerges from behind the trailer before I can make the intercept.

"Hey, what the fuck you doin' back there?" the driver challenges.

Scotto takes her own advice, shrugging and backing away, pretending she doesn't understand English.

"I asked what you were doing, bitch!" He grabs Scotto's arm and shoves her in the direction of the cab, then sees me coming and pounds on it with his fist. "Harlan?! Harlan, we got us a problem here!"

I'm waiting for Scotto to go for her gun, waiting for the other agents to come to our rescue, but I wait in vain. They're nowhere to be seen, and she continues playing the confused foreigner, telling the driver to go fuck himself in her New York-accented Russian.

"Excuse please," I call out, purposely fracturing my syntax. "Excuse please. She is not speaking the English yet."

"No shit!" the driver growls. He pounds on the cab again. "Harlan?!"

The door opens, revealing Harlan to be a sleepy-eyed young fellow in a baseball cap, cradling a shotgun. "What the fuck's going on?"

"Caught her nosing around the rig."

Harlan jumps to the ground and levels the weapon at us menacingly.

My eyes widen at the double-barreled muzzle. The thought that a twitch of this kid's finger could cut me in half has my knees knocking. "I couldn't stop him," I say to Scotto in Russian, the words sticking in my throat. "What are we going to do now?"

"Lighten up," Scotto counsels coolly in Russian. "Give him some bullshit about me getting lost on the way back from the ladies room."

"Sir? Sir, excuse please again? She is not nosing the rig; she is coming from the room for the ladies, and . . . and her way became lost. Please, we are on the, how you say? The honeyball?"

"Honeyball?" the driver echoes with a cocky smirk. "You aren't speaking the English yet either, pal. You may be balling her, but the fuckin' word's *honeymoon.*"

"Oh, yes, we are balling on the honey-*moon,* and for the first time in the free country too. Is wonderful."

Scotto forces an insipid smile and clings to me like a frightened waif. "Be affectionate, dammit," she orders sweetly in Russian, as if she's relishing every minute of this. "You told this asshole we're on our honeymoon. It better look it."

The driver bristles with paranoia. "What? What's that?" he challenges as I wrap an arm around Scotto protectively. "She make some crack about me?"

"No. No, she . . . she is asking if you know of the sights to be seeing?"

"Yeah," he smirks. "Ever been to Siberia?"

"C'mon, Curtis," Harlan says, lowering the shotgun. "They're jus' tourists. Leave 'em be."

"Leave my fucking rig be, bitch." He glares at us, then unhooks his keys from his belt loop and struts toward the cab, his boots pounding the tarmac.

The kid lingers, his pronounced brow knitted with remorse. "I never met no Russians before. I don't want y'all getting the wrong idea. Americans are good people. I mean, if it wasn't for Reagan and Bush, them Commies'd still be running the show, right?" He turns toward the cab, then brightens with a thought. "Disney World. Yeah, that's where y'all oughta go."

"Diz-nee-vherl?" Scotto repeats, sounding it out like a Russian who's never heard it before.

"Hey, she's really getting the hang of it. It's in Florida. Orlando. Me an' my girl went once?" he says, his voice rising with childish wonder. "Fan-fuckin-tastic!"

"Come on, Harlan, let's roll!" the driver calls out from the cab.

"Y'all go down there," the kid concludes, hurrying off with his shotgun. "Y'all go down there, and find out what Americans are all about."

We force smiles and head for the Buick, arms around each other's waists. Scotto's wired, living on the edge again. I'm relieved, yet seething with indignation. "Regan and Bush?" I exclaim through clenched teeth. "Reagan and Bush destroyed Communism? Self-delusion is what you Americans are all about!"

"Come on, at least give us credit for putting a banana peel or two in Lenin's path, will you?"

"They were totally unnecessary. Communism is an absurd idea. It was doomed from the start."

"Okay, okay. Lighten up. We're on our honeyball, remember? Come on, grab my ass or something. This is a truck stop." Her hand drops to my buttock and squeezes it so hard that I yelp. She opens the trunk, rummages in one of the boxes, and hands me the bottle of vodka. "You earned it, Katkov. You did real good."

"Thanks." I steady my hands, unscrew the cap, and take a long swallow. "I was quite terrified. Still am."

"Me too."

"Shit of the bull, Scotto. You were enjoying it, immensely, and you know it."

"I guess so," she says with a laugh that ends in a reflective smile. "I can't explain it, but it's a rush every time. When I think of the things I've done...." The husky roar of a diesel kicking over pulls her out of it. We clamber into the Buick. I toss the bottle into the box on the backseat. Scotto pokes her fingers under the cuff of her jacket and pulls the ice pick from the sleeve. "Stick this in there, will you?"

"Quite frankly, I was waiting for you to stick it in him."

"I came close," she admits, adrenaline still pumping, "but it would've blown everything."

"What did you do with it, anyway?"

She starts the engine and smiles. "You'll see."

Across the grounds, the eighteen-wheeler starts rolling toward the highway, then suddenly turns in our direction. I'm blinded, not by the alcohol, but by headlights that are closing fast. The tractor's massive grille is within a car length of hitting the sedan head-on before the driver brakes and swerves sharply. The Buick shudders violently as the forty-ton semi thunders past. It rumbles onto the highway with a deafening blast from its air horns, followed by the other two rigs—also hauling containers numbered 95824.

"Jerk," Scotto mutters. She lays back, giving them a head start, then pulls out and pursues. The eighteen-wheelers merge into heavy commercial traffic, barreling south at a steady 75 mph; but I've no trouble tailing our target now. Dead center in each of its taillights, a blinding white point of light burns from the hole Scotto made with the ice pick, each a distinct beacon in the panorama of red lenses bobbing in the darkness.

We've gone a short distance when Scotto's radio comes to life. The crackle gives way to heavy breathing followed by laughter. "We saw her grabbing your ass, Zhivago," an agent in one of the other pursuit units cracks. "You want to file sexual harrassment charges? You've got witnesses."

Scotto scoops up her radio. "Okay, you guys," she warns, trying to keep her cool. "I've had enough."

"Hey, she uses that one on me all the time, Zhivago," another agent cracks. "Don't believe her."

"The only reason you clowns are getting away with this," Scotto counters, fuming, "is because you stayed out of it back there. Nice to see you using your heads instead of your dicks for a change."

We're well south of the Tennessee border when dawn breaks, silhouetting distant mountains. The interstate rises and falls, transporting us in and out of wispy ground fog that cloaks our target; but the pinpoints of light coming from the flatbed's tail-lights cut through the haze like lasers. We're outside Jefferson City, approaching the intersection of 40 East, when the second decoy peels off, taking one of the pursuit units with it. About an hour later, twenty miles south of Knoxville, agents in the remaining unit report that their target has split off west. That leaves Scotto and me tailing the Virginia rig with the two billion in cash. It's a hundred-mile sprint to Chattanooga on the Tennessee-Georgia border, and another hundred or so to Atlanta. It's late morning by the time the city's tightly packed mass of glass and steel appears on the horizon.

"Forgive me for saying it, Scotto, but we could've just as well flown down here with Krauss and camped out at the recycling plant until our target arrived."

"Yeah, but look at all the fun we would've missed. I mean, is this a story or what?"

"A fan-fucking-tastic story."

She laughs, then her brow furrows with concern. "Let's hope *somebody's* camped out here." She reaches for her radio and thumbs the transmit button. "Hel-lo At-lan-ta," she says, sing-songing it. "This is Shell Game Leader to Nutcracker One. Leader to Nutcracker One. Do you read?"

"This is Nutcracker," the agent in charge of the Atlanta task force replies. "Coming through loud and clear. Go ahead."

"Target is two miles north of the Two-eighty-five turnoff. ETA to your location, ten minutes."

"Copy that. All our units are in position."

"Sounds good," Scotto acknowledges. "I'll hang in here and count it down for you: one mile . . . a half . . . a quarter . . . coming up on the turnoff. Yeah, yeah, he's going for it. We got brake lights; we got a turn signal." She pumps the air with a fist. "Okay, we're rolling west on Two-eight-five now."

She clicks off and has me retrieve her shoulder bag from the backseat. One of the pockets contains a detailed street map of Atlanta. Highway 285 crosses the interstate about ten miles north of the city. Like the boulevards that encircle Moscow, it rings the congested downtown area, routing commercial traffic to surrounding manufacturing districts. Container 95824's ultimate destination is located near Fulton County Airport off a highway access road. Easy-to-spot landmarks are identified on the map, and the distance to destination is written next to each. I read off the miles aloud as each landmark flashes past. Scotto radios the data to Nutcracker. "Three miles," she reports as the rig changes lanes up ahead.

"That's a read. We're ready for him."

"Two miles . . . one . . ."

"Nice work, Shell Game. Back off when he makes the turn and hold at the foot of the access road. We're hanging tight until the creeps take possession of the cargo. Wouldn't want 'em claiming it was delivered to the wrong address, would we?"

"Copy that," Scotto replies as the sprawling recycling plant appears in the distance. "A thousand yards . . . five hundred . . . smokestacks . . . nice sign on the roof. He's turning into the access road riiiiight . . ." She draws it out in anticipation of adding 'now!'—but she never gets to say it. Instead of slowing to make the turn, the eighteen-wheeler blows right past it. "Hold it, hold it, he kept going!"

"Fuck," Nutcracker growls. "They're pulling a fast one. We better roll some units and take him."

"Negative," Scotto barks sharply. "Negative. Don't overreact, dammit. Tom Krauss there?"

"Yeah."

"Put him on, will you?"

"Gabby?" Krauss's voice crackles tensely.

"Yeah. Pour some cold water on that guy, will you? I've been tailing this rig for over twelve hours. I don't want to blow this end now. Let's lay back and see what he's up to."

"Yeah, maybe he's meeting the mayor for lunch?" Nutcracker says facetiously.

"Talk to me, Gabby," Krauss commands. "You got any idea what?"

"Negative. We can always take him. I want to give him some rope, see if he hangs somebody with it."

"That's a read. I'll take care of it."

Scotto clicks off and swings me a concerned look. "He better hang somebody soon." She points to the instrument panel in response to my look. "Running on fumes again. Let's hope our boy is too."

28

Dammit, Scotto," Banzer's voice crackles over the cellular. "I thought you were coordinating?" Scotto's car phone is an amazing gadget by Russian standards, with a hands-free mode that allows both of us to listen and respond via a tiny speaker and microphone.

"Makes two of us," Scotto fires back. "But they pulled a couple of fast ones. For openers, what am I bid for four eighteen-wheelers and four containers with the same number?"

"Geezus. Why didn't you call me?"

"What for? We had enough units to sustain pursuit. Each one took a rig."

"God help you if we lost track of the cash."

"No way. We had the plate number of the rig that's carrying it."

"Ah, and you just happened to tail that one?"

"Hey, I got lucky. The recycling plant was a decoy too."

"Great. Any idea where the cash is headed?"

"For a train ride."

"A train ride."

"Uh-huh. Me and Katkov are sitting on it in the Atlanta yards right now. The eighteen-wheeler's crew dropped it off, trailer and all, and split."

"What's the drill?"

"Nutcracker wanted to take it down before it gets out of his jurisdiction, but I got Krauss to talk him out of it. The money's going to end up on somebody's doorstep, and I want to know whose."

"You and me both. What about the rig's crew?"

"We're holding off on them too, for now. Better if they think it's all going according to plan."

"Good. You have backup?"

"Uh-huh. Nutcracker's got a couple of units covering us; they're also putting a chopper on standby. Too chancy tailing a truck by air, but a freight shouldn't be a problem."

"Yeah, but why standby? I mean, it's going to be moving. We know that."

"But we don't know when, Joe. Nutcracker said it could sit here for weeks. The chopper's a National Guard loaner, and they can't tie it up that long. I couldn't argue."

"Well you're a loaner too, and I can't tie you up that long either. And don't argue."

"*Joe.*"

"Hold on a sec. I know a guy on the Amtrak PD. Maybe we can find out where it's going and when."

Scotto does a slow burn and waits, listening to the hum of the line.

I keep the binoculars trained on our target. Container 95824 is one of hundreds in the section of the train yard where long lines of flatcars wait to be loaded with containerized cargo. A gargantuan bridge crane straddles them, gliding back and forth on tracks of its own as it goes about transferring two of the forty-foot-long aluminum boxes to each flatcar.

We're parked on an overpass at one end of the yard. It arches between the deserted hulks of once thriving mills and factories that crowd the right of way. Like most of the streets in this desolate area, the graffiti-covered span is littered with abandoned vehicles. Dents, dings, faded paint, and a heavy coat of road grime keep Scotto's Buick from standing out.

From this vantage point, the entire network of track stretches out before us. Several husky diesels patrol it, picking up their charges. One by one each railcar is guided to a central spur, where it joins others moving up one side of an incline and down the other. Trainmen, working in a control tower atop the hump, open and close combinations of switches, directing each car to the proper train.

"It's still sitting there, huh?" Scotto prompts, squirming in her seat impatiently.

I nod and lower the binoculars. "What's Amtrak?"

"National train system—for passengers."

"National?" I echo, astonished at this breach of capitalist ideology. "You mean it's run by the government?"

"Subsidized."

"Still, whatever happened to free enterprise?"

"It ran into the Wright brothers. The airlines were putting passenger trains out of business, so the government got into it, bought 'em all out, and merged 'em into one."

"And it has its own police department?"

"Uh-huh. Covers about twenty thousand miles of track, everything within a couple hundred feet on either side of it, and everything that travels on it. Passenger, freight, whatever. Carved it out of FBI turf back in the seventies. A little before my time." She's smiling, savoring the thought, when the cellular comes back to life.

"Gabby?" Banzer's voice crackles. "Good news and bad news. According to my guy, whoever's running this show is pretty damned sharp. Atlanta is the hub for the entire southeast. More than a dozen railroads run in and out of there."

"Great," Scotto groans sarcastically. "The target could be going anywhere, on any one of 'em, at any time. Now, give me the bad news."

Banzer laughs. "Listen, it's a computerized yard. They use these scanners to read a code on each railcar. It's racked up in a sleeve on the side. You get me the code, my guy can get into their data base and find out date and time of departure and destination."

"Way to go, Joe. One little problem. The container's not on a flatcar yet. We'll have to hang in here until it is."

"I thought Nutcracker said that might take weeks? Listen, Scotto, I think you ought to get your butt back here and let his people . . ."

Scotto's eyes bug. She scoops up her radio and holds down one of the buttons. It emits a constant stream of loud, scratchy static that's picked up by the cellular's mike. "Joe? Joe? We're losing you, Joe. Say again? Joe? Joe, do you read?" She sets down the radio with a little smile and flicks the cellular to off. "Satellite must be picking up some kind of interference."

It's been at least thirty-six hours since either of us have had any sleep. We take turns napping and keeping an eye on the target. There's nothing terribly demanding about it. Nothing that tests one's skills or acuity. Nothing vital, other than remaining awake. Container 95824 spends the afternoon sitting in the yard on its trailer. Before we know it, darkness is falling and our stomachs are growling. The Buick's trunk seems to have an inexhaustible supply of junk food and beverages, but we're both craving a hot meal. I volunteer to take the car and get us something.

"No, I gotta go," Scotto protests. "You stay here and mind the store."

"Really, I'd be more than happy to—"

"You didn't hear me, Katkov," she interrupts urgently, pressing her knees together. "I said I gotta *go*." She digs a pager out of the glove box and hands it to me. "That container starts moving, hit this button. We won't be able to talk, but the radio'll pick up the signal, and I'll come running."

The Buick's taillights are soon red specks in the darkness. I'm fine-tuning the focus on the binoculars when the screech of grinding metal raises my pores. Far below, a long freight enters the yard and snakes through a series of switches, filling the air with the harsh scent of burnt steel. Containers come and go; but 95824 isn't one of them. About a half hour later, headlights appear at the far end of the overpass and come toward me. It's Scotto. She gets out of the sedan with an ear-to-ear grin on her face and a flat, square box in her arms. Bright red letters that slash across the top proclaim PIZZA HUT.

I break up with laughter. "In honor of my homeless status?"

"By default. I spotted this neat-looking Texas Chili joint across from where I gassed up, but decided against it."

"Doesn't agree with you?"

"Hell no, I could live on the stuff. Did live on it when I was working the border down in Brownsville. It was the thought of running into our favorite trucking crew that gave me a pain in my gut."

"You mean the two who were—?"

"Uh-huh. Mr. Don't Touch My Rig, Bitch and his shotgun-hugging flunky. Their tractor was parked right outside the place."

"Any chance they saw you?"

Scotto shrugs. "Hard to say. I didn't see them." We settle on the tailgate of an abandoned pickup truck and dig into the pizza. She devours the first piece, then stares off into the darkness, ignoring the rest.

"Rather tasty. Come on, have another."

"Lost my appetite," she mutters, preoccupied. "I keep thinking about this thing . . . you know . . . with my husband. I don't know what I'm going to do."

"As a very smart person once told me, 'Just be your pushy, pain-in-the-ass self. You'll do fine.' "

"Very funny."

"You will."

"How the hell do you know? You write a column for the lovelorn in your spare time?"

"No, but I could. It seems everyone I know in Moscow is either divorced or on the verge of it."

"No kidding? It was like that in the seventies here. We raised our consciences so high, we lost sight of what really counted. What's the problem in Russia?"

"High unemployment, long winters, alcoholism."

"Not exactly a prescription for wedded bliss, huh? What's yours?"

"Political activism. It had a rather negative impact on my ex's medical practice. That was part of it, anyway."

"And the other part?"

I lower the binoculars and look Scotto square in the eye. "I'm an alcoholic."

Her face falls. "Gosh, I feel kind of funny about before. I mean, I wouldn't have . . . I'm really sorry."

"I could've said no. I decided otherwise."

She smiles sadly. "That's what they all say, isn't it?"

"Classic denial. I know. Strange as it sounds, the cravings seem to have diminished as of late."

"As of late? Very strange. I mean, this job drives people to drink, not the reverse."

"Not at all surprising. But since leaving Moscow, I don't know, I feel different."

"Well, change of environment sometimes—"

"Hey?! Hey, it's moving!" I interrupt, raising the binoculars.

"What?"

"The container, it's moving!"

Number 95824 hangs in a crossfire of work lights beneath the bridge crane's boom. A rectangular frame of massive beams and pulleys grips the perimeter at the roofline. With surprising speed and precision, the huge, articulated structure rolls on its tracks, then stops, swivels, extends, and deftly deposits the forty-foot-long aluminum box in the bed of a flatcar.

"Can you see the code?" Scotto prompts anxiously.

"No, the angle's all wrong."

"Come on," she orders, jumping from the tailgate. "We better find one that's right."

I keep my eyes pressed to the binoculars for a moment. One of the patrolling diesels hooks up to the flatcar and starts moving the two-billion-dollar cargo through the yard. "Hold it. I'm afraid we're not going to have time."

Scotto fetches the radio and thumbs the transmit button. "Nutcracker . . . Nutcracker, this is Shell Game. It's moving. The target's moving; we need that chopper."

"Copy that. Bird is on standby as planned. ETA your location . . . twenty minutes. Any fix on target's destination?"

"Negative."

"That's a copy. Be advised max range for chopper is three hundred miles."

"Yeah, yeah, just make it fast, dammit." Scotto clicks off the radio with an angry scowl.

The diesel negotiates a combination of switches and maneuvers to the incline, where the flatcar begins its ascent. Moments later, it rolls down the other side and couples to a long freight that's being assembled. A half-dozen more railcars swiftly follow. The last one is a caboose. Within minutes, the three-unit diesel at the head of the train unleashes its awesome power and lunges forward. The grinding of drive wheels on rails, the angry creak of stressed metal, the rapid-fire bang-bang-bang of engaging couplers blend with haunting blasts from air horns that announce the fifty-plus-car freight's departure.

"I don't know about you, Scotto, but after coming this far, there's no way I'm stopping now."

"What are you talking about?"

"Following the money. After what's happened, even if we

knew the destination, where that container goes, I go. You coming?"

Scotto glances to the sky forlornly. Still no sign of the chopper. I dash to the Buick and climb behind the wheel. I've just started the engine when she comes after me and rips open the door. "Scoot over, Katkov." I hesitate. "Scoot over, dammit. Now!" I clamber over the transmission console. She shoves the shift lever into drive and takes off. The acceleration pins me to the seat. She weaves between the abandoned vehicles to the far end of the overpass. The cross street runs parallel to a concrete embankment that slopes sharply to the yard. Scotto puts the Buick into a high-speed slide and fishtails through the corner. As the car is settling down, long-haul halogens suddenly blast from between the vacant factories. An all-too-familiar tractor charges into view and tries to cut us off. Scotto instinctively snaps the wheel right-left-right. The sedan responds and slithers around the tractor. It's so close I can read PETERBILT on the cowl.

"What are they doing here?!"

"Waiting for us. What else? One of 'em must've spotted me before."

I look back for the tractor. It swerves to avoid going over the embankment, then comes out of it and pursues. The entrance to the train yard is dead ahead. Scotto blows past some slow-moving trucks and rockets into the access road. The steep incline leads to a network of service roads. One parallels the tracks. She races the length of the yard—past the control tower, past lines of railcars, past signal towers and distance markers—in pursuit of the departing train.

I'm watching with wide-eyed amazement.

She senses it and grins. "Driving school. They teach us how to handle everything from motorcycles to that thing that's trying to kill us."

I glance back over my shoulder again. The tractor is gaining. It's a hell of a lot faster without that forty-ton trailer behind it.

Scotto is radioing the backup units for help. A blast from an air horn interrupts. One of the other diesels is coming toward us on an intersecting spur, pulling a long string of boxcars. The engineer leans on his horn again. Scotto flicks a glance to the mirror and curses. The tractor is still coming like a runaway freight. So is the thundering diesel. The word CONRAIL is stenciled across its stubby snout. My heart's climbing into my mouth. My brain's screaming, Hit the brakes! Hit the brakes! The air horn's still blasting. Scotto's still ignoring it. She steels herself and stands on the gas instead. The Buick zips across the tracks. The onrushing train misses us by millimeters and roars across the service road, blocking the pursuing tractor.

The freight carrying container 95824 is up ahead, traveling at the posted yard speed of 5 mph. We overtake it easily. Scotto keeps the pedal to the floor, racing along the service road that parallels the outbound spur. Railcar after railcar flashes past. The numbers on the target go by in a blur. She keeps going until we're so far ahead of the train, it's completely out of sight by the time she stops.

We waste no time getting out of the car. Scotto starts stuffing a nylon gym bag with things from the trunk. I'm pulling my typewriter from the backseat with one hand and a suitcase with the other. Headlights sweep through a distant turn, startling us. If it's the train, it's moving so fast we'll never get aboard. I'm not sure if our luck is holding or running out, but it's not the train—it's the tractor! Tinted two-piece windshield bridging its cowl like a pair of Ray-Bans, engine snarling behind vicious chrome teeth, stacks snorting fire into the darkness, the monster-on-wheels comes at us at high speed.

We literally run for our lives, putting as much distance as possible between us and the Buick that blocks the narrow service road. The driver redlines every gear. The speeding tractor closes the distance in an eyeblink. It's heading right for the sedan.

"Shit!" Scotto exclaims, glancing back. "That son-of-a-bitch is gonna total my car!" She drops her bags, then pulls her pistol, steadies it with both hands, and coolly fires at the onrushing vehicle. The windshield shatters. The engine growls like a broken lawn mower. A tire blows. The tractor swerves wildly out of control, narrowly missing the Buick. It rockets across a median, sending up a shower of gravel, and crashes into an embankment.

"Yes!" Scotto whoops, pumping a fist in triumph.

Despite the circumstances, I can't help thinking it's amazing the things people become attached to.

"Stay back," she orders, pushing me aside before advancing on the tractor cautiously. The door cracks open before she gets

there. The shotgun emerges. She advances swiftly, then grasps
the barrel and pulls hard, yanking Harlan from the cab. He gets
a face full of gravel. Scotto gets his weapon. "Police officer!
Don't move!" she commands sharply, pressing a foot against
the back of his neck. He remains facedown on the ground. She
hands me the shotgun. "Shoot him if he moves." She swings
the door open wide, leveling her pistol at the driver. "Police!
Out. Now. Move it!" He stumbles from the cab, blood trickling
into his beard from a cut on his cheek. "Hit the deck," Scotto
orders, holding the pistol on him as she steps back.

The wail of sirens rises as he flops facedown in the gravel
next to his colleague. The backup units race along the service
road and converge on the tractor. Krauss and Nutcracker are at
the forefront of the agents who pile out of the vehicles, guns
drawn.

"All yours, Tom," Scotto says coolly as they move in around
the two truckers. Then, noticing a single headlight streaking
through the darkness, she breaks into a cocky grin and adds,
"Come on, Katkov. Don't want to miss our train."

The long freight seems to be picking up speed as it exits the
yard. At the least, we're going to need a running start. Krauss
and the other agents are wide-eyed as we scoop up our bags
and start sprinting parallel to the tracks. The ground shudders
violently as the throbbing diesel approaches, pushing air with
jolting force as it passes.

We're running clumsily with our cargo alongside an empty
boxcar. I toss the typewriter and suitcase through the open
door. Scotto does the same with the canvas sack and her shoulder bag. There's a boarding handle welded to the doorframe. It
takes me several tries, but I finally get hold of it and belly flop
aboard. The train is moving faster. Scotto is running like crazy
to keep up. She accelerates and makes a desperate headfirst
lunge for the doorway. I manage to get hold of her wrist. She
hooks a leg over the sill—half of her in, the other half hanging
perilously out—and claws at the floor for a handhold. I grab
the seat of her pants with my free hand and drag her inside.
We stumble away from the door and fall against opposite walls
of the boxcar, gasping for breath.

"You . . . you okay?" I finally ask.

She nods, unable to speak.

"I . . . I . . . think . . . I'm starting to understand."

"You . . . you mean about . . . getting back into the field?"

"Uh-huh. . . . You're . . . you're amazing."

"I know . . ." she wheezes with a grin. "But I think . . . maybe . . . I've lost a step or two. . . . Gotten a little . . . broad in the beam."

"I believe . . . I mentioned that when we first met."

"A born diplomat."

"Think positively. . . . It gave me something to hang on to."

"That's what my husband says. Don't start getting sexual on me, Katkov."

"Thought's never crossed my mind."

"Nice to know I can always count on you for an ego boost."

I smile. So does she. We're sitting there like rag dolls, watching the city go by, when it dawns on me we haven't the slightest idea where we're going.

29

I'm jolted by a sharp poke in the ribs. An elbow, to be exact. Scotto's elbow. I don't know why, but it seems she's always waking me up. I roll over, eyes gritty and heavy with sleep. She's lying on the floor next to me, alternating the painful jabs with angry tugs of a small blanket that barely covers us.

"Katkov? Come on, shake out the cobwebs, dammit."

I'm staring at her face as if I've never seen it before. My disorientation lasts a few seconds. Then the train's rhythmic clack penetrates the haze, and the last forty-eight hours come back in a numbing rush.

"What? . . . What?" I rasp, worried something's happened to the container. "Something wrong?"

"Bet your ass," she snaps. "Why aren't you over there where you belong?"

I groan, relieved, despite her shrill pitch. "Well, it got quite chilly for a while. I figured there'd be no harm in sharing the blanket. So . . . I slipped beneath it."

"Next to me."

"Next to you. Yes. I had little choice. Unless you'd prefer I'd taken it back to where I belong." I angrily toss it aside. My body is sore and stiff from the boxcar's hard floor, and I've no

232

tolerance for her pettiness. I let my head clear, then stagger to my feet and roll the corrugated steel door aside.

A thin shaft of daylight knifes into the darkness and gradually widens. Humid air with a sharp, salty bite follows. I inhale deeply, squinting at the glare. Beyond the lush tropical foliage that borders the right of way, a sparkling expanse of ocean stretches to a faint horizon and blends into a cloudless sky. The climate and vegetation leave little doubt we're traveling south.

Scotto drifts over and stands next to me, looking appropriately contrite. "Sorry 'bout that," she says, raising her voice over the sound of clacking wheels and rushing air that snaps at her hair. "I'm one of these people who wake up grouchy."

"Forget it."

"Hey, it was selfish of me to hog the blanket in the first place. Okay?"

"Okay," I reply, feigning I'm still offended.

"Something's bugging you, isn't it?" she prompts, taking the bait.

"No, really."

"Come on, I can tell. Spit it out."

"Well, it's nothing of any consequence; but I found it a little unsettling last night when you started moaning, 'Marty! Oh, Marty!' in the middle of your orgasm. Other than that . . ."

She laughs lustily. "Only in your dreams, Katkov. Only in your dreams."

We're standing in the doorway, watching the coastline go by, when the train leans into a curve. The freight is soon stretched out over its entire length, and we can see container 95824 at the other end. I doubt anyone else is keeping an eye on it. I heard rotors several times during the night, but we must be well beyond the three-hundred-mile range by now, because there's no helicopter in sight.

We settle on the floor and go to work on the junk food and bottled water Scotto hastily stuffed into the gym bag along with the blanket and some clothing. Once fortified, she slips her pistol from its holster, extracts the clip, and checks there isn't a bullet in the chamber. Then, with sure-handed authority, she begins breaking the weapon down. This is a satisfying ritual, not a chore; and, like Vorontsov's medals on the lace tablecloth, the precisely machined parts are soon neatly arranged between us on the blanket, along with the box of shells and cleaning kit Scotto takes from the gym bag.

I'm reflecting on how she handled those truckers and wondering why she craves living on the edge instead of in a house in the suburbs. "Tell me something, will you, Scotto?"

"Do my best."

"Why'd you become a cop?"

"Easy one. I dated a guy in college who was a criminology major. Much more interesting than European History—than him, for that matter. Definite FBI type. So I switched."

"That's how you became a cop. I asked you why."

"It's exciting. Makes me feel secure, and"—she inserts a long brush into the pistol's barrel, then looks up at me and giggles— "I get to play with guns. Last but not least, there's my Uncle Angelo."

"The one who taught you to shoot craps?"

"Uh-huh."

"You followed in his footsteps?"

She bursts into laughter and shakes her head no. "I'd be in the slammer if I did that."

"He's in prison?"

"Was. I said he was a bit of a hood. Got caught running numbers out of his *trattoria.*" She deftly slips the hammer assembly into the housing and locks it in position. "Made the best Sicilian pizza in Bensonhurst. Unfortunately, he wasn't as skilled when it came to making bail."

"So then what? You got into law enforcement to prove that all Italians aren't mobsters?"

"Nothing that idealistic." One by one, her fingers insert bullets into the clip as she explains. "He was a great guy, lots of laughs, affectionate. All the guys in my neighborhood were like that, but a lot of them had a sort of—I don't know—a pathological split in their personalities. They'd be hugging their kids one minute and pistol-whipping a shopkeeper who wouldn't pay protection the next."

"There's a lot of pistol-whipping going on in Moscow these days."

"Yeah, well, my girlfriends married those guys. They stayed home, cleaned house, cooked, and had kids—perfect little housewives who are still lying to themselves about where the money comes from."

"And you figured getting into law enforcement would keep all the split personalities at bay."

"Yeah, and it worked. I'm married to a decent guy who wants a little house in the 'burbs with a wife, kids, and a dog." She slaps the clip into the handgrip, holsters the weapon, and fastens the tie-down. "All that figuring sure came back and bit me on the ass, didn't it?"

Several blasts on the locomotive's air horns save me from having to reply. The insistent clanging of a bell follows as the train thunders through a crossing on the outskirts of a town. A quaint, steepled station with a sign that reads PORT ST. LUCIE flashes past.

"Florida," Scotto announces brightly. "We're in Florida, Katkov. My Aunt Adele lives down here."

"Uncle Angelo's wife?"

"No. Uncle Hank's. He was a golf pro."

"You had an uncle who was a golf pro?"

"Yeah," she replies indignantly. "They weren't all hoods. He had a driving range when I was a kid. Way ahead of his time."

"Way ahead of mine too. People try to hit a little ball into a hole from five hundred meters away. I don't get it."

"Me neither. They're always grousing about a hook, or a slice, or getting up and down, whatever the hell that means."

"Something to do with impotence, I imagine."

Scotto laughs. "Beats me, but I can tell you where we're going. . . ." She lets it tail off with that look she gets when pieces fall into place. "Miami."

"Miami? How do you know that?"

"It's the fluff-and-fold capital of America. The creeps get that cash into the banking system down there, they can wire it anywhere in the world. I mean, there's more than a hundred international banks with branches in south Florida. Some collaborate outright, some are negligent, some are just plain stupid. We've been leaning on 'em pretty hard lately."

"I'm sure you'll correct me if I'm wrong, but I've been under the impression your banking system is rather highly regulated."

"Up to a point. Ten thou is the magic number. Anything over that has to be reported to the IRS."

"So they keep each transaction under the limit, and you're none the wiser."

"You got it."

GREG DINALLO

"But two billion dollars. It'd take forever to launder that much, wouldn't it?"

"Depends. Doesn't take more than a couple of seconds to run an electronic rinse."

"What's that?"

"A wire transfer. A trillion bucks a day is wired among the world's banks, Katkov—that's *trillion*. Every penny goes through this massive computer setup in Manhattan called CHIPS."

"An acronym for . . . ?"

"Clearing House Interbank Payments System. They've got more electronic security than the CIA and KGB put together: codes, passwords, backup systems, screening systems, over a hundred dedicated phone lines to member banks. Five out of every six dollars that move in our economy go through the place, not to mention eighty percent of worldwide payments—and all for eighteen cents a pop."

"Per transaction?"

Scotto nods smartly. "Regardless of the amount."

"In other words, they could wire the entire two billion, anywhere in the world, for eighteen cents?"

"Uh-huh. But, like I said, they have to get it into the banking system first."

"Despite all that technology, there's still no way to distinguish dirty money from clean?"

"Not once it's on the wire. Bankers have the best shot. Unfortunately, the very institutions that are in a position to do it have the least incentive."

"Because they're making money off it."

"Getting rich off it. Anywhere from seven to ten percent off the top."

For the next four hours, temperature and humidity continue to rise, and stations zip past more frequently: Palm Beach, Boca Raton, Pompano, Fort Lauderdale. It's late afternoon by the time Miami's beachfront hotels come into view across Biscayne Bay. Bathed in the glow of fading sunlight, the pastel facades appear as if they've been dusted with powdered sugar. Long, narrow bridges that Scotto calls causeways connect the overdeveloped strip of sand to the mainland.

The train begins slowing down, then enters a short tunnel that takes it into the railyards in northeast Miami. Long lines of freight and passenger cars line the tracks. Work diesels patrol in search of their charges. Yardmen scurry between them checking couplers.

Scotto and I gather our things and prepare to jump from the boxcar when it stops, but the train seems to be maintaining its speed. Indeed, instead of being directed through a series of switches, instead of being shunted onto a siding, it continues straight ahead, bypassing the network of tracks. We exchange nervous glances as it becomes clear that we're waiting in vain, that it isn't going to stop, that, as we fear, it's going in one end of the yard and out the other.

"What the hell's going on now?" Scotto groans, her tone a mixture of exhaustion and exasperation.

"Maybe there's another yard someplace?"

"Yeah, sure," she says cynically, taking an angry swipe at the gym bag with her foot.

The long freight continues through a section of town that reminds me of East Baltimore, passing beneath a traffic interchange where expressways, interstates, and causeways come together in a gigantic concrete knot. Towering futuristic skyscrapers are looming up ahead when the tracks suddenly curve sharply eastward toward a short causeway that angles out across the water.

In the distance, an immense man-made island of passenger terminals, warehouses, and piers hovers above the placid bay. A sign proclaims PORT OF MIAMI DODGE ISLAND TERMINUS. The superstructures of cruise ships and ocean-going freighters beyond make it painfully clear that the money isn't going into Miami's banking system to be laundered electronically, as Scotto theorized. It's going into one of those cargo vessels, going out of the country, going to an unknown destination, where it will be scrubbed by hand.

30

*L*ike an exhausted marathoner, the long freight wheezes, screeches, and finally grinds to a stop somewhere in the middle of the immense island terminus.

The sun is below the rooftops when Scotto and I heft our bags and slip from the stuffy boxcar. Warmer on this spring night than Moscow on the hottest summer day, Miami lolls beneath a magenta sky that silhouettes the booms of freighters and skeletons of bridge cranes straddling the lines of railcars.

We make our way through a maze of narrow corridors created by the hundreds of shipping containers on the wharf, then turn a corner and come upon a massive containerized freighter straining at its hawsers. In the distance, the white, military-style shirts of Customs agents catch the fading twilight. Armed and vigilant, they're posted at the entrances and along the perimeter of this section of the terminus. Signs that proclaim RESTRICTED AREA OFF LIMITS TO UNAUTHORIZED PERSONNEL appear at intervals along a high fence that encloses it.

"The place is crawling with cops," Scotto whispers.

"You think Customs or DEA somehow beat us to the container?"

"Sure as hell hope not; they could blow the whole business before we—"

"Hey! Hey, hold it right there," a man's voice calls out sharply.

We freeze and turn to see a Customs agent leveling his side-arm at us with one hand and a flashlight with the other. I expect Scotto to identify herself, but she raises her hands instead and, through clenched teeth, says, "Keep your mouth shut and follow my lead."

The agent has us face one of the containers, hands raised, palms pressed against the gritty metal, feet spread wide apart; then he exchanges flashlight for radio and calls for assistance.

Moments later, I'm still trying to figure out what Scotto's up to when headlights come across the pier at high speed. A gray van screeches to a stop nearby, and three more agents, one of them a sergeant, pile out and frisk us. One finds Scotto's pistol and hands it to the sergeant with an incriminating smirk.

"I've got ID to go with that, Sergeant," Scotto says in a taut whisper. "Inside right jacket pocket."

The sergeant turns us around and shines his flashlight in Scotto's face; then he cautiously removes and examines her identification. The badge shimmers in the light as he shifts the beam to the plastic laminated photo and back. "U.S. Treasury."

Scotto nods imperceptibly. "I don't want to advertise. Understand?"

"I'm listening," he says, challengingly.

"We're working a money-laundering op. Make like we're a couple of vagrants in case the dry cleaners are watching, okay?"

"I doubt it. This place is buttoned up pretty damned tight."

"Yeah, next time we'll remember to knock. I'd rather be safe than sorry, okay?"

The sergeant reddens slightly and signals his men. They cuff us brusquely and shove us into the van. It heads for the Customs Building at the far end of the terminus. Once inside, the handcuffs come off and we're ushered into a cramped office with furniture that makes FinCEN's look like fine antiques. The sign on the door reads SHIFT SUPERVISOR.

The senior Customs inspector is a round-faced man with captain's bars on his epaulets and a mustache as coarse as a hairbrush beneath his broad nose. His name tag reads AGUILAR. He's cocked back in his chair, staring at us with a befuddled expression. "I want to make sure I have this right," he says, scrutinizing our ID. "He's a Russian journalist, and you're working with him?"

"It's a long story," Scotto replies. "He gave us some key data, and we're reciprocating by—"

"A journalist?" Aguilar interrupts, flabbergasted. "A journalist gave you data?"

"I know. They're different over there."

"She means we take sides."

"I mean you're taking our side," Scotto corrects. "That's the difference."

"No difference to me," Aguilar growls. "I don't want anything to do with journalists."

I can't hold my tongue any longer. "What's your problem, Inspector?"

"Scar tissue. Every time I talk to you people, I get burned. You tell lies, call it the truth, stir up trouble and walk away from it."

"Not me. I usually hop a freight."

Scotto arches a brow in vindication. Then she gets back to business and briefs Aguilar on the saga of container 95824.

"Two billion in cash!" he exclaims when she finishes, his eyes glowing like chandeliers in the Moscow Metro. "That's quite a haul, Scotto. We'd be happy to inspect, interdict, whatever you need."

"Appreciate the offer, Inspector, but I can't take you up on it," she replies gently. "Don't get me wrong. It's not that your happiness isn't high on my list, but we want to take down the creeps at the other end. So what I really need is a fix on where that container's going. Switzerland? Liechtenstein? Caymans? Panama? Gotta be one of your friendly neighborhood laundromats."

Aguilar leans back in his chair and smiles to himself. I get the feeling he's thinking "The joke's on you," and is deciding whether or not he'll let us in on it. Then he nods, and, in a mischievous whisper, replies, "Havana."

"No way," Scotto's fires back.

"Oh, yeah. Every container on that restricted section of pier is going to *Ha-ba-na.*"

"But we don't ship anything to Cuba," Scotto argues, perplexed. "The way I hear it, the embargo was just extended. The screws are being tightened, not loosened."

Aguilar nods smugly. "Yes, as a matter of fact, the screw-tighteners were good enough to send me a copy of the latest directive. Naturally, it makes this shipment all the more sensitive."

"Shipment of what?" Scotto prompts, still a little flustered.

Aguilar pulls himself from the chair and fetches a thick binder. Then he perches on the corner of his desk and, with cocky snaps of his wrist, flips through a sheaf of computer printouts and enumerates: "Dressers, side chairs, mirrors, beds, artwork, linen, drapery, carpet, glassware, china, desks, lamps, televisions—thousands and thousands of 'em."

"Geezus," Scotto groans. She's shaking her head in dismay. Inspector Aguilar's smiling beneath his mustache. I'm reflecting on that morning in Barkhin's Mercedes, on his remarks about Cuba's economy, about Castro getting back into tourism. "Sounds to me like furnishings for a hotel or something, no?"

"Close, but no cigar," Aguilar quips, flipping more pages in his binder. "We also have containers chock-full of slot machines, blackjack and roulette tables, playing cards, chips—need I go on?"

Scotto holds up her hands in surrender and whistles. "Cuba's back in the casino business?"

Aguilar nods and scowls disapprovingly.

"Who's the consignee?"

"Company called Turistica Internacional."

"Never heard of 'em."

"Me neither, but there've been dozens of shipments over the last couple of years. All signed, sealed, and sanctioned by the USG."

Scotto's expression hardens, and she glances over at me. "Sounds to me like your buddy Rubineau's mixed up in this."

"Thought's crossed my mind."

"You ever run across that name?" she asks Aguilar, spelling it out for him.

"Rubineau?" He shrugs and shakes his head no.

"What about Rubinowitz?"

"I think one of the crane operators is a guy named Rubinowitz. Naw, naw, maybe it's Liebowitz? I don't know. Something like that."

"This guy's an operator, but cranes aren't his thing. Any idea when that freighter sails?"

"Well, she berthed this morning," Aguilar replies. "Full cargo, unload, load—it'll be a while."

"When?" Scotto demands.

Aguilar swivels to a computer, types a few keystrokes. "Let's see . . . *Halifax* puts to sea—"

"*Halifax?*" Scotto interrupts suspiciously. "Canadian registry?"

Aguilar nods.

Scotto's eyes widen and dart to mine. The puzzle's making a little more sense now. "You getting this, Katkov?"

"Canada has diplomatic ties to Cuba and the USA."

"You're getting it. The shipper of container nine-five-eight-two-four on that list, Inspector?"

Aguilar turns to his binder and runs a stubby finger down the columns of numbers. "Coppelia Paper Products Limited."

Another look from Scotto. "Okay. Now, when does this sad excuse for the QE2 sail?"

Aguilar's eyes shift to the computer screen. "She sails . . . Monday . . . eighteen-thirty hours."

"Four days," Scotto sighs, relieved. "Gives us some time to shower and catch our breaths."

"Anything I can do to help?" he offers.

"Nothing. Please. Do absolutely nothing. Agreed?"

"Agreed," he replies halfheartedly.

"And I need to use a phone."

Aguilar shows us into an unoccupied office and leaves. Scotto punches out a number. "It's Scotto. Is he there?" She holds briefly, then winces and pulls the phone from her ear. I can hear Banzer reading her the riot act. He vents his spleen, then peppers her with questions. "Miami. . . . Freighter. . . . Havana," she replies evenly. As I expected, it's the last one that quiets him. After she briefs him on the details, he offers to run FinCEN's data bases for the owner of Turistica Internacional, then get back to us.

An hour later, Scotto and I are settled into adjoining rooms in the Best Western Hotel. It's a wicker-filled extravaganza in a waterfront park at the foot of the terminus causeway.

I'm standing beneath a steaming shower in another one of those bathrooms Muscovites would kill for. This one even has a telephone. The shower must be back-to-back with Scotto's because I can hear it going. In my mind, I suddenly hear her lusty admonition, "Only in your dreams, Katkov. Only in your dreams." Well, she may not know it, but here we are next to each other stark naked, and I'm dreaming.

The wall that separates us dissolves in a cloud of steam. Now we're face-to-face, the water running through her hair, swirling sensuously over her tawny Sicilian flesh that glistens like wet amber. She hands me a bar of soap and tosses her head back with abandon. I'm having visions of spreading the creamy lather over her generous swells when the soap suddenly shoots from my grasp and rockets over the top of the enclosure. I roll back the glass door in search of it. The bathroom is hazy with steam. The bar of soap is nowhere in sight, and now, to my utter dismay, neither is Special Agent Scotto.

I've just finished shaving when she knocks on the door that connects our rooms. "Katkov? Hey, Katkov, open up." I pull on a pair of slacks and let her in. She's barefoot; dressed in white jeans and starched blue denim shirt. Her hair hangs around her scrubbed face in a mass of wet tangles. "You have the boob tube on?" she asks, sounding refreshed.

"Please, after twelve hours on that train I was rather enjoying the quiet."

"Well, there's something coming up on CNN you might want to catch." She saunters across the room, drying her hair with a towel, and uses the remote to turn on the television.

A commercial for flashlight batteries in which a pink mechanical rabbit propels itself into a police shoot-out is in progress. If this were Moscow, it would be an old woman on a street corner holding a packet of batteries in one hand and a jar of mayonnaise in the other. The rabbit keeps going and going. Then the anchorman appears and, in grave tones, says, "Recapping today's top story: Less than a year after dissolving Parliament for refusing to endorse his policies and attempting to usurp his powers by force, Russian President Boris Yeltsin is, once again, threatening to declare emergency rule. Here with a live update from Moscow is CNN correspondent Jill Doherty."

Though, as of late, such crises seem to be the rule rather than the exception in my country, this is still shocking news. I'm trying to comprehend its meaning when an attractive woman appears on the screen. Bundled against the cold, she stands in Red Square with the illuminated onion-shaped domes of St. Basil's behind her and reports:

"Angrily denouncing the lethargic pace of the newly elected Congress, President Yeltsin said he will govern by decree, if necessary, to get the nation's economy moving, and will ask for yet another vote of confidence in a national referendum in the fall. In an effort to rally his followers, he doubled the minimum wage and confirmed that large-scale private ownership of land and industry is still his top priority.

"Though some believe the country is, once again, teetering on the brink of chaos, others cite Russia's privatization program as evidence to the contrary. Ninety-eight percent of the vouchers entitling citizens to buy shares in state-owned industries—GUM, the Moscow department store; Zil, the luxury auto maker; and the Volgograd tractor factory, among them— have been claimed, and enough citizens may have a financial stake in Yeltsin's reforms to make them irreversible. But experts still insist private investment is the key to this experiment in democracy."

"What do you think?" Scotto prompts as the correspondent drones on.

"This could be quite a disaster for Russia."

"Why? You really think the Communists could take over again?"

"They never left."

"Pardon me?"

"You're simplifying a very complex matter, Scotto. Yeltsin was a Communist. An extremely accomplished one, I might add. All the reformers were. They joined the Party because they were ambitious, not patriotic. Since its main function was to grant or deny permission to do things, the free market made them obsolete, and they became capitalists. Except Zhirinovsky, of course."

"Never heard of him."

"Good. I hope you never do. He's a nationalist lunatic, an ethnic cleanser in-waiting. But this isn't about ideology. It's about power. When Yeltsin dissolved Parliament and called for new elections, Zhirinovsky's party won the most votes—twenty percent. The Communists got twelve. He makes them look like human rights activists. People have short memories, Scotto. Look what happened in Poland last year."

"They dumped Walesa."

I nod glumly. "Believe me, the hard-liners are never going to let go."

"Yeah, but there'll be other elections. And sooner or later, they're going to get kicked out of office."

"Maybe. Unfortunately, this has nothing to do with the quality of life in Russia—which is unimaginably rotten—and is getting worse daily. Massive unemployment, rampant inflation, homelessness, hunger, not to mention a resurgence of anti-Semitism."

"Sounds like Germany in the thirties."

"Perfect analogy."

"So the danger is the people will throw in their lot with whoever convinces them they can better it."

"Worse than that." I pause, loath to validate the thought by verbalizing it. "The danger is, they'll remember things were better under Brezhnev—which they were—and decide freedom isn't worth the price."

"Come on, under Brezhnev there's no way you'd be sitting here today."

"True."

"I mean now you could even emigrate, if you wanted to. Right?"

"If I wanted to."

"You saying you never thought of getting out? Starting a new life somewhere? Israel, Brighton Beach . . ."

"All the time."

Scotto smiles and goes back to drying her hair with the towel as the television screen fills with demonstrators jammed into Red Square.

I can't take my eyes off them or the word LIVE next to the CNN logo. Live? I feel so distant, so out of touch. Everything here has moved so fast, I haven't had the inclination, let alone the time, to think about Russia. Now I can't get it out of my mind. For a brief moment, I'm seized by a compulsion to make a dash for the nearest airport. I decide to call Yuri for a firsthand report instead. I need to touch base, need to hear his reassuring voice. I follow instructions on a plastic card affixed to the phone and direct-dial his apartment in Moscow. Amazing. It rings in a matter of seconds, then rings and rings and rings.

"No answer?" Scotto prompts.

I nod glumly and hang up. "The time difference is eight hours, isn't it?"

Scotto nods, glancing to her watch. "It's two in the morning there."

"I don't understand. It's not like him. Yuri's always home at this hour."

"Maybe he's at that demonstration?"

"Yuri? I doubt it."

"He's not into reform?"

"Totally into it. Scientists make the best dissidents."

"How come?"

"Because they're always searching for the truth—"

"Walked right into that one."

"—and therefore have little tolerance for propaganda. Yuri's an economist, the quiet, behind-the-scenes type; goes to see his mother every Saturday."

She smiles. "Let's get some dinner, and you can try him again when we—" The phone in Scotto's room rings, interrupting. She hurries off to answer it.

I remain and stare numbly at the television, my eyes searching the faces of my countrymen, searching the crowd for Yuri— searching it madly, if I'm honest with myself, for Vera. Barely a week has passed since I left, but it seems so much longer. I cross to the windows, feeling vulnerable and homesick. The lights across the bay twinkle hypnotically in the darkness.

"That was Joe," Scotto announces brightly, pulling me out of it. "He's coming down tomorrow."

"That bad, huh?"

"Well, he talked to some people at State. For openers, Turistica Internacional is an American company. It's been granted special permission to work with the Cuban Government and redevelop their tourism and gaming industries."

"So much for the hard-nosed embargo. I imagine that explains why Jennifer couldn't get into their data base."

"Sure as hell does. It gets better. TI is a subsidiary of Travis Enterprises."

"Travis? That's Rubineau's holding company."

"Uh-huh," she says, her eyes brightening with an idea. "Now he can add the initials TI to it and call it travesty."

I can't help but laugh.

"By the way," Scotto goes on, "after talking with Joe, I had a brief chat with your pal Jennifer in Ops. Guess where Rubineau's jet is cooling its turbines this week?"

"Miami International."

Scotto nods emphatically.

"He's working out of his Miami office."

She nods again and breaks into a devilish smile. "I think it's time Mr. Rubinowitz and I got to know each other."

31

Sunlight streams through the windows of my hotel room. An impeccably dressed, terminally earnest black man in a pair of owlish glasses stares at me from the television. "Russia's Parliament threatens to impeach President Yeltsin," he announces with grave authority. "We'll be talking about it with former Ambassador Robert Strauss when *Today* continues." No mechanical rabbit selling batteries scampers across the screen this time. Instead, a massive cockroach crawls out of a drain threatening to devour everything in sight. It has to be stopped before it multiplies! Naturally, the pitchman has the answer. I can't help thinking it's a perfect metaphor for what's going on in Russia.

It's midafternoon in Moscow. I try Yuri again, this time at his office in the Interior Ministry. His secretary says he took the week off to care for his mother, who's ill. Very ill, I'm afraid, for Yuri to be out of the office that long with his work load. I finish dressing and head for the restaurant to meet Scotto. The hotel concession catches my eye en route. I've never seen so many brands of cigarettes in my life. The choices are overwhelming, but the time is short, so I quickly select several at random along with a pack of Marlboros as backup. Over breakfast, Scotto and I discuss how to approach Rubineau.

She sees the element of surprise as an advantage and decides against calling ahead for an appointment.

The Southeast Financial Center is a short walk from our hotel. The fifty-five-story tower rises from a plaza where towering palms sway beneath a steel-and-glass space frame. Rubineau occupies a choice suite on the top floor. On the wall behind the reception desk, an illuminated graphic diagrams the complex interlocking of his various companies. Travis Enterprises, ITZ, and Turistica Internacional are among the many names.

He handles Scotto's "surprise" with the aplomb and graciousness I anticipated and receives us in a sleek corner office that overlooks downtown Miami and Biscayne Bay beyond. The decor is severely modern: glass, chrome, and leather furnishings; artwork that rivals the pieces in his New York apartment; a full complement of executive toys, including computer terminal, stock market quotron, golf clubs, telescope, and impressive communications console.

Rubineau wastes no time showing off his favorite—a scale model of a sprawling resort complex that takes up the entire conference area. The detailed facades of literally dozens of beachfront hotels soar to eye level; charming bungalows cluster around Olympic-size swimming pools; chic condominiums line the fairways of championship golf courses. Basking in the sunny glow of spotlights, the development sweeps majestically into the sea on a finger of white sand. The sound of crashing surf is the only thing missing.

I'm staring at it in amazement. Scotto is staring at Rubineau. He's smiling like a grandfather showing off the long-awaited heir who will carry on the family legacy. The dark, pin-striped business suit he wore in New York has been replaced by cream-colored linen that sets off his deep tan.

"Varadero," he says, gesturing grandly as he walks around the gleaming model. "Less than two hours by car from Havana, an hour by plane from Miami." He whirls to the telescope and adds, "On a clear day, you can almost see it from here."

"That's fascinating, Mr. Rubineau," Scotto says brightly. "And one of your companies, Turistica Internacional, is developing it. Correct?"

"Correct."

"Then perhaps I'm also correct in assuming you can tell us why a container with two billion dollars in illicit cash—that's *billion*—is part of a shipment consigned to Turistica Internacional in Cuba?"

"Two billion?" Rubineau echoes coolly, circling in our direction.

Scotto nods. "In that ballpark. I haven't had the opportunity to count it yet."

"In a container being shipped to TI in Cuba?"

"That's what I said."

"That's a hell of a pile of money."

"Drug money. One of several piles that've turned up on your doorstep lately."

Rubineau pauses and fires an angry look between the scale model hotel towers. "That sounds like a threat, Agent Scotto."

"No, Mr. Rubineau. It's a fact."

"I thought this was going to be a friendly off-the-record chat. If I'm being accused of something, I'll call my lawyers now."

"Call whoever you like. Be sure to mention that you also own a building in Baltimore where close to five hundred million more turned up."

Rubineau's eyes lock onto Scotto's like a pair of angry lasers. I'm wondering what he'll do: Blow his top? Throw us out? Call security? Instead, he surprises me and nods grudgingly. "I'll tell you what I told Katkov. I'm not responsible for what's stored in a building leased from me, and you know it." His eyes leave hers and capture mine; then he shifts into Russian and challenges, "What the hell is this, Katkov? I thought I told you to tell her she was wasting her time. Now she's here wasting mine."

I can see Scotto out of the corner of my eye. Skillful as ever, she looks appropriately baffled by the sudden shift in languages. "That's a matter of opinion, Mr. Rubineau," I reply sharply in Russian, annoyed that he's treating me as if I'm on his payroll, or at the least on his side. "Quite frankly, if I were you, I'd be hoping that's the case. Furthermore—"

"Listen, Katkov," he interrupts, continuing to speak in Russian. "When I want advice from you, I'll ask for it. Understood?"

More Russian. "Understood. Now there's something *you* have to understand. I'm not your errand boy. I don't answer to you, and I don't like your implying it."

"Fair enough."

Scotto rewards me with a cocky smile. Rubineau picks up on it, but isn't certain what it means. I do. I've known all along what's coming now. "You know, maybe you should call those lawyers," Scotto suggests coyly in Russian. She pauses briefly, letting Rubineau squirm, then adds, "While you're at it, you might mention you also own a trucking depot in Maryland that dispatched the container with the two billion."

"The one in Hagerstown," he says in English, unwilling to acknowledge she topped him.

Scotto nods incriminatingly.

"Come on, Agent Scotto, they don't inspect cargo, they ship it."

"It's your company."

"I'm not personally responsible for everything that goes through the place."

"Somebody is."

"Are you suggesting I'm being used?"

"Are you?"

"Anything's possible."

"Then I expect you'd want to do something about it?"

"Who said I don't? Look, I checked my records. A company called Coppelia Paper Products leases that building in Baltimore."

"That's not news."

"Did they also ship that container?"

"Sure as hell did."

"Well, for the record," Rubineau says, indicating the architectural model, "this development is a coventure with the Cuban Government. My half is being financed with profits from my other businesses."

"The State Department will verify that?"

"You can count on it."

"You can count on me checking with them. I also plan to ask why they're breaking their own embargo."

"I'll save you the time. It's the old carrot and stick routine. The diplomatic version of good cop, bad cop. Smack 'em with one hand, massage 'em with the other, and let them decide which they prefer."

"I'm familiar with the technique."

"I thought you might be."

"No offense, but with your background, why would the United States Government—"

Rubineau's eyes flare with indignation. "Hold it right there. Am I to assume that means you're referring to Mr. Lansky?"

"That's right."

"Then I do take offense."

"Suit yourself, Mr. Rubineau. Now, let's get back to my question. With all the people in the hotel and gaming business, why would the USG come to you?"

"They didn't." A smug grin tugs at a corner of his mouth. He straightens his tie, letting her live with it for a moment, then delivers the punch line. "Castro did—*personally.*"

Scotto's jaw drops.

So does mine.

"And the USG agreed to it?" she asks, stunned.

Rubineau smiles, pleased by her reaction. "It's a very long story. You have a half hour? I want to show you something." He turns and leads the way from the office without waiting for a reply.

32

The high-speed elevator deposits us in the financial center's underground garage, where a Lincoln limousine is waiting. Sleek, sensuous, with the finish of a black mirror, it makes the Russian Zil look like an armored personnel carrier. The license plate reads TRAVIS. Rubineau and I settle in the backseat, Scotto in one of the jump seats facing us. The chauffeur swings up the spiraling ramp, onto Biscayne Boulevard, then takes Flagler west across the Miami River.

We're gliding through the sweltering streets in air-conditioned comfort when I notice the fronts of the bars and markets are gradually becoming sprinkled with Spanish. Soon, we're in a quarter of the city alive with an earthy gaiety that reminds me of Havana when I was there twenty years ago. Colorful explosions of neon, plastic, and paint advertise: CAFÉ CUBANO, LOS PINARENOS, MAXIMO GOMEZ PARK, LAS CASA DE LOS TRUCOS, EL CRÉDITO, VARADERO MARKET. Old men in embroidered shirts that Rubineau calls *guayaberas* shuffle about blithely. Dark-haired women bargain fiercely with merchants who hawk their wares from pushcarts and rickety stands.

Without any prompting from Rubineau, the chauffeur slows and parks in front of a flower shop. It's bursting with displays that spill out across the sidewalk.

"Don't go 'way," Rubineau says as the chauffeur opens the door for him. He unfolds his lanky frame and crosses to the Cuban proprietor, who greets him warmly.

"What the hell's he up to?" I wonder after the door closes.

"Beats me," Scotto replies. "But I think he's lying through his teeth."

It catches me a little off guard. "Why?"

"You see the telescope in his office?"

I nod, still unable to imagine where she's headed.

"But you didn't notice it was aimed right at the piers, did you? Ten to one he's keeping an eye on container nine-five-eight-two-four."

"You don't know that for a fact."

"No, but I don't believe that bullshit about keeping an eye on Varadero, either. I mean—" She bites it off as Rubineau's shadow falls across the window and the chauffeur opens the door.

Scotto and I exchange curious looks as Rubineau settles next to me with a spray of lilies. His behavior only deepens the intrigue, as does his silence. The limousine resumes its journey. A series of rights and lefts takes us to a flagstone gatehouse. An elderly attendant looks up and nods blankly. A weathered bronze plaque reads MOUNT NEBO CEMETERY.

"You know your Old Testament, Katkov?" Rubineau prompts as the limousine follows the winding road.

"I'm afraid the study of religion was rather frowned upon when I was growing up."

"Well, Mount Nebo is the mountain in Canaan where Moses died."

"Ah, yes, I have a dim recollection of reading that somewhere. If you don't mind my asking, what's a Jewish cemetery doing in the middle of Little Havana?"

"It was a Jewish neighborhood called Shenandoah in the fifties. The intriguing part is, as the Cubans began mingling with the Jews, they realized they had something in common."

"You mean they've both been exiled from their homelands."

"Right. And one group still is—which explains the fascination Cuban refugees have for Israel. It stands as a symbol of what can be attained if you hang in there long enough."

The limousine comes to a stop. Rubineau takes two black yarmulkes from a compartment between the jump seats. He dons one, hands me the other, and gets out of the car. I haven't worn one in years, and it takes a moment to get the skullcap situated atop my unruly locks; then Scotto and I hurry after him. The narrow path is lined with headstones that proclaim ROTHER, LEVINE, GOLDBERG, ABRAMOWITZ. It leads to a grove of trees that shade a slab of chest-high granite flanked by octagonal columns, resembling mezuzahs. Simple block letters chiseled across its face spell out the name LANSKY.

Rubineau places the flowers atop the monument and spends a moment in solemn contemplation, then turns to us and says, "It's fitting that Meyer's buried here. He loved Cuba, loved the people. He also had a love of history and was very politically astute. He predicted what was going to happen in Cuba. As a matter of fact, he went to the FBI and told them, because he loved his country as well."

"That's very moving, Mr. Rubineau," Scotto says, clearly unmoved.

"I don't like your tone, Agent Scotto. For your edification, Meyer's son, Paul, went to West Point."

"So did Noriega's chief of staff. I don't mean to be disrespectful of the dead, but it was a selfish act, and you know it. Lansky had a huge investment there."

"You bet. Every penny Meyer had went into the Riviera. It was the finest hotel and best-run casino in Havana."

"That's my point. He had a lot to lose."

"So did the United States," Rubineau fires back. "But they ignored his warning, and look what happened. Soviet missiles ended up a stone's throw from Miami, and we ended up on the brink of nuclear war."

Scotto scowls. "We didn't come here for a history lesson, Mr. Rubineau. What's all this got to do with Castro hiring you?"

"Not very patient, is she, Katkov?" he prompts with one of his disarming smiles.

I can't help but return it.

Scotto is stone-faced.

"It all began back in the late forties," Rubineau explains. "After years of collaboration, Meyer and the Italians had a falling out over Las Vegas. Costello thought it would be a loser and didn't want to invest. Meyer disagreed and sided with Siegel, who was pushing it. What can I say? The man was a genius. Look at the town today."

"Yeah," Scotto snorts facetiously, "A showcase of American integrity and family values."

"And tax revenues," Rubineau adds without missing a beat. He winks at me. "Imagine an agent of the U.S. Treasury overlooking taxes? Anyway, it was every man for himself after that. So, when Meyer found out the Italians were in cahoots with the CIA to take out Castro, he decided to take care of Meyer."

"I recall they tried everything short of nuclear weapons to kill him."

"Tell me about it," Scotto replies, disgusted. "It was a comedy of errors. Cyanide pills smuggled into his bedroom by his mistress, a thing with shoe polish to make his beard fall out, poisoned cigars. Nothing worked. Somehow, he always managed to survive."

"Amazing," Rubineau concludes with a wiley smile. "At the snap of a finger, they could take out a rival capo protected by an army of wise guys, but they couldn't get to Castro. How lucky can a guy get?"

Scotto looks from Rubineau to the headstone and back, putting the pieces together. "Lansky tipped Castro to the hits."

Rubineau nods and allows himself a little smile. "I don't mean to be immodest, but it was my idea."

"An idea that eventually got you disbarred."

"Let's not get into that," Rubineau snaps, seething at the memory. "Meyer was against it at first; but once he realized Castro was a *fait accompli,* he knew he had to take action to save the Riviera."

"Well, he may have been a genius," Scotto intones, "but he sure blew the call on that one."

Rubineau waggles his hand. "The Riviera actually reopened for a while, but then Castro hooked up with the Kremlin, and it was nationalized—along with Kodak, Westinghouse, Woolworth, and Goodyear, I might add. Hell, the Riviera's still in business. For years, all the Russian big shots stayed there. Politicians, generals, engineers. They turned the casino into a convention center." He laughs ironically at a thought. "Now, you can gamble in Moscow but not in Havana."

"So then it didn't pay off," Scotto says, still trying to provoke him.

"It didn't pay off *then* . . ." Rubineau says with a mischievous twinkle. He lets it trail off, picks a blossom from a low-hanging branch, and hands it to Scotto. "But it has now."

Scotto's eyes come alive, matching the sparkle in his. The final piece to the puzzle falls into place. "That's the answer to my question, isn't it?"

Rubineau nods. "Thirty years ago, Castro destroyed the tourist industry and replaced the income with Soviet aid. Now it's gone. The economy's in the toilet, and he's desperate to turn it around. Reestablishing Cuba as a tourist mecca is the only move he's got. Legalized gambling is the key. And I'm the guy he hired to make it happen."

"Castro's way of saying thanks."

"One way of putting it. Keep in mind, he didn't settle for a second-string player just to repay a debt. As a matter of fact, I happen to know he talked to the top guys at Radisson and Hyatt to keep me honest. Sure, they could handle it, but no better than Mike Rubineau. Varadero's already in the black. The hotels are running at an eighty-six percent occupancy rate. The place is becoming a playground for Canadians, Italians, Russians."

Scotto shakes her head incredulously. "I still can't believe the State Department agreed to do business with you."

"Why not? They cooperated with Italian gangsters to kick Castro's butt. Why not a Jewish entrepreneur to pull Cuba's out of the fire?"

"An entrepreneur Castro trusts."

"Very good, Katkov. Besides, compared to what some of our financial wizards have been up to lately, I'm Mr. Clean as far as the USG is concerned."

"Don't blow that horn too loud, Mr. Rubineau," Scotto cautions. "You still have to deal with that two billion in drug money consigned to Turistica Internacional."

Rubineau nods and runs a hand across the top of Lansky's tombstone thoughtfully. "You willing to give me the benefit of the doubt?"

"What do you mean?"

"Let that container go to Cuba. I mean, if somebody's using me, I want to find out who it is as badly as you do."

"Food for thought," Scotto muses, studying him obliquely; then she pointedly adds, "If somebody is using you, Mr. Rubineau, we'll find him. If not, we'll find that out too."

33

The message light is flashing on Scotto's phone when we return to the hotel. Banzer and Krauss have checked in. We waste no time heading down the corridor to Banzer's room. Nothing pretentious. Bland and provincial, just like ours. Just like him. Though, in short-sleeve shirt with nautical motif, elastic-waistband trousers, and deck shoes, FinCEN's portly director does look a little out of his element. Krauss, on the other hand, appears to be clearly at home in Levi's, polo shirt, and athletic shoes.

Scotto takes one look at her boss and bites a lip to keep from bursting into laughter. "Hey, you guys didn't have to do this," she gushes facetiously. "I mean, imagine leaving winter wonderland to tough it out in Miami Beach? If this doesn't get Congress to pass the budget, nothing will."

"Come on," Banzer protests self-consciously. "I've been looking for an excuse to wear this stuff since Christmas."

"Of 'seventy-three," Krauss cracks.

Scotto can no longer suppress it. Neither can I. The room rocks with laughter. "So, what's going on?" she finally asks, still fighting for control.

"I'm sure you'll correct me if I'm wrong, Gabby," Banzer replies with a good-natured grin, "but I believe I'm the one who gets to ask that question." He settles back in his chair and listens intently as she reviews our meeting with Rubineau. "Well," the director says after she finishes, "if the man isn't clean, he's playing the game as well as it's ever been played."

"And he's gonna win big," Scotto adds smartly. She shifts her attention to Krauss. "Any news on Coppelia? Like a tie to Rubineau, maybe?"

"Nothing," the Ops chief reports. "No connection to any of his companies. Matter of fact, as you may suspect . . ." He lets it trail off and gestures to Scotto to finish the sentence.

"Coppelia Paper Products doesn't exist," she fires back, "except on paper."

Banzer grunts in disgust. "A name with a bank account to which funds are wired."

"From where?"

"We're still working on that."

"Not surprising," Scotto intones glumly. She falls into a chair opposite Banzer. I settle on a stool next to the wet bar. Krauss slips behind it and opens the small refrigerator. "Interest anybody in a brew?"

"Right here," Banzer replies.

"Ditto," Scotto chirps.

"Katkov?"

"Coke, please."

Krauss starts pitching cans about the room like a circus juggler. "So, what're our options?"

"One from column A and one from column A," Scotto replies in a sassy tone. "We either take Rubineau down or we"—she hooks her finger in the pull ring and opens her beer with a loud pop—"take Rubineau down."

"Why?" I wonder, baffled by her rashness. "Unless I missed something, he isn't culpable until he takes possession of the money."

"That's right," Krauss says. "And there's no way he's going to do that here."

Scotto frowns. "He may not do it anywhere. That's why I figure if we complicate his life a little, he might agree to cooperate."

"I'm sure you'll correct me if I'm wrong, Agent Scotto," I say, catching Banzer's eye, "but less than an hour ago, Rubineau offered to do just that."

"You mean that crap about letting the container go to Cuba?" Scotto scoffs.

"Precisely."

"Not a chance."

"Why not? We've come all this way. I thought the idea was to let the container take us to whoever's at the other end?"

"It is. But that wouldn't be cooperation, that'd be collusion—in the strictest criminal sense."

"You're playing word games with me, Scotto. You want the other end or not?"

"Bet your ass I do."

"Well, then you can just as well bet your ass that it's Russia."

A look passes between Banzer and Krauss. "You're positive that's where it's going?" the latter prompts, taken by the theory.

"Positive. I'm afraid your colleague is either unwilling or unable to see it."

"And you can?!" Scotto challenges, getting out of the chair to confront me.

"Indeed, and I'll be more than happy to explain what's going on. When I first got involved in this, I thought it had to do with moving money out of Russia."

"Capital flight," Banzer interjects.

"Yes, but I was wrong. It's the opposite. It's about moving money in. Russia needs hard currency. The cartels and crime bosses have it. But, thanks to you folks, the traditional laundering venues—wire transfers, check-cashing operations, unnumbered bank accounts, et cetera—are becoming less and less viable. Therefore, they need a new—"

"Big of you to point that out, Katkov," Scotto cracks, her tone dripping with sarcasm.

"Knock it off, Gabby," Banzer orders sharply. "Let him finish."

"My point is, they need a new mechanism, and Rubineau's the key. He's bitter over the past and driven by the future, by this late-in-life allegiance to his homeland. So what does he do? He uses his USG-sanctioned deal in Cuba to set himself up as the pipeline. All the dirty cash that's locked in the USA, that's rotting in basements, can be quite efficiently moved and invested in Russia."

"Quite cleverly too," Krauss says. "One container going directly to Russia stands a much greater chance of being nailed by Customs than one of thousands going to Cuba under special sanction."

Banzer's eyes widen with intrigue. "All his deals in Russia are legit, but he's using mob money to pay for them. That's pretty good."

"Better than good. Rubineau actually told me he was bringing money in; however, he didn't say whose."

"Okay, okay, assuming Katkov's right, *assuming* . . ." Scotto emphasizes, running with the theory, "then Russia's privatization program would play right into the mob's hands, wouldn't it?"

"Keep talking," Banzer prompts.

"Well, it's a voucher system. That means if they buy them from private citizens with the dirty cash, they'll be laundering it in lots of small pieces, rather than in huge chunks."

"Like a check-cashing operation," Krauss concludes.

"Exactly."

"No," I protest gently. "You're complicating the matter. There's no need to launder it in Russia. No one questions cash there. You simply place several large suitcases on the table, and the deal is done."

"Direct investment," Krauss concludes.

"Whatever."

"If Katkov's right," Banzer reasons, nursing his beer, "if this money is going into Russia to pay for ITZ deals, there still has to be somebody on the inside."

"That'd be Arkady Barkhin, I imagine."

"No way," Banzer declares. "He'll come away with a piece of the action, but the Russian government owns the industries ITZ is buying, correct?"

"Uh-huh."

"Then there has to be a transition point for the money; and that means someone inside the government."

"I thought it might've been Vorontsov, early on," I venture, having no idea who else it could be. "But now I'm quite certain he was clean."

"Me too," Scotto chimes in. She drains her beer and launches the can into the air with a flick of her wrist. "They killed him because he was about to blow the whistle on organized crime buying into Russian businesses." The can lands in a trash pail next to the wet bar. She nods smartly, suggesting her accuracy validates her theory.

"Yes, but someone had to finger him first," Banzer argues, hitching up trousers that keep slipping despite the elastic waist. "They had to know Vorontsov was going to blow the whistle. Which leaves us with an insider who blew it on him."

Scotto's head bobs with uncertainty. "That works if the money's going to Russia, but there's an equally good chance it's staying in Cuba, or—"

"Organized crime. Running Havana's casinos like in the old days," Banzer interrupts, jumping on it.

"Yeah. It's pretty obvious Rubineau still feels the weight of Lansky's legacy." Scotto cocks her head in my direction, soliciting confirmation.

"I agree. He's quite burdened with it, but—"

"Thank you," she says curtly, cutting me off. "On the other hand, it could be going anywhere from there. Havana's what? About two-hundred-fifty miles from the Caymans, less than a thou from Bolivia or Panama. Not to mention Switzerland, Liechtenstein . . ."

"A third angle," Krauss offers, "is that Castro's setting up Cuba as a clearinghouse. From the missile base of the sixties to the monetary base of the nineties."

Banzer grunts in agreement. "If he was smart, he'd do it by the book and model it after the Cays: easy incorporation, regulatory flexibility, strict confidentiality, no taxes, ten percent off the top."

"Two hundred million for doing nothing," Scotto calculates.

"Beats working for a living," Krauss quips.

"Well, if I were you," I say, fueling the fire, "I'd sure want to know if that's what he's up to."

Banzer nods thoughtfully and swings a look to Krauss. "Tom?"

"Well, I guess we could play ball with Rubineau for a while."

"Gabby?"

"I don't trust him. I mean, which came first here, the chicken or the egg?"

"I've waited years for the answer," Banzer jokes.

"Look, Rubineau claims Castro came to him out of undying gratitude. That's a pun, guys. Anyway, there's every chance it was the other way around."

"You mean Rubineau had a line to the money and instigated the whole thing?" Krauss speculates.

Scotto nods emphatically.

"It doesn't matter, dammit," I say, frustration getting the best of me. "You're all forgetting it started in Moscow, and that's where it's ending. But you have to let that container go."

"Why? Because it's better for your story?" Scotto challenges.

"Better for my country. It's rife with corruption. Letting crime syndicates control our distribution systems isn't going to clean it up."

"Getting the two billion into Russia might be better for your country too, Katkov."

"What do you mean by that?"

A sly smile creeps across her face. "Oh, just that it's possible he's won you over."

"Who?"

"Your newly found countryman."

"Rubineau? Are you accusing me of something?"

"No. I'm wondering if you haven't fallen victim to the same misguided motives. It wouldn't be the first time someone with a strong ethical compass lost their way. Things get bad enough, it's easy to convince yourself the end justifies the means."

"Well, since we're talking about purity of motive, Agent Scotto, was your friend Woodruff's death an excuse to get back into the field? Or do you really want to bring those responsible to justice?"

Scotto seethes. I've struck the nerve dead center, as I intended. Even Banzer waits expectantly for her reply. "That was a low blow, Katkov," she says through clenched teeth.

"As you Americans are so fond of saying, it comes with the territory. A Russian may not have pulled the trigger; but once again, I hasten to remind you, that this began in Moscow, and—"

"What if you're wrong? Two billion slips through our fingers, and—"

"I'm not wrong."

"Easy to say, but—"

"Hold it, hold it," Banzer interrupts. He has a weird look on his face. As if he's been stunned by a thought. "You two chased that container for fifteen hundred miles, right?"

Scotto grunts. I nod.

"Either of you happen to get a look inside it?"

We both shake our heads no.

"No one's actually seen the two billion?"

From Scotto's expression I suspect her gut is feeling hollow like mine. "Katkov raised the issue when the decoy rigs showed up," she offers generously. "But it wasn't in the cards. Any word on them?"

"Yeah. Two were empty. They were dropped off at depots for reuse. We lost track of the third."

"So," Krauss concludes in his incisive way, "we're fighting over whether or not we let a container of evidence go; and for all we know it could be filled with kitty litter?"

Scotto nods somberly.

Banzer winces with apprehension.

I drain my Coke in response to the bile rising in the back of my throat.

34

The Fincen gang spends the afternoon making arrangements with Customs to inspect container 95824. I spend it satisfying an overwhelming compulsion to write. Within minutes of returning to my room, the typewriter is out of its scarred case, and I'm ripping off page after page of notes on what's happened since Scotto and I left Arlington.

As soon as darkness falls, the four of us pile into Banzer's rented sedan and cross the short causeway to Dodge Island. Several cruise ships are about to sail. The passenger terminals are ablaze with light and buzzing with bon voyage festivities. Banzer parks in front of the Customs building.

Inspector Aguilar is out of his chair the instant he sees us coming down the corridor toward his office. One eye on the time clock, the other on his pension, he'd do quite well at any Ministry in Moscow. But this could be the biggest money-laundering interdiction in history, and he wants to be part of it so badly, he can taste it. After some perfunctory paper shuffling with Banzer, Aguilar consults his computer for the location of container 95824. "Aisle thirty-four, slot twenty-one," he announces from beneath his mustache before leading the way outside.

The sergeant who took Scotto and me into custody packs the

group into a gray Customs van. It proceeds along Port Boulevard to the far end of the harbor where cargo vessels are berthed. Bridge cranes stilled, work lights off, longshoremen headed home, the massive pier is deserted and painted with deep shadows that recede into hard-edged blackness.

The guard at the security gate salutes Aguilar and waves the van through. It crosses the restricted area and turns into a narrow aisle between the containers destined for the hold of the Havana-bound freighter. Somewhere deep in the corrugated-steel maze, the van slows and stops.

The numerals 95824 are visible through the window next to me. My heart starts pounding. Aguilar rolls back the door, and the six of us pile out of the van. Anxious glances. Tense silence. An air of finality. The pungent odor of creosote rises as we gather around one end of the grimy container.

Aguilar nods.

The sergeant breaks the Customs seals and uses a master key to open the padlock, then retracts the dead bolts that secure the doors. The weathered hinges grind unnervingly as he opens one, then the other, and turns on a flashlight. Krauss and Aguilar do the same. The beams slash the darkness like dueling sabers, and there—behind the plastic webbing that prevents the cargo from shifting—the overlapping circles of light find an eight-foot-square wall of United States currency. Clear plastic bags stuffed with bundles of cash are piled side-to-side and top-to-bottom like tightly packed stones. They all seem to contain hundred-dollar bills from which Benjamin Franklin's stern visage stares back at us.

We're stunned by the sight of it. Even Scotto is at a loss for words. The collective sigh of relief is probably loud enough to be heard back at FinCEN headquarters in Arlington.

Scotto tightens a fist in triumph.

"Yessss," Krauss hisses under his breath.

"Fuck-ing A!" Aguilar exclaims jubilantly.

"Let's not break out the champagne yet," Banzer cautions. He leads the group around to the container's side door. "Better crack this one too, just to be sure."

The sergeant opens it swiftly. More plastic bags stuffed with hundreds are jammed across the opening.

"It's—it's unbelievable," I stutter.

"Well, I'll tell you something else you won't believe, Mr.

Katkov," Banzer says in a confidential tone. "At this very moment, despite strict Federal Reserve monitoring of the money supply, the USG has no idea where eighty percent of the bills printed by the Treasury are located."

"Eighty percent?" I echo, flabbergasted.

"Eighty," he repeats, pleased by my reaction.

"Well, we located a few of them, didn't we?" Aguilar prompts, mustache twitching with anticipation.

Banzer forces a weak smile. "Okay, button it up."

Aguilar stops the sergeant with a look. "Care to run that by me again?" he challenges caustically.

"I'll run it over you, if I have to," Banzer threatens. "We have a decision to make, and the lid stays screwed on tight until we do. Am I coming through?"

Aguilar holds Banzer's look, then breaks it off. "Loud and clear." He nods to the sergeant, who goes about slamming doors, setting dead bolts, and securing levers and locks.

A thought occurs to me. I motion Scotto aside. "You have something sharp in there?"

"Uh-huh." She digs in her shoulder bag, and, to my amazement, removes a hunting knife. "Why?"

"Just a feeling." I use it to scratch my initials into the side of the container next to the number. "There were four of these with the same number; but one is still unaccounted for, right?"

Scotto raises a brow in tribute and whispers, "Fuck-ing A."

A short time later, we're packed into Aguilar's office in the Customs building. Banzer leans against the edge of the desk, arms folded across his chest as he holds court. Aguilar is beside himself, pacing the tiny space like a caged animal. "We let that container out of the country"—he pauses to glare at me—"we can kiss it good-bye."

"I beg to differ. I—"

"Beg all you like," he interrupts, "there's no way in hell I'm signing off on it."

"Be advised, Inspector," Banzer says, making no effort to hide his disdain, "that in the event we decide to let the container go on, my ass'll be on the line, not yours." He pushes off the edge of the desk and hitches up his pants. "If you need verification, give Assistant Commissioner Morrison a call. I have the number if you need it." He shifts his look to Krauss without waiting for a reply. "What's your take on this, Tom?"

"I don't know, boss. I mean, if it ends up in Cuba, we have no legal recourse; nothing."

"And if it doesn't, if it goes on," Scotto adds with a nod that acknowledges my theory, "we have no way to trace it."

Three heads bob sharply in agreement.

"Yes, you do," I say mysteriously, pausing to light a cigarette now that I have their attention. "You have me."

"You?" Banzer prompts, baffled.

"That's right, Mr. Banzer. Me. Maybe none of you can go to Cuba, but I can."

"That's ridiculous," Aguilar scoffs loudly, spinning his chair to show his anger.

"Why? I can book passage on that freighter as a tourist, and be as close to that container when it gets to Cuba—and when it leaves—as we were tonight."

Banzer groans with exasperation. "Look, we got away with letting you hook up with Scotto, but I'm afraid that's as far as it goes."

Aguilar grunts in agreement. "I mean, no way I'm putting two billion dollars in the hands of a Russian journalist."

I exhale slowly, adding to the haze that hangs beneath the fluorescents. "Are you implying I'm not trustworthy, Inspector?"

"No. I'm saying it."

"Hey, hey," Banzer says in a conciliatory tone. "It's not a matter of trust. It's a matter of competence."

"That's right," Krauss says. "No offense, Katkov, but you're not qualified to handle this."

Scotto has a strange look on her face, as if something of monumental significance just occurred to her. "I don't know about that. I mean, as partners go, he's sure as hell held up his end so far."

"He what?" Banzer blurts.

"You heard me. Held up mine on occasion too," she says with a mischievous grin. "Didn't you, Katkov?"

I'm speechless. Along with Banzer and Krauss, she's caught me completely off guard, and I can barely manage an astonished grunt.

"Geezus," Banzer finally exclaims incredulously. "Am I actually hearing this?"

"What can I tell you, guys? I got this thing for journalists who put their ass on the line. It never dawned on me Katkov could go to Cuba. All things considered, I think it's worth a shot."

"All things considered, I think you're nuts."

"Come on, Joe. We—"

"Don't start with that Joe business again."

"Look," Scotto argues. "We already nailed a half billion in that basement, right?"

Banzer nods impatiently.

"And we already nailed the truck depot."

"Gabby—"

"And if Rubineau's a bad penny, we can nail him whenever we want. We're already batting .750, Joe. Why not swing away? Come on, let the damned container go."

"Give me one good reason."

"Other than the three I just gave you?"

Banzer grunts affirmatively.

"This." She points to the pit of her stomach. "My gut is telling me Katkov's right about it going to Russia—"

"Not good enough."

"And you'll be getting me back," she adds brightly.

Banzer grins wryly and waggles a hand.

"Okay, Joe, but you're asking for both barrels."

"Woody?" Banzer prompts warily. "Again? You want me to go along with this for Woody?"

Scotto nods solemnly.

"What do you think he'd say?"

"I'd give anything to be able to ask him, Joe."

Banzer removes his glasses and pinches the bridge of his nose, then holds the lenses up to the light, scrutinizing them as he thinks it through. "The Halifax sails on Monday, right?"

Scotto and I both nod.

"Well, if I were you, Katkov," Banzer concludes, "I'd spend the weekend working on my tan."

"You saying what I think you're saying?" Scotto asks expectantly.

"I'm saying that if he's going to Cuba as a tourist, and Miami was his last stop, he damn well better look it."

"Shit," Aguilar mutters under his breath.

"You don't like it?" Banzer shoves the phone across the desk. "God is waiting for your call."

Aguilar glances to the phone, then slumps in his chair and seethes.

Banzer grins at Scotto. "Since you Sicilians seem to have the technique down, Agent Scotto, I'm leaving Katkov in your capable hands. Get him some clothes, a camera, sunglasses, a T-shirt from Disney World, whatever."

"Diz-nee-vherl?" Scotto says, breaking up.

I burst into laughter along with her.

"What? What?" Banzer wonders, preoccupied. "I miss something here?"

"No, Joe, it's an inside joke."

Banzer puts the glasses back on and zeroes in on Aguilar. "We'll be counting on your cooperation."

Aguilar nods sullenly.

"What was that?" Banzer prompts, a hand to his ear.

"I said, you can count on it."

"Okay," Banzer exclaims with a clap of his hands as if he's wrapped up another day at the office. "Where we going for dinner? I'm starving."

Scotto decides it should be a bon voyage party in my honor and tracks down a place in Little Havana called Versailles. The strangely named restaurant is sweaty, raucous, and alive with rapid-fire Spanish and the thump of canned congas that echo off walls of faded mirrors. The customers are smoking like chimneys. The dishes of earthy Cuban food are massive. The beer is strong and dark, the coffee stronger and darker. I'm nursing my third piña colada. Banzer is absentmindedly stirring what's left of his café Cubano. Scotto's counting the turns of the spoon. "What's bugging you, Joe?"

"Huh?"

"You're drilling a hole in your cup. You always do that when something's on your mind."

He nods grimly. "This damned insider."

"The one we figure blew the whistle on Vorontsov," Krauss declares.

"Yeah. They cross paths, chances are he'll know Katkov, but Katkov won't know him. None of us would. He could be sitting at the next table."

Scotto arches a brow in agreement. Her eyes dart back and forth between us.

Banzer's search mine for a reaction.

"Well, as you might imagine, I've been giving that some thought."

Banzer sets the spoon aside and takes a sip of coffee. "I'd be worried if you hadn't."

"It has to be someone in the Interior Ministry, and I'm . . . I'm fairly certain I know who." That gets their attention. I'm not so sure I want it. I stub out my cigarette, wondering if I went too far, wondering if what I'm about to say will offend them. More importantly, if it will affect Banzer's decision to let the container go to Cuba. "It's a police officer." I stiffen with apprehension but not one of them bats an eye; not one appears defensive. Evidently, I'm still too conditioned by the past, by thoughts of what would happen if they were KGB agents. "His name's Gudonov. He was in charge of Economic Crimes. Now he's the new chief investigator."

Banzer winces. "Geezus." He's disgusted, not angry.

"Figures," Scotto growls, knowingly. "An arrogant asshole if ever there was one."

"Not to mention devious. He pulled the case out from under Shevchenko, handed my story to another journalist, and used him to allege Vorontsov was killed because he was blackmailing some bureaucrats."

"Over what?" Krauss asks.

"He supposedly caught them embezzling from the Party to buy State assets. My friend Yuri thinks it's part of a cover-up. So do I."

Banzer lets out a long breath. "And you're certain you still want to do this?"

"Try and stop me."

Banzer smiles and mulls it over. "Okay. We'll take care of the travel arrangements soon as we get back. Speaking of which . . ." He glances to his watch, then flags the waiter for the check. "Better move it. By the time we drop you at the hotel, we'll be lucky to make our flight."

"Go," Scotto says. "We'll grab a cab."

"You sure?"

"Uh-huh. I promised Katkov a piece of key lime pie, and we've got some shopping to do."

"Good luck, Katkov," Banzer says. It's a joke, but the levity in his voice is missing from his eyes.

"Thanks. I'm in Agent Scotto's quite capable hands, am I not?"

A little look flicks between Banzer and Krauss.

Scotto sees it. "That's it," she snarls good-naturedly. "Get the hell out of here."

They push back their chairs, feigning they've been unjustly accused. Krauss shakes my hand, then slips sideways between the tables. Banzer lingers with a thought. "Remember, Gabby, we're talking Wal-mart here, not Saks and Neiman's."

Scotto gives him the finger.

He laughs, then pays the check and shoulders his way after Krauss. My eyes are drifting back toward Scotto when they catch sight of a man at the bar. Detached countenance, unremarkable features, gold neck chains, loose-fitting tropical shirt—the details come in fleeting glimpses through openings in the crowd that surges around the bar. I have an uneasy feeling I've seen him before. But I can't place him. I'm falling back into old habits. Hell, he probably resembles someone I've seen in passing lately. *Pravda?* The passport office? Arlington Cemetery?

"So," Scotto says a little too brightly, pulling me out of it. "How are you doing, Katkov?"

"After three piña coladas? Hey, this has been great fun. Thanks. How about you?"

"I'm doing . . . okay." She lowers her eyes and draws circles in some bread crumbs with a fingertip. "I called my husband last night. Invited him down for a couple of days."

"Good for you."

"Well, not really. He . . . he declined. Made up some excuse about having to be away on business. He's an architect, and—aggghhh—what's the point?"

"I'm sorry, Scotto."

"Yeah, well, I sort of figured he might, but . . ." She sighs wistfully and works the crumbs to the edge of the table, then sweeps them to the floor with the back of her hand.

"Maybe we should skip the pie?" I suggest in deference to her mood.

She nods and thanks me with a sad smile, then leads the way through the crowd. I resist the temptation to look back over my shoulder. We're nearing the exit when I catch sight of the bar in one of the faded mirrors. The man is gone.

35

We're at a sidewalk stand on Calle Ocha, Little Havana's main shopping street. Scotto is looking at sunglasses. Mirrored, polarized, photo-sensitive. I'm looking over my shoulder for the man at the bar. She has me try on damn near every pair before deciding on the "Vuarnet knockoffs"—heavy black plastic frame, dark wine-colored lenses; then, pitting her Italian against the vendor's Spanish, she has a ball haggling over the price. It does wonders for her spirits, and we spend the next hour or so on a mini shopping spree amid the carts and stalls, then take a cab back to the hotel with our booty.

The next morning, I'm dutifully attired in my new swim trunks—fully committed to putting in time around the pool to work on my tourist disguise—when Scotto knocks on the door that connects our rooms. She's wrapped in one of the hotel's terry-cloth robes. Thigh length, tied at the waist, it accentuates her hourglass figure and shows off her long, bronze legs to advantage. I'm sweeping my eyes over them when she recoils with a gasp. "What? What is it?" I wonder, baffled. "You look rather like you've seen a ghost or something."

"I have," she replies, sweeping her eyes over *me.* "That body looks like it hasn't seen sun since Castro took Havana."

"Moscow isn't exactly on the equator, you know."

"Tell me about it. You'll be burned to a crisp in ten minutes."

"I thought that was the idea."

"The idea is to get a tan, not sun poisoning. She takes a tube of lotion from a pocket, then turns me around, squeezes some out across my shoulders, and begins working it in. The scent is heavy and sweet.

"What is that stuff?"

"Italian cocoa butter," she jokes. "It's made from olive oil and garlic. You turn brown and ward off the evil spirits at the same time."

Her hands are expert and strong. Her fingertips glide over my skin, awakening every pore. Her bare legs brush gently against mine. Pleasurable sensations begin radiating from deep inside me. Is she aware of it? Does she know exactly what she's doing? Or is this another one of my fantasies? *Only in your dreams, Katkov. Only in your dreams.* But this time I'm not dreaming. The choreography is fluid and subtle, and soon we're face to face, gazing into each other's eyes. There's a gentleness in hers that I haven't seen before.

"Are you sure about this?" I ask in a whisper, our lips dangerously close. "I mean . . . your husband . . . you're certain that you—" She puts a finger to my lips to silence me. I nibble at it. She pulls it back with a sexy giggle. "I just want you to be sure."

"Are you?"

"Me?"

"Uh-huh. You talked to Vera since you left?"

I shake my head no.

"Well?"

I shrug. "I don't seem to be sure of anything, anymore. Your turn."

"I'm sure it would be very nice, but that's all I'm sure of."

"Do you love him?"

She smiles demurely and whispers, "Yes, I do."

"Then I'd say it's time for a cold, refreshing swim, wouldn't you?"

She nods, then forces a laugh and tosses me the tube of suntan lotion. "I missed a few spots."

We spend the weekend languishing about the pool in bone-warming sun, reading trashy paperbacks from the hotel shop, and dining in beachfront restaurants. On Monday afternoon a courier delivers a prepaid ticket for my passage on the *Halifax*.

Sailing time 6:30 P.M. tonight.

A crescent moon hangs in the twilight as Scotto and I cross the pier in the Customs van with Inspector Aguilar. It proceeds through the security gate to a boarding ramp near the freighter's stern, where the superstructure that houses the bridge, crew quarters, and passenger cabins is located. The *Halifax* sits low in the water now, her hold filled with containers. They're secured in an impressive jungle gym of steel racks and extend three levels above the deck.

Aguilar handles the paperwork with the first mate.

I go about unloading my things from the van.

Scotto's eyes dart to my typewriter. She latches onto the handle possessively. "This one stays with me," she says, taking me aside.

"Why?"

"It's not exactly tourist gear, is it?"

"Never occurred to me," I reply, a little unsettled.

"That's okay. You've got fourteen hours to get in the right frame of mind. Don't waste them."

"I won't. Make sure you bring that when you come to Moscow."

"That's a promise."

"I'll call you as soon as I know what's going on."

"Don't wait that long."

I smile.

"I want to know you're all right, Katkov. I do." She grabs my shoulders, thinks about it for a moment, then hugs me. "Take care of yourself." A foghorn beckons, then again. I disengage, grab my bags, and hurry up the ramp onto the deck. Longshoremen are wrestling with hawsers. A husky tugboat nudges the vessel away from the pier. I'm standing at the rail, watching Scotto recede into the darkness. She's waving with one hand and hanging on to my typewriter with the other. I wave back until she's gone, then light a cigarette. The flashy gold script on the matchbook spells out Versailles. It plunges me into a world of smoky mirrors and shimmering reflections. I stare at it for a long moment, thinking about the other night, about the man I noticed sitting at the bar, the familiar looking one who was there and gone. It was only a fleeting glimpse, but the hazy image has stayed with me, and now, as it slowly sharpens, I've no doubt that I've seen him before, no doubt whatsoever that he was the same man who frisked me in the elevator on the way up to Rubineau's apartment.

36

The *Halifax* slips between two islands that flank the narrow mouth of Miami Harbor. The steady throb of her engines courses through every compartment as she builds up steam and sweeps in a southwest arc along the Florida Keys to open sea. Her running lights glide through the darkness like tiny spaceships flying in precise formation.

The passenger cabins are below the bridge adjacent to the captain's and first mate's quarters. Mine is clean, comfortable, and almost free of the scent of diesel oil that permeates everything aboard. A pleasurable sense of escape comes over me as I get settled in, but my mind soon drifts to the fellow at the bar in the Versailles. He didn't seem interested in me. I'm not even sure he saw me. Furthermore, Rubineau has an affinity for Little Havana. It's possible he's hooked on the food and sent his errand boy to fetch a spicy order of *ropa vieja*. But it's far more probable he's hooked on me and assigned his thug to play watchdog—though I didn't notice anyone following us to the pier tonight.

The *Halifax*'s captain is a loquatious fellow with a Scottish burr who jabbers on over dinner about Bosnia and the recent Truman biography he's reading. He can't recall the last time he had a passenger, can't imagine why anyone would travel on a container ship. I explain I'm not terribly keen on flying and avoid it whenever possible. The crewmen who join us are a friendly enough lot, and despite a mean-looking Puerto Rican who eats noisily and leaves without a word, they dispel the notion that all seamen are tattooed cretins.

It's close to midnight when we break up. I spend a few minutes at the rail staring into magnificent star-studded darkness; then cross the deck still in search of my sea legs and wobble down the passageway toward my cabin.

The door is ajar.

I closed it when I left. At least I'm fairly certain I did. I can vaguely recall the sound of the latch engaging. I advance cautiously, then sense a presence in the passageway behind me. I whirl in time to glimpse a fleeting shadow, which turns the corner, and hurry after it. Muffled footsteps quickly fade. A rusty hinge creaks in protest. The intersecting passageway is empty. At the far end, an open hatch is swinging to and fro with the roll of the ship. It leads to an exterior landing that overlooks the stern.

There's no one in sight.

No one is dashing down the companionway to the main deck; nor up the one that zigzags overhead to the bridge; and no one is hurrying in the gunnels toward the racks of containers stacked in the cargo hold; nor slinking along the catwalks that run between them. There's no movement. No footsteps. No human sound whatsoever, only the muted throb of engines and whisper of the breeze that comes off the water.

Did I surprise a thief going through my things? One of the crewmen? The Puerto Rican? My cabin doesn't appear at all disturbed when I return. Closer inspection confirms that nothing is missing. If not a thief, then what? An assassin? Rubineau's thug keeping tabs on me? The captain or a member of the crew stopping by to rehash our dinner conversation? My mind playing tricks? My KGB-born paranoia coming back to haunt me again? I lock the door, climb into my bunk in an unsettled state, and sleep fitfully, if at all.

I'm on deck before sunrise, my head turned into a stiff wind I hope will clear it, when Havana's lights begin winking in the distance like a swarm of fireflies floating just above the sea. I return to the cabin for the camera Scotto and I purchased in Miami. It's a technological tour de force by Russian standards:

auto-load, -focus, -flash, -advance, and -rewind; 35- to 115-millimeter motorized zoom; push-button settings to compensate for backlighting, shooting through glass, and haze in distant landscapes; small enough to fit in a shirt pocket; and priced under two hundred dollars. I drop in a roll of film—DX-coded, thirty-six exposures, 400 ASA—then close the back, setting off a series of reassuring electronic sounds, and shift into tourist mode.

The sun is well above the horizon when the *Halifax* glides past the crumbling castle at the entrance to Havana Harbor. The brackish waters are alive with an armada of rusting freighters and weary, paint-encrusted ferries. The miles of battered seawall are lined with old tires. Indeed, on closer inspection the idyllic-looking island is in dire need of repair, the level of decay equaling, if not exceeding, Moscow's.

After disembarking, I'm directed to a weathered, two-story building where a Customs official takes my passport. I speak no Spanish. He speaks neither Russian nor English. There's no way we can communicate. *"Intérprete, intérprete,"* he mutters, escorting me to a room on the second floor. A few rickety chairs, a small table, a framed photograph of Fidel Castro, and a window that overlooks the pier. No *intérprete.* The Customs official forces a smile, insists I take a seat, and leaves. It's going to be a long wait. I pass the time watching containers being unloaded from the freighter onto the flatbeds of eighteen-wheelers, keeping my eyes peeled for 95824.

Several hours later, still no sign of the *intérprete* or the container. Is it remaining aboard? Going elsewhere? I'm still wondering when the Customs official finally returns with the interpreter, a short, bony fellow with a thin mustache and jaundiced eyes that do little to ease my anxiety.

He apologizes for the delay and explains that though the *Halifax* radioed ahead, Russians never arrive on freighters from Miami—actually from anywhere lately, thanks to the ruble's massive devaluation—and an interpreter wasn't available at such an early hour. I sense "early hour" is the operative phrase here. After several exchanges in rapid-fire Spanish with the Customs officer, he turns to me and says, "He wants to know what you were doing in Miami, Mr. Katkov."

"Sightseeing," I reply, indicating my Disney World T-shirt. "I'm a tourist."

The Customs official makes a notation on an official-looking form. More bursts of Spanish. The interpreter smirks. "He's puzzled. He says you're a Russian. An ally. Yet you spend money in the United States when Cuba needs all it can get. Why?"

"Tell him it was a mistake. I didn't like it."

"You didn't like Disney World?"

"No," I reply with as much indignation as I can muster. "It's a false view of life. A capitalist-pig fantasy. That's why I came to Cuba."

Another exchange in Spanish. The Customs officer sweeps his eyes over me warily. They leave the room to decide my fate. I return to the window. Several more containers are unloaded. I'm about to turn away when 95824 is suddenly lifted from the freighter's hold and deposited in the flatbed of an eighteen-wheeler.

Damn. Is it staying in Cuba? Being transferred to another ship? A plane? I've got to get out of here and keep track of it. I'm beside myself by the time they return. The Customs official hands me my passport. "You're free to go, Mr. Katkov," the interpreter says. "Enjoy your stay in Cuba."

"Thanks," I reply as calmly as possible. "Is there a place nearby where I can rent a car?"

"The next pier," he replies, to my surprise. "Where the cruise ships berth."

"Thanks." I force a smile and head for the door.

"Only tourists and seamen with hard currency can afford them now," he goes on, blocking my way. "Fuel is very scarce. The price outrageous. It's gotten so bad, we have power blackouts to conserve energy. Five to eight P.M. every day." He pauses and shakes his head, disgusted. "We have that fool Gorbachev to thank for it. He let the Soviet Union go down the toilet, and we went with it. No more troops spending their pay, no more aid, no trade, nothing."

"For what it's worth, things aren't much better in Moscow, believe me." I shake his hand, then slip past him and head downstairs to collect my bags. A tough-looking man clutching a thick sheaf of paperwork exits an office and comes toward me. I'm stunned by the sight of him. Stunned by the aggressive stride, the flattened nose, designer sunglasses, and shaved head dotted with stubble that are eerily familiar; not to mention the jeans, leather jacket, and gloves—worn despite the stifling heat—that confirm the skinhead's identity. It's Arkady Barkhin's thug, Ray-Ban!

I'm trapped. No alcove, no doorway, no escape. He charges straight down the center of the corridor. I cringe and hug the wall, anticipating the encounter. His shoulder brushes mine as he blows past without so much as a glance. All business. Preoccupied. As if I don't exist. Of course. He's not expecting to run into me here, let alone in Vuarnet knockoffs, Disney World T-shirt, Miami Beach tan, and camera hanging from my neck. No, that's not at all the image he has of me.

I hurry to a nearby window. Ray-Ban exits the building and crosses to the eighteen-wheeler with 95824 in its flatbed. He climbs into the cab next to the driver. It belches black smoke and thunders off, merging into the line of rigs leaving the pier.

It's midmorning by the time I rent a car. The dusty Lada 1600 is part of a small fleet of Russian-made vehicles on the waterfront lot. Eighty-five thousand kilometers on the odometer, worn tires, faded paint, but it has a full tank of gas and a detailed map of Cuba and the streets of Havana on the threadbare driver's seat. Container 95824 is long gone, but I know where it's going. Rubineau told me. Varadero. Ninety miles due east of Havana. Where the Turistica Internacional resort complexes are being completed. That's where it's going. That's where they're all going.

Via Blanca, the superhighway that connects Havana and Varadero, circles the harbor, then winds eastward along the coast. Lest I have any doubts about the scarcity of fuel, its broad, smoothly paved lanes are free of automotive traffic. Clusters of pedestrians and hundreds of bicycles in long caravans travel on them instead. Except for the occasional car or motor scooter, and decrepit buses with passengers hanging out the doors, the container-laden eighteen-wheelers are the only motorized traffic. They travel in small convoys. Each time the Lada overtakes one, I anxiously scrutinize the numbers; each time, 95824 isn't among them.

On one side of the highway, fields of sugarcane stretch to the horizon. Workers with machetes do the work of fuel-starved combines. On the other side, miles of pristine beaches and picturesque villages with musical names go by: Santa Maria Del

Mar, Boca Ciega, Playas del Este, Santa Cruz del Norte, Carbonera.

Rubineau may be a deceitful son of a bitch, but he wasn't lying about Varadero. Bathed in sunshine, dotted with swaying palms, cooled by gentle trade winds, it's a dream come true; actually, dream in progress would be more accurate. Some hotels are open for business, others in various stages of construction.

It's noon by the time I arrive and get my bearings. The narrow peninsula is barely a thousand meters at its widest point. The main street, Avenida Primera, runs the entire length, joining intermittent grids of short cross streets. The simple layout makes it easy to conduct an organized search. I cruise the ten-mile strip of sand with my map, checking out construction sites and the loading docks of every hotel, office building, and warehouse. Containers are everywhere, arriving, unloading, baking in the sun; but to my profound dismay, 95824 isn't one of them either. It's not like I'm looking for a needle in a haystack. The massive aluminum boxes are difficult to conceal, the large numbers easily spotted.

The sun is setting when I come upon a hotel that's nearing completion. Containers from the *Halifax* are aligned in the parking lot. Furniture, gaming tables, and slot machines are being unloaded and moved inside on dollies. I'm circling the lot in search of my elusive target when I notice a Zil limousine pulled up alongside the loading dock. A few moments later, I'm stunned to see Rubineau and Barkhin emerge from the hotel.

Rubineau said they had a business relationship. Banzer said he thought Barkhin would get a piece of the action. And from the looks of things, running the casinos in Varadero is it.

They have a brief exchange with a man supervising the operation, then get into the limousine and drive off. The clumsy vehicle lumbers down Avenida Primera, crosses the bridge that spans the narrow lagoon, and instead of swinging into Via Blanca toward Havana, turns into Varadero Airport, where numerous private and commercial jets are parked. Rubineau's Gulfstream is one of them. It buttons up and taxis the instant they're aboard.

I'm back to square one. No sign of the container, or Ray-Ban, for that matter. I've no choice but to conclude that I was wrong; that despite my logic, despite the convoys of eighteen-wheelers, despite Rubineau and Barkhin's presence, container 95824 wasn't taken to Varadero.

I head back to Havana. Darkness falls en route, deepening my mood. The power blackout follows. The coastal villages are lifeless, as if abandoned to an invading army. Every so often, the distant flicker of a candle alleviates the monotony. Nothing alleviates my sense of failure. Scotto put her trust in me. I haven't been in Cuba a day, and I've already blown it. How can I tell her I've lost track of the container? Dammit. It has to be here somewhere. I'm exhausted. My brain refuses to function. I decide to check into a hotel, get some sleep, and regroup in the morning.

Havana is dark when I arrive, an earthly black hole with a faint glow from the harbor at its center. I'm proceeding cautiously through the pitch-black streets when the power suddenly comes back on. Every window in the city lights up at once. The cool glow of television screens reflect off ceilings. Rock music blares from open windows. Signs flicker to life. Streetlights pop on with startling brilliance. Havana's sweltering citizens pour out of their apartments. The dusty neighborhoods are soon crowded with strollers escaping the stifling heat indoors.

I'm stopped at a traffic light. My eyes drift to a wall in a small shopping plaza covered with posters, then blink in weary disbelief at their message. Maybe I've been on the road too long. maybe it's a mirage, a desperate man's fantasy. But no. No, there, plastered at odd angles across the sun-bleached stucco, dozens of posters with colorful typography proclaim: COPPELIA.

37

"Excuse me? Excuse me?" I'm out of the car and hurrying into the cobblestoned shopping plaza. A group of old men around a table outside a coffeehouse look up as I approach. Two are playing dominos. The others, arms sagely folded across ample stomachs, kibitz between sips of café Cubano. "Coppelia?" I demand, pointing to the posters on the wall. "Coppelia? What's Coppelia?"

They're taken aback by my intensity at first; then their eyes crinkle with recognition. "Coppelia. *Sí, sí,* Coppelia." One of the kibitzers pokes his corpulent colleague in the stomach. It swallows his finger to the knuckle. "Coppelia!" They all explode with laughter. A barrage of rapid Spanish follows. I make out words, phrases. *"Izquierdo . . . Calzada de Infanta . . . Vedado . . . contiguo Habana Libre."* They're pointing and gesturing this way and that. Directions! They're giving me directions!

I hold up my hands to stop them and fetch the map from the car. The fat one screws his cigar into the corner of his mouth and takes the map from me. He angles it toward the light that comes from inside the shop, then finds what he's after and begins to laugh.

I'm baffled. "What's so funny? What?"

He points to something and shows it to the others. They're

pointing and roaring with laughter again. The map finally makes its way back to me. One of them stabs a gnarled finger at it; and there, smack in the middle of downtown Havana, is the word COPPELIA.

I shrug and grin sheepishly. Like Havana's major hotels and places of interest, Coppelia's location is marked with a symbol and labeled in block letters. Whatever the hell it is, I've no doubt I'll find the cash-filled container there.

"Gracias, gracias," I call back as I return to the Lada wondering about Coppelia. A wax doll. A factory that makes dolls? Dolls exported to Russia?! Coppelia. A ballet. The national ballet? Founded by expatriate Russians? Where a touring company is performing. A touring Russian company?! Yes, that sounds more like it. The container will join others in which costumes, lighting gear, and theatrical sets are shipped, and be smuggled into Russia when the troupe returns home!

Calzada de Infanta, a broad boulevard that cuts diagonally across the city, takes me to the Vedado District. The lights are brighter here, the streets progressively more crowded with pedestrians. I maneuver the creaking Lada between them and turn into Avenida Rampa. Up ahead, a large illuminated sign flashes COPPELIA. A long line of people snakes around the corner from the entrance. Ballet. It has to be the ballet. That's odd. The building doesn't resemble any theater I've ever seen. The two-story, star-shaped structure looks more like something from outer space that landed in a park. If I was curious before, I'm totally baffled now. Coppelia isn't a doll factory. It isn't a ballet. It isn't a paper company either. Coppelia is a gigantic ice cream parlor.

A vague uneasiness begins gnawing at me. I leave the car and stroll through the park. It's like a festive picnic ground filled with tables and chairs. There are two queues. One to buy tickets, the other to exchange them for immense scoops of ice cream. Very Russian. Very frustrating. Despite it, Coppelia is packed. Flirting teenagers. Couples holding hands. Children clutching melting cones, faces smeared with their favorite flavor.

I stop at one of the small tables and notice that the napkins bulging from the plastic dispenser do more than clean sticky hands and faces. They also tell the "Story of Coppelia" in several languages, explaining that twenty-five years ago Fidel Castro decided his people would have quality ice cream. He put Celia Sanchez, his cultured revolutionary companion, in charge of the project. She named it Coppelia after her favorite ballet; she also designed the plaid skirts worn by the waitresses. It has since become a national institution, functioning as the heart of the city.

By the time I finish reading, I've circled the building. My eyes widen at the sight of a truck at the delivery entrance. It turns out to be a refrigerated van. The driver is stacking cardboard drums of ice cream on a handcart. A delivery at eight-thirty in the evening? Evidently, as the napkin boasts, Coppelia has never run out of ice cream and never will. There's no sign of container 95824 anywhere.

I'm reeling with disappointment. Suddenly the vague uneasiness snaps into focus. Chilling, insidious, too painful to contemplate, it points an ugly finger at the identity of the insider. The thought makes me shudder. Losing track of the container is nothing compared to this. No, this—this *betrayal*—threatens everything: my sense of judgment, my confidence, my hunger for the truth. Indeed, if this is it, I've no desire to know it. I can't accept what it portends. I can't. No. No, it's Gudonov. I know it is. It has to be Gudonov who's on the inside.

I'm in need of sustenance, but it's not ice cream that I crave. I plunge into a darkened lane behind the park. There's one on every street here. No need to look for the sign. I can smell it at ten paces. The inside is dingy and decrepit like the rest of Havana. Like Moscow. About a dozen men perch on stools, brown arms encircling their beers, eyes riveted to a television where a baseball game is in progress. At the other end of the bar, a woman with heavy makeup and skimpy, tight-fitting clothes watches them with amusement.

The bartender drifts in my direction. *"Cerveza?"* he prompts, his head cocked to the television.

I put some money on the stained hardwood. "Vodka."

One hand comes up with the bottle. The other with a squat tumbler. He fills it to the line without ever taking his eyes from the game.

"You have any ice? Ice. *Lyot. Khalodni.* Cold."

"No. No hielo. Beisbol." He gestures to the television. "Linares." He says it with pride and reverence. As if referring to a god.

The vodka goes down like water. The batter swings and misses. The men at the bar groan in unison. Linares is a god—as best I can gather, the star of the Cuban national team. He swings and misses again, and then again. My bar mates are devastated. The woman with the heavy makeup and skimpy clothes moves in to console them. This entrepreneur knows her market well.

An hour later, I'm staring into my third tumbler of room-temperature vodka, alternately feeling sorry for myself and wracking my brain for the whereabouts of the elusive container. I'm replaying the conversations I had with Rubineau in search of a clue when the pieces fall into place. There's only one other spot in all of Havana it could be.

38

I'm barreling west on the Malecon with my map of Havana spread across the steering wheel. Except for a few fishermen on bicycles, the Lada is the only thing with wheels moving on the six-lane boulevard that parallels the seawall.

In the distance, a modernistic Y-shaped building dominates the skyline. Sheathed in turquoise tile and cantilevered balconies, the twenty-story hotel towers over the placid ocean. Next to it, the infamous casino-turned-convention-center nestles like a gigantic Fabergé egg, its gilded shell shimmering in the darkness. A large sign flickers RIVIERA in green neon.

The service entrance is adjacent to the parking lot. A long driveway leads to a turnaround large enough to accommodate tractor-trailers. It's blocked by a wooden barricade, but I'm close enough to see the eighteen-wheeler backed up to one of the loading docks. The steel shutter is rolled up, and the container on the rig's flatbed mates neatly to the opening. Shafts of light stream from the narrow space around it, raking across the number on the container—number 95824! It's clear and unmistakable. I stare at it for a long moment, verifying each numeral anyway.

My excitement is short-lived. The area beyond the barricade is fenced. Razor wire spirals across the top of the chain link.

Armed guards are posted at the gate. A German shepherd heels next to the one with the bulletproof vest. It's a two-billion-dollar security package. Impenetrable.

I shift into reverse and swing around to leave. Two guards are standing in the Lada's headlights. One levels his rifle at me. The other advances with a cocky stride and shines a flashlight in my face, then shifts it about the car's interior. The map, the tan, the T-shirt, the camera on the passenger seat do their job. *"Turista,"* he grunts with a tired scowl.

The other nods sullenly. *"Parque de automóviles."* He points toward the guest parking lot and steps aside. *"Parque de automóviles por convidados."*

"Ah," I reply with an insipid smile. *"Gracias, señor. Gracias."* I resist the temptation to floor it and drive off slowly instead. Okay, Katkov. You've been officially declared a tourist; it's time to act like one. Time to stop sneaking around. Time to hang the camera around your neck and walk in the front door. Why the hell not? After my face-to-face with Ray-Ban, I've little fear of being recognized.

The Riviera's entrance is marked by a reflecting pool and large sculpture of a stylized mermaid and sea horse who seem entwined in procreative bliss. Like the rest of Havana, Meyer Lansky's once-grand gaming palace is in desperate need of repair. The glass doors open into a shabby lobby where dusty chandeliers burn dimly. The marble floors look gritty and dull, the carpeting, drapery, and furniture threadbare. A few loiterers. A yawning bellman. An old man reading a newspaper. The Russian engineers who once frequented the convention center felt perfectly at home here.

The check-in desk is empty. I stroll past and come upon a marble atrium. A bank of hotel elevators on one side, the main entrance to the convention center on the other. It's obvious this juxtaposition is no accident, obvious that in the old days, whether coming or going, guests had an inviting sightline into the casino. It's blocked by a row of steel doors now. Closed. Locked. Sealed like a vault. A line of velvet ropes wards off straying guests. Small signs atop the stanchions warn CLOSED TO THE PUBLIC in several languages. No need for armed guards here. No need to call attention to the convention center's current event.

Impenetrable security or not, there's no way I'm leaving without getting a look at the two-billion-dollar extravaganza going on inside. It dawns on me that the gaming equipment and furnishings were long ago removed, but from the looks of this place, there's little chance the casino has even been repainted, let alone renovated. If that's the case, if the interior is still intact, I've got a pretty good idea how I can pull it off.

I slip behind the velvet ropes and past the steel doors into a corridor that turns left and then right before reaching a door labeled *ADMINISTRACION.* It opens into what looks like a converted backstage area—high ceilings, concrete floor, a walled-off proscenium. The dressing rooms where famous entertainers once held court serve as convention offices now. Like the lobby, they're shabby, ill-furnished, and unoccupied at this hour. They're also disorienting. I'm searching for the convention center's curving wall. A loud whirring noise comes from one of the offices. I freeze at the sound, then advance cautiously and peer through the doorway. An old woman, reminiscent of Moscow's *babushkas* with their birch-twig brooms, is vacuuming the worn carpet. I wait until her back is turned and slip past the door, the sound of footsteps on concrete covered by the racket.

I finally come upon a curved section of corridor that rings the egg-shaped building. It leads to a makeshift storage area. Boxes of supplies are piled neatly in one corner. I'm about to move on when it dawns on me that they're piled too neatly, rising in stepped tiers—rising like the staircase on which they're stored! This is what I've been looking for.

The thought of how close I came to missing it makes me shudder. It's obvious that the staircase isn't used, that, as I suspected, the place hasn't been renovated, that my plan to get a look inside the convention center might be about to pay off.

I pick my way between the cartons, climbing in darkness. The stairs lead to a landing that's strung with cobwebs. I claw them aside and feel my way along the wall. My hand finds a light switch. Click-click. Nothing happens. It's pitch-black up here. I strike a match. There's only one door. It's locked. The latch is formidable. The hinges are on the other side. The flame stings my fingers. I light another match to get my bearings and start back down.

The maid has moved on, her vacuum a distant hum now. I find the largest office, ostensibly that of the center's manager, and rifle the desk. The kneehole drawer is cluttered with the

usual assortment of junk: pens, paperclips, pads, family snapshots, calculator, and a flashlight, which I pocket. In the back,
beneath sheafs of notes and outdated schedules, I unearth two
rings of keys. There must be several dozen on each. Some have
paper tags affixed, but the notations are scribbled in Spanish.

I return to the landing. The flashlight makes the task a little
easier, but the keys don't. I'm into the second ring before one
even slips into the lock. It's a short-lived high. The key stead-
fastly refuses to turn. Maybe the lock's jammed from lack of
use. I jiggle the key, then force it left and right. It still won't
budge. I'm down to the last few keys when one finally engages
the tumblers with a crisp click, and turns smoothly, withdraw-
ing the dead bolt.

The door opens into the space above the convention center's
ceiling. I *am* right. It's no longer a casino, but it's all still here:
security office, observation platforms, and two-way mirrors
through which the gaming tables below were once surveilled.
A pale glow comes through them, illuminating the network of
catwalks above the hung ceiling. I crouch to one of the mirrors.
It's like being on a roof at night and looking down through a
skylight. The massive hall below appears empty. Am I too late?
Has the money already come and gone? Damn. It hasn't been
twenty-four hours. The rig and container are still here. I'm getting that hollow feeling when a muted, shuffling sound rises. I
trace it to a group of angled mirrors in the center of the ceiling;
and there, directly below me, is a mountain of plastic bags
filled with money.

Other two-way mirrors reveal an assembly line operation,
cranking at full tilt. No dealers, no pit bosses, no feverish players; but diligent money handlers, their machines, and two
armed watchdogs: Ray-Ban, perched vigilantly atop a stool cradling a compact machine gun; and Rubineau's bodyguard, the
one from the elevator, outfitted in an impressive shoulder holster that hangs from his armpit to his waist.

I slip the camera from my pocket—the LCD panel indicates
I used four of thirty-six exposures on the *Halifax*—and begin
taking pictures through the mirrors. One gives me an angle on
tables where the bags are opened and emptied, where the crude
bundles of currency—all hundreds—are broken down.

Another mirror is positioned above a group of automated
money-counting machines. Here, the currency is racked up in

long chutes and processed in lightning-fast bursts that pump out identical bundles of cash.

Another provides a vantage point of machines that square, compress, and then wrap a wide paper band around the individual bundles. Each is about the thickness of a five-hundred-sheet package of heavy-weight stationery. Each contains only hundreds. Each therefore contains fifty-thousand dollars.

Yet another mirror reveals equipment that packages the finished product. It combines twenty of these fifty-thousand-dollar bundles—five wide, two deep, two high—into a precise, rectangular volume about the size of a large attaché case, then wraps it tightly in heat-sealed plastic. These million-dollar packages are stacked on the floor like concrete building blocks.

Though the crew and every piece of equipment are operating at breakneck speed, there's still a long way to go. I'm exhausted, hungry, and fearful of being discovered, but there's no way I'm leaving now. I pocket the camera and follow the catwalks back to the security office. From here, eagle-eyed observers phoned reports about cheaters and complicit dealers to security personnel working the floor below. It's obvious no one's been up here in decades. There's probably no safer place in all Havana. I'm about to stretch out on a dusty sofa when I notice the phone. Is it still connected? I'm suddenly taken by an impulse to call Scotto.

"Hi. Guess where I am?"

"In the arms of a sizzling, dark-eyed Latina?"

"Well, I am rather irresistible, but at the moment it would be more accurate to say I'm a voyeur."

"You've stooped to peeking in keyholes?"

"Much better than that. I'm taking pictures through two-way mirrors—"

"Katkov."

"—from the ceiling of the Riviera's casino."

"What the hell are you doing up there?"

"Watching the high rollers count their winnings before they're hatched."

Dare I chance it? I lift the handset. The line is dead. I fall on the sofa wondering what Scotto's doing, listening to the muted shuffle of the counting machines below. The last thing I remember is the scent of her perfume. Direct, full bodied, a little brassy at first blush; but enticing and surprisingly pleasant if given time to mellow. Like her. I don't know how many hours I slept; but the machines are still going full tilt when I awaken and squint at my watch. Five in the morning. No wonder I feel so rotten. I pull myself together and make my way across the catwalks to the observation platforms. Bundles of cash still cover the tables, but the mountain of bags is gone; the operation is winding down.

The million-dollar packages are separated into two stacks now—but not into halves. Indeed, one appears to be ten times larger than the other. Still, something tells me I'm looking at a two-way split. The small stack—eight wide, five deep, and five high—contains two hundred packages. Assuming a two-billion-dollar total and one million dollars per package, that's a ten-percent or two-hundred-million-dollar cut, probably for the Cuban government. That leaves ninety percent—eighteen hundred packages—1.8 billion dollars to be invested in Russia by Rubineau.

A few hours later, a garage-sized door in the wall of the convention center rumbles open. People begin arriving in vehicles that are driven right onto the floor. Zil limousines. Official staff cars. Several spanking new Mercedes sedans. I begin moving from one mirror to the next with the camera, getting the best angle, zooming in on their faces. Members of the Cuban government resplendent in military uniforms. Nameless, faceless crime bosses in baggy suits. Drug lords in gaudy jewelry and designer sunglasses. Then Arkady Barkhin, who gravitates toward Ray-Ban. And finally, ever dapper in beige linen, Michael Rubineau, smiling, loquacious, taking center stage. I can hear him now, reminiscing about the old days, about how fitting it is that this historic transaction is taking place in the Riviera's casino, about how the house always wins—and wins big—in the end, about how proud and fulfilled Meyer would be if he knew.

Like high rollers cashing out after an incredible run of luck, they hover about the stacks of money, barely able to contain their delight. Several reach out to touch them. Others pace anxiously. All appear to be waiting for someone; and suddenly, so am I. The representative from the Russian government—Banzer's dangerous insider, the official who can execute the industries-for-cash deal—has yet to arrive. I've been too caught up in all that's been going on even to think about him until now.

Another Zil pulls in. Several men get out. I scurry across the catwalks to a mirror that affords a better angle. Eye pressed to the camera. Poised to fire. A face moves into the lens. Zoom. Focus. Red hair. Pock-marked complexion. Bad teeth. Yes! Yes, I was right. It's Gudonov! He's the insider. My worst fears were unwarranted. Coppelia was a coincidence. I take a shot. The autowind whirrs. The shutter cocks. It's still Gudonov. I'm sighing with relief when I notice the man who's with him. There's something familiar about his carriage as he steps forward; but my sightline is blocked. Rubineau towers over him. Gudonov stands in front of him. The Cubans and the others encircle him in a display of respect and deference. Then documents. Signatures. The deal is being consummated. Smiles all around.

I scurry across the catwalks to get a better angle, then crouch to a two-way mirror. Eye pressed to the camera. Waiting. The group parts. The man turns. Zoom. Focus. He's short. Thin-boned. I take a shot. The autowind whirrs. The film advances. Another shot. Click. Whirr. Advance and fire. Another. And another. But nothing changes. The sharp cheekbones, the rodentlike countenance, the neatly razored mustache. Each shot confirms the ugly truth. Each confirms, that sick mother or no, he isn't away taking care of her! He's here betraying me! Deny it, dislike it, condemn it as I might, the face centered in the lens is Yuri's.

39

Devastated, betrayed, infuriated—the feelings are over-whelming and complex. I'm staring blankly through the two-way mirror on the verge of wretching. Yuri is preening like a peacock below. Yuri? Yuri?! Quiet, unassuming, sup-portive *Yuri?!* Half of me wants to crawl in a hole and die. The other half wants to go down there and beat him to a pulp. He was the first person I went to about Vorontsov. Fucking bastard.

My mind is racing. Like one's life at the moment of death, the entire sequence of events flashes before my eyes in an illu-minating rush. Suddenly I understand why Yuri couldn't get me copies of the documents, why he suggested I look up Bar-khin. He knew I'd track down the medal dealers sooner or later; better to have control, better, as Shevchenko said, to have Rafik baby-sitting me. And why I wasn't killed—I wasn't a target. Rafik didn't save my life; Yuri protected me. He had Rafik killed to scare me off and, as Shevchenko also said, to sever the only link to who hired him.

It also explains why Ray-Ban went to Mrs. Parfenov looking for me. Keep the heat on, make sure I stayed scared. And why Yuri played word games with ITZ. Turn it into a joke, make it impossible to decipher. Lastly, it explains how Rubineau knew

I was working with FinCEN. It wasn't Shevchenko who tipped him off; it was Yuri.

But it raises as many questions as it answers. First and foremost, how could Yuri be in a position to orchestrate something of this magnitude? It's no secret that his star at the Interior Ministry has been on the rise; and decades spent concealing his free-market mind-set from the KGB could account for his guile. But neither his career path nor personality suggest, even remotely, that field work is his forte. On the other hand, he certainly has the intellectual capacity and wouldn't be the first introvert to acquire the skills and power—those four telephones on his desk go a long way to confirming the latter.

However, having done so, why let me go to Washington? He made an obligatory effort to dissuade me; but I've no doubt he could've easily had me stopped. Not killed. A broken leg or two would've sufficed. Instead, he gives me carte blanche use of his phone, and drives me to the airport. And what's driving him? Was Yuri KGB all these years? Is that how he "eluded" them? Is that how they always seemed to know what I was up to? He sure as hell knew what Vorontsov was up to. Found out he was going to blow the whistle and blew it on him first. I feel so blind, so naively loyal. I mean, didn't Yuri warn me? Wasn't he the one who said government thugs are much harder to identify now? Was it a slip? Was he toying with me insidiously? Was it a subtle warning to a friend?

I'm sitting cross-legged on the observation platform trying to pull myself together and sort it out. This is no time to lose my nerve. Nerve? Come on, Katkov. Gall, stupidity, suicidal bent would be more like it. I'm in the ceiling of a defunct casino in Havana up against ruthless thugs, guards with machine guns, and killer dogs—any one of whom would gladly hunt me down and kill me like a cockroach—and I'm armed with a camera and a flashlight.

My eyes drift back to the two-way mirror. The million-dollar packages of cash in the large stack are being put into cardboard cartons that are labeled CUBAN CANE SUGAR in Spanish and Russian. One package per carton, cushioned and concealed with bags of raw sugar packed around it. The two hundred packages of plastic-wrapped cash in the smaller stack are being loaded into a military van. The cartons—the eighteen hundred that I'm betting are going to Russia—are being loaded on wooden pallets that are speared by a small forklift and returned to container 95824.

There's nothing I can do about Yuri, not at the moment anyway; but I can get some shots of this packing and loading operation. Especially from one of the other observation platforms that might give me a better angle. I'm about to move off when I notice Barkhin—who's standing directly below me—brushing something from the sleeve of his suit jacket. A few seconds later, he reacts and does it again. It's as if dust is falling on it. Curious, puzzled, he glances up at the ceiling, at the mirror where I'm located, then back to his sleeve and brushes it again. Dust *is* falling on it! He waves Ray-Ban over and points to the ceiling. An urgent, animated conversation follows. Ray-Ban nods resolutely and storms off with his machine gun slung beneath his arm.

I know where he's going; I know how he's getting there; and I'd better be long gone when he does. I leave the observation platform, in search of another way out, and spot a fire exit on the opposite side of the ceiling. I scurry across the catwalks, sprint the last twenty feet, and slam my palms against the emergency bar. Nothing happens. The door is locked. It's probably walled off on the other side. I'm trapped. There's no way I can get across the catwalks and down the stairs before Ray-Ban reaches them and starts up.

If I can't get out, I've got to keep Ray-Ban from getting in. Did I lock the door last night?! I start back across the catwalks. Zigzagging. Running. I'm a few steps from the door. Boots are pounding on the staircase on the other side. The rhythm changes. Swifter. Louder. Ray-Ban must've reached the landing and is running for the door. I lunge for it and throw the dead bolt an instant before he grabs the knob. It jiggles, then shakes as Ray-Ban turns it left, then right, pushing and pulling it in frustration. Several dull thuds, as if he's slamming a shoulder into it, follow. Then sharper, louder whacks as if he's kicking it with the heel of his boot. He kicks again and again. The steel jamb and dead bolt refuse to budge.

I overcome an impulse to run. Retreating would be a huge mistake. I'd be trapped on the catwalks. No, that door is the only way out of here; I've got to stick as close to it as I can. Stick close, let him burst in, and slip out behind him. But the door swings flat against the railing when it opens. There's no place to stand behind it. I'm looking frantically for a hiding place. A burst from Ray-Ban's machine gun rips through the metal around the dead bolt.

I'm on the verge of panicking when I notice the catwalks aren't built directly on the ceiling. There's a space between the top of one structure and the underside of the other—enough space for a man to hide. I'm climbing off the catwalk onto the ceiling when another burst from the machine gun turns the dead bolt assembly into a chunk of twisted metal. I'm lying on the ceiling—my back and legs bridging the gaps in the egg crate structure—and sliding beneath the catwalk when the door opens and smashes into the railing with a loud bang.

Ray-Ban thunders onto the catwalks. The entire structure creaks and sways. Decades-old dust falls on my face, dotting my glasses. Ray-Ban advances a few steps, then pauses. I can see the texture of his soles through the spaces in the decking. He's standing directly above me. A sneeze, a cough, a sigh, and I'm a dead man. The beam of his flashlight bends across the curved shell of the convention center roof and flickers through the hangers and cross braces that support the ceiling and catwalks. I have to get him to move off, to move deeper into the ceiling space in search of me.

Uncomfortable, cramped, terrified of making a sound, I work a hand into a pocket with painstaking care and get hold of a coin. My fingers are moist with sweat and slippery. The thought of dropping it makes me shudder. I squeeze it tightly, waiting until Ray-Ban takes a few more steps, until his back is to me and to the door. Then I extend my arm out from beneath the catwalk and fling the coin as hard as I can. It zips through the air, ricochets off the window of the security office with a loud ping, and clinks through the metal ceiling structure.

Ray-Ban dashes off in the direction of the sound. The entire catwalk structure begins bouncing up and down. It slams painfully against my chest, the rise and fall alternately freeing and pinning me beneath it. The pounding finally stops, which means Ray-Ban has stopped. I crane my neck, trying to get a fix on his location. He's advancing on the security office in a catlike crouch. Machine gun locked, loaded, and ready to fire. I wait until he works his way around to the far side, which blocks his view, then ease my way out from beneath the catwalk and roll up onto it.

I'm getting to my feet when a shoelace snags the edge of the decking. I stumble in my haste to free it and almost go sprawling headlong across the catwalk. My hand catches the railing, keeping me upright, but my shoulder hits the door. It swings back against the railing with a loud slam. I run onto the landing and down the staircase taking the steps two, three at a time, jumping over the boxes at the bottom. I'm dashing through the storage area when I hear Ray-Ban thundering down the stairs behind me.

The convention center offices are still unoccupied except for a few early birds. One of them is accepting a package and signing the deliveryman's clipboard. They go by in a blur as I exit the administration area, continuing past the main entrance and velvet rope barricade into the lobby. It's busier than it was last night. Guests are checking out, streaming toward the dining room for breakfast, waiting in groups for tour buses.

Did Ray-Ban get a look at me when I stumbled? Will he recognize me? He won't need to if he sees someone dashing through the lobby. Better to assume he hasn't. Better to slip in among the milling tourists than to run for my life. I take a moment to catch my breath and straighten my clothes, then walk casually past the check-in desk toward the cashiers' windows.

The young woman smiles as I approach. To my surprise, she's green-eyed and freckled like the British students who tour Moscow.

I put a twenty-dollar bill on the counter. "May I have pesos, please?" I ask in English.

"Certainly, sir," she replies in a slight brogue. She pauses, studies the bill, then looks up at me. "You know, with that accent I half expected pounds."

The knot in my gut tightens. I'm sure she's just being friendly, but under the circumstances everything is threatening. "I had business in Miami."

She opens the cash drawer and begins peeling off bills. "Well, I hope you're enjoying your stay at the Riviera?"

"Oh, yes, very much."

"Good. Most of our guests find it relaxing."

I force a smile and glance back over my shoulder in time to see Ray-Ban explode from the corridor. His weapon hangs discretely beneath his arm. He freezes and scans the crowd. His eyes sweep right past me.

The cashier presents me with a neat stack of bills. "I've worked at hotels in Madrid, Rio, Mexico City," she says brightly. "But I fell in love with Havana's easy pace."

"Me too. Thanks." I scoop up the pesos and turn from the window ready to bolt.

Ray-Ban is poised to spring at anything that moves. His head ratchets around. His eyes sweep over me. The deliveryman emerges from the corridor behind him. Ray-Ban spots him out of the corner of his eye and is on him like an attack dog, gloved hands going for his throat, dragging him back into the corridor and slamming him against wall. The poor fellow is terrified, sputtering in Spanish, and gesturing frantically to his clipboard as Ray-Ban grills him unrelentingly in Russian.

I'm paralyzed; I want to help, but there's nothing I can do, no way I can chance coming forward.

The commotion attracts a small crowd, including the employee who signed for the delivery. She manages to communicate with Ray-Ban, who releases his victim and begins grilling her instead. She's alternately nodding and shaking her head no amid a garble of Spanish and Russian. From Ray-Ban's side of the conversation, I gather the woman saw a man run past her office; but it was just a glimpse, and she can't describe him.

Lest the sight of me jog her memory, I stroll out of the lobby and across the parking lot toward the Lada. My pace is casual. It's my heart rate that's nearing the speed of light. If stress doesn't break it, Yuri's betrayal will. I don't know what's driving him. I may never know. One thing I'm certain of—the Riviera isn't the last stop for the cash-filled container. I'm still shaken by my narrow escape and, though I've never been one to see life in religious terms, I can't help thinking that it sure feels like Passover.

40

Whatever its destination, container 95824 isn't going anywhere for a while. Not until all eighteen hundred packages are sealed into cardboard cartons, stacked on pallets, and loaded inside. I check into an inexpensive motel down the street from the Riviera. After a quick shower, shave, and change of clothes, I get some breakfast in a touristy bar next door. The walls are papered with grainy, coffee-stained photo blowups of Hemingway. Worn copies of his novels are stuffed into every nook and cranny. I eat quickly, order several cups of the pitch-black coffee to go—which wouldn't be possible in Moscow—and drive back to the Riviera.

Opposite the hotel, on the ocean side of the Malecon, there's a large paved area where fishermen once parked their vehicles. But there are only a few cars now, a dozen or so bicycles, and a clear view of the Riviera's service road—which is why I'm here. There's no way the eighteen-wheeler can leave without my seeing it.

I spend the better part of the day sitting on the seawall with the fishermen, and most of the night in the Lada drinking coffee to stay awake. Actually it's not the caffeine that keeps my adrenaline pumping and my gut churning. It's Yuri. He's obviously staying at the hotel, and I'm more than tempted to track him down and confront him. But I've come too far to let a moment of satisfaction endanger everything.

Early the next morning, the clanking of a poorly maintained diesel shatters the silence. Then, belching thick blue-black smoke into the darkness, the lumbering eighteen-wheeler emerges from behind the Riviera. The military van, a Cuban government staff car, and two Zil limousines follow.

The caravan exits the service road and turns into Paseo, a main boulevard with towering palms that march down the median. I fire up the Lada and wait. There's virtually no traffic at this hour, greatly increasing the chances of being spotted. I keep the headlights off and follow at a distance. The divided roadway cuts a triumphant path across the city to the Revolutionary Palace. The State Treasury or Ministry of Finance must be located here, because the cash-filled military van and government staff car turn into the grounds. The eighteen-wheeler and the two limousines angle into Avenida de la Independencia and continue south on the empty, arrow-straight highway. A half hour later, the caravan passes beneath a sign that reads JOSE MARTI INTERNATIONAL AIRPORT.

The main approach road runs parallel to a high chain link fence that encloses it. The three vehicles continue past the entrance to the passenger terminals and turn into a brightly lighted street that leads to a security kiosk. It's manned by two uniformed guards. One carries a sidearm. The other cradles an automatic rifle. I pull over behind a bus shelter. Evidently, the guards have their orders—no inspection, no probing questions, no time wasted—because the gate arm rises almost immediately, and the vehicles proceed onto the airport grounds.

I've no chance of getting past the guards, but I can see the caravan through the chain link. I continue driving parallel to the fence. I've got one eye on the road, the other on the vehicles, when they disappear behind a row of hangars and maintenance sheds. Is that it? Have they stopped? Damn. I can't see a thing from here. I'm about to get out and climb the fence when I spot headlights streaming between the buildings. The three vehicles finally emerge and swing onto the tarmac, where two jets are waiting.

One is Rubineau's Gulfstream.

The other is a cargo plane that I recognize as a Russian-made Antonov-22. I used to hop flights on them when I was covering the war in Afghanistan. Massive, extremely slow, built very close to the ground, its wide-bodied, hundred-foot-long cargo hold can easily accommodate a pair of scud missiles on mobile launchers with room left over for a squad of battle tanks, their crews, equipment, and a hitchhiking journalist or two.

The eighteen-wheeler circles around and approaches from the rear. The underside of the plane's sharply angled tail section lowers hydraulically like a space-age drawbridge and becomes a loading ramp. A member of the ground crew guides the tractor-trailer into proper alignment. Without coming to a stop, the rig accelerates up the gentle slope and vanishes inside the turboprop's cavernous fuselage.

Simultaneously, the two limousines stop next to the Gulfstream. Barkhin, Ray-Ban, Rubineau, and his bodyguard get out of one; Gudonov and Yuri out of the other. They all board Rubineau's sleek corporate jet. The crew wastes no time buttoning up and taxiing. The Antonov's crew does the same. Container 95824 is on its way to Russia.

I make a beeline for the passenger terminal. The sun is creeping over the horizon, sending shafts of light across the near-empty parking lots. I drop off the Lada, proceed to the Aeroflot ticketing counter, and book a seat on the day's only flight to Moscow. My next stop is a row of public phone booths. Several are marked for international calls. Are they bugged? Does the Cuban government listen in on those dialing outside the country? I've no choice but to take the chance; and I make it collect to Scotto at FinCEN Headquarters.

The woman who answers recognizes my name, accepts the charges, and explains Scotto hasn't come in yet. She's rarely there by nine, let alone seven, but she left instructions that my calls be forwarded whatever the hour.

The phone rings a half-dozen times before I finally hear the sounds of someone grappling with the receiver. "Yeah? Yeah, hello?" A sleepy voice answers—a sleepy *man's* voice.

"This is FinCEN calling," the woman says. "I have a Mr. Katkov on the line for Agent Scotto."

"Sure. Sure, y'all hang on a sec, okay?" the man replies in the soft drawl I've heard before. "Gabby? Gabby, come on, it's for you. It's that guy, Katkov."

"Go ahead," the woman says, dropping off the line. A groan. The rustle of bedding. "Katkov?" Scotto rasps groggily; then more alertly, her New York accent ringing with concern, "Katkov? Katkov, you okay?"

"Yes. Yes, I'm fine. Listen, I'm sorry to wake you, Scotto, but—"

"No problem. Hang on, I want to change phones." She puts me on hold. I listen to the hum of the line, thinking about that morning in Miami with the suntan lotion. "Hi," she says a little more brightly, pulling me out of it. "That was Marty. He was here when I got back from Florida." She makes a sound that's somewhere between a giggle and a gush. "Something's going on. I'm not sure what. I'm just going to go with it. See what happens."

"Sounds delightful, but I'm afraid I'm going to ruin it for you."

"The container's moving, right?"

"As we speak. They drove it, rig and all, into one of those big cargo jets."

"They? Who's they?"

I knew she was going to ask. I've been wrestling with what to do about Yuri all night, and I still don't have the answer. It's sort of like being told you have terminal cancer. Shock, denial, anger, acceptance. Only instead of progressing through them in a straight line, I'm ricocheting wildly from one to the other, unwilling to deal with any of them.

"Katkov? Katkov, you there?"

"Yes. Sorry. We've a poor connection, I'm afraid. I couldn't hear you very well."

"Who was there?"

"Barkhin, Rubineau, a couple of officious-looking Cubans, several repulsive thugs from the drug cartels and crime syndicates, and my friend—Gudonov."

"Gudonov? No kidding? Then I guess he's the insider, isn't he?"

"Right," I reply, glad she can't see my eyes.

"Way to go, Katkov. You did good. Real good. That means we can trust Schevchenko."

"We have to trust someone. The only flight out of here doesn't leave until late afternoon. I certainly won't get to Moscow in time. What about you?"

"I don't know. There's one out of Dulles at nine. At least, there was when I went over for that seminar. If I can get on it."

"If? Get tough. Pull rank. Use the Special Agent Scotto U.S. Treasury routine. That cargo jet has the speed of a flying hippo—add on a refueling stop—you can pull it off."

"You get the hippo's tail number?"

"Yes. It's—"

"Good. Save it. Call Shevchenko and give it to him. He can verify the destination and ETA from his end. Bring him up to speed in case I don't get there in time; and make sure he knows the idea is to tail it and take down the creeps at the other end."

"That's a given. He does it at the airport, I'll kill him. Safe flight."

"You too. And thanks. Thanks a lot."

"For what?"

"For being a nice guy. I owe you one. We owe you one—I think."

"We'll settle up in Moscow. Dollars. Not rubles."

"That's a deal. Look, this is going to be history by the time you get in. Where can I reach you?"

"Reach me?"

"Yeah. You going to be staying at your friend's place again?"

"At Yuri's?"

"Right. I couldn't think of his name."

"Yes, yes, I'll be staying there," I reply in as casual a tone as I can muster. I'm still not sure why I didn't tell her. Maybe I'm not up to facing the truth yet. Maybe her accusation that journalists have no regard for its consequences has affected me. Maybe it's the loyalty of a lifelong friendship. Maybe it's because knowing who is one thing, and knowing why is a totally different matter. Only Yuri can tell me that. If I don't like what he has to say—well, I haven't covered his ass, I just haven't been the one to kick it—though it's going to be hard to resist the temptation. Damn. None of this really matters, anyway. Like Scotto said, it'll be over by the time I get back to Moscow, and chances are pretty good that any conversation I have with Yuri is going to take place through prison bars.

I've got ten hours to kill before departure and fifteen more in the air to come to grips with it. I'm dialing Shevchenko's number when the implication hits me. It will be over by the time I get there. *All* over. I've risked my life, been betrayed by my best friend, chased this story all over the world, and now I'm going to miss the grand finale.

"Shevchenko," the senior investigator answers sharply, snapping me out of it.

"Hi. It's Katkov."

"Katkov? Been a while. What's going on?"

"I have a question for you."

"What else is new?"

"Your marriage still on the rocks?"

"Yes, I'm afraid so."

"You're sure your wife's not going to turn up on your doorstep in the next couple of hours begging to put it back together?"

"Not a chance in hell. Why?"

"Because you're going to be working late tonight."

41

Darkness is falling as Aeroflot Su-416 circles the desolate countryside north of Moscow and touches down with a thump on one of Sheremetyevo's runways. Fifteen hours in the air, plus the eight-hour time difference, means the Ilyushin jumbo glides to a stop at the gate about the same time it departed Havana. I've lost an entire day. The Antonov-22 with the eighteen-wheeler and cash-filled container in its flatbed arrived sometime this morning, Rubineau's swifter Gulfstream at least several hours earlier. Probably before dawn.

The airport's cavernous baggage hall is dimly lit and even gloomier than I remember; the queues for Customs and Passport Control move at the same glacial pace. The instant I'm cleared, I hurry to the taxi stand, anxious to hear about the takedown and what happened to Yuri. I'm lugging my bags past the barrier that restrains those waiting to meet arriving passengers when I hear my name.

"Katkov? Hey, Katkov, over here!"

It's Scotto. She's knifing sideways through the crowd to keep up with me. What's she doing here? And why isn't she smiling? Whatever the reason, she looks shaken. Something's drastically wrong.

"What happened?" I call out, quickening my pace.

"A disaster."

"Shevchenko moved too soon? I told him, dammit. I warned him—"

"No," she interrupts sharply as we come together at the end of the barrier. "Gudonov did."

"Gudonov?!" I echo, astonished.

She nods grimly. "The Gulfstream got in first, like you figured. Shevchenko had it under surveillance; but neither Gudonov nor the other passengers stuck around to claim their prize. My flight got in next. Shevchenko and I hung out until the Antonov showed, then tailed the eighteen-wheeler."

"Follow the money. Your favorite game."

"Not when I get beat. We were a couple miles south of the airport when all hell broke loose. I've never seen so many cops and reporters in my life. Like a Hollywood extravaganza."

"Starring Gudonov?"

Scotto grunts in the affirmative.

"It doesn't make sense. He was in the thick of things in Havana. He's up to his ass in this."

"He claims," Scotto says in a cynical tone, "that he was working undercover."

"Bullshit."

"That's what Shevchenko said. He can't believe it."

"Neither can I."

Scotto shrugs as if to say "I'm ready to believe anything," then leads the way to a rented Zhiguli in the parking lot across from the terminal. There's a hint of spring in the air, an almost balmy sweetness that surfaces when the temperature finally gets above freezing and stays there. I toss my luggage into the backseat and settle next to her. "Shevchenko thought you'd want to see this." She drops a newspaper in my lap, starts the engine, and drives off.

It's a copy of *Pravda*. The headline reads MILITIA MONEY LAUNDERING STING. Beneath it is a photograph of the eighteen-wheeler pulled to the side of the highway. It's surrounded by police vehicles and personnel. Container 95824 is the center of attention. The doors at one end are opened. Several sugar cartons have been torn open and the million-dollar packages of cash removed and prominently displayed in the foreground. Gudonov poses next to them like a conquering invader. I'm angered—but not the least bit surprised—that the by-line on the accompanying article reads M. I. Drevnya.

This morning, while Muscovites slept, Chief Investigator Yevgeny Gudonov led a crack militia task force in a money-laundering sting. The brilliantly executed operation netted more than a billion and a half U.S. dollars. American crime czars were planning to use the profits from their illicit drug deals to buy Russian industries. Gudonov, who's been working on the case for months, risked his life to go undercover inside the smuggling operation. The scheme was . . .

"Risked his life to go undercover?!" I exclaim, infuriated. "What a sham!"

"Tell me about it. Who's his PR agent?"

"You."

"Me?"

"Yeah, it's all your doing, Scotto. You and your damned seminar, whatever the hell it's called. Gudonov probably learned everything he knows about using the media from you."

She concedes the point with a smile, then swings out of the airport onto Leningradsky Prospekt and heads south toward Moscow. "I have to admit he'd have gotten an A-plus for this caper. Keep reading. You haven't gotten to the good part yet."

The good part? Yuri. It has to be Yuri. She knows about him, and she's making me squirm for not telling her. My eyes swiftly scan the long article. Vorontsov's name is ubiquitous, as is Rubineau's, Barkhin's, and, of course, Gudonov's. They're all here, all except Yuri's—which means she doesn't know. I start over, reading the text more carefully.

Dammit. It's immediately obvious that Sergei was right. The kid's style has punch and pace, but he's still an unprincipled jerk as far as I'm concerned. It's the next to last paragraph that really gets my attention. I read it aloud in shock and disbelief. " 'Highly reliable sources have told *Pravda* that Investigator Gudonov plans to destroy the contraband at Moscow's Garbage Incinerating Plant this evening'?! His reputation's gone to his head."

"Shevchenko told me all about that."

"I can't believe he's burning all that money?!"

"Burning the *evidence*. Cost me my badge, gun, and pension if I did something like that."

"This is Russia, Scotto."

"I've noticed. Shevchenko's trying to stop him anyway. We're meeting him there."

"You know where you're going?"

"No. You think I picked you up out of the goodness of my heart?"

"Well, I wouldn't go quite that far, but you could've easily gone with Shevchenko and let me fend for myself."

"Shut up, smartass."

"Take the MKAD turnoff, Agent Scotto."

About ten minutes later, she angles into the Outer Ring that circumvents the city. We're soon spiraling down the Rizhskiy Interchange into a service road that winds through the marshlands. Thick smoke stretches in dense layers below the night sky. The Zhiguli climbs a steep hill, comes over the crest, and approaches the incineration plant. Like gigantic Roman candles, its towering stacks send bursts of orange sparks shooting into the darkness.

The promise of a headline that reads TWO BILLION UP IN SMOKE has brought out the media in full force: print journalists, still photographers, television reporters, and satellite vans, sporting the logos of American, European, and Russian networks. All are gathered around one of the huge incinerators. The flaming beast roars with the intensity of a blast furnace. Its gaping cast-iron jaws could swallow a shipping container whole. No longer on the eighteen-wheeler's flatbed, 95824 sits on the ground next to a work platform that leads to the inferno. From this simmering perch, Gudonov supervises the operation, playing to the media throng below.

Scotto and I hurry from the car and push through the crowd in search of Shevchenko. She spots him off to one side of the container where a noisy forklift prowls. Evidently most of the cartons have already been removed and incinerated, because the forklift travels deep into the forty-foot tunnel in search of the next pallet.

"Last one," Shevchenko says, clearly demoralized.

"Why the hell wouldn't he wait?"

"Wait?!" Shevchenko snaps angrily. "The cocky little bastard wouldn't even listen."

"Can't say I blame him," Scotto says impassively.

Shevchenko and I fire looks in her direction. "What do you mean by that?!"

"We're talking show business here, guys. You sell this many tickets to a performance, there's no way you can cancel it."

With a throaty rumble and clank of steel, the forklift backs out of the container. The operator swings it around, guns the throttle, and heads for the incinerator; then, hands pushing and pulling on a rack of levers, he raises the pallet high into the air and deposits it on the platform. Rollers built into the decking allow workers to manhandle it easily toward the fire-breathing incinerator.

Gudonov holds up a hand, giving the pallet a brief stay of execution, and instructs the workers to open several of the cartons. Then with much fanfare, he removes one of the million-dollar packages of currency and holds it high overhead before tossing it into the roaring inferno. Another soon follows and then another. Sparks fly. Cameras whir. Strobes flash. The chief investigator struts triumphantly, then signals the workers, who roll the entire pallet of cartons into the roaring flames. Gudonov jumps down from the platform.

The media surges around him, shouting his name, firing off questions. "How long have you been working on this case? How high up in the Interior Ministry will your investigation reach? Do you know if—"

"Ask him why he's burning evidence," Shevchenko calls out.

"What about that?!" one of the reporters prompts. "Good question!" another chimes in. "Care to comment, Chief?!"

"Yes, but I'd prefer to introduce my colleague first. You all know Senior Homicide Investigator Shevchenko." The TV cameras and lights swing around and focus on Shevchenko with blinding intensity. "I like to give credit where credit is due," Gudonov goes on with a smug grin. His face is pock-marked, his suit is rumpled and his delivery is crude, but his tactics and timing are polished. "This all began with a homicide—a homicide that Investigator Shevchenko solved with customary brilliance. In light of his firsthand knowledge of the case, I've no doubt he's aware that Comrade Vorontsov—the corrupt Interior Ministry official who masterminded this scheme—got involved with people who settle disputes in ways he wasn't accustomed to and is now deceased, as is the assassin who killed him. Nor do I doubt the senior investigator also knows that the militia can't prosecute the dead—which makes his so-called evidence useless."

"What about the coconspirators?" Shevchenko challenges. "What about prosecuting them? I can give you their names if you like."

"So can anyone who reads the newspapers or watches television. Unfortunately, they've cleverly distanced themselves, and there's no way to connect them to the case."

"Thanks to you," Shevchenko counters angrily.

"You're right," Scotto says, leaning to me. "Something weird's going on. This doesn't make a goddamned bit of sense."

"However," Gudonov resumes, ignoring Shevchenko's barb, "just because we can't prosecute doesn't mean we can't prevent." He pauses, gestures dramatically to the conflagration behind him, and grins at what he's about to say. "This serves strong notice that we're turning up the heat, that Russian justice is ruthless and swift, that whether they smuggle in two billion or twenty billion, every last penny will go up in smoke; that neither this nation's economy, nor her integrity, can be bought by agents of the American underworld who traffic in filth."

Shevchenko scowls in disgust, then makes his way through the crowd to his Moskvitch and drives off without a word.

Gudonov drones on in self-aggrandizement.

Scotto looks like she's about to barf. "Come on, Katkov. I'll buy you a drink."

We're crossing to her car when an intriguing thought occurs to me. It's probably a waste of time, but what the hell. The way this has turned out, I've been wasting it since the night Vera beeped me in Moscow Beginners anyway. "Hold on a minute, Scotto. There's something I want to check." I circle the container, examining it. Same number. Same off-white color. Same gritty accumulation of grime and salt. Same cartons of sugar labeled in Spanish and Russian. Indeed, it has everything essential to identify it as the cash-filled target we've been tailing—everything except my initials scratched into the paint.

42

"A decoy?!" Shevchenko exclaims, kicking back in his desk chair, astonished. "Did I see Gudonov tossing millions into that incinerator, or what?"

"Cost of doing business," Scotto replies in a tone that implies it's obvious. "They sacrificed a couple mill for effect."

Shevchenko nods thoughtfully. "Then we were right all along. Gudonov's in cahoots, not undercover."

"Whatever. The bottom line is, it wasn't the same container."

"Hold it. You and I saw it come out of the plane. Katkov saw it go in. . . ." His eyes shift to mine in search of confirmation. "Right?"

"Yes, right. Unless . . ."

"Unless, what?"

"The decoy was already aboard when I got there."

Scotto frowns skeptically. "Two eighteen-wheelers fit in that thing?"

"In an Antonov twenty-two? Easy."

"Well, if you're right about that," Shevchenko muses, brightening at the prospect, "then maybe the one with the cash is still in the plane."

"It's been damn near fifteen hours," Scotto challenges. "No way they're letting two billion sit there that long."

Shevchenko nods resignedly. He's exhausted. We all are. He stares blankly at the ceiling for a moment, then lifts the phone, dials an extension, and puts out an All-Units-Alert for container 95824. As an afterthought, he also dispatches an investigative team to the airport to check out the Antonov. "Can't hurt. It's either still aboard, or out there somewhere."

"Yeah," Scotto says wearily. "It's big. It's got a number on it. We shouldn't have too much trouble finding it."

"This is Russia, Scotto."

"Dammit, Katkov. You keep saying that."

"Things are different here. You know what they say about winter, don't you?"

Shevchenko winces. "I sure as hell hope you're wrong about that."

"What? What?" Scotto prompts, feeling left out.

"They say, 'It doesn't wait.' "

"No shit? Is this some Russian male-bonding thing or what?"

"No," I reply. "It's some Russian way of saying no matter how hard you try, some things can't be—interdicted."

Scotto smiles.

Shevchenko looks smug. "Hate to say I told you so, Katkov, but—"

"Another Russian thing?" Scotto interrupts.

"A Shevchenko thing. He's one of those people who thinks a free society has its baggage."

"So do my hips. I didn't stand around spouting poetry about them, for Chrissakes. Look, this didn't make sense before, and it makes less now. Assuming Gudonov's involved, and assuming that container's a decoy, why didn't they lead us on a wild-goose chase to Siberia while the other container slipped quietly into the country? Why take it down?"

"She's got a point, Shevchenko. I mean why the fanfare? Why burn it? Why all this media hype? There has to be a reason."

"Diversion. Distraction. Call it what you want. I don't really care," Shevchenko replies impatiently. He pushes up from his chair and crosses to a street map of Moscow on the opposite wall. "Where? Where would they take it?"

"Someplace real safe," Scotto says, crossing to the window as she puzzles it out. "If this was Miami, it'd already be in the banking system ticketed for an electronic rinse."

"How about a former bank?"

"A what?"

I stab a finger at the map, pointing to the Frunze District. "The Paradise Club. It used to be a bank. It's got a vault the size of an Antonov."

"You sure?"

"I took the guided tour."

Shevchenko bristles with renewed energy. He snatches up the phone and punches out an extension. "This is Shevchenko. I need three teams. Who's on call? . . . Uh-huh . . . uh-huh. . . . They'll do. . . . The Paradise Club on Luzhniki. We'll rendezvous outside at twenty-three thirty."

"That's barely a half hour," Scotto challenges. "You get a search warrant that fast?"

"Search warrant?" Shevchenko echoes with an amused chuckle. "The instant I request it, some paper pusher at Justice'll be on the phone to Barkhin."

"He's that powerful?"

"No. His hard currency is."

"You may find this hard to believe, but graft isn't unique to Russia. I just don't want to blow this takedown on a technicality, okay?"

"No problem," Shevchenko replies. He heads for the door, slipping on his jacket. "Russian law is like a harness, Agent Scotto. It—"

"Tell me about it," Scotto interrupts, as we hurry after him down the corridor. "That's one Russian thing I understand. It's constraining, frustrating, stacked in favor of the bad guys, and—"

"No. No, Scotto, you *don't* understand," he interrupts, turning into the elevator lobby. "I was comparing our legal system to a team of horses. Left, right, straight ahead, a skilled teamster can use the harness to make it go wherever he wants."

"Not where I come from."

"Yes, well, every system has its baggage. In this one, for every law there's another that contradicts it. Frankly, they're often built into the same statute. It's wonderful." He thumbs the elevator button impatiently. "We call this one the self-sac-stat."

"The self what?"

"Sac as in sacrifice. The bad guys are protected from self-incrimination; the good guys are protected from self-destruction. " The elevator door opens. He grins wickedly and charges into it. "Naturally, I'm invoking the latter clause."

Scotto and I leave the rented Zhiguli in the courtyard and pile into the Moskvitch with Shevchenko. He turns south into Petrovka and heads across town to the Paradise Club. It's almost midnight when we arrive. The street is deserted except for a few parked cars and a homeless woman in a doorway. A breeze blows litter against the club's graffiti-plastered facade.

Shevchenko clicks on his radio and verifies the other teams are in position, then cruises past the granite edifice and turns into the service alley that runs behind it. The loading dock where armored cars once made their pickups and deliveries is empty. No sign of container 95824 anywhere.

"Not surprising," Scotto observes. "They've had plenty of time to unload it."

"I'm counting on it," Shevchenko says cagily. He drives back around to the main entrance, then gathers his troops and briefs them. "Okay, Katkov," he says as they take up positions behind the columns that flank the huge bronze doors. "You're on."

I take a deep breath and ring the buzzer. "It's Katkov," I announce to the natty thug who peers from the security slot. "Nikolai Katkov."

He grunts in acknowledgment and throws the latch. The door opens with a weighty shudder.

"Moscow Militia," Shevchenko announces, blowing through it. He shoves his ID in the thug's face and leads the charge of detectives and uniformed officers into the club. Scotto and I follow through the lounge and a series of interior doors into the main hall, where the floor show is in full swing.

Bare-breasted dancers stop gyrating and hurry off-stage. Gamblers stiffen apprehensively. Dealers freeze in mid-shuffle. The club is suddenly still and silent, save for the occasional squawking parrot.

Shevchenko ignores them, along with the Tahitian landscapes and towering palms, and crosses to the corner table. I follow apprehensively, wondering if Yuri is here celebrating with his fellow conspirators. My eyes dart from Barkhin, to Rubineau, to the phalanx of bodyguards lurking in the background; but there's no sign of him. No caviar, no champagne, and no scantily clad young women either. They're shrewdly keeping a low profile. It's for naught now. Indeed, despite a week in sunny Havana, both men look pale and tense. They look angry. Very angry. At me. I return their stares unflinchingly as Shevchenko displays his badge and identifies himself.

"Nice of you to drop in, Mr. Investigator," Barkhin says with as much bravado as he can muster. "Unfortunately, we're all booked. With a party of this size, I suggest you call for a reservation next time."

"I'm making this one in person," Shevchenko counters, his face raked by spotlights that turn his sharp features into a craggy mask.

"For what?"

"A tour of your vault."

Barkhin stands and comes forward to confront him. "You won't find any rubles in it, if that's what you're looking for," he says indignantly. "This is a strictly legal operation, Shevchenko. Hard currency only."

"We're not looking for rubles. We're looking for dollars. Two billion in U.S. hundreds."

Barkhin's brows arch in reaction. "Two billion. I have to admit the club is doing well, but I think that estimate's a little excessive." He turns to Rubineau with a cocky smile and prompts, "You agree?"

"Well, I've run up sizable markers on occasion," he replies, matching Barkhin's aplomb. "But rarely more than what? A billion or so?"

"Or so. Of course, if Investigator Shevchenko feels I've been neglecting my responsibilities . . ." Barkhin pauses and reaches inside his jacket.

"Hold it," Scotto orders, drawing her pistol.

Barkhin freezes.

"That won't be necessary, Agent Scotto," Shevchenko says calmly, nodding to a detective who opens his coat, revealing a compact machine gun leveled at Barkhin's gut. "If it's money, bust him for bribery. If it's a gun, kill him."

Barkhin slowly removes his hand from his jacket. Empty. No money. No gun. "Agent Scotto," he says in a patronizing tone. "And all along I thought you were in the restaurant business. What would make an attractive woman like you forsake all that glamour for police work?"

"The class of people. In case you've forgotten, we ask the questions, you answer them. Two billion was smuggled into

Moscow in a shipping container this morning. Ring a bell now?"

"Ah, I vaguely recall seeing it in the newspaper."

"I distinctly recall your seeing it in Havana," I counter pointedly.

Barkhin snorts smugly and brushes some imaginary dust from his sleeve. "Bad time to be away, Katkov." He fetches a copy of *Pravda* from the table. "Somebody beat you to the story."

"Yes, but he blew the ending. You're going to help me rewrite it."

"What about Mr. Clean, here?" Scotto prompts, glaring at Rubineau. "Maybe he can help too?"

"My mission in life," Rubineau replies facetiously. "What do you need?"

"That container. You remember it, don't you? The one you begged us to let go to Havana? The one you said was going to lead us to whoever was using you?"

Rubineau grins and flicks an amused look to Barkhin. "I also remember saying you were wasting your time. You're still wasting it, believe me."

"The man's right," Barkhin says, brandishing the newspaper. "I hate to be the one to burst your bubble, but it looks like somebody beat you out too."

"Nice try. Not going to work," Shevchenko says.

"Pardon me?"

"Not a chance of that happening either," Scotto quips. "Murder? Money laundering? Not even Nixon could swing it. You guys are going away."

Barkhin and Rubineau exchange looks and chuckle to themselves, as if sharing an inside joke.

"The vault," Shevchenko prompts, losing patience.

"Of course," Barkhin says magnanimously. He's cocky, too cocky. They both are. Something's wrong. They don't seem at all threatened. He leads the way down the marble staircase to his elegant office. At the touch of a button, the hardwood panels slide back revealing the vault's gleaming door. He sets the tumblers, then spins the retracting wheel, swinging aside the enormous disk of case-hardened steel.

Shevchenko leads the charge inside and anxiously sweeps his eyes over the shelving bays filled with hard currency. His posture slackens. The immense space could easily hold the contents of four containers, but not a single heat-sealed million-dollar package is to be found, let alone eighteen hundred of them.

"Waste of time," Scotto says forlornly.

"Where have I heard that before?" Barkhin gloats, bringing a sardonic smile to Rubineau's face.

Shevchenko mutters an embarrassed apology and leads the group of officers from the club. "Son of a bitch," he exclaims angrily as the three of us pile into the Moskvitch and drive off.

"Back to square one," Scotto groans. "There's a container out there somewhere. We have to find it, and I don't want to hear any more of this 'Winter doesn't wait' bullshit. Matter of fact, I don't want to hear anything for a while. I want to think." We drive in silence through the Frunze District and head north on the Inner Ring. Traffic is light at this hour, and the Moskvitch travels at a steady clip. "I keep coming back to the same thing," Scotto finally says. "They could've led us on a wild-goose chase with that decoy, right? So, why the takedown? There has to be a reason."

"Maybe Gudonov didn't know it was a decoy," Shevchenko says, brightening at a thought. "Maybe he *was* working under-cover. He tried to beat us out, went for the fake, and shot him-self in the foot."

"But he was at the airport in Havana," Scotto protests. "He'd have known there were two containers."

"No. No, he never got a look inside the cargo plane," I ex-plain. "None of them did."

"Come on, he had custody of that container since this morn-ing. He has to know it's a decoy."

"So? Maybe he does!" Shevchenko says, chuckling with de-light. "That's why he burned the 'evidence'!"

"Of course," I conclude, "he was going through the motions to save face."

"He also burned a couple of million bucks, for Chrissakes," Scotto cracks. "Where'd he get it?"

Silence. None of us have the answer to that one.

We're crossing Tverskoi Bulvar about a mile from Militia Headquarters when the radio comes alive. The team Shev-chenko dispatched to check out the Antonov reports the con-tainer wasn't in the cargo hold; but something else of interest was. The two detectives are waiting in Shevchenko's office when we enter. Centered beneath the desk lamp are several cans of spray paint and a numeral stencil.

"Great," Shevchenko groans. "They changed the fucking number. That container could be downstairs in the courtyard, and we wouldn't know it. We'll never find it now. Let alone nail whoever's at the other end!" He kicks a trash pail in frustration. "In the old days, the KGB would seal off every road, airport, train station. It couldn't travel ten kilometers without being spotted!"

"Neither could I," I retort with a grin.

"Yeah, well, every system has its baggage," Scotto chimes in with a little look to Shevchenko.

"Anything more on the guy with Gudonov?" he asks offhandedly, ignoring us.

The detective shakes his head no.

I'm rocked. They know someone was with Gudonov?! But Yuri's name still hasn't surfaced?! I wait until my heart rate returns to normal, then, as nonchalantly as possible, prompt, "What guy?"

"Good question," Shevchenko replies. "We ran the Gulfstream's manifest this morning: "Rubineau, Barkhin, their flunkies, and two other names we didn't recognize. The passport office had no record of them, so we know they were traveling on phony IDs. Obviously one was Gudonov, but we've no fix on the other."

"Probably his flunky," the detective offers.

"Maybe," Shevchenko concedes. "Then again, he could be a key player. We don't know."

I do. I know who it is, but I still can't get the pieces to fit: Yuri is the only one not mentioned in *Pravda;* he wasn't at the incinerating plant; he wasn't at the Paradise Club; and he's not on the Gulfstream's manifest. There has to be a reason. If Gudonov was undercover, is it possible Yuri was too? Like Gudonov, he had cover ID. Like Gudonov, he works for the Interior Ministry. Damn. I'm asking myself the same questions about Yuri now that I was asking about Vorontsov in the beginning. Onto it? Or into it? Under the circumstances, I'm not sure it matters. I'm not even sure Yuri does. "I have a question. Why are we shifting our focus to people?"

"You have a problem with that?" Shevchenko challenges irritably.

"No, but we've been following the money all along and unless I misunderstood, regardless of who the players are, we don't have a case without the money. It'd be like trying to prosecute a homicide without a corpse, wouldn't it?"

"He's right," Scotto says forcefully. "No money, no case. The world thinks it went up in smoke. We have to prove it didn't. We find that container, we'll have a shot at nailing the creeps. We don't, it doesn't matter who they are, because they're all gonna walk."

Shevchenko nods grudgingly and stares at the map. We're wracking our brains and jumping at every ringing phone when I hear myself say, "I know where it is."

Two heads snap around as if reacting to a gunshot. "What? Where?"

"At least, I think I do."

"Come on, come on," Scotto urges frantically, her eyes locked onto mine.

I hold them for a long moment, deciding; then look away. "No. No, this one's personal. I'm going to have to do it alone."

"Chrissakes, Katkov!" Scotto erupts.

"No fucking way," Shevchenko roars. "You tell us what you have, or I'm going to bust your ass for withholding evidence."

"I'm afraid I don't have evidence. Frankly, it's little more than a vague hunch. You let me run with it, I might get you some."

Shevchenko glares at me.

Scotto throws up her hands. "I don't believe this."

"I didn't have to say anything you know."

They exchange looks, reconsidering.

"You said you owe me one, Scotto. Why don't we—"

"That was personal."

"So is this, dammit."

"Vera?"

"No, thank God."

"Well, you're the agent-in-charge, Shevchenko," Scotto finally says, "but if you don't mind me putting my two cents in, I figure we've got nothing to lose."

Shevchenko scowls in thought, then nods grudgingly.

"I'm going to need your car, Scotto."

Her eyes are hard and threatening. "Don't fuck me on this, Katkov."

"Not in your wildest dreams."

Scotto holds the look for a moment, then smiles and drops the keys in my palm. "Katkov?" she calls out as I head for the door. I stop and turn back toward her. She takes the pistol from her holster and hands it to me. "I hope you don't need it."

43

The city is virtually free of traffic, and the Zhiguli makes quick work of Moscow's streets. It's soon barreling north on the Yaroslavl Highway through rolling countryside. Occasionally, light from a window glimmers in the blackness. Despite the empty roads, the trip to Sudilova takes well over two hours. After several wrong turns in the maze of ancient streets, I find the narrow thoroughfare that snakes west into the Ustye Valley.

Dirt roads branch off in every direction. The wind-lashed tree that marks the one I want finally appears in the Zhiguli's headlights. I shut them off, and make the turn past the mailbox without a name. Patches of melting snow dot long-neglected fields that flank the bumpy road. Weathered farm buildings loom like ghostly apparitions in the darkness. No lights. No vehicles. No sentries. No sign of life save a curl of smoke that comes from the chimney of the old house.

I park the Zhiguli behind the stand of pines where the road forks. The air is cool, the ground soft as I get out of the car clutching Scotto's pistol. I take cover in the trees, scoop up a handful of rocks, and throw them at the barn's sagging door. I don't have to see the container to know it's inside. The sudden appearance of armed guards would send me slinking back to the Zhiguli with sufficient proof. None respond to the salvo. I fire another to be certain. Nothing. Maybe I took the wrong road? Maybe I'm wrong about this hunch? Nothing but stillness and the sound of wind in the trees as I advance toward the barn.

Deep tire ruts lead right to the door. A tractor pulling a plow? Or an eighteen-wheeler pulling a cash-filled container? The hasp is thrown, but a rusty horseshoe nail, not a padlock, secures it. The overhead tracks and rollers chatter in protest as I roll the door back just enough to slip inside.

As if sent by an angry God, a shaft of moonlight slices through the narrow opening and strikes the huge shipping container. The eighteen-wheeler is gone, and the forty-ton box sits on the floor between the empty horse stalls. It's not going anywhere. There's no need to advertise its presence; no need to deploy guards who might be tempted to help themselves to the money, or worse, brag about it. Rubineau and Barkhin aren't the only ones keeping a low profile. There's no need to check for my initials, or the restenciled number either. I've found what I'm after. My emotions soar, running the gamut from satisfaction to extreme disappointment. I stare at the container for a few heady moments, then leave the barn and stride swiftly up the hill to the house.

A light burns dimly in one of the windows now. I slither along the wall and peer inside. Almost wider than she is high, wrapped in her coarse wool sweater and ever-present scarf, Yuri's mother is leaning into a massive stone fireplace vigorously stoking the embers to life. I slip the pistol under my jacket and knock on the windowpane. "Mrs. Ternyak?"

She straightens and turns to the sound. "Who's there?" she calls out, her voice wavering with age and apprehension.

"It's Nikolai, Mrs. Ternyak. Nikolai Katkov."

She shuffles to the door and opens it. "Nikolai?" she repeats, a little confused, eyes straining to see through the cataracts that cloud them. She hugs me with surprising strength, then leans to one side, looking around me. "Is Yuri with you?"

"No. I'm sorry if I startled you."

"Well, he always comes on Saturday for breakfast. He shouldn't be long." Her brow furrows with confusion. "You know, I think he was here this week. Yesterday? The day before?" She sighs, angry at herself. "He told me he put some equipment in the barn."

"Ah, he said he wanted to show me something. I guess that's it. Why don't I wait there for him?"

I have many questions to ask Yuri, but one in particular. I also have time, the element of surprise, and an idea or two about how to get at the truth. I return to the Zhiguli and drive it around to the side of the barn away from the road. It suddenly dawns on me that I have something for Yuri, and this is the perfect time to give it to him. I rummage through my bags in the backseat until I find it, then hurry inside the barn.

The shaft of moonlight is gradually replaced by the pale wash of morning. Several hours later, the sound of an approaching car breaks the silence. I pull the pistol from my waistband and step behind the door. The old wooden planks are warped and uneven, and through the spaces I can see Yuri's Lada approaching on the road. It reaches the fork and lurches to a stop. Yuri is staring at the barn, staring right at the door. I had no doubt that he'd notice it's open, no doubt that instead of continuing to the house, he'd detour here.

The car angles left, curves down the gentle slope, and creaks to a stop in front of the barn. The ratchet of the hand brake sends a chill through me. I watch from behind the door as Yuri gets out and looks about curiously. He's alone and doesn't appear to be armed. I back away, slip into one of the horse stalls where some hay bales are stored, and crouch behind them.

The hollow thunk of the car door follows. A few footsteps. A shadow. Yuri leans into the barn. "Mom?" he calls out warily. "Mom? It's Yuri. You in there? Mom?" He enters, squinting at the darkness, and sweeps his eyes over the container. Satisfied that the locks are secure, he turns to leave, then stops suddenly and stiffens as if stabbed between the shoulder blades. I've no doubt his eyes are staring at the word *Coppelia,* staring at the napkin that I've affixed to the inside of the door. He fingers it curiously and removes it from the nail.

I conceal the pistol beneath my jacket and step out behind him. "Hello, Yuri."

He turns slowly, his face taut with uncertainty. "Nikolai?" he wonders weakly.

"I thought that might get your attention."

He stares at me for a long moment. My mind is racing. Is he armed? Will he go for his gun? Should I go for mine? Instead, he shrugs and smiles wanly in concession. "Did you have some when you were there?"

"No, I'm afraid I lost my taste for ice cream when I realized what it meant."

"Shame. It's much better than anything we have here. One of the few things Castro did well, actually. That and baseball, as I understand it. Boring game. Barkhin insisted I go to one."

"So you needed a name for a dummy corporation; naturally 'Coppelia' came to mind."

"Naturally. Seemed like a good idea at the time."

"I thought privatization deals were outside your area? You've come a long way, but empowered to act on behalf of the government? I'd no idea."

"Well, as you know, there's been quite a bit of restructuring going on lately; and there may have been a promotion or two I didn't get around to mentioning," he explains, pleased with himself. "I don't mean to be immodest, but my superiors were so taken by my ideas on reform, they eventually made me responsible for carrying them out."

"Really? Sounds like it's time to get rid of that crummy apartment and the wreck you've been driving. Upgrade your lifestyle to something more befitting a man with four phones on his desk."

"As you may have noticed," he counters in a sarcastic tone that equals mine, "I've been dealing with more pressing matters. That was you in the ceiling at the Riviera, wasn't it?"

"Yes. Took some rather interesting pictures too." Yuri's eyes neither blink nor narrow in reaction; he seems wholly unthreatened. "Why did you let me go in the first place?"

"You mean to Washington? As you recall, I tried to dissuade you at first. Then it dawned on me that you couldn't hurt, you could only help."

"I don't understand."

Yuri breaks into a smug grin that sends the tips of his mustache toward the corners of his eyes. "I figured if push came to shove, you'd be arguing to let the container go. I was right, wasn't I?"

"How—how could you be so sure?"

"You're not a cop, Nikolai, you're a journalist. A Russian journalist. That container doesn't get to Moscow, you don't get your story."

My eyes flare at the insult. "How could you do this? After all we've been through. How?!"

"I haven't done anything, Nikasha. I—"

"Don't Nikasha me, you bastard!" I pull the pistol from inside my jacket and come at him in a rage. "All these years, you and the fucking KGB!"

"KGB?! No! You're wrong!" he shouts hysterically, backing away. "Never! You don't understand. Listen, I—"

"Lying fuck! I'm going to splatter your brains all over this barn!" Yuri is backed up against the wall. I level the pistol at his head, letting him squirm for a few seconds before pulling the trigger. A blue-orange flash. A loud crack. The bullet whistles past his ear, punching a hole in the siding.

Yuri emits a terrified yelp. He's frantic, like a cornered rat. I take aim and fire another shot over his head. Blam! Wood chips fill the air. He's cowering, close to panic. "On second thought, maybe I'll just beat the shit out of you!" I raise the pistol and charge, threatening to smash him with the butt. He grasps my wrist with one hand and throws a punch with the other. We tumble to the floor, struggling for control of the weapon. It slips from my grasp and skitters away. I lunge for it, but Yuri is wiry and quicker, and swipes it from beneath my hand. We both scramble to our feet. He backs away, leveling the pistol at me. "Now calm down and listen, dammit!" he shouts, gasping for breath. "I'm a patriot, Nikolai. I care about Russia as much as you do."

"Bullshit!"

"Listen, dammit, will you! I spent my life trying to bring the Communists down, and you know it! This is our chance to get rid of them forever, but it will take money, lots of it."

"You know where this comes from?!"

"I could care less!"

"You want American crime syndicates to take over our industries?!"

"They're putting money into the country, Nikolai. The Russian mobsters are taking it out!"

"We don't need it, dammit! The United States gave us a billion and a half dollars. The G-Seven countries will soon—"

"Aggghh! You're so naive! Whether we have a Communist, fascist, or democratic government, it's still going to be a *Russian* government—a bottomless pit of bureaucratic quicksand that'll suck up everything in its path. None of that money'll ever get to the people."

"And this will?!" I protest angrily, gesturing to the container.

"Yes, it's bypassing the system completely! I'm going to distribute it directly to small businessmen, manufacturers, entrepreneurs. Thanks to the ministry I've access to a wealth of data, Nikolai. I've spent hours analyzing it and compiling lists of those citizens who'd use the money well. I'm not talking loans, mind you, I'm talking subsidies. To buy equipment and raw materials, to create jobs and fill empty stomachs, to put meat on the table and bread on the shelves! It's going to insure that the average Russian doesn't give up on democracy before this wretched economy gets turned around."

I'm stunned. That's the last thing I expected him to say. "I may be mistaken, Yuri, but I thought Rubineau was investing it in our distribution systems."

Yuri breaks into that rodent's smile. "So did he."

The pieces have suddenly fallen into place with staggering impact. The reason we didn't crash a party at the Paradise Club last night had nothing to do with Barkhin and Rubineau keeping a low profile. They weren't holding off the celebration. They were holding a wake—a wake for a container of cash that never came. Their cockiness wasn't due to the thrill of victory, but to the delicious irony of defeat, the realization that they'd have been caught red-handed by Shevchenko if they hadn't been duped. "You double-crossed him?"

Another smile. *"Used* him would be more accurate. He wanted to help Russia, and he has. A one-point-eight-billion-dollar donation. At the current exchange rate, it would take less than half of it to buy all the privatization vouchers the government has issued. Of course, Rubineau can't very well invest money that's been incinerated by the police now, can he? And, as far as he's concerned"—Yuri chuckles delightedly—"I'm as upset over it as he is."

"Gudonov."

Yuri nods. "Couldn't have done it without him."

"I can't believe you're doing business with that asshole."

"Ass*holes,* Nikolai. Plural. You're forgetting his pal at *Pravda."*

"Drevnya?"

Yuri smiles.

I groan in disgust. My eyes drift to the pistol.

"Not my favorite people either," he concedes. "But I'd deal with the devil himself if it'd buy us enough time. You know what's been going on here since you left?"

I nod glumly.

"Well, I'm pleased to report Yeltsin survived again. Three out of three isn't bad, but how long can he keep this up?"

"The law of averages is bound to catch up with him. I know."

"And do you know what today is?"

"Saturday, isn't it? Why?"

"It's also May Day, Nikolai."

"May Day? My God."

"How quickly we forget: the constant fear, the terror, the gulag, the KGB listening to every call, watching every move. You want the hard-liners back? You've forgotten what it was like?"

"Forgotten?! I'm the one who lived it, Yuri, not you! Why didn't you confide in me?"

"Please, Nikolai, be realistic. You were hooked on the story. Unstoppable. Like a pit bull. Look at you. You still are."

"Come on, dammit! You know how I get when I—"

"I rest my case," he interrupts smugly. "Don't get defensive. I'm not faulting you. I'm asking you to understand that I feel just as strongly about this."

"Fair enough." I study his eyes for a moment. "There's something else I have to know. You had Vorontsov killed?"

Yuri winces as if offended, then glances self-consciously to the gun, wishing he wasn't holding it. "It wasn't quite that cold-blooded. You recall what Henry the Second said of Becket?"

" 'Who will free me from this' . . . this pain in the ass, or whatever the hell it was."

" 'Turbulent priest.' Vorontsov was becoming a problem, and Barkhin was quick to—to take it on, for want of a better phrase."

"You're no better than him."

Yuri's face flushes with anger. "Vorontsov was a pompous fool, Nikolai! He didn't care about Russia. He was only interested in himself, in holding on to power like these idiots in Parliament! I begged, pleaded, cajoled him not to blow the whistle. I even told him what I was going to do. He wouldn't back down. Kept going on about his fucking integrity."

"So the end justifies the means?"

"Yes, dammit! Throughout history, I might add. And I'm sick and tired of it being used pejoratively. I couldn't let one man stand in the way."

The latter has the tone of an afterthought, but the implications are unmistakable. "Do you feel that way now?" I ask, taking a step toward him.

Yuri tightens his grip on the pistol. "Don't force me to make that choice, Nikolai."

"You're forcing *me* to make one."

He cocks his head and studies me obliquely, then his eyes soften and hold mine. "I'm asking you to put your country before yourself. You've been doing it all your life. I can't imagine you're going to stop now."

"I don't recall saying I was."

"Then don't."

"I'll think about it."

We hold a look. I push the muzzle of the gun aside and walk out of the barn into the sunlight. After I've taken about a half-dozen steps, Yuri calls out, "Nikolai?!" I keep walking, waiting for him to pull the trigger. "Dammit, Nikolai?!" he calls out again as I reach the end of the barn. Nothing. I turn the corner, then get into the Zhiguli, start the engine, and circle back to Yuri. He's standing in front of the barn with an astonished look on his face.

The pistol is at his side.

I stop next to him and roll down the window. "May I have that back, please? It's not mine."

Yuri nods curiously and hands me the weapon. "How did you know I wouldn't use it?"

"I didn't, but it was important to find out whether or not you would."

His eyes narrow with confusion.

"Here." I reach out the window. "You'd have had a hard time killing me without these." I open my hand to reveal the bullets I'd removed from the gun, drop them into his palm, and drive off.

44

 he willows along the river are dotted with fresh growth and bathed in sunlight that strikes the House on the Embankment at a flattering angle. Like hibernating bears, the residents venture from their caves to thaw frozen marrow and stretch long-dormant muscles. The benches are jammed with elderly sun worshipers, the paths crowded with chatting strollers, the grounds alive with the playful shrieks of children. A bouncing ball. A soaring kite. Tricycles. The smell of cottonwoods. I remember days like this.

I park the Zhiguli on Morisa Toreza, put Scotto's pistol in the glove box, and make my way across the grounds to the entrance, taking the elevator to Mrs. Churkin's apartment.

She reacts as if she's never seen me before when she opens the door. "Nikolai?" she finally exclaims, brightening. "You look so—so healthy. I didn't recognize you. Please come in." Her fashionable skirt swirls gracefully as she turns and leads the way. "I've been hoping to hear from you. I thought you might call from Washington. I couldn't imagine what happened."

"I wanted to be sure one way or the other, first."

"And now you are?" she prompts apprehensively as we cross the grandly proportioned living room, taking seats near the windows.

I wait until I can capture her eyes with mine. "Yes. You were right. He was wholly innocent."

She sighs, the pent-up anxiety released like air escaping from a balloon. "Oh. Thank God."

"He was murdered to prevent him from doing his job."

She smiles weakly, then looks off with a thought. "Then why are they still saying otherwise? First they called him a blackmailer. Now, he's the mastermind."

"It's all part of the cover-up. He was neither, Mrs. Churkin, believe me. Your father was an honest man—honest to a fault."

"Will you write that?"

"Of course I will."

"Thank you, Nikolai," she says, beaming. "Thank you for everything." She leaves the chair and fetches her jacket from a closet near the door. It makes a metallic tinkling sound as she slips it on. My eyes dart to a cascade of brightly colored ribbons and shimmering medals arranged in neat rows on the black wool. She notices me staring. "There's a demonstration in Red Square this morning," she explains. "I'm taking the children. Thank you again. This is going to be the most wonderful May Day."

My gut tightens. My face falls. I can't hide my reaction. May Day was always the symbol of everything I despised; the endless parade of tanks, missiles, and troops. Mile after mile of them marching like robots, marching in the same goose step as the hated Nazis. The bizarre military affectation always baffled me. As did the huge portraits—Marx, a Jew: Engels, a German; and Lenin, a Western-educated lawyer—that hung above the latter's tomb, where members of the Politburo stood in precise pecking order, their beaming faces failing to conceal the flinty malevolence in their eyes.

"You disapprove, don't you?" Mrs. Churkin prompts.

"I disapprove of anything that glorifies tyrants and dictators."

"My father was neither. He was a war hero, a patriot, and a great man."

"A Communist."

"True. It's part of my children's heritage. You're not suggesting I lie about it, are you?"

"On the contrary. I think it's important they know the truth."

"Which is?"

"Seventy-five years of totalitarian rule, of repression, terror, the denial of human rights."

"It wasn't the Communists who took away my father's human rights, was it?" she declares pointedly.

I stiffen, stung by the penetrating accuracy of her remark. "No, it wasn't."

"Do you know who?"

"Yes, I asked him about your father. That's why I'm so positive of his innocence."

Her eyes narrow in suspicion. "Why aren't you telling me his name? Aren't you going to reveal it?"

"I'm not sure."

"I don't understand."

"I thought you wanted to restore your father's reputation?"

"Yes, I'd also like to see the man responsible for his death punished."

"The man who killed him is dead, Mrs. Churkin."

"I said the man *responsible.*"

"What if I told you it might hurt Russia?"

"What do you mean?"

"Democracy. Our commitment to a free society. What you're asking me to do could have consequences that—"

"This has nothing to do with that, as far as I'm concerned," she interrupts indignantly. "My father was killed in cold blood, Nikolai. I want justice. I have a right to it. So does he."

"To use the common analogy, justice is best served by weighing opposing views, and I assure you, that's what I'm doing."

"Yes, and eventually one side of the scale goes up and the other goes down."

"I'm afraid you're forgetting that there's always a slim chance they'll balance."

She stares at me for a long moment, then nods resignedly and crosses to a doorway. "Children? Children, we don't want to be late."

They come running excitedly from their rooms. Their faces are brighter than I recall. Their posture straighter. Both are impeccably dressed. The boy struts proudly in his white shirt, tie, and blazer adorned with several of his grandfather's medals. His sister, immaculate in a flowery spring dress and prim white gloves, holds a stick to which a small Soviet flag is affixed. The

Hammer and Sickle against the bright red field still raises my hackles and sends shivers of terror up my spine.

We leave the apartment and take the elevator to the lobby in silence. "I used to live here," I say, as we exit and cross toward the big wooden door. "Did I ever mention that?"

Mrs. Churkin brightens, pleasantly surprised. I sense that this revelation, more than retrieving the medals, or determining her father's innocence, somehow validates me. "Your family? Here?"

"Uh-huh," I reply, opening the door for them. "Until my father was arrested by the KGB."

The children dash through it enthusiastically. Mrs. Churkin hesitates. "Why?"

"He didn't think Soviet tanks belonged in Prague."

"Neither did mine, as I recall."

"Yes, well, mine made the mistake of saying it."

"What happened to him?"

"He died in a labor camp. Many years ago. He was a good man. Educated. Compassionate. He had every bit as much integrity and love for his country as yours."

She smiles sympathetically and hurries down the steps, then pauses and turns back to face me. "I'm counting on you, Nikolai."

I force a smile as she goes after the children, then return to the Zhiguli. It seems to be giving off a faint electronic twitter when I open the door. The sound is coming from the backseat. I pull my briefcase from beneath the suitcases and throw back the flap. The sound gets louder. It's my beeper. It's been in there since I left Moscow. I'd forgotten all about it. I jog across the grounds to a phone kiosk, thumb two kopeks into the slot, and dial Militia Headquarters.

"Dispatcher seventeen."

"Vera? Vera, it's Nikolai. You beep me?"

"Of course. Who else? Several times in the last few weeks, I might add."

"I was away for a while. What's going on?"

"You're in trouble with the militia."

"Gudonov?"

"No, Shevchenko. He put out an alert for a rented Zhiguli and identified you as the driver."

"Oh," I sigh, relieved. "That's okay. We're still working on that story. It's been a long night. He's probably wondering what happened."

"I don't know about that. The alert carries a warning that you're armed."

"Great. Listen, Vera, I'm at the Embankment. Can you meet me?"

"No, I'm working."

"Get someone to cover for you. I'm in a quandary over this. I need to talk."

"I can't. What about Yuri? Call him."

"It's about Yuri. Please, it's important. You've no idea how important."

"All right, Niko. I'm on my way."

My stomach flutters at the thought of seeing her. I settle on one of the benches, wondering if she meant it, if she's really going to come. Fifteen minutes. A half hour. I'm lighting one cigarette from the next and on the verge of giving up hope when I spot Vera's lithe figure weaving through the crowd.

She apologizes for taking so long, explaining that the May Day demonstration has snarled traffic and the taxi couldn't get through. She's predictably intrigued and impressed by my tale of adventure, and as shocked and confused by my dilemma as I am. "I can't tell you what to do, Nikolai," she replies with a comely shrug. "I've no idea how to handle it. Besides, you never listened to me before. Why would you start now?"

"I'm desperate," I reply with a little smile. "And anyone who could come up with those documents is well worth listening to. I'm sorry. I never thanked you. None of this could've happened without them."

"I'm not sure how to take that."

"That makes two of us. Want to tell me how you did it?"

"I didn't. I have a friend in the mail room who owed me a favor. She intercepted the envelope before it got out of the building." Vera splays her hands and grins. "You still want advice from me?"

"You have some?"

"Uh-huh."

"What? Join a monastery?"

She chuckles and throws her hair back over her shoulder. "No. Just be yourself. It's always served you well."

"I'm not sure I know who I am anymore."

"You don't seem different."

"I'm not. Everything else is. It all used to be so clear. So simple. The assholes in the Kremlin were the bad guys. We were the good guys. It's all muddled now."

"Trust your instincts. Do what feels right. You'll be okay, Nikolai. I know you will." She smiles, then glances to her watch. "I have to go." She turns to leave, then pauses and lunges into my arms. Her eyes are brimming with emotion. "I missed you. Will you call me?"

"If you really want me to."

"Of course I do." She kisses my cheek, steps back, then turns and hurries off.

I watch until she disappears in the crowd, then walk along the river lost in my thoughts. A half hour later, I find myself back at the Zhiguli. As I'm opening the door, I hear the shuffle of feet and I whirl to see four men running toward me brandishing guns.

"Police!" one of them shouts. "Turn around and put your hands on the car!"

"I'm not armed," I call out, complying with the order. "The gun's in the glove box."

One of the officers fetches it. They frisk me anyway, confiscating my wallet and car keys, then spin me around to face them. "Nikolai Katkov?"

I nod wearily.

"Investigator Shevchenko wants to see you. You'll have to come with us."

Two of them hustle me into a patrol car. As we drive off, another gets behind the wheel of the Zhiguli and follows. The driver avoids the demonstration-clogged streets, and makes quick work of the drive to Militia Headquarters. In less than fifteen minutes, we're hurrying down the corridor to Shevchenko's office.

"Katkov. Katkov, you okay?" Scotto asks anxiously as we enter.

"Yeah, I'm fine."

"Good, because I'm gonna kill you, dammit. Now, what the hell's going on?"

"Going on?" I'm stalling, vacillating like a flickering light bulb. "What do you mean?"

"Come on, Katkov!" Shevchenko growls, jumping out of his

chair and circling the desk to confront me. "Twelve hours to check out a hunch?!"

"Some take longer than others."

"Am I to assume that means you've completed your investigation into the container's whereabouts?" he asks sardonically.

I nod, buying every last second before deciding.

"And?" he groans, exasperated.

Silence. I could hear a pin drop. A long moment passes before I shrug and hear myself say, "I was wrong."

45

Drop you somewhere?" Scotto asks curtly as we leave Militia Headquarters and walk across the courtyard toward the Zhiguli.

"Thanks. That's okay. I'll take my things out of the car and catch a taxi."

"You sure? Plenty of time before my flight."

She's fuming, seething in silence. I've no doubt her gesture is genuine; it's the motive that's a little vague. I have a feeling something's on her mind, and she needs a little time to get around to it. "Okay. I'm going to Yuri's place, I guess. It's not far."

We drive in silence for a few blocks. She's still distant. We're stopped at a traffic light when she finally glances over. "You found it, didn't you, Katkov?"

"You sound like you already know the answer."

"Uh-huh," she says with a sassy nod.

"Then there's no need for a reply, is there?"

"You protecting someone?"

"Really, Scotto. You know I'd never do that."

"Then why, dammit? Why?"

"Because it's not what I thought. It's—it's more complicated. It's not black and white."

"Thanks for clarifying it," she says facetiously. "Look, I'm a fairly bright person. Why don't you run it past me? Who knows, I might understand."

"I've a better idea. Make a left at the corner."

She turns into Tverskoy and drives south to the Moskva Hotel. We leave the car in the parking area and walk to Red Square. A barbarous roar echoes off the towering walls of brick. The diehard Communists are out in full force. Hundreds of thousands of them. In their midst, a group of furiously intense men with bullhorns stand Lenin-style, in the bed of a truck, inciting the burgeoning throng. Old soldiers exhibiting grand mustaches, rotund women flashing gold-toothed smiles, children clutching tiny red flags—their proud chests shimmering with medals—are chanting, "Le-nin! Le-nin! Le-nin!" A sea of Soviet regalia, flags, banners, and posters surges through the Square. The Hammer and Sickle. The glowering images of Lenin and Stalin. A mass of humanity eagerly protesting the fall of tyranny and the advent of freedom. It's a staggering sight.

"It'll be a long time before Russia is anything like the United States, Scotto."

"Hey, whether you agree with these clowns or not, it's a step in the right direction. Dissent is the cornerstone of a free society."

"Thanks for clarifying it," I say pointedly.

She reddens slightly and apologizes with a smile.

"My point is, no matter how violently you people disagree, it's always over how to make it work better. There aren't hordes of Americans in the streets protesting democracy."

"Not lately anyway, but the right to do it, to advocate an idea that you or I might totally despise, has to be preserved at all costs."

"Easier said than done."

"Bet your ass. But if you want to be a democracy, Katkov, you have to act like one. You can't have it both ways."

"We can't have it overnight either. The framework is barely in place. It's unsteady and very fragile. The slightest push could bring the whole thing down."

"And these clowns are pushing."

"Right. I don't want to stop them; I want to buy enough time to reinforce the foundation."

"One-point-eight-billion dollars' worth?"

"I think you're starting to understand. At the moment, there are more important things in Russia than the letter of the law."

"More important than the truth?"

"I'm not sure."

"But you know what it is."

"Uh-huh. Just not sure what to do with it."

Scotto brightens with a thought. "Come on, I have something that might help you decide." She leads the way back to the parking area next to the hotel and opens the Zhiguli's trunk. "Here," she says, presenting me with my typewriter.

I stare at it in stunned silence for a moment, struck by the realization that I'd—quite conveniently—forgotten all about it. "I assure you, you've made your point."

"Just keeping a promise," she says, pulling the typewriter back with a giggle when I reach for it. "Trade you for the camera."

"The camera?"

"You know Joe," she replies a little too casually. "With this damn budget crunch, I'm gonna have to account for it one way or the other."

I lean into the backseat of the Zhiguli and get the camera from my briefcase. "Come on, we better go," Scotto says, pocketing it. She's reaching for the door handle when she notices I'm removing my luggage from the backseat. "What're you doing?"

"Changing my mind. Something tells me I've worn out my welcome at Yuri's, and I'm not terribly keen on leaving my things in storage. I think I'll take a room here for a few days, then find a place of my own."

She studies me for a moment. "I've no doubt you'll know it when you find it," she says, poignantly.

"I just want to do the right thing, Scotto."

"Make sure you try real hard."

"You know, a fairly bright person once told me she didn't like journalists because they think that as long as they tell the truth, they're not responsible for the consequences."

Scotto smiles at the irony and opens the Zhiguli's door. "Hey, who knows? Maybe they'll give you a medal?" She kisses my cheek, slides behind the wheel, and drives off with a tap of her horn.

The car winds down the hill past the Kremlin, past crenellated turrets and stands of towering pines that send long shadows across the expanse of centuries-old cobblestones. I watch